To DAD —

A STORY OF THE OLD
STOMPING GROUND OF
THE WILLCOCKSON'S
AND THE BOONE'S;
NORTH CAROLINA.

LOVE,

Marshall Ray Wilcoxen

CANTON, ILLINOIS
AUGUST 5, 2001.

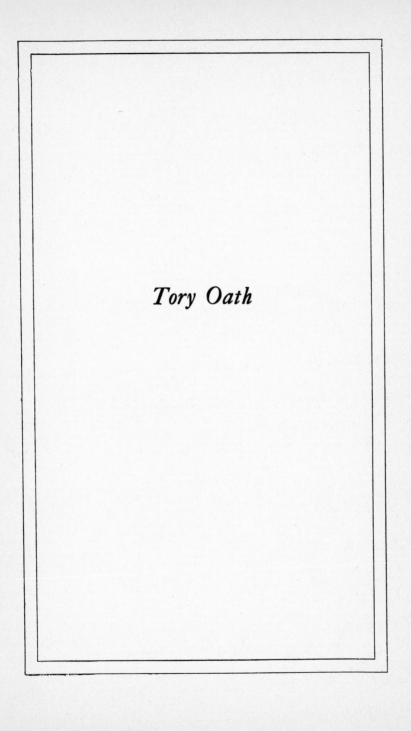

Tory Oath

Tory Oath

TIM PRIDGEN

GARDEN CITY, N. Y.

Doubleday, Doran and Company, Inc.

1941

PRINTED AT THE *Country Life Press*, GARDEN CITY, N. Y., U. S. A.

To
E. P. P.

AUTHOR'S NOTE

*The story of "*TORY OATH*" and history, where they join, are in fairly intimate agreement. One explanation is made: the indicated time of the Battle of Elizabethtown is slightly out of historical order.*

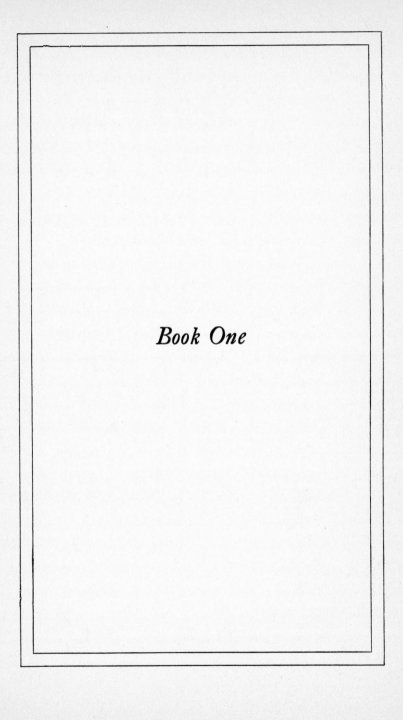

Book One

Book One

CHAPTER 1

THE AUTUMN OF 1774 A.D. writhed in birth. The sultry, vixenish summer gave up to spawn it in torture. The equinoctial storm wailed in from the sea. Ragged clouds, tattered by the cold winds which sliced across Frying Pan Shoals and howled through the rigging of the luckless ships that strove for haven, swayed dismally swift over the Tidewater and plunged in hunger upon the remaining summerlands up the Cape Fear.

The suddenly chill rice fields and cornlands belched their black slaves shivering to quarters, and houseboys toted armloads of pine and oak to the great fireplaces in the manor houses. In the evening's gloom, while the planters drank their toddies and entertained their guests and awaited supper, warm lights glowed from the hall windows into the disturbed darkness.

It was a long way from the high-ceilinged palaces of the Tidewater up the winding Cape Fear to the sturdy, wood-pinned domiciles of the Scottish Highlanders along the upper waters— and a longer way yet from the thoughts of one to the thoughts of the other. As far—aye—as from gray moss to purple heather. Even so, the racing clouds blanketed all the fire-flushed groups at the hearths before the night was black.

The storm came upon Duncan Stuart, at the tar kilns, that afternoon from down the river. The cloud line was straight across what had been a fair sky, and a knife edge of silver sheared off the summer as keenly as his own drawing knife carved the riven pine

3

slats for tar-barrel staves. He was busy. The weather mattered little. Hoop poles and barrel staves and headings mattered much, and these were corded around him under the shed.

He worked with a certain rhythm, a certain sureness of strength and habit. He sat astride a cooper horse, with his foot on the treadle. Thus he held the cream-white staves in place to shape them with his drawing knife—first the big slice, with the wood shrieking and buckling into sudden curving flowers; next, purling ribbons to twirl thin and fall like lines of poetry. Then a kick, a careless toss, an empty clatter, and a new stave was in place.

It was interesting, absorbing, to the strange woman who sat on her horse behind him and watched. The sand was deep. The horse had made no noise. Duncan worked on, unaware. His long, flexing arms went through their stint as without direction. His yellow hair, with its roll of curl about his neck, swayed as his broad shoulders swayed.

Now he stopped and listened into the swamp. Its green blanket stretched flatly toward the horizon and merged with the trees on a far highland so distant that one could not see where. His fair face was grave, not particularly handsome, not unhandsome, but sound and even with an air of strength. His nose was full-sized and straight, and his lips were a straight line with a bit of dip at the corners. His brows, brassy rugged swipes over bulges, would have made his blue eyes seem inset if they had not been so large.

Across the swamp came the faint creak of wooden axles in hubs. Somewhere, down under the green, a yoke of oxen strained at a cart. The load was golden yellow split heart pine, cut from the logs in the islands. Gillie Black, the slave lad, hauled it in to the kilns. The trail was black mud, half-spoke deep, and as the oxen groaned and heaved, gobs of ooze slopped down the spokes of the creeping wheels and dropped back to the ground. Duncan saw that as though he were there.

He looked long and intently, not at the blue-green shadow which flowed from the cloud upon the swamp, nor at the proud cypresses which here and there lofted their green feathered leaves above the trees, but to listen to the distressed cart hubs.

He lifted his voice in a far-carrying, thrusting cry. "Whig up! Whig up!" he shouted, hand at mouth.

Back from the swamp Gillie Black's energized "Gee up! Gee up!" came back over the green, and now the slave burst into a rolling, musical halloo as smooth and silvery as a thrush's call.

His little empire again in hand, Duncan laid his two-handled drawing knife in a box, drew his palm over the yellow bristles on his forearm and leaned for a moment on the block of the stave vise. He was still. After the shouting the silence of the wilderness came back like an ethereal echo.

Like those much alone, Duncan spoke to himself, grumbling: "Ten lashes for his back—then he'll remember."

The woman said: "Serves him right, if it is about the dry axles."

"Aye," said Duncan, "I told him—— Eh?"

His surprise jerked him upright, straddling the cooper horse, twisting to stare over his shoulder.

She laughed down at him. She had fine white teeth. Her eyes, which were lively dark blue under black brows, laughed, too, quite as daringly as her lips. She spoke and laughed from her chest, full and deep and abruptly pleasant.

Duncan, smiling, astonished, questioning, all in one grunt lifted his foot over the sill and faced her. And rather breathlessly, for he was only twenty-three and not bold with women.

"Did you see a wagonload of beeswax and skins headed for Wilmington, I wonder?"

"Na," Duncan said, still confused. "Wilmington? On this side o' the river?"

"Aye, Highlander," she half mocked him. "On this side. The Rockfish bridge is out, so I sent it down this way. But I lost it."

"Aye," Duncan frowned. "No wonder. On this side we nigh to make our trails as we go. Na, I didna see a wagon today. He bore to the east o' the lake, likely."

The woman sidled her tall, rangy horse to a pine stump and stepped off. Then she steadied herself with one hand on the horn of the saddle and dropped to the ground handily. Duncan did not have time to aid, after he had thought to do so. But she made a sprightly jump for one her size.

She was a big woman and good-looking. Firm enough and soft enough and bold enough. She asked no quarter for her womanhood, and her two pistols gave her the air of being quite able to fend for herself. Duncan had the impulse to step back at her quick advance, but big men are not nimble, and he remained in his tracks. Smiling still, she looked him up and down, from his stock-inged legs to his bare head, as she might have appraised a horse. His leveled eyes caught the crown of her mannish felt hat and held there for the ordeal.

"You're a big devil!" she approved him saucily.

"Y're na sae wee y'rsel'," he came alive. They laughed, Duncan now more at ease. One was not long merely abashed in the presence of the Widow Martha McGee, of Deep River valley. She breathed life and challenge, and one either gave her blow for blow or fled ingloriously. She was in the full glory of her sex, she knew proudly. Failing to know, she would have been oft reminded by the trenchant and sometimes uncouth admiring males in the back settlements.

She shook her head ruefully. "I'm the wrong size. Too big for little men—and big men want little women."

"Zounds—I shouldna think ye'd be long waitin'."

"You'd be surprised. Where'm I to spend the night?"

"Weel—t'other side of the river, Brompton Hall, Oakland, Bel-font, but 'twill take ye past dark tae get there. Yon way, around Granston Lake to South River, the Cromarties, the Murphys, the Merediths—but it's o'er half a day's journey. In the swamp there are cabins, but hard tae find."

"Then I'll stay here."

"Na!" Duncan was alarmed. "There are no women! Only me—and my nigger."

She chuckled softly. Women had a way of chuckling softly at Duncan.

"You don't make a practice of ravishing women, I hope," she demanded.

"Na! Na! I winna rape ye, woman! Losh! What maun ye think o' me? But——".

"Well, then—what's to forbid?"

"Naething—only——"

"Think I'm going to ride out in a storm just to save the yammer-yammer of flat-chested women? To hell with 'em!"

"Weel—anyway—ye're not," Duncan agreed.

"Not what? Flat-chested?" She grinned impishly. Her hands on her hips, she stood erect and twisted her shoulders, flaunting her ample physical charms. "I hope to say I'm not!"

It were prudish out here where Nature reared her children to blush over those subjects wherein Nature was frank and unashamed. That was civilization's sicklied gift, and civilization in these fastnesses clung timorously to riverbanks and high roads.

"It wi' be cold tonight, wi' this wind makin' up," Duncan commented. They were through with their joshing, done with their challenging and testing. They were interested in each other's affairs, and Duncan was showing Martha his place. They were standing on the charcoal-saturated ground beside the tar kilns.

"The swamp," said Duncan, waving his arm, "is a' mine. I hae plans for't. This way," waving to the left, "I hae eight hunder acres o' sandhill and low ground, wi' more pine than I can tend. I wi' save that until I hae slaves."

Martha looked curiously at the long kilns—long slanting funnels in the ground, pitched to disgorge their tar into barrel-like pits at the low ends. One smoking kiln, filled with corded, slanting pine, covered with pine straw and heaped over with dirt, was partly burned. The wall of fire was eating its way down to the deep narrow end. The other kiln, face to face with it and pointing in the opposite direction, was half filled with pine. The creaking cart was bringing more.

"When one burns out," Duncan explained, "we are ready for the next and, so, keep tar running a' the while. It's bad f'r sleep, but when next I raft tar tae Wilmington I wi' hae enough money tae buy bricks f'r my pillars and, mayhap, chimneys f'r my stout house."

"Stout house?"

"Aye—I'll show ye."

They walked across the sand. They went carefully across a footlog over a clear-water creek and up a sandhill into a grove of live oaks. Duncan was as eager as his natural taciturnity would allow.

"It's na much tae look at now," he said, standing beside large cypress sills, running his hands over their smoothness. Scarcely a splinter stood out from where his broadaxe had hewn them clean and true. "But here it wi' stand. Solid. Strong. I wi' hew every timber mysel', and build the house wi' my own hands. It is my will."

"What kind of house?" Martha asked doubtfully.

"A frame house of two stories and dormer windows in the third, wi' columns f'r the porch here—wi' glass windows—on the front, anyway—and a chimney there"—Duncan was taking long quick steps, pointing as though he saw these things in fact—"and a chimney over there—and the kitchen ell this way, and——"

"A house that fine," Martha protested, "here on the side of a boggy swamp?"

"Aye—but the swamp winna be a swamp." Duncan's eyes grew bright as he unfolded his great plan. "When I hae taken out the pine and hae cut the cypress, then, in a dry spell, I shall have a grand burnin'. A' that"—pointing down beyond the grove—"wi' be a lake, wi' a dam and a gristmill and a sawmill at yon low end. It shall be known as Stuart's Lake, and the stout house shall be known as Stuart's Hall, and the mill shall be——"

Martha laughed. "I know. I know. Stuart's Mill. You will have a grand lane up from the water. You will have a fine, proud wife to be a sort of little queen——"

"Na sae little," Duncan said.

"—to sit at the other end of a long table with three white linen tablecloths on it. She will pour coffee——"

"And tea."

"Damn tea—once for the King. And pour coffee in china cups and little nigger girls will pass them up the table. And your great hall will have a great fireplace, and you'll have grand visitors up from Wilmington and down from Cross Creek to sit before your fire and drink toddies on cold nights, and your nigger slaves will care for the horses and shine their carriages, and a big fat one will tend to your towheaded children——"

"One brown-headed, one yellow and the rest mixed."

"Towheaded, I said, and your little wife——"

"Na sae little."

"How little?"

"Like Flora MacDonald, perhaps."

"I don't like her. Who is she?"

"Don't you know Flora——"

"I don't want to know her."

"But, my God, woman! Ye should——"

"What's the difference? You can't do all this, anyhow."

Duncan bristled. "And why na?"

"Because you've got to sell tar and turpentine to get the money, and the Whigs are going to embargo everything. You Tories won't be able to ship even a spoonful of tar to the West Indies."

Martha was spiteful, and Duncan took it as his own fault. What marriageable woman loves to hear such fine plans for another woman? Moreover, she was a Whig, and Whig women spoke their minds most independently. But he didn't care. She had stepped on his toes, too.

"Whigs!" he grunted disdainfully. " 'Tax on tea!' 'Tax on tea!' What do you care about either tea or taxes?"

"Nothing."

"Then why all the plots and schemes and sedition?"

"On account of tax on tea!"

"But it doesna make sense."

"Then call it what you like—tax on tea—the Cause of Boston— the King's tyranny—we're through with the King, if he could take a hint."

" 'Tis rebellion! Ye'll do well to cease it before the King's patience gives way to bloody wrath!"

"Just the same," she shrugged, "you'll be longer buildin' your house than you think."

She turned and walked away, waving her hands to the swamp and to the backlands, as though he dreamed preposterous dreams.

The sweet, thrilling silence of twilight, blue, chill, like the hush of a time long gone, settled down, and Duncan and Martha made their way back over the footlog toward his log cabin on the next sandhill. He admired—grudgingly, for she had roiled him—the supple sway of her back, the easy swing of her legs, the proud balance of her upright head. The thought that had popped into his mind when he first saw her came back. She was a good-looking woman.

Her resentment over small things was not as long-lasting as his.

When she had stepped from the log she waited for him, smiling again. She took his arm when he stepped to the sand and leaned on it. Her soft flesh where it rested on his was warm and good. His chest first felt tight, and then it was loose and expanding.

"Mad at me?" she begged like a wee lass.

"F'r what?" he demanded like a lord. "Na."

She took her arm from his and spoke of the soft soil in Bladen and how different it was from the rocky clay on Deep River. She stood beside him in the cabin while he found a tinderbox on the fireboard and stooped to the hearth to strike sparks into the scorched linen. From the smoldering rag he coaxed a sulphur match to sickly blue flame. From that he ignited fat pine splinters and started fire in the clay fireplace. While the blaze grew he stood erect. They were near together. They did not speak. Something in her spirit met his and held them vibrantly. He had the excited impulse to kiss her. He knew he could. Miles deep in the wilderness, with her alone, and she was willing. But the moment passed.

"My God!" she turned about, looking. Now that the light illuminated the room, her housewifely instincts leaped uppermost. "Don't you ever clean house?"

Duncan's eyes followed her, surprised. "Aye!" he asserted. "It's clean."

"Look at that bed!"

She snatched the quilt off, and things rattled to the floor—horseshoe nails, a dirk, a squirrelskin cap and a bag of shot. "Hand me the *broom!*"

He gave her the stumpy bundle of sedge grass which had served so well until this minute, and then fled.

"The cart has come in," he almost shouted.

The wind was rising, and each puff was colder than the one before. It cut through Duncan's thin shirt, but he did not notice. Martha McGee had set him swirling in his mind. A braw, robust man could not come in this intimate contact with a buxom siren like Martha without the thought to hold her. Yet she was an honest woman, no doubt.

"I wish I kenned," he worried. "She nigh o'erpowers a man."

He plowed on toward the kiln, frowning. Martha McGee looked out the cabin door after him and smiled, but he did not see that.

A puff of wind swirled the tarry smoke full upon him, and he groped his way through, holding his breath.

In the clear, two solemn-faced oxen, Bo and Jay—Bo with the blazed face, Jay with the black—looked at him without concern.

Bruce, the black-and-tan dog, trotted up and squatted on his haunches, looking eagerly to his master for approbation for bringing in the ox team and Gillie Black. He laid his throat against Duncan's leg and whined contentedly at the gentle scratch behind his ears. Then, suddenly, he was away.

Gillie Black, short, strong, square-shouldered, was black down to his eyeballs and down to his teeth, and these in the twilight shone white like something from the graveyard. He was four years younger than Duncan.

Gillie loosed the oxen. They moved off to the creek, side by side, as though still pulling the cart.

"The ox whup," Duncan said sternly, holding out his hand.

Gillie batted his eyes, then glared. "Yas'h," he said and handed Duncan the whip.

"Strup!"

Gillie glared angrily yet, but he cast off his galluses and his clothes fell to his feet. He bellied across a barrel, his glare rolling back over his shoulder.

"Ye get ten lashes f'r not putting tallow on the cart axles as ye were told."

Gillie sprang up, his hands out, trembling, not in fear but in passionate protest.

"I tallied 'em, Mas' Dunk—'fo' God, I tallied 'em!"

"Ye lie. F'r y'r triflin' incompetence the oxen today drew extra burdens on their bare necks. Get back."

Gillie shook his head and spat, trying to conjure up something else to say. Then resignedly he went to the barrel.

The leather whip whirred through the air and splatted sharply. The Negro cringed but did not cry. After that he did not cringe. Not until the eighth lash. Then he groaned. The ninth fell across his black skin and jerked unbearable pain into him. He screamed. His hands spread out frantically over the ground and seized upon a green hickory stick.

Duncan stood poised with his whip.

"Ye hae y'r club," he said coldly. "Use it."

Gillie cast the club from him and waved it away. His whine was like the dog's, but it was broken by sobs. The tenth lash fell lightly, more the gesture than the punishment.

"Run tae the creek and wash y'rself," Duncan ordered. "Then feed Donald Bane and the extra horse i' the stall. Ye needna cook supper tonight, I'm thinkin'."

Gillie, trembling in the agony of listening to orders while his pains stung, dashed away.

Duncan shook his head in regret.

"Sometimes, a'most," he said doubtfully, "ye'd think the black bugger was human."

Duncan, having seen to the evening chores, battled his conscience on the way to the cabin and surrendered completely.

"She's a good woman, f'r a' her boldness," he conceded. "And as compelling in her grand body as she be, for a' o' my concern she can stay so. Right's right."

Even so, he walked with high knees and loose hips and a feeling of adventure. And no small sense of self-righteousness.

"Losh!" he exclaimed, stepping in the door. It was like a different place. Inward misgivings at all this neatly packed cleanliness disturbed him, but he spoke words of pleasure. The bed never had been so well made. Its quilt was tucked in, and the pillow had a clean casing. His clothes had been taken from the chairs and hung on the wooden pegs along the wall. His Highland coat and kilt, of the proud Stuart tartan, were hung on separate pegs, and his basket-hilted broadsword lay over them. He stood and looked around, and his shoes grated on the thick sprinkle of white sand with which Martha had crowned her efforts.

" 'Tis bonnie—bonnie!"

She answered tartly: "Then see that it's not like a pigpen my next time around."

Martha already had started supper. A skillet of peas was being warmed over, huddling close to the blaze, with live coals on the iron cover. Ash boards lay around the fire, with thin loaves of bread clinging to them and beginning to brown. A wide skillet was full of white-and-red slices of bacon, prepared to fry when she was ready. A tall coffeepot, smudged with many fires, rested on the coals but had not begun to steam. And sweet potatoes roasted in the ashes.

For lack of something better to do while Martha was busy with the meal, Duncan took down his broadsword and began to sharpen its double edge with a whetstone—a round section of petrified hickory from the creek.

"Where'd you get it?" she asked, looking at the weapon in dislike.

"My father's. He brought it to this country the year after the 'Forty-five. Smuggled in a roll of bedding."

Duncan hefted the stout old sword with both hands, looking at it proudly.

"Well, I don't think it is so fine," she said, tilting the bread nearer the fire.

"It's been wi' the Stuarts," he mused, "since no soul knows when. My father swung it in the ring o' clansmen around his chief on Drummossie Moor in the Battle o' Culloden. He was cut down there, and fourteen dead clansmen fell on him. The British roamed the field and cracked every skull that moved, and my father stayed there a' the day and a' the night while the corpses stiffened on him. He said the most horrifyin' sound he e'er heard was when his own bare bones scraped upon the bare bones o' the dead when he crawled out."

Martha McGee grimaced and turned back to her cooking.

"The Whigs," he said, "make me think often o' this blade. I hope tae God they cease their rebellious contentions before His Majesty commands the Hielanders tae march out and clear the country o' 'em. I hae some good friends wi' the Whigs."

"Don't be too certain," Martha took umbrage, "they don't clear the country o' you!"

"Uh? Eh?" He was astonished. He laughed. His full-throated guffaw filled the cabin with sound. Martha's face flushed with quick anger, and she smiled at him through her spite.

"I speak o' the *Hielanders* marchin' on the Whigs," he explained, as though she hadn't understood.

They ate supper on a table of pine boards before the fire and talked of many things as the storm howled. Duncan looked at her in amazement when she told of her big house up on Deep River, of her farm; of her store where the men from the mountains and from as far east as the Hawfields and from up on Troublesome Creek fetched in their skins and beeswax to trade for nails and salt and coffee. She spoke of her gristmill and how it had to run three days a week and sometimes more.

"But," he protested, "I thought ye were concerned only wi' midwifin'?"

"La!" she laughed. Martha McGee's good round laugh sounded bonnie and comforting in the room after his nights of loneliness. "Grannyin' is not a smidget—just a little fun on the side. That and tendin' the sick. I've got the gift of healin'. I can pull 'em through, 'most every time."

"D'ye hae t' gae far frae home on y'r missions?"

"Once I rode a hundred miles, night and day. The woman was almost dead when I got there. I saved her and I saved the baby. It was a bastard."

"How do they pay you?"

"I don't take pay. I don't need money. I've got plenty."

She made a plate of supper and handed it out the door to Gillie Black. Duncan followed her with his eyes and said nothing, awed somehow by her bumptious goodness.

They lifted back the table and sat before the fire for greater comfort. For a time they were silent, thinking.

"Martha McGee," Duncan said, "ye're a grand, strong, good woman. Ye hae sae much t' give, and ye give sae freely."

"Shut up!" she said testily.

Duncan twisted his mouth. He looked at her curiously and kept silent. She crossed her feet before the blaze, smoothed her skirt over her extended legs, and gazed moodily into the coals.

"I'm not a good woman," she said in a low tone. "I'm mean and sharp-tongued. I hurt people's feelings. I can't help it. The Almighty put a curse on me, and I can't get satisfied. I am as strong as most men, and bigger than a woman ought to be. I don't fit in. I'd give my soul to be a snivelin', whinin' little woman, with just a common tobacco-spittin' man to pat me on the shoulder and tell me I was just fine. Or else——"

She went silent and kept her eyes on the fire. Duncan saw her face, smooth, pink, and thought that the fire had made it quite red.

"Eh? Else?"

She shook her head defiantly. "Or else, by God, I wish I had a man my size! As strong as a buffalo, to make me feel littler and weaker than he was."

"Weel," Duncan reasoned, "seems tae me—'twould take an extra——"

"Seems, the devil! I never saw but two such men in my life. One is Steve Lewis, up my way. Oh, he's much of a man! And mean! Broad-shouldered, like you, except he's got smaller ankles and is quicker on his feet. He makes advances at me every chance he gets, the polecat! He figgers that sooner or later—— But he's married. More than that, he's a Tory. I hope I don't meet him in the woods some moonlight night when I feel like I feel now."

Martha McGee was silent again, strangely subdued.

"Perhaps, Martha," Duncan offered, also looking stonily in the fire, "I know how ye feel. I myself hae had the yearn tae put my arms about a woman and feel 'em full o' bigness and strength, and the softness and shyness which only a woman has."

"Yes, yes!"

"Only——"

Martha interrupted briskly, deliberately changing the subject: "Who is this Flora MacDonald?"

"Oh," Duncan brightened. "She is a grand, lovely lady o' the Hielands—o' the ancient Clanranald stock—o' song and story concerning Bonnie Prince Charlie. She comes to America to mend the family fortune——"

"Yeh!" Martha twisted her mouth. "All full of heather and lochs and philibegs and haggis and bagpipes. I don't want to hear any more about her!"

"But, Martha," Duncan said in pained surprise, "she is a grand lady o' culture and loyalty, and she wi' stand proud i' the Cape Fear clans, and, perhaps——"

"Yeh! And make two Tories where one was before! She better stay home, for the good she'll do."

Bedtime came quickly after dark in the woods. Martha McGee soon yawned and stood before the fire. Duncan likewise. It was time for him to wrap himself in his tartan in the shed beside the kiln; there, sleeping and waking, to tend the running tar. But he lingered. Martha, too, lingered near him. She took down her hair and ran her fingers through it and listened to it crackle.

"You never did ask who the other man was?" she suggested.

Duncan was looking at her in fascination, her smooth, flushed face in her dark hair. He scarcely knew what he said.

"Na. Who?"

"Just another damned Tory," she said in mock bitterness.

Duncan leaned toward her, and she did not retreat. "Who?" he asked. He was tingling strangely—all mixtie-maxtie. He didn't care who the man was. "Who?"

Their faces were close together, he could feel the warmth of her breath.

"You," she almost wailed.

The muscles of her back were sliding and soft to his hands. She was against his breast, and her hair was over his face like a cloud. She was in him and through him and around him to tear him apart inside, to make his head whirl and his heart hammer and to send ten thousand hot surges coursing through him. Her lips were an intoxicating fire upon his. She threw back her head and laughed into his face. He kissed her eyes and her cheeks and her mouth again. They stood immovable, and his hand began to rove and draw her closer. It gripped into her shoulder, and she laughed again and with her own arms drew herself so close that not even a sheet of paper could come between them, much less his hand.

"Duncan," she whispered, and he heard as though from a far distance. He did not answer.

"Duncan." The whole length of her quivered against him, and he did not answer then.

"Duncan." She was pleading now, like the little lass she was for the moment at the footlog.

"Aye, Martha," he struggled to say.

"Come with me to Deep River, and take my store and mill, and be my husband. Be a good patriot and love our country and love me."

He said nothing. He tried to think. She wanted him to be a Whig. Why? Why a Whig?

"Na."

"Please."

"Na."

"Will you think it over?"

He drew her closer. She was asking questions. He didn't want to bother with questions. He kissed her.

"Aye."

Her hands pushed against his chest. The sudden movement thrust his arms from her. She stepped back. He followed her.

"Get back! Get back!" She threw his hands aside. He pressed on.

"Stop!"

He did stop. He shook his head, looked at her again, stepped toward her.

"Get that bull glaze out of your eyes!" she said sharply.

But he wanted to feel the fullness and richness and strength of her in his arms again and pressed forward.

He squinted and shook his head. He looked into the muzzles of two pistols. She held them most expertly.

"Before God, Duncan," she said, "I'll kill you. Get your senses back. I never saw such a stubborn mule."

"Martha, I'm bristlin' wi' love f'r ye," he pleaded. "Ye winna kiss me?"

"I winna! You're passion-drunk and you've got no sense. Get out and cool down. Think it over. I'll not unbolt the door until midnight. After that—if you want to—come back, and come looking for an honest woman. Ye'd promise too quick now."

Duncan sat by his tar kiln fire, hot on one side and cold on the other. His mind was muddled. He gave no thought to Martha's proposal. He could think, only, that she was in his cabin and that he wanted to be in there with her. He jumped to his feet to go back, to break the door down. He ran halfway to the cabin and returned to the kiln. Caution battered him. It commanded him to think first. He couldn't think. He shook his head sullenly. He still wanted to go.

Then he jumped up, running. He would settle at least one issue. He had sense enough to know what it was. He raced down a trail that led to the east, pounding the sand. Enough miles on the giving soil would let down his sap. He would come back with a clear head. The wind tore through the scrub oaks, and the pines writhed and shrilled. The cold sliced against his right ear and his cheek and felt good, for his blood raced hot. The cold sweet air poured into his hungry lungs. He was running strong and had a long way to go yet before he could stumble back to his tar kiln fire weak enough to think straight.

Some things began to take shape in his mind as he ran. They frightened him, because they were different from his thoughts before. His lands suddenly were shabby, no solid house and mill and barns and well-broken fields, such as Martha had, and his dream of Stuart Hall was just that—an empty dream. Martha's plantation, his for opening a door, was bonnie and rich, and he could have mastery upon it without all this hard work. Strangely, the King, his symbol of stability, now was far away and unimportant. And, as strangely, the despicable Whigs, who would not let well enough alone, of a sudden were not so bad. One might mix among 'em and still not be the damned fool. Then he thought on the ancient Highlands, their songs, their glories, his heritage of Wallace and the Bruce, Flora MacDonald, his kinship with the clansmen of the Cape Fear, and his soul balked.

It was torture. He wanted Martha McGee with a hunger that wrung him, but she tore ruthlessly into all that life was. She had made his dream of achieving and building and mastering and holding secure in the strength of the Crown a thing of no account. He hated her. He loved her. He wanted her. He despised her. He ran the harder, as if by speed he could escape the anguish.

Duncan, full-winded, finally panted back to his tar kilns, and he had no thought of women. He wanted, gaspingly, to lie down and ease the pains in his chest and legs and feel the comfort of his pine-straw bed before the fire.

Gillie Black ran out from his bunk in the stable loft and stammered with his eyes. Duncan stiffly ran by.

"Whuffo?"

Duncan gave him no answer.

For himself there was no answer. He had no passion now except the passion for rest. He could think better, but that only increased his confusion. Martha offered him her wealth and herself, but she demanded a great price. Just how great was not clear, but something vague that he had always held priceless. Should he give it to her? He did not know. He did not know what it was or what it was worth. If he had been forced to make answer he would have said that it was loyalty to the King. But it was more. Something that flooded down to him in a bold course of blood and glory from the ancient Highlanders. It was that which made him tight-throated when he thought to hear Flora MacDonald sing the old songs. It was nought of commodities or politics, but of the spiritual intangibles, and he knew no way to make a trading price on it. Nevertheless Martha offered handsomely. She was a Whig, and of those Ulster Scots who had discarded the flavor of the Highlands, and she was older than he, but . . .

Weel—he would think on't. She was worth considering. Aye!

He thought but little, for suddenly there was an ungodly hammering over on his cabin door.

"Open up!" some blunt-speaking Highlander demanded, banging louder yet.

Duncan cried his alarm: "Come awa'!"

No one heard, because the exploding roar of Martha's pistol answered the Scot and he ran, yelling.

"Come, man! Come!" Duncan shouted again. "Ye hurted?"

The kilted man raced over to the kiln, swearing terrible oaths.

"Calm y'rsel'!" Duncan chuckled, eyeing him curiously. "Calm y'rsel'. Ye're na harmed."

"Calm, hell! He shot at me!"

"Weel—ye dinna understand. The honest soul i' the house mistook ye for one worthy t' be shot, did he break that door."

The angered Scot sputtered and cast fierce glances through the darkness toward the cabin. "Ye speak riddles!"

"'Tis na y'r concern," Duncan ended the talk and explained nothing. "Ye're one o' the MacDougalls o' Cross Creek. I recognize the favor. What fetches ye here on a night so stormy?"

"I've a message for ye."

The MacDougall was a courier from the Highland citadel at Cross Creek. He had been sent to rally the clansmen to welcome Flora, to save her mind stainless from the persuasion of the Tidewater Whigs.

"Wi' ye gae?"

Duncan cringed inside. Sudden pains clamped him, the same as if he had been squeezed in his own cooper-shop vise. If he took up with Martha, and she pulled him tremendously, then he would be out of place among the Loyal Scots gathering to Flora. But . . . so did Flora call to him tremendously.

"Wi' ye gae?" the Highlander repeated.

Duncan twisted his body and his face and made no answer. He led the visitor to the log which he used for a bench. Sitting down under the brush shelter, he faced the MacDougall intently.

"The MacDougalls," he hesitated, "hae the name o' men o' gumption. Before I make answer t' ye, I want y'r counsel on a particular matter."

The MacDougall nodded solemnly and settled back to listen, as befitted one called upon to give advice. "As far as my sma' wisdom goes," he offered, "ye shall hae it."

"Then—would ye wed a widow woman older than y'rsel'?"

The visitor spread his mouth under his black mustache and bared his teeth, the better to give thought.

"A young widow," he said, "e'en wi' comely form and feature, but wi' bairns and no property—no."

"Though ye loved her?"

"E'en I loved her. But—one ten years older, wi' five hundred acres—aye. One fifteen years older wi' a thousand acres, aye. One wi' a thousand acres, and a mill, and stock and slaves—the older the better."

"E'en on condition ye become a Whig?"

"Hauld man! Ye didna mention that. For me—no. For ye—weel —it is a matter a man must decide for hi'sel', accordin' to his oath and attitude."

"Ye hae given me vera useless counsel."

"Doubtless."

Duncan scratched thoughtfully behind his ear.

"Wi' ye go to meet Flora?"

"I dinna ken. I maun gi' thought yet. 'Twill take time. Weel— aye. I wi' go. But I do not say, now, that I wi' greet Flora, or be wi' anither who goes to the Tidewater."

"If ye plan to turn to the damned Whigs," the MacDougall said shortly, "ye needna gae, 's far as I'm concerned."

"Weel," Duncan gave that thought and spoke without rancor, more to himself than to his guest, "ye may go to the devil and take y'r concerns wi' ye, 's far's I'm concerned."

MacDougall shook out his plaid and calmly prepared to bed down for the night. Duncan sat still and looked into the fire, and Martha's image looked back at him from the smoke in a way to drive a man wild.

But Duncan, even so, would not take his yearning to be comforted in Martha McGee's embrace. The marriage bed summoned him imperiously, but a fiendish caution gripped him and held him away, to think upon it still.

He awoke at dawn, leaning against the log. The Highlander was gone. So was Martha McGee. Gillie Black was yoking the oxen.

"De 'ooman," said Gillie, "she say tell you she shoot you again, you try dat some mo'."

Duncan shouted: "I did na! She misunderstood!"

Gillie backed away. It was not his argument.

CHAPTER 2

THE COMING OF Flora MacDonald was the crowning grace of the Scottish Cape Fear. For forty years, since the MacLean fetched his three hundred to Bladen, the snug little empire of the rupturing clans grew in the valley, first ten thousand strong, then twenty, then forty, and finally fifty or sixty—none ever knew how many, because of the confusion which came—there to dream its dreams of future glories sired by splendors of the past.

From a day's journey above Tidewater to the Piedmont they filled the land—bold, proud people, great of stature and bred to rule. But the wilderness was loose, like the meandering flow of the river, and the King's government was as loose. Butcher Cumberland had crushed the clans and imposed the oath which forbade them to reorganize, and that was irksome, for the Scots loved a chief, a strong center of power. They hated uncertainties and indecision. They built their cabins and their big houses along the riverbanks and up its tributaries and beside its swamps. They made wealth and birthed their bairns and knew promise of well-being beyond anything the old Highlands had given, but their hearts remained tender for the ancient grandeur. Clanship was dead on earth but not in their souls. And that is why Flora MacDonald came so eagerly to Carolina and why the clansmen so eagerly welcomed her. She, in spirit at least, would bind them together and make them whole again.

So, joyously, they journeyed down to Wilmington, by couples, by families, by clans, on the river in boats, and on the King's Highway beside it. They came all the way from Cross Creek and above, toward Deep River, and from Anson in the west, nearly to the Yadkin. It was as though the old river became an enormous tree shaken in a wind, its kilted fruit falling to the roots. It was as if, by the pure force of longing for the heather, the lochs, the mists of Skye, and the water's roar in the Uists, for the soul-twisting voice in which Caledonia ever spoke to her children, the Carolinians finally had prevailed and Scotland shared with them her own heart.

Coming with Flora in the ship *Baliol* were leading MacDonalds and MacLeods and MacCrimmons and other proud clansmen of the Hebrides. They were proud only in what had been, for now their castles were going to the highest bidder. The interminable herds of sheep were grazing their fields, and men of warrior stock must either become herdsmen for the moneyed men of the towns, or starve, or leave. The Hanovers had broken the clan economy, and its crumbling now was complete. So, to Carolina. Some were coming free. Some, bound. Some were of ruling houses, some of the septs and slaves. Some had paid their way. Some indentured themselves for five years for the passage. All were escaping Scottish poverty.

It made more poignant the foretelling of the sinister Coinneach Odhar, the seer of the MacKenzies, who, more than a century before, had prophesied: ". . . the day will come when the raven

will drink its three fulls of the blood of the Clan MacDonald."
And he also said: ". . . the day will come when the clans will flee
from their native country before an army of sheep, and they will
go to lands now unknown, but which shall yet be discovered in
the boundless oceans."

And now, as the MacDonalds sailed a stormy sea to America,
all these sayings of the evil speaker had come to pass. The Mac-
Donald blood *had* flowed upon many a battlefield. The sheep
grazers *had* invaded the Highlands to wreak starvation upon the
shattered clans. The people, in countless numbers, *had* escaped to
lands which were unknown to the ancient prophet.

Duncan, still in the anguish of indecision, although three days
had passed since he had seen Martha, rode over the sand ridges
and crossed the river at Elizabethtown to watch the clansmen and
their womenfolk go down the highway.

There was wealthy Farquard Campbell's grand coach and horses
with outriders and grooms, all in kilts and fine style. There was
Hector MacNeill's slave-rowed boat, with easy chairs and awning.
These two leaders of Cross Creek would vie for the honor of bringing Flora back into the Cape Fear. There was fine old Alexander
MacAlister, riding his great horse, wearing his kilt—plain old
honest Kenneth Black, making no pretensions, but the peer of
them all in unassuming loyalty—far-seeing old Gilbert Johnston,
of Brompton Hall, not an hour's ride up the road—these and other
Scottish strong men. They were burdened with their forebodings
of what evil of turmoil might disrupt America, yet, for this moment, joyful, proud of their mission and eager to pay this tribute.

And there were other groups, some huddling together because,
forsooth, though bold and ready, they were Gaelic-speakers from
the innermost Highlands and were unable to understand the mod-
ern Scots who spoke only English. There were families and there
were groups of kin. Some were going merely to meet Flora Mac-
Donald. Many of them were going to meet brothers and sisters
and children and mates. There were tears in their hearts, if not
in their eyes, for no happiness is so searching to the Scot as reunion.

Even Duncan, Carolina-born, was shaken. He, too, caught the
urge. He could decide afterward. On Donald Bane, his horse, he

pushed forward in the line so that none should speak to him. There were carts and coaches and people who walked. There were men whose kilts, tartans of the MacLeans, the MacNeills, the MacCallums, the MacMurdocks, the MacKenzies, swung beside their horses' heads while their womenfolk, sometimes two and three, rode the horses' backs. Here were the quietly happy family groups, going solidly together to meet those left behind. Here was a fierce oldster, with bristling beard, militantly facing Duncan and demanding something in a wild burst of Gaelic. Here was a heavy-eyed woman, trudging alone, for now she was a widow and her brothers were coming to till her lands. Here was a bare-kneed husband, marching proudly, for now he had cleared the new ground and built the hut, and he went to receive his wife and bairns. And here was the wealthier planter, one of the early Carolina Scots, not haughty, not disdainful, but aloof only as wealth imposes its distinction. He bowed with kindly air and spoke here and there as his spirited horses passed those on the road, but his fine horses and his vauntie slaves were not conducive to the fellowship which the less-favored knew.

So they moved, the road mile by mile becoming softer in deeper sand and deeper mud. There was the purl of wheels in watered ruts, the tinkle of water dripping from the wheels in clear streams, the crackle of dry grit between tire and felloe in the dusty ruts, the padded clop-clop of horses pounding the sand. Far away might be heard the blasting skirl of a bagpipe, and just beyond Donald Bane's pricking ears, in a cart, looking back shyly, laughing at Duncan's yellow hair, a bevy of lassies sang:

"An' Charlie, he's my darlin',
My darlin', my darlin',
Charlie, he's my darlin',
The Young Chevalier!"

Duncan rode on proudly. His heart sang. He had the glow of belonging. The finest gifts of the finest Whigs and all they hoped to have was nothing to compare with e'en the bit of a locket which hung at Flora MacDonald's breast. End his dilemma he must, but first he would meet Flora.

CHAPTER 3

THE TIDE WAS RUNNING OUT. The mighty flood of the Tidewater Cape Fear rolled free. Tart autumn breezes scooped whitecaps. On yon greater half of the river the water was amber, but on this side, splashing at the barnacled wharf timbers, it was black. Upstream a rifleshot distant, at Nigger Head Point, the clay-tinged Cape Fear and its northeast branch, from out the upper plain, came together and flowed side by side, curiously black and amber, thirty miles to the sea.

Downstream three or four miles in the Flats the ship *Baliol* lay against the wind. She was dark-bodied and ivory-sailed, still proud and staunch after the storms which had beset her course from Campbelltown, Kintyre. The Cape Fear Scots had gauged their time well, and now lined Wilmington's Market Street dock, hundreds strong, to welcome the newcomers. With only low murmurs to break the silence and betray their tenseness, they had waited and watched the ship for an hour; they were patiently set for another.

Then the Cape Fear current became slow, and slower yet. It barely crept. Finally, as though a wind ceased, it stopped. The river, its black and amber undisturbed, performed the phenomenon of lying still in its bed, somehow helplessly prostrate and confused. Whereupon, reluctantly, as in protest, the water began to creep back upstream.

Duncan Stuart, wearing his best kilt, his chin proudly high, looked over his left shoulder to speak. "The tide," he said, "has tur-r-ned."

"Yes, turned," said middle-aged Cornelius Harnett. His voice had the quick, soft twist of the Irish, though he was a Carolinian and a full generation out of the Green Isle.

They looked back at the ship, for destiny rode in those ivory sails, and if at moments the sails lagged empty, it was because the strong winds yet did not blow. Not yet. The scene was flat and green and tinted with the first pastels of autumn. In their lush setting, the mansions of the rice planters reposed in placid luxury. Their tall chimneys reached above the monotonous green background which here and there was lighted by the blazing reds and yellows of the early-turning sweet gums. It was a sight to enthrall the MacDonalds, for it was richness and peace and welcome. The Tidewater barons were to be envied. The Scots must have a strong grip if they were to escape the Whig snare with Flora MacDonald.

The sweetness of the plantations made Nelson's grogshop across the wharf and the dingy town house behind the crowd and the crowding small buildings along Market Street look the part of a shabby village, which they were. But the finer houses were on the hill and not visible from where they stood.

Duncan Stuart was not thinking of the scene, except to wonder, perhaps, what Flora and her gallant Allan might think on't, but of what Cornelius Harnett had said. There was the hint of a double meaning in the tone. The Whigs were tricky. He looked back to see.

"It always tur-r-ns!" he said truculently.

The suave Harnett was not one to clash blades to no end. He waited as though his hazel eyes listened. Harnett was wealthy and his mansion magnificently set. It was a place to which the noted came in their travels. But no man feared to speak his mind before Cornelius Harnett. He was one of the people.

"Aye, Duncan," he said softly, even persuasively, "but you never forget, my lad, that more flows out than flows in."

Duncan Stuart was not subtle, but he understood. He stood alert, searching for a reply.

Harnett continued to speak soothingly: "And remember, too, that far upstream, where the water runs out from the rot in the swamps, it flows, always downhill. It is only on tidewater, Duncan, where the flow ever stops. Change will not be denied."

Duncan thought hard. The Irishman's smooth words were too convincing for their truth. Harnett's benign look was deceptive.

"The in-tide," he said stoutly, "neither will be denied."

"That is true," Harnett said, agreeable. "Still—swamp water always reaches the sea. Is it not so?"

"Swamp water!" Duncan said disdainfully.

"Yes," Cornelius Harnett mused. "Swamp water it is."

"Good for nothing but to turn mill wheels."

"So many think so," Cornelius Harnett sighed.

They dropped the conversation, turning to look at a chaise-and-four which clattered in from the Brunswick Ferry Road. The equipage whirled to a theatrical stop before the docks, and two liveried Negroes ran to the heads of the horses. The coachman went to the door and opened it with a bow and a flourish.

The man who stepped to the running board was elegantly dressed. His lacy white stock was crisp. His blue, tailed coat was without a wrinkle and fitted his stocky shoulders with a perfection that bespoke his trips to London and fittings with his tailor. Leisurely on the running board, his thin cane at an angle beside his glistening shoe buckles, Robert Howe, of Howe's Point, appraised the crowd on the wharf. His eyes rested searchingly on the Scottish women down from the Upper Cape Fear. Bob Howe kept up an unremitting search for new beauties. The plain brown garb of farm folk made no difference. But his eye passed on, dark and piercing, to the men. His slow smile broadened as the flicking tap of his glance caught first one acquaintance and then another.

It was so for Duncan Stuart, who nodded his head and set swinging his yellow hair. Duncan's nod was not warm, for he disliked Robert Howe, disliked the manner in which Howe separated from his wife and the way in which he so arrogantly pursued women. But Howe was charming, a man's man as well as a woman's man, and Duncan looked at him and, resentfully, felt his pull. These Scot Highland women—Duncan loved them, loved their plain clothes and their simple pleasures and their kindly firmness. It galled him to have them raked by Bob Howe's lustful eye, though Howe's glance was no more for them than for all women.

Howe was waving to Cornelius Harnett and calling: "Evenin', Connie. Come, we need a drink—you and Duncan."

Bob Howe lifted his cane lightly toward the tavern invitingly.

Duncan shook his head, and Cornelius Harnett said: "No. Don't want one."

Of all the men of the Tidewater, Duncan liked Cornelius Harnett most, although the Lord knew he had little enough confidence in the whole pack. Where Bob Howe was more than forty, Cornelius Hartnett was fifty and more, where Howe was black and driving, cutting his eye like a rapier, subduing women for his pleasure and men for his following, Cornelius Harnett was chestnut-haired and calm, with a lanky grace and darkly hazel eyes that waited and studied and sought to agree. But Harnett had a power that was deep and compelling. Both were subverters and troublemakers and enemies to the King's peace.

They watched Howe enter the saloon, arm on the off shoulder of the Herculean Alexander Lillington, reaching up to attain it.

"I reckon we may as well," Cornelius Harnett said as though he had reconsidered. He made it seem to Duncan that he, Duncan, too, had decided, after all, to drink with Bob Howe. With no more discussion they sauntered over the timbers toward the tavern.

The place was crowded and dark and rumbling with talk. They pushed into the door, and the pounding noise of half-drunken mouthing smote their ears. The sweetish reek of hard liquor and tobacco smoke met them in a wave. Through the dim light of the river window thirty or forty men were to be seen, standing, disregarding the chairs and tables, holding their liquor glasses in little groups, some shouting, some laughing. Their dark clothes melted into the lower shadows, but the light caught their ludicrously earnest faces, the flash of their teeth, the whites of their eyes.

The scene stopped Duncan in his tracks. A sudden hard suspicion burned in him. The Whigs were at work. His eyes leaped fiercely from group to group. In the near group was Hector MacNeill, a strong man among the Highlanders. Colonel John Ashe, of the Tidewater, was plying him with fine English liquor, flattering him, and Hector was mellow with Ashe's liquor and flattery.

Beyond stood Farquard Campbell, one of the wealthiest of the Cumberland planters, listening and smiling, his light hair and pink face lit by the uncertain light, and his milky blue eyes, so easy to shift, held steady under the pleasure of drinking to his and his companion's ancestors—he, Farquard Campbell, son of Scottish nobility, and James Moore, descendant of the Irish kings.

Yonder, Duncan Stuart saw with increasing sullenness, stood Gilbert Johnston, of Brompton Hall, a Scot of his own Bladen County settlement—Gilbert Johnston, who had fought shoulder to shoulder with Duncan's father at Culloden. At Gilbert's elbow stood the loud-mouthed William Dry of Brunswick, an arrant Whig, and out of prison purely by the mercy of a lenient King George.

And now Alexander Lillington was standing beside the solid old Kenneth Black, the upper-country man and a giant among the Scots. The huge Lillington towered like an amiable mastodon above him. The elegant Howe was making his way toward Archibald MacDougall.

In every group was a staunch Scot, a man of influence, and ever at his elbow was a low-country Whig of purling tongue and flattering word. And nary a Highlander was buying a drink. Liquor was free—fine liquor. Scotch money, Duncan noted, wouldn't pass. Well, by God, he'd see.

Cornelius Harnett was pushing at his elbow, urging him on to the bar. Nelson was sweating, rubbing the oak planks with a towel, looking up at them in inquiry. But Cornelius Harnett was looking at Duncan and gauging his hard-set eyes and his grim mouth. Cornelius Harnett was shrewd.

"Wut! Wut!" Duncan muttered. "What's this?"

"Little enough," Harnett shrugged amiably, "when old friends get together."

"Fr-r-iends!" Duncan scoffed.

"Yes, friends," Cornelius Harnett answered casually as though that ended the matter. But he did not invite Duncan to drink. Instead he demanded: "Aren't you going to buy me a drink, fellow?"

Duncan's chest swelled. He blurted: "Aye! That I am!" and his heavy fist pounded the bar.

"Scots!" he thundered. "Array—Glengarry, Skye, Raasay, Kintyre, Benbecula!"

The talk ceased, and the Highlanders and their friends turned curiously and met his glare.

"A toast!" he said.

If the seasoned oldsters, wily in their tricks and proud of bold records, failed to understand why this youngster should call them to silence and demand a toast, it mattered little. He was a Scot, and he had called.

"Aye!" they answered, and gulped down one drink to take another. They pushed to the bar, taking their companions with them.

"Aye, Doon-kan!" Hearty old Hector MacNeill slapped his back. "A braw drinkie, with a braw laddie—f'r auld lang syne!"

"Na!" said Duncan. "Be still. I'll speak the toast."

"What matters?" Hector shrugged. "A drink's a drink."

Nelson, with a bottle in each hand, clinked the bottle necks against the glasses and made gurgling music swiftly down the bar.

"My toast!" said Duncan stepping back, holding his glass high. The men stood back and raised their glasses, and the agile-minded young Alfred Moore looked at him amusedly.

"To a name, which, as Dr Johnson said and as Boswell wrote, will be mentioned in history, and if courage and fidelity be virtues, mentioned with honor—Flora MacDonald!"

The response was a blast of "Ayes!" and the Tidewater Whigs led all the rest. The liquor was whipped down, and the men cheered once more. One might have taken it for a Tidewater demonstration. The ceremony ended. The Scots turned back to their Whig friends and fell to talking again. Duncan angrily turned to pay for the round of drinks.

As he waited for his change, someone tugged at his arm, and Farquard Campbell smiled there.

" 'Twas with a good will ye did it, lad—but save y'r money. It takes more than Irish blarney to change the mind of a Scot. Aye—and more toddy than the Tidewater fops can carry."

"But it galls a man!"

"Aye—well. Ye'll be older, y'rsel', someday."

Farquard turned back to the fount of his joviality, and Duncan leaned on the rail morosely.

For all his efforts to break the Scots out of the smooth clutches of the rice planters and bring them a sense of duty, he had only served to spend his money and make his countrymen drunker. How long he stood thus he did not know. He awoke to a man standing before him. His eyes were grave, he had a sweet smile, and there was no hint of guile in him. It was Cornelius Harnett again, and he pressed a drink into Duncan's hand.

"It is your turn to drink with me now," Harnett said.

Duncan drew a breath of indignation. He sought a proper retort for a whipsawing politician.

"For a toast!" Cornelius insisted quickly. "A toast to—King George!"

The glass was in Duncan's left hand, but his right drew convulsively into a fist.

"Cornelius Harnett, do you sneer at my king?"

Cornelius' chuckle flowed with mellow good nature. "Yours— *alone?* Come, Duncan, don't be so selfish with your king. He is my king, too."

"Yours!"

"Aye! Not a rebellious word have I spoken yet—nor will. Not if His Majesty but grants me the same rights as a London cockney."

"His Majesty will grant ye your entitlements!" Duncan declared stoutly.

"Let us hope so," and Cornelius Harnett looked out the window with a flicker of anxiety upon his mobile countenance. Harnett had much wealth to go into these balances.

Duncan's anger, under Farquard's canny advice and Harnett's irresistable good nature, began to cool.

"An' it will be well," he said in the tone of giving fair counsel, "to bide His Majesty's sound decisions. I hold you too much a friend to take pleasure in an order for us Hielanders to march down the river and lay our broadswords across your necks."

Harnett laughed and shook his head. "Drink, Duncan. Drink!"

That was one trouble wi' the damned Whigs. They laughed too much.

A woman went white, stumbled to her knees, her arms still outstretched, her eyes strained in the joy of reunion, and swooned. They lifted her away, her stiff, heavy shoes showing incongruously from out her brown skirt. The mad excitement was turmoil. Bagpipes on board the ship and on the dock shrieked ruthless clamor. Men shouted and women cried. Ship's officers bawled their orders and could not be heard. The scream of the winches and the grumble of cables were drowned in the tumult of hysterical welcome.

Women thrust babies over the slowly moving rail and held

them high for men on the dock to see. Old men and old women stood back from the crush, their leathered faces streamed with tears. Men shouted hoarsely, as though by ferocious voices they could bridge twenty feet of water and crush loved ones once more to their hearts. Young people squealed and tugged at restraining hands.

On the dock the front lines were a frenzied mass, waving over the water to hurry the landing. Behind them, excited, too, but able better to restrain themselves, were the Scots of property and influence. They waited patiently, for it was apparent from the first that there would be a wild scramble, a reunion so fiercely joyous that all other business must wait until it had spent itself. Duncan Stuart, queer new feelings throttling his breast, stood in this group.

Against him a woman stumbled, desolated and unseeing.

"He didna come!" she wailed. "He didna come."

Courteously at one side the Cape Fear rice planters stood, their trim long coats and slender legs comparing strikingly with the swinging kilts and bare knees of the Scots.

A round-faced, pleasant-eyed man of distinction tripped up hurriedly, nearly out of breath. He shook hands quickly with some of the up-river Scots, bowing to his neighbors of the town.

"I thought—I thought—" he explained anxiously, "that Mrs Sikes' new baby would never—would never . . ."

The up-river and down-river groups, both, looked relieved, for he was Dr Thomas Cobham, himself a Scot, the ideal person to be the spokesman.

In the storm of noise the timbers touched, and the two lines of people were at each other like waves. All others stood back. The moan, the whine, the muffled cries were too much a prayer, too sacred a happiness for one to do aught but attend it respectfully.

Soon the stream of people began to flow down the gangways, some still clutching each other. Others bore on their shoulders bales of clothing, bundles of chairs, clanking pots and pans. One woman, who had feared there were no oaks in Carolina, drew from her pockets a handful of acorns and threw them overboard, laughing gaily.

As the deck cleared, the piles of household goods, the home treasures which had been brought to the new huts, began to show up as little hills.

On the afterdeck, standing beyond the tumult, suppressing their excitement, were the Kingsburgh Scots. Duncan stared o'erbold at them, with a surging new pride—tall, handsome, kilted men—silk-gowned, comely women. The men were like a military escort for the grand lady who stood modestly in the center.

Flora MacDonald was happy. Her eyes, to Duncan, were a blue mist, moved by the wild joy of the reunited. Her smile, too, was as full of warmth and sympathy as her look, but it came and went as she willed. She was not large and not small, but firm and round, her fifty-two winters having passed over her most kindly. The wavering pink of her cheek was still that of her maidenhood when Allan Ramsay and his contemporary artists matched their skill against its gentle bloom. Her hair was still soft brown and abundant, still with its wind-blown flair to match a soul born to venture. Her dress was of black silk, a rich remnant of the years before poverty became a threat in the Highlands. Over her left shoulder was the green, gray and red crossing of the Stuart tartan. If she felt aught of the stares from the dock, she took it in easy grace while the Kingsburghers waited for the committee.

The shrill whisper of a lassie on the wharf, quickly hushed to politeness, exclaimed: "The locket! With Bonnie Charlie's hair!"

And that was true. The little round locket rested snug on the cushion of her breast as it had done these twenty-eight years.

The Americans who picked their way across the deck had no hesitation on whom to address. Dr Cobham was the least abashed of them all, but the Scots who followed him were fierce and back-shouldered in their self-consciousness. The Tidewater planters, for all their lordly presumptions, held back both from courtesy and a certain timidity in approaching the famed heroine.

Allan MacDonald of Kingsburgh had been represented to them as they now saw him, a large, stately man of sensible, military cast. His jet-black hair, tied behind, was topped with a large Highland blue bonnet. Though Flora's own age, he seemed older, more incisive, with a touch of the eagle about his eye and beaked nose. For this dress appearance he wore the tartan of the MacDonalds of Glengarry, broad blue crossings on red, with philibeg matching the plaid thrown back from the black rosette on his left shoulder. He was one to make Highlanders proud of the ancient garb.

But where Allan had the eagle eye of daring, Duncan thought that it was Flora who saw this raw scene with the clarity to gauge it dubiously, to be afraid and yet meet the challenge. It was not all rice fields and serenity, and that was known to her and accepted.

As eager as he was, Duncan held back to the wharf, his foot resting on the gang board. He wished to hold the hand of Flora MacDonald and radiate to her the reverence in his soul, to stand with those other more favored Highlanders who were like a guard about her. But he had no license to intrude. He would wait, and later—today, tomorrow, when the great ones had ceased to monopolize her—he would approach quietly but without fear.

He knew now what she was. It was in her eyes. There was gentleness and common sense and an understanding of pain. And more yet. In the blue something was hidden, a flash to go with the thrust of her jaw. And the thrust, too, was hidden in the smooth curve of her chin. Duncan sensed now that one might come to love Flora's gentleness long before he felt the force which made her a heroine.

Dr Cobham introduced himself to Allan, and Allan presented him to Flora, then to Anne, their daughter; to a young Miss MacLeod, to a Mrs MacDougall and to a Mrs MacKenzie. Turning to the men, to Anne's middle-aged, soldierly husband, Alexander MacLeod of Lochbay, then to MacLoreds, and Clan-ranald MacDonalds and Glengarry MacDonalds. These, in turn, were introduced to the waiting Scots and to the Wilmington citizens who by now had lost their sense of order and were an undivided group pressing eagerly forward in their delight and their welcome.

"And this, Mrs MacDonald," said Dr Cobham, causing Duncan to start guiltily, for he had not realized that he had followed so deeply into the crowd, "is one of your handsomest, most devoted worshipers on the Cape Fear—Duncan Stuart."

Duncan's first mad impulse was to turn and burst through the crowd, away. His hands, his knees, his feet were around him, like great leaden things to move about. Flora MacDonald, her blue-lighted eyes suddenly warm, put her hand on his possessively.

"Sweet boy," she said, "I love the land that gives me such friends." Her voice was rich and smooth, like velvet.

Duncan began to mumble something and turn away, but she held him. "No, no, you stand here with us." She made a way through the line for him between her daughter Anne and the Miss MacLeod, whose hand she fixed on his arm lightly. "Keep him, Mary, child," she smiled, "for our own." The little group closed again, and Duncan felt himself to be something large and ungainly crushed in a bale of roses. He looked over the top of Flora MacDonald's head in stony silence up the terrifying vista of Market Street. Cornelius Harnett looked at him and smiled, strangely pleased. Flora MacDonald was speaking to others. Allan was beside her, as tall as Duncan himself, entirely unruffled by the things which made him quake. He'd prefer, aye, ten times over, to fight with a Cape Fear alligator than to stand here helpless in the daintiness of lace and the tinkle of cultured voices and the intangible fragrance of perfume. Old Kenneth Black was passing before the group, unafraid, kindly, eyes atwinkle.

"*Fionnaghal nighean Raonuill 'ic Aonghais Oig, an Airidh Mhuilinn*—I hae admiration for ye, lass."

"Oh-h-h-h!" Flora beamed, patting the back of his hand, "that's the first time my full name has been spoken in years. Do you speak Gaelic freely?"

"Na unco guid, but there's them that's fair glib-gabbet on't e'en yet. Ye maun gab wi' them aften, dochter. They be saire lanely f'r the auld heather."

The sun was dropping low upon Eagle's Island across the river, and Dr Cobham sped his introductions.

"Before we go to my house," he said to Flora, "you must know Bob Howe. He has placed his chaise at your disposal. He is jealous of me because you are not going to his fine mansion, down in Brunswick, instead."

"You are so good," Flora smiled, giving him her hand.

Howe bowed, kissed her fingers, did it with that grace which made it seem quite the normal thing in the colony. He raised his eyes and became erect, audaciously apologetic.

"Dr Johnson," he pleaded, "left me unprepared. He was so—ah—conservative."

Flora scoffed, pressing his arm. They chatted for a moment. Flora referred to Dr Johnson as a "stormy-headed old dear." Bob Howe spoke easily of London and of Edinburgh.

But even as they talked, Howe's roving eye leaped over Flora's shoulder and rested on the MacLeod lass whose hand was on Duncan Stuart's arm. Duncan scowled at him. The girl had said no word to him, but now she tightened her clasp. She laughed and raised her face to his. He started, as out of a daze, and bent down to listen.

She said something. Something about a storm at sea, he thought. He didn't quite catch it. She had a round, firmly soft face, with warm pink coursing close under the white. Her lips were soft, too, and firm like her cheeks, and her eyes were warm like her cheeks. But they were brown and steady—and excited. Her hair was like brown silk beside the yellow lock of his own that fell beside it as he bent down.

"Don't you think so, too?" she was asking urgently.

Duncan Stuart looked long into her face. Surely, he thought, what she said, though she was but a glaikit lassie, required an answer.

"Aye," he said solemnly, and stood straight again and stared up Market Street. Bob Howe had turned away, and she stopped preening for the old philanderer.

That night Duncan saw Mary MacLeod again. He would not have, but circumstance made it so. The Kingsburgh party and many others had gone to the Cobhams'. There was to be an elaborate reception. He might have gone. An invitation was not required. But he was confused, and the purple shadows that lay upon the water called him to stay at the wharf. He had the feeling of defeat. Flora MacDonald had come. She was all that he had dreamed, and more. But she had the touch and tone and delicate lilt of the Whigs more than the braw bluffness of the up-country Scots. She was more at home with Maurice Moore than with Hector MacNeill. And, b'God, the damned Whigs had run away with her, to dazzle her with their uniformed niggers and spermaceti candles and silver candlesticks and flowing draperies. The Scots were there, in truth, but they would play second fiddle. The Whigs would see to that. He didn't want to be there. They'd make him look more the backwoods gawk, just to brighten their own glow.

Better, here, where the shadows were purple, where he could sit in the dark and look through the ratlines of the *Baliol* and hear the splash of the water and the murmur of the Scots in the covered carts as they ate their suppers and prepared for the all-night plod up the King's Highway. Bob Howe, no doubt, had cornered Mary MacLeod in some nook and was smothering her will with protestations of sudden love. Aye, and she believed it.

The gloom which called to him so richly, however, soon was broken by the coming of a rude back-countryman in whom there was nothing placid. Short, compact, questing, the young fellow came into the ship's light abruptly. He wore a red silk skullcap. So young for a skullcap, he must have lost his hair by the filthy scaldhead, the tetterworm. It added to Duncan's feeling of inhospitality. The woodsman carried a knobby hickory stick, shaved white, which he gripped at halfway and handled as a club. He was vigorously at leisure. Exploringly he whacked at the ship's rail, he whacked at a wharf timber. He clubbed a washpot on the dock, and it rang like a bell. He whacked at the cable which moored the ship. He looked into the shadow where Duncan sat as if minded to club him, too.

"Is that a big ship or a little ship?" he demanded.

Duncan looked up to frown. The man had blue, hard eyes, which disbelieved one's word even before it was spoken.

Duncan hesitated, but came out of his funk to find an answer: "Some are bigger yet, some smaller."

"Sure?" The tone was suspicion.

"Would I make ye a damned lie for sport?"

The skullcapped one flashed a quick smile, as though he had drawn first blood, and walked on, whacking a cart wheel.

While he was yet in sight, Cornelius Harnett strolled down from Front Street and stood on the dock, watching the water. He was near Duncan and peered into the shadow.

"You, Duncan?"

"Aye."

They were silent a full minute.

"The water at night," said Cornelius—"I like it. You can feel it flow, but you can't see it. It is like the undercurrents of mankind."

"Aye?" Duncan was not interested.

"I came for you."

"I kenned. Why?"

"Because I wish you to see for yourself that we design nothing on Flora MacDonald. We welcome her. We admire her. That is all. She is a beautiful woman, and she honors us with her presence. That makes us happy. But for intrigue—no."

"Who said I tho't ye designed on her?"

Cornelius Harnett laughed softly. "No one had to. You've bristled like a field nettle all day."

"Weel—I'm not comin'. Why should you fiddle your time with me, when a'ready y've inveigled Hector MacNeill and Farquard Campbell and the old ones?"

Cornelius said nothing, but looked at the water.

"Ye're wrong, Cornelius—bad wrong—wi' your committees an' schemes by night. 'Tis bad enough for you, but when you seek to trap my ain folk, already struck down to oppression, and bring on them once more the wrath o' the King, ye make shame to yoursel'."

Cornelius was not disturbed, but stood quietly, his hands in his pockets, listening, nearly smiling. "But what do you think of a king, Duncan," he asked in reasoning tone, "that takes money from your purse to give it to a fat London merchant?"

"Deil ma care! I hae no time t' disturb mysel' wi' considerations o' high finance. I'll build my stout house. I'll worship my God. I'll serve my king. I'll burn my tar and till my ground, and I'll hae plenty. Gin a Lon'on merchant swindle me a bit, like the rats in my corn crib, he's on'y a whit less than welcome. I'll na rebel on my king for it."

Cornelius heard this, his interested smile barely changing.

"But, tell me, Duncan—suppose the King should wax extremely

wroth and order you and the clansmen to march upon us and
strike us down. Would you do so?"

The two men eyed each other, smiling dry. Duncan said: "At
the King's command, there is no question. At his word I would
split you frae your pate t' y'r thrapple. I couldna do else."

"But you wouldn't enjoy it, Duncan?" Cornelius urged. His
smile was wry but still amiably pleased.

"Na, Cornelius Harnett—'twould grieve me sore. I count ye
a fool and a Whig, but a friend."

"Fine! Fine! I can't imagine being more pleasantly slaughtered
than by a sorrowful Scot."

The elder man chuckled and changed the subject.

"They're having good times at the ball. Everyone is trying to
show the famous Flora how perfectly correct he can be."

"Aye."

"By the way, the pretty MacLeod girl has vanished. No one
could find her as I left."

"Uh?"

"No. And Bob Howe was nowhere to be found."

"They're thegither!" Duncan cried, starting up.

"No doubt," Cornelius Harnett said equably. "If you have
any interest in her you'd best find her—for Bob Howe is fast
and sure with women."

Duncan shook his fist in Cornelius Harnett's face. "I'll wring
his neck! I'll——"

"Slowly, slowly with the fist. I did not abduct the girl. Moreover, it isn't likely that he can entirely subjugate her in a mere
two hours. Still, if you're interested, it would be safer to make
sure."

"What hae I to do with it?" Duncan demanded, suddenly
defensive. "Only that she is a Scottish lass and Robert Howe shall
do her no harm. She's but a bit of a giglet and no match for him."

But now they were marching fast up Market Street, and Cornelius Harnett had to step lively to keep up with Duncan's
plowing stride.

It was "Doon-kan," the deep liquid music he had known in
his mind, when Flora MacDonald turned from the group and

came on the red-carpeted floor to him. No flat "Dunkkin" here.
And no reserve. She had seen him on the ship and had known
him and had taken him as friend. His timidity in the splendor
of the silk and the silver and the tinkle of the voices once more
gripped him, and he fought a sudden foolish desire to drop to
one knee and bow before her. But she had his hand in her warm
two hands, pressing it. "You bonnie boy!" her eyes holding on
his, smiling, and then she was like an aunt, a very dear aunt, and
he no longer was blate, but at ease. Mary Harnett watched him
quietly smiling, as though saying to herself: "It is as I said."

Women in lace dresses and silk dresses, their ruffles flaring
stiff, except in the soft curves of their bosoms, were on the floor.
Some were sitting, some standing. Beyond the wide doors to
the library the men were smoking pipes. From somewhere came
soft violin music. Flora's chair was next to the spinet, but no one
was playing.

Mrs Cobham joined them. She called him "Duncan," though he
had never been introduced. "We've been trying to persuade
Mistress MacDonald to sing some of the Scottish songs," she
said. Duncan eyed her without approval. A woman should not be
a Whig when her husband was a king's friend.

A girl, a very tall girl, joined them in the middle of the large
parlor. "I've looked everywhere——" Then she said: "Oh!" and
waited. Mrs Cobham introduced Duncan. She was Ann Fergus,
light-haired, with a sly roguish look.

"And I would," said Flora, "but no one can find Mary MacLeod
to play the accompaniment. Perhaps, you, Duncan——"

"But, please—oh, please—Mistress MacDonald, may I ask——"
Flora turned to the girl and smiled.

". . . did you really—re-e-e-ally—sleep in the arms of Bonnie
Prince Charlie that night in the storm on the Minch?"

All the women laughed and gathered quickly to hear the
answer.

"Well"—Flora's lips were a pursed smile—"the romanticists
and the poets would have it that way. One young woman actually
stormed the ship when I was being taken to the Tower of London,
and nothing would do but that she must sleep with me. She
wanted to say she had slept in the same bed with the girl who

had slept in the Bonnie Prince's arms. I let her. It seemed a pity
to tell her otherwise."

The women smiled, but they were disappointed.

"One would scarcely tell it, anyway," Duncan said, manlike,
and started, for that was the first time he had heard his own
voice in the room.

"Well, all I know," Flora shrugged and smiled, "is that I
was most weary and leaned against the side of the boat. The
Prince told me to have no fear, that he would keep the oarsmen
from stepping on me. Well—when I wakened—no one had
stepped on me."

Everyone laughed. Duncan said stoutly: "I'll find her."

He did. Very soon. In just such a place as he suspected. Mary
and Robert Howe were on the second-story piazza in the shadow
behind the vines. Howe was murmuring so insistently that Duncan heard him. Duncan stepped up resentfully—angry with Howe
for attempting to kiss one so young, angry with Mary for not
repulsing him. His own awkward position did not occur to him.
He merely plowed forward with the assurance of delegated
authority.

"Lass, Flora said come there."

Robert Howe sprang to his feet, meeting him. It was dark,
but Duncan knew his fury by the rasp in his voice.

"Miss MacLeod's name," said Howe, "is Miss MacLeod, and
please address her that way. And in future kindly avoid these—
unheralded arrivals."

"When there is occasion," Duncan said bluntly, "I'll come
as I please."

"I don't like your tone!"

"I don't like yours. Come, giglet."

Mary was so humiliated and so bitter at Duncan's intrusion
that she had no smart reply. She ran toward him and stopped.
She stamped her foot. She gasped: "I—— Oh-h-h!" She trembled
in the helplessness of emotion too swiftly turned from romance
to rage.

Duncan, for all his anger, paused to chuckle, and she
stormed:

"I hae you understand that I am a grown woman, to be treated as such! I hae worn the snood this twalmont, fourteen months e'en. I am no giglet!"

"Aye, aye," said Duncan. "Even so, ye'll come. Flora said so."

"I'll not!"

"And," said Robert Howe, "that settles it. The lady says she will not be ordered about, and I will see that she isn't."

"Ye'll do well, Robert Howe, to keep silent. 'Tis not your concern."

The two men leaped at each other. Duncan's anger was slow and sullen, goaded by the tricks of fashion which he had encountered through the day; Robert Howe's, flamed and quick. Duncan was bigger, and younger by twenty years. Howe, nevertheless, was strong and agile. Moreover he was agile-minded, which was a golden asset at the moment, when he was about to make an implacable enemy of a man he needed for a friend.

He smiled, and his flash of anger seemed to disappear with it. The girl was important, certainly, but there were girls and girls. His hand went placatingly to Duncan's tensed arm, and he laughed.

"How silly!" he said. "What must Miss MacLeod think of us Americans! Certainly we will go. We all will go." He moved as if to lead the way. But Duncan was not so quick-minded.

"I hae the mind to slap ye o'er the rail, still," he said.

"Oh!" Robert Howe laughed, waving his hand, as if wiping out all that had been.

"Come, girl," said Duncan. He placed his arm around her back, as he would treat a child. She was stubborn and braced against him. Her strength surprised him. He dropped his hand, and she stepped away.

Robert Howe bowed her through the door, murmuring: "Another, better time?"

They all went down to the parlor together. Mary did not look at Duncan again that night, but the square set of her shoulders was eloquent enough. Nor did she again look at Robert Howe, who soon left.

She sat at the spinet, in back of Flora MacDonald, and in the sweep of other things Duncan soon ceased to give her thought. To his mind, if she but knew, she should be grateful instead of clabbered with spite. As she tried the keys, Flora's eyes turned slowly on her and clouded for the moment. Then Flora forgot Mary and began to sing.

It was one of the old Gaelic folk songs, a wild and haunting ballad the clans of the Western Isles had sung since a time no one remembered. Only Flora knew the words. Some knew the tune. There was no applause. Some of the Wilmingtonians attempted it, but it seemed a desecration upon the silence of the up-the-river people. The men had left their pipes and their liquor and had joined the women. The Scots made no effort to find seats but stood in the middle of the room, their arms crossed, frowning darkly.

Then Flora swung into the rippling "Charlie, He's My Darling!" and the Scottish faces went from pinkly fierce to red, and their faces glowed. Flora's voice was rich and lilting, and she had that trick that the Scots knew as truly Caledonian. She ended it: ". . . Charlie, he's my darling, my darling, the Young Chevalier!" and the crashing, raucous, wailing smash was laughter. Wild laughter.

The pent-up, homesick yearnings of the Scottish bosoms exploded as thunder. One dark little knobby Scot stood in the middle of the floor in a daze, beating time to the ended tune with his fist. Others lifted their knees and slapped them with their hands. Old Hector MacNeill and Archibald MacDougall shouted and circled gaily in the first few steps of a Highland fling. Flora smiled delightedly. Duncan looked at her with shining eyes, marveling.

As a compliment to Farquard, Flora then sang: "The Campbells are comin', oho, oho; the Campbells are comin', oho, oho . . ." and the MacDonalds and the MacLeods, who had an ancient grudge against the Campbells, stood silent, grimly, but Farquard was hugely pleased with the song and, too, with the resentment in their breasts. He smiled sly and triumphant, and the others glowered at him. Still it was something from Scotia and from Flora MacDonald, and when she turned from the Campbellian boast they nodded and asked for more of it.

Flora laughed derisively at the Macs and then softened their bristles with the old ditty:

> *"Oh, tarry wool is ill to spin;*
> *Card it weel ere ye begin—*
> *Card it weel and draw it sma'.*
> *Tarry wool is best of a'."*

Now they were smiling again, the MacDonalds and the MacEacherns and the MacLeans and the Campbells, all—smiling slowly and hungrily. Flora was feeding them bits of music of the old heather, and they leaned forward for the next. She sang:

> *"Oh, gin my love were yon red rose*
> *That grows upon the castle wa'*
> *And I mysel a drap o' dew*
> *Into her bonny breast tae fa'."*

Then she sang a bit from the lament of the old Highland free-booter, MacPherson, who fiddled gallantly his way to the hangman:

> *"But dantonly and wantonly*
> *And rantingly I'll gae;*
> *I'll play a tune and dance it round*
> *Beneath the gallows tree."*

Flora looked around at the Wilmingtonians and smiled saucily. "There are no Whigs present, I hope?"

"No!" John Ashe declared, and everybody laughed. "Particularly no, when you sing of gallows trees!"

"Go ahead! Go ahead!" the Whigs urged, and she sang the complaint of the early Scottish Tories:

> *"Our thistles flourished fresh and fair,*
> *And bonny bloomed our roses,*
> *But Whigs came like frost in June*
> *And withered a' our posies!*
>   *Awa, Whigs, awa!*
>   *Awa, Whigs, awa!*
>   *Ye're but a pack o' traitor louns—*
>   *Ye'll do nae guid at a'!"*

Scots roared at that and pounded Whig backs and then pounded them again to make sure there were no hard feelings. The Whigs were hugely pleased if their guffaws spoke truth, and Flora stood most tickled at the success of her daring little jibe.

While the laughter still rumbled, she swung into the bit of a song which had this folksy chorus:

> *"Oh, corn rigs and rye rigs!*
> *Oh, corn rigs are bonnie,*
> *And where'er ye meet a bonnie lass*
> *Preen up her cockernonnie."*

Duncan detected a sobering change come into the blue of Flora MacDonald's eyes. At first, at the instant explosion of soul-hungry approval by the Scots, she had seemed surprised and delighted. Then she had suppressed what almost was a gloating assurance when she found that the Highlanders laid their hearts bare before her. Now she was gentle. " 'Lord Randal'?" she asked them, looking around the circle, referring to the ancient ballad which all Scots knew and loved.

"Aye!" Kenneth Black beamed. "Aye!" And so she sang:

> *" 'Oh, where hae ye been, Lord Randal, my son?*
> *Oh, where hae ye been, my handsome young man?'*
> *'I hae been to the wildwood; Mother, make my bed soon,*
> *For I'm weary wi' hunting, and fain wald lie doon.' "*

After the manner of the old ballad singers she sang and waited, and one by one the others took up the story while Mary MacLeod accompanied them. Hector MacNeill, powerfully abashed when his voice first boomed, sang: "I dined wi' my true love; Mother, make my bed . . ." Allan MacDonald carried the story to: "I gat eels boiled in broo; Mother, make my bed . . ." Gilbert Johnston forsook his dignity enough to explain about the dogs: "Oh, they swelled and they died; Mother, make my bed . . ." And Flora sang the last stanza:

> *" 'Oh, I fear ye are poisoned, Lord Randal, my son!*
> *Oh, I fear ye are poisoned, my handsome young man!'*
> *'Oh yes! I am poisoned; Mother, make my bed soon,*
> *For I'm sick at the heart and I fain wald lie doon.' "*

The doleful old song came to its funereal end, and Flora and the Scots stood chuckling wishfully. She sighed, and swung into a ditty:

"Oh, hon, my Highland man!
Oh my bonny Highland man!
Weel wad I my true love ken,
Amang ten thousand Highland men!"

Without waiting, Flora then sang "Annie Laurie" and did not pause, perhaps because her voice was rich and uncertain with the feeling that throbbed in the room:

"My heart's in the Highlands, my heart is not here.
My heart's in the Highlands, a-chasing the deer . . ."

Cornelius Harnett and John Slingsby sensed what would come soon and were prepared. When Flora struck the first word of Ramsay's "Auld Lang Syne," they placed "a cup o' kindness" in the hand of each Highlander:

"Should auld acquaintance be forgot
And never thought upon,
The flames of love extinguished
And freely past and gone?"

A congealing change came upon the Highlanders. Their faces no longer glowed red in their grim pleasure. Now there was a far hunger in their eyes, and they crept close upon Flora MacDonald as she sang. They breathed almost in sobs.

"If e'er I have a house, my dear,
That truly is call'd mine . . ."

They stood, mute, as though they listened to the tumbling of the Minch on the rocks or beheld the gray crags of Glengarry. Some gulped their liquor without seeming to know they did so, others did not drink at all, their perfect tribute of soul-riving emotion to Flora's gift of song.

"Though thou wert rebel to the king
And beat with wind and rain . . ."

Old Kenneth Black stood straight, his head up, and tears trembled on his cheeks. Hector MacNeill grasped his glass as though it were the hilt of a claymore, his chin drawn in, his lips curved down. Farquard Campbell sniffled and wiped his eyes and was not ashamed.

> *"Assure thyself of welcome love,*
> *For auld lang syne."*

"Stap!" Gilbert Johnston strangled. "Stap, lass! I canna bear more."

Mary MacLeod turned from the spinet, and Flora looked upon them gently, her own eyes quivering with unshed tears. None more than she knew what turmoil of homesickness raged.

"Good nights" were spoken, quietly and quickly. None dared inject a new note to break the spell. The Scots left in a group, and the Tidewater men followed.

Catherine Cobham put her arm around Flora and led her to the stairs.

CHAPTER 4

THE SUN ROSE the next morning on queer scenes for the new Scots. Their carts and gigs and walking groups lined many weary flat miles as they toiled out of the Tidewater toward their new homes in the upper reaches. The breaking day brought them sights to dishearten them and make them doubt the fine promises which brought them here.

Only the last-comers out of Wilmington had light to see the whitening rice fields, like little seas of tall, green grass, with lines of Negro slaves in the far distance to give the feeling of industry and plenty. But the night had hidden these sights from those higher in the line.

For them the day brought a wilderness not worth the taming. For one group the brightening dawn revealed a savannah, a dismal level of wire grass and soured soil, fit only for stunted pines and huddling green clumps of gallberry bushes. For another was a white sandhill, barely keeping alive the scrub oaks which lived desperately on its breast. For yet another was a sandy waste, with nothing on it to move but an intermittent clear stream too unstable even to bear shrubs on its bare banks. Another group labored over the corduroy logs of a swamp road and had for their unprepossessing glimpse of the new country black muck gravied with green moss and ferns, with bamboo briers and honeysuckle vines racing from the stench of rot to the tops of the trees.

It was no wonder that the newcomers looked upon the drear sweeps in panic. Their course, demonstrably, was a march into starvation.

Duncan Stuart comforted them, adding his assurances to those of the other old Scots. He was well up the line of them now, although he had been one of the last to ferry from Wilmington. Only the women and the children had slept. The men, servants and masters alike, had spent most of the night unloading the ship and carrying house furnishings and supplies into vehicles and river boats. Most of their belongings were shabby enough and use-smoothed, but some, like Alexander MacLeod and Allan Mac-Donald, had brought fine furniture and books and cook stoves and chests of cloths and finery still lasting from more prosperous days. They and their servants—Allan and Flora had brought eight indentured folk—loaded their goods on lighters, and these even now were being poled up the Cape Fear. Others, too, had gone by boat. Alexander MacLeod and Anne and their baby and others of the gentle strain had taken the river trip. But Flora and some of the women preferred the carriages and since long before daylight had been pushing on ahead of the more lowly carts and wagons.

Duncan, though he had left Wilmington long after Farquard Campbell and Flora's party, rode his swift-striding Donald Bane and planned soon to overtake them. He wanted to be one of those to ride in her train, to hear her speak of what she saw—for by the time he came upon her they would be in the firmer, richer country.

There would be grapes to gather for her. And, barely possibly, a few ripe persimmons. And the yellow goldenrod flower. And a drape or two of gray moss. And, with luck, he might point out to her a leaping deer beyond a swamp. There would be the first fruit of the hickory tree. Mayhap a small alligator.

But as he rode up to the carriage, the alligator was large and not small, and the men of the carriages were down in the woods shooting harmless bullets into its ten-foot skin.

"Get away! Get away! He'll swing his tail an' break your back!" Duncan cried. He chopped excitedly at the foot of a young hickory tree with his handaxe. Flora MacDonald and the women were at the carriages, frantic. Flora's sons—Sandy and James, husky youths and bold—were leading the fight on the swamp monster.

Duncan, with his long, sharp-pointed pike, waded into the fray in that effective but not pretty manner of the low-country people. It was hard, fierce, indelicate work, and the hog-killing reptile was far from beautiful when Duncan had finished with him. The men followed him out of the woods singing his praises, which was bad enough, but when the women gathered to him and made him a hero it nigh unstrung him.

"It was nothing! Nothing!" he protested, backing away.

"But it was magnificent!" Flora made it worse. "We saw you from here—that horrible beast lunging at you, you lunging at it, back and forth in the brush! We were terrified, but we were thrilled!"

"Na! Na!" Duncan was red-faced and wished to lay violent hands on Farquard Campbell who grinned at him amusedly. He turned and went to his horse, but even here was one of the women from the carriages. She was sitting on his saddle, waiting for him.

"Ye're the great master of every situation, it seems."

He frowned to look the better. Her lips were set thin and her brown eyes cold. It was the mutinous brat of last night—the Mac-Leod girl that Flora had fetched.

"Na, na, lass—what do ye mean?"

"I will ride your nag while ye walk beside me and I will speak my thoughts."

"Aye." She was like to become a nuisance. She was a harbinger of ill. He had seen her four times, and each time it was in a moment of great trouble of spirit.

"Aye," he said again, absently, and spanked Donald Bane on the rump to get along. At least, she said nothing of heroism.

There was no pillion, but the saddle served. Mary sat quite well

on it. The coach horses plodded on, and Donald Bane strode on
by them. Duncan, glumly enough, walked at his shoulder.

They picked their way in silence over the puncheon road of a
little swamp, and when they reached the high ground the carriages were well behind them.

"And what had ye to say to me?" Duncan asked. He felt better
now. He was moving toward home, getting away from the dainty
nettlings of Tidewater society.

"I wanted"—Mary's voice was clear and sharp, as though her
thoughts were little hard crystals that clinked one upon the other
—"to say how unspeakably detestable ye be!"

Duncan was back in his own woods, in his own world. Neither
the wilderness nor the people in it, its great silences nor its brooding dreariness, were his masters. Free of the sheen and pinpricks
of fashion, he was in balance again. He felt it and it was good.
His own strength was his citadel. Therefore Mary's sudden attack,
which surprised him, was not overwhelming. By the standards
of the Cape Fear he was not detestable. He knew that. He would
harm no person wrongfully. He would aid the weak. He would
mind his own matters and not interfere with others. He would
give shelter to the traveler. It was a simple code and he lived to it.
If a lass declared him to be detestable, then it was a feminine
whim and not a declaration of common sense. His shyness of
women disappeared at such twaddle.

"Aye?" he asked lightly.

"Aye!"

"Then it must have been a deadly insult when I intruded upon
ye and the auld philanderer yestreen."

Duncan walked slightly ahead of Mary, with his hand on the
horse's mane. He had given the child a sound answer to a silly
plaint. He looked back over his shoulder to laugh.

"Eh?" Dismay shook him.

She, dumfoundingly, was no giglet! She was a grown woman!
Yesterday he had caught her flavor on the ship. Then she was a
part of the enchantment, the glamor, the dizzying perfume, and
under the dominant presence of the grand Flora and the older
ones she was but a lass. He had gained no other impression. But
now, by the gods, she was a full-blown woman in her own right.

Her round, lithe leg bracing under her skirt against the stirrup, the funneling rise of her body from her neat waist, these said as much. Also did the fullness and proudness of her bosom, and her jimply set head which seemed to move at the dictates of her round chin.

Aye, it was her chin which told the story—soft and round, but under its softness and roundness was firmness, like Flora Mac-Donald's. She had strength and maturity, as well as youth, and Duncan had been wrong in supposing her a giglet. So now he gave fearful respect to the heat of her brown eyes and the chill of her voice.

That was painful, for Duncan was in the wrong, and he had no nimble arts of speech to make it right.

"It is na that," she said bitterly.

"What, then?" he asked cautiously.

She did not answer. She seethed, but she held her tongue.

Duncan sighed. He had swapped the petulant lass for the shrewish woman and had lost by the trade. "Spitfire," was the word. He had heard of such women, bitter, capricious, with sharp little souls. That was strange, for she did not look the part.

"Weel," he sighed, not very penitently, "if ye dinna propound my offense, except to say I was born detestable, what can I answer?"

She still said nothing, and Duncan, feeling surer of himself, looked up at her with a slow smile. And a frown, for why should she, or anyone, belittle him without a cause?

"Pig!" she spat.

Duncan laughed, but with no mirth.

"Smug backwoods loon!"

He turned to her in amazement, one of his eyes nearly closed, his mouth open wide on one side.

Donald Bane, wise to the trails of the sandhills, turned from the highway down a dim path to the right. It was a short cut which would come again to the highway on beyond.

She said nothing to that. She was too engrossed in her almost speechless and unexplained displeasure.

"I hate you! Oh, I loathe you!"

Duncan shrugged. She needed to be cut down to the size of her breeches. A bold kiss would do it.

Aye. That would wilt her—provided she didn't like it—and, in case she did, aye, also. Nothing of harm could come of it, either way. The more he thought of it, the more brilliant the idea seemed.

"D'ye expect a man to stand such recrimination and not stand up for himsel'?" he demanded.

"Say it, then!" she snapped.

"It need not be words."

"Say it!"

"Men can humble women without talk, if need be."

She tossed her head as though he spoke senselessly. "Idiot!"

"Very well," Duncan warned her. "Remember ye brought it on yoursel'."

If she heard him she made no sign. While the carriages wound up the creek for an easier crossing, Donald Bane continued down the path to the ravine near the river. At the foot of the hill where the creek flowed into a lily-padded pool, they turned into an alcove under the trees. It was as if the Almighty had fashioned a grand woodland cathedral. Tree branches and gray moss hung down to make a dome over the walls of sand and fern. A wild tangle of brush veiled the swamp. At one side a clear spring jetted from the bank and made a rivulet through white sand down to the black polished cove.

At the sight of the water Donald Bane, now hot and sweating, champed his bit and started forward eagerly. But Duncan caught the bridle rein and stopped him.

"Now," he said to Mary, "ye winna talk to me as a woman might talk to a man, sae I wi' speak to ye in the talk of a man to a maid."

Mary did not guess his purpose until he had lifted her from the saddle, and then she struggled wildly. His body tingled and his heart pounded and he was lifted in a fierce, quick exhilaration as she twisted and squirmed and threw her bulk against him to break away.

As she struggled he looked into her face. Her lips curled and bared her teeth. Her gasps were little gusts upon his throat. Her palm shoved futilely at his chin. "Now," he muttered, "ye maun heal the hurts ye sae mercilessly inflicted."

She was so extraordinarily small against him, so thrillingly alive and vital as she struggled, her eyes were so hotly vibrantly angry. Her strong young body so flowing under his fingers. Now she was so intensely silent. He kissed her forehead and her cheek, and then, slowly, her lips. He released her and laughed loudly, more triumphantly and more arrogantly than he had chosen.

She walked away from him. He looked after her and fought against shame. She was so little and so crushed. It was unfair, he struggled not to think, opposing his strength to hers. Even as sharp-tongued as she had been. She was in a strange land. She was excited. She was . . . "Great God!" he forgave himself, "men have robbed maids of kisses since Eve!"

But he uncomfortably gave attention to Donald Bane. He took off the saddle and laid it on the ground. He led the horse to the pool and gave him one draught and checked him. It was not good for a hot horse to drink as he would like. In a few minutes he would cool and could drink his fill.

Then, assuming arrogance again, he looked at Mary and stared. He was unstrung and betrayed. She was sitting on a sand bank, weeping.

He had seen women weep, at funerals. He had heard backwoods strumpets rail and curse and spice their tears with epithets, but he had never caused a woman to weep. His breast twisted and his stomach went cold, and he had the impulse to grovel.

He went to her, one slow remorseful step at a time.

"Mary." His voice trembled, but her sobs did not cease.

"Mary."

She did not heed him, and he came nearer yet. He dropped to his knees in the sand and leaned forward to beg with his eyes.

"Mary—I hae been the fool. Ye needna be afeared o' me."

He waited. Her face was still in her hands and remained so for another long time.

"Mary," he whispered, "ye hae no harm frae me, lass."

And so they were fixed through the spinning moments, the big bright Scot on his knees, pleading; the little brown Scot on the sand, weeping, while Donald Bane stamped angrily and demanded water.

Mary quivered as though the storm gave her a final wrench.

"I am twisted wi' shame, Mary, and I'd hae ye know it."

Then she spoke. Her voice was little and strained: "I ken, Doon-kan. I ken. Ye're na to faut. I'm to faut. Wholly. I came wi' a' my pride. I determined to surrender naething to the new country. I was too vauntie, and it is good, I ween, that if someone maun bring me humility, it should be y'rsel'."

"Na, Mary! I wish ye no humility. I wish ye to hae pride, to give sparkle to the brown o' your eye!"

She looked at him in wonder. Her eyes were round and brown and bright with unfallen tears.

"Then ye dinna ken?"

He shook his head. "Ken what?"

"Flora did na say?"

"Flora said nothing."

"But, Doon-kan, then I maun tell ye. I hae misjudged y'r pur-poses. I hae na the right tae do as I please. I thought ye had been told and instructed tae humble me last e'en. I am so bound that my life is na my own. For time to come."

Her mouth curved down as if to weep again, and Duncan frowned, bewildered. She continued:

"I took the part of a free lady last e'en, as ye well ken, and that was but a prank o' pride. But I wanted, and, against Flora's coun-sel, I took, one last night as the equal o' polite people. And, now, today—is today—and I'm o'ersorry I didna take my place wi' my brither among the indented."

"Indentured, lass? Ye'll na be indented—ye're na the kind!"

"In truth I tried to believe so, but when ye came last night and ordered my presence to Flora MacDonald sae peremptorily—I felt, for the first time, that I was indeed what I am, a maidservant."

"Na!" Duncan stared. "Na! Ye're gentle folk. I canna believe it, Mary. Who indented ye? Who holds y'r papers?"

"Ye'll understand, Doon-kan. There are no papers. My brither and I gied our words."

"Aye. But I still dinna comprehend."

"Weel—it was like unto this: Malcolm and I were the last o' our kind, and Malcolm is bookish and not brisk in business. So—what we had in Raasay was taken frae us bit by bit. We were vera poor, and I was being sore pressed tae marry Thamas MacDonald o' Glengarry—but, Doon-kan, I couldna, I couldna!"

"Aye!" Duncan agreed heartily, though he had never heard of Thamas MacDonald.

"Malcolm blamed me smartly, for Thamas has a cozy thatched house o' stone and many herds o' sheep, well tended—but Doonkan, I couldna! Malcolm, being the head o' the house, made gestures tae force me tae wedlock, but I couldna! I didna love Thamas and I couldna give mysel' tae him."

"Aye!" said Duncan, with even more satisfaction.

"So—we were acquaint with a cousin of the captain of the *Baliol* ship. It was irregular, but the captain had sympathy for the oppressed people o' the Hielands. We gied our words as our bonds to make the captain's price good by indentin' oursel's in Carolina. Flora MacDonald stood sponsor, to keep watch on us and be our guardian to the captain. So—we are here." Mary hung her head and whispered, "I stand and wait to be bought and sold by whosoe'er shall bid money for me."

Her eyes were still brown liquid with tears. One teardrop rested and trembled on the round of her cheek where Duncan had kissed her. But her eyes were haunted with the new anguish.

"But how," Duncan asked her gently, "if ye were unwillin' to sell yoursel' for Thamas' herds o' sheep, can ye be willin' to make yoursel' a market piece in a strange land?"

"Oh, I dinna ken!" she wailed, shaking her head so that she twisted her whole body. "I dinna ken!"

Then she looked at Duncan steadily, and something welled in her to give her strength. Her round, brown eyes took on the cast of defiance.

"Aye. I do know," she told him. She leaned forward to make him feel what she said. "It is because I am dishonest. I am an untrue woman. I hae inveigled the captain o' the *Baliol* ship tae trust me when I am not tae be trusted. I hae caused Flora MacDonald t' be my sponsor, when a' the while I knew I would desert her protection at the first chance. That is why."

Duncan dug in the sand and let the grains run between his fingers, looking at her uncomfortably. She was a strange lass and not to be understood.

"And," she lifted her chin, "I am na sorry."

Duncan put his elbows on his thighs and crossed his hands to his knees, to bend down and look into her face. It was queer talk for one so young, but her face did not give way, but remained close to his, and her eyes did not waver. He said:

"I dinna comprehend, lass. Ye speak straight o' y'r infidelity, but the deceitfu' ne'er expose themsel's so brashly. What's *really* in y'r heart?"

Her glance now was cool, and she smiled. Almost it was a gentle sneer. "Ye'd make an honest woman o' me despite myself," she objected.

"Tell," Duncan insisted.

"Oh, what matters," she flung her head, "by what name I ca' it? I'll be judged by ithers in terms o' their own. Be my way e'er sae justified in my heart, still when they say 'ungratefu' hissie,' then an ungratefu' hissie I'll be tae them. So what matters what I say? It only matters what I do."

"Tell," Duncan said again, and frowned. Her laugh was hard and reckless and grated against the gentleness which marked her face.

"Nothing t' tell," she said. "I took stock o' mysel' in Raasay, and what did I find? Tradesmen and property owners to filch me plackless—laws to take the wee scrapin's o' gold which my mither hoarded for me—tacksmen tae grasp the last cog o' barley—selfish men tae scratch an' pick, tae grasp an' grip, tae take and hold! And beyond the water in Glengarry was Thamas, a-breedin' his sheep and lookin' on me and gi'in' thought tae breedin' childer. He ne'er heeded me beyond bed and board. All I was tae him was a human ewe!"

Duncan shook his head.

"So!" She stood up, and Duncan rose with her. Her eyes battled his. "So! If under the auld laws my charms fetch only the price o' stinkin' sheep, and the institutions ring me about and bind me down—if I'm tae be bought and sold and treated as a chattel— then at least I'll do my own bargainin'! I'm here tae see what the new land offers. I'm through wi' oppression, Duncan! If I hae tae live in a cave and run naked through the woods, I'm through wi' it, I tell ye!"

Duncan bent his neck and narrowed his eyes and looked at her under his brows. "Ye speak desperate, lass," he said without approval.

"I am desperate! I'll break wi' my kin—I'll be despised—I'll be cast out frae the clans—but, Duncan, hear what I say, I'll never more be thwarted and frustrated and bound down by my own!"

"Ye speak o' breakin' y'r word, where't as a broom straw."

"Word!" she spat. "Am I to be loyal to kin and kind which so reduce me? Me, Mary MacLeod, o' the proudest o' Scottish blood, to be peddled about frae farm tae farm and sold tae one who takes fancy t' my sound wind and strong limbs?"

"The MacLeods," the Stuart made a concession, "were vera good, but na the proudest."

If she heard she made no response. Her breast pumped fast, and she battled his look as if daring him to strike. Her eyes now wavered as though she had thrust her uttermost against him and he still were unruffled.

"Say it!" she challenged. "Say I am a false woman, a word-breaker, a disgrace t' honest Highland blood!"

"I say no such," Duncan frowned. "I say ye're nigh doited wi' anxiety, and ye shall forget such thoughts until ye emerge frae y'r ignorance o' the new land. It is na as ye think."

In one of those swift changes so easy to her and so bewildering to Duncan she leaned forward, pleading. His eye caught the curve of her throat and lingered.

"Doon-kan, are indented servants sae ill thought of and ill treated in Carolina?"

"No, lass. Hae no fear. The bound come free and nought is held against them."

She looked up, half hoping, half disbelieving.

"Then it is the grand country, the place of freedom and fortune they promised in Scotland? Freedom, Duncan?"

"Aye! 'Tis a braw land, which yields to them as test it."

"But it seemed sae dowie, sae distressed, when I first saw it frae the sea—great white sandhills, like tombstones—trees, hanging wi' mournfu' moss, weepin' sore—terrible barren wastes o' grass—high pines soughin' o' defeat and desolation——"

"Aye," said Duncan, "ye'll come to love that."

"But how?" she quavered. "Can I love such dreariness?"

"Aye. It winna be drear, but a bonnie song o' comfort and content." He was looking at her mouth, thinking how firm and soft and warm it had felt.

"E'en I be sold to someone who'll drive me hard to get every bawbee o' his money back?"

Duncan flushed. "Aye. E'en then." He spoke absently. He was looking at her more hungrily than he knew. At her roundly square shoulders, at the quick fire and spirit in her eyes, at her good round arms with their smooth skin and grace of motion. And comparing her to Martha McGee, whose fire burned in him yet. Na! Martha was not for him. He would take Mary. He would not wait to finish his stout house, but he would take her now and live with her while they built his prosperity. The thought was as clear and sound to him as if he had known it all his life.

Mary came softly to him, not shyly, but uncertainly. She put the fingers of both hands on his arm and he looked down on her curiously.

"Doon-kan," she whispered, looking up into his eyes.

"Aye, lass."

"Could ye, perhaps, kiss me just once—na like before, but like a brither—and hold me in y'r arms—just a wee bit? Ye are strong, and ye gie me strength for what may befa'."

He was speechless, but his arm thrust convulsively around her and swept her in to him.

"Na!" she cried in alarm. "Na!" and pressed against his breast with both hands. "Na that way!" But he crushed her and held her and silenced her mouth with his. He felt her body resisting madly, but he held her and kissed her. He pressed his lips into the softness of her face until she went limp and hung in his arms.

When he loosed his hold she walked away as calmly as though she had just picked a flower. She was pale, but her voice was clear.

"Now," she said, turning back, "wi' ye kiss me as I asked?"

It was a bit of a cool peck, the brush of a breeze against his hot lips, and she stepped from him again, just as cool. The rebuke stung, and Duncan's pain was in his voice:

"But I wi' *marry* ye, lass!" he protested. "I wi' take ye home wi' me and I——"

"I will na wed ye," she declared, not smiling.

"But, aye, ye shall!" he almost shouted. "I wi' pay y'r passage. I wi' make it right wi' Flora. I wi' marry ye and——"

Her voice did not change, but remained light and clear. "Listen, Duncan. I said I will *na* wed ye, and I spoke truly. For a' y'r vauntie ambitions, ye hae but a shack and a swamp, and 'tis na enough. If I maun sell my body, I shall seek better markets."

"My God, lass! Ye speak like a strumpet!"

"I wi' do as I will. Ye can make me such words as ye think befit. I dinna care."

She walked away from him again and sat calmly on the sand bank where so recently she had wept.

"I wi' see to't," he said roughly, angry, still wanting her. "I wi' see Flora!"

She tossed her head but only made marks in the sand with her finger. Duncan stamped over to Donald Bane and gave him all the water he wished.

It was a tribute to the fine management of Gilbert Johnston's good wife that when the moonlit cavalcade turned into the lane that night the belated supper began to go on the table as though it had been planned for that moment. The air had sharpened to put edge on a grand, peaceful night. The blue-green light produced a pretty picture for the weary travelers. First was the long straight line of zigzag rail fence, with fields of stripped corn to the right and left. At the end of the lane the plantation gates creaked and opened wide. They were held open by slave boys while the coaches and the gigs and the carts and saddle horses filed through and debouched under the oaks. Through the limbs the soft glow of candles gleamed from the windows and beckoned the sojourners to the repast.

Here was abundance, but not the elegance of the socially more adept in the Tidewater. The house was big and roomy, but it made no pretensions to cultured architecture. It was what it pretended to be, no more, and, definitely, no less—a big sound house, hospitable, comfortable, a shelter for all who belonged there and a haven for any wayfarer who should lay claim to its benefits. Duncan had been there often and was at home in it.

The first hint of formality was at the instigation of old Ben, the head Negro. Proudly displaying his master's property, he had the slave men lined up in a column, twenty of them, to receive the horses. A man was assigned to each horse.

"Take dat'n, deh, Jebo," he commanded. "Put he in de fur stall 'n' hang he bridle 'n' saddle on dat do'—an' no uddeh do'. Ain' gwine gits dese saddles an' bridles mixed up. Skeet, you tek dat nex' hoss."

Bright-eyed Negro boys stood lined up near the vehicles, waiting to carry the baggage. They were excited, twitching their fingers, half of them dragging their feet back, practising the "scrape 'n' bob" old Ben had taught them as a curtsy for "extra special quality." This was new glory for Brompton, greater than they had ever known.

Gilbert Johnston, burry-voiced, gray-haired, stalwart, distinguished only by his simple dignity, helped the ladies to the ground.

"You're welcome," he said ceremoniously. "Everything at Brompton Hall is yours."

Mrs Johnston and her daughters were in the hall. There was no "take on." The welcome was simple and cordial, with no self-consciousness. The mother and the girls conducted Flora and the other women to their rooms, where were to be found washstands with basins and water.

Gilbert took charge of the men. "There's water in your rooms," he explained, "but if you like best to wash at the well, it's out this way." And the thunder of their hard-leather shoes flowed through the back halls to the yard.

In this interval Duncan had opportunity to speak to Gilbert of Mary MacLeod and her brother Malcolm and their graceless predicament in the new country. Old Gilbert showed Whiggish streaks at times, but he had sound common sense otherwise. He listened well and said he would put thought to it for what might be done.

The supper was a grand spread. If some of the guests moved with unseemly haste to get to it, that was both a compliment to the housewife and a very sincere rebellion against hunger.

The linen tablecloth glistened white, Mrs Johnston being one who had preserved the Scottish housewifely art of bleaching washing. The wax candles in their pewter holders sparkled in a double line from master to mistress.

Here, again, was not the delicacy of the Wilmingtonians, with their courses and triple tablecloths and dainty chinaware, for which Duncan thanked his Maker. Sixty miles from the coast, with difficulty in replacing broken pieces, household wares were selected for their sturdiness. Rather, the scene was more reminiscent of the dining hall of an old Highland chief—the long table, the food piled high, many hall servants to fetch and carry, the guests being urged constantly to eat more. And that was not to say that the natural refinement of most of those present had no opportunity to exercise itself. It was more that the motif was abundance and heartiness. Honest hunger was no disgrace and was dealt with frankly and in pleasure.

Where daintiness surrendered to profusion, the qualms of the finicky were eased by the quality of the cooking. There was a roasted wild turkey, golden, hot, battling with the appealing odor of rich red fried ham flanked by fried eggs. More retiring was the heavy flank of roast beef, and farther down the table was a platter piled high with sausage. Between the meats were biscuits—buttermilk biscuits baked brown and freckled with the process of cooking—and at intervals platters heaping with cornbread. Black-eyed peas and collards and sweet potatoes were the vegetables, with the collards ringed around with patties of white corn dumpling. There was only one course—except for the pie, to be sure, which was brought in at the last.

Gilbert Johnston sat at the head of the table, Flora MacDonald on his left, Allan on his right. The others chose their seats as they liked.

Gilbert Johnston was quite wonderful about it, Duncan thought. After he had said grace and asked a special blessing upon the visitors within the portals, he looked inquiringly down the lines of those seated before him.

"But where is—Malcolm MacLeod? Where is your brother, Mary?"

Mary was startled and showed her distress. "He's—He——"

Gilbert interrupted her: "I remember. I saw him talking to one of the servants. Inquiring about the new country, I shouldn't wonder. Go fetch him, Abednego. Quickly."

The Negro faded through the door, and Gilbert fell to carving the turkey. A sudden clatter arose when everyone passed dishes to everyone else. Before this preliminary was complete the tall, red-haired Malcolm, abashed and vague, was shown in and invited to a seat. Mary blushed full rosy, but only Duncan noticed that. The others looked on the newcomer with interest, most of them wondering why they hadn't seen him before. He was looking quizzically about, as if trying to divine what inspired the summons.

"We've been separated through the day," Gilbert Johnston explained to him, "but before you go up the river I wanted some of our neighbors here to know you better. Malcolm MacLeod, gentlemen—a man of great learning. His presence suggests the need of a schoolmaster."

"Eh?" Malcolm faltered.

Mary grasped the significance of the offer and was startled. She looked at Duncan with suspicion, not knowing whether to be pleased or offended.

Malcolm was hesitant. His head rose from his long neck as though he tried to swallow, and his voice came strident and combative: "You wouldn't want me! The world is flat. It has four corners. I can't teach otherwise. It's in the Bible. But Americans must have it round."

Gilbert laughed tolerantly. "How do you explain these voyages around the world, then?"

"I don't. I can't. It's driving me insane. But, anyway, the world is flat, and it has four corners. The Bible says so implicitly."

"So the Bible does," Gilbert said solemnly. "It troubles me, too. What I might think, myself, is due, for all I know, to the devil himself. For my children, they must take the safe course."

As an occasion for social intercourse the supper was quite a failure, and no one regretted it. Weary and hungry, the guests fell to with a zest that well repaid the solicitous Mrs Johnston for what may have been lost in repartee. The turkey quickly disappeared, but no one knew when, for girls from the kitchen brought in fresh platters of the same. The ham and the roast shrank like ice in the sun, and the bread and the vegetables likewise. Spicing these were jelly and preserves and sugar-cane syrup. Servants constantly refilled coffee cups from gallon-size pots, offering tea to those who preferred it.

There was little talk, except toward the end of the meal, when men, unabashed, unbuttoned their waistcoats to give themselves ease in the belly and brief interludes in which to make comment. But not for long. The vigorous business of eating was of chief importance.

Just what Flora MacDonald thought of it did not appear. After the long day's toss-about from Wilmington the lady, no doubt, was quite willing to take food and customs as they came. At any rate, toward the end of the meal she was quite as drowsy as anyone. One or two of the guests were under the torpor of food and nodded in sleep.

After supper the general movement was for bed. Mrs Johnston, quite pleased with the success of her feast, showed the guests to rooms. The large number, of course, quite overran the house, but Duncan and other young men, attempting no new thing, did very well with blankets on the front-porch floor. Not for nothing had their ancestors these centuries wrapped themselves in tartan plaids and slept upon the ground as they went through the country.

It was nearly noon the next morning, what with breakfast and the arrival of neighbors to pay their respects to Flora MacDonald, before Duncan could ask Flora to see him and Mary together. He had lain awake on the porch the night before and had given thought to his plan. He had tried to renew his determination not to marry until he had built his house, but the more he thought, the more he envisioned Mary's rebellious brown eyes and the thrill of her kisses. And finally it had seemed to him a point of common sense to marry a Highland girl, untainted of the new American thought, and have that protection against the most powerful invitation of Martha McGee. Mary's refusal he looked upon as a small obstacle which Flora would brush aside. Mary was young and full of whims. Flora would settle her mind.

He waited in the dark parlor for them to come. He had considered it to be easy, but now as he waited the interview seemed more and more terrifying. He made up little speeches to say to Flora. When the door opened he forgot them all.

Flora had mischief in her smile when she looked on him, but Mary was set-faced. She had changed none since yesterday, except that now she sidled her eyes and held her hands and stood still, coldly resigned to this ordeal, but not agreeing.

"You wished to see us, Doon-kan?" Flora asked, still smiling a wicked enjoyment of his discomfort. She smiled, too, on Mary and quite evidently knew nothing of her refusal.

"Aye," Duncan blurted. "I would marry Mary."

Flora laughed; her laugh was a delighted gurgle. "Poor lad," she sympathized. "It is a terrible torment, asking for a woman's hand, isn't it?"

"Aye." But now, thank God, Flora was in charge. He had said it, and now she would do the rest. He sat back and waited.

"Close the door, Mary," she said, "and then we will talk."

Anyone could see that Flora was in favor. She was pleased. And now she was ready to arrange everything. Losh, the woman was able! Duncan began to feel good, a'ready.

"Ye sit here, Mary, so we can converse," Flora ordered the situation. "Now!" she said, sitting down. "Now." She turned to him. "I suspected this might happen from the first. So"—she closed her eye roguishly—"I made it a point to make inquiry about you yesterday. Ah—I wish my Allan and me were young again and might have such prospects!" She changed her tone: "Of course ye know Mary's unfortunate condition. All of us new arrivals are vera poor. She has no tocher. She has only herself to offer—but that, Duncan, is a great treasure."

"Aye!"

"And, there is a matter of the balance due on her passage—the captain o' the ship holds her liable for twelve pounds. You are willing to pay it?"

"Aye," said Duncan. "I hae been told a' that."

"Well, *then*,"—she spread her hands happily—"what's to prevent?"

"Weel," Duncan suggested, "Mary refuses me."

Flora's eyes narrowed as at something unthinkable and turned amazedly to Mary. "Ye heard what Duncan said, lassie." She spoke kindly, but weight was in her tone. Duncan, too, looked at Mary for what she might say. The light was dim, but the shadow that darkened her eye was that of rebellion, as yesterday. She sat up-right and gazed steadily at Mrs Johnston's drapes of dried sea grass over the fireplace.

"I'll be good to her," Duncan urged, looking at Mary but speaking to Flora. "I wi' build my house twice as big as she had in Scotland. I wi' spend money on her. She shall have ribbons and braids and, now and then, when tar sells brisk, silk to go wi' the cloths she makes at her own loom. I wi' give her pin money to spend as she wills. I wi' get her the best granny women when she births my bairns. And when my plantation grows full wi' slaves, she shall hae house servants and be the proud mistress o' Stuart's Hall. It is my plan."

Duncan sat back, satisfied. He had spoken generously. For a lass without tocher, and twelve pounds less, he had promised munificently. Flora would see the sense o't and bring her around. He waited. He wondered if he had promised too freely. But, no. He nodded to himself. Unwise or not, the perfume of the lass was still in his nostrils and made him a'most choke for her. He had promised rashly, but he would stand to it.

Mary said: "Pish!" She kept her eyes on the sea grass and deigned to answer both Flora and Duncan with the one chill sibilant.

Duncan grasped his knees and stared at her, with his mouth open. He closed it.

Flora raised her head and looked down on Mary querulously, with big eyes. "Child!" she gasped.

And Mary turned direct to her and in the same cold voice said: "Pish!"

Duncan was dumfounded at such disrespect to Flora, and Flora seemed hardly less so. But Flora's eyebrows slowly came down. She was not to be routed by trifles.

"Mary!" she said sharply, as a mother to a child. "Ye're impudent. I dinna understand such an attitude. Gather your senses, lassie. Remember your trainin' i' your father's house!"

"Pish!"

Flora's impatience waxed, and she jerked at the scarf about her shoulders.

"Take heed, Mary," she said ominously. "If ye persist in mutiny,

Duncan may take the privilege o' withdrawin' his offer. And keep in mind that I have undertaken responsibility for ye. Ye are word-bound, and I wi' ye, to be indented for five years to pay your passage. If ye rebel on it ye become an ungratefu'——"

"Hissie!" Mary interjected and laughed defiantly.

"—child, and must be dealt wi'. Duncan has made ye an honorable proposal. As your guardian, I approve it. Now, wi' ye agree?"

Mary was full white. The red had gone from her lips, and they were stretched across her teeth. She was not pretty, and Duncan took pain in his breast because he knew that Mary had pain greater than he could feel.

"Lass!" he cried. He would tell her that he loved her. He would say that she should order her life as she willed, that he would stand in her support. But they paid him no heed, and it was silly, any-way. How could a woman, in the ancient and honored Scottish customs, order her life independently? That was worse than Whig thinking.

"I winna wed him!" Mary's darkened brown eyes fairly shrieked into Flora's worried blue eyes, and her voice was vibrant almost to the breaking place. "Can a body not live a life wi'out being hawked about, like a swine's ham? Can a woman not breathe God's air and eat Nature's food, wi'out havin' t' smile an' smirk and simper and praise Heaven when some man looks on her to lust and say: 'I want you'? Lacking gold, as I do, have I nothing else o' my own? Have my proud ancestors left nothing of their glory in my blood? Have I no privileges? No rights? No richness of body or charm of soul t' do wi' as I please? Na! I winna wed him."

Flora, instead of sweeping upward in emotion as Mary had done, now merely smiled in tolerant amusement. Duncan was more torn than Flora. For all its rashness, for all its crashing against the bed-rocks of Scottish convention which were known to be good, something in what she said smacked of justice, and he was troubled by it.

"We wi' discuss it anither time," said Duncan, rising.

"No!" Flora exclaimed, alarmed. "We will settle it now. Sit down. Mary has broached her rebellion and can talk sense again."

"We have talked sense," Mary said to her, "and it is settled."

"Then," Flora asked as an ultimatum, "shall I advertise among the colonists that I have a maidservant for indenture? We must do one of two things, and that soon."

"Must I answer now?"

"Yes, sooner than I planned, for I see the possibility o' great trouble wi' you, and my Allan and me are borne down too much a'ready to take on more. I have no wish to be unkind, but wi' your wild way o' talkin', it were kindness to all to impose the rule o' common sense and carry out the agreement which we made and pledged wi' our words." Flora spoke firmly, as though she propounded the final thought. "Ye may"—she held up two fingers and checked them as she spoke—"take Duncan, if he be so gracious as still to desire ye, or ye may prepare t' be indented. Ye must decide now."

"But have I no rights? Not even the right to consider?" Mary shrilled, a flash of fear coming to her eyes.

"Aye," Flora said grimly. "Ye have all the rights ye have strength to uphold. My own widowed young mither, when I was a wee bairn, had the right to refuse to marry Hugh MacDonald of Armadale. But he took her by force, and she was without the benefit of marriage until later. But, for a' that, they lived many happy years togither. Ye are not being asked to do more than many a good Hieland woman has seen the wisdom to do before ye."

Duncan shook his head. "I'll not force her," he declared.

"I'd kill ye, an ye did." Mary did not take her eyes from Flora's, and then she added: "Wait, please. I'll answer ye soon." She swung to the door and lashed them with her eyes as she went.

Flora cried: "Where d'ye go? Come here!" but Mary was gone.

Flora gasped again. The strange demeanor of her ward had twice made her gasp. She shook her head helplessly and looked at Duncan.

"I canna explain to ye, lad. She seems a'most daft, wi' her queer thinkin'. She talks o' spurnin' sweet privileges for the sake o' empty rights."

"Whig talk," Duncan frowned.

"Aye," Flora condemned it. "Whig talk."

"Where could she ha' learned it?" Duncan wondered.

"La, me! The young people these days—I dinna ken what the world may be comin' to. 'Tis comfortin' to find one like y'rsel', wi' respect for the auld ways. Mary should——"

But the door burst open and Mary came in excitedly, tugging at Gilbert Johnston's arm.

"There!" Mary pointed, as though to a pair of culprits. "There they are!"

Gilbert came in slowly, his pipe in his hand. His eyes half smiled, dubiously. He was tall, and his walnut-dyed coat hung loosely. It had the muttony smell of homespun. His gray hair fluffed lightly under his hat.

"Aye, dochter,"—he puffed at his pipe in quiet good humor—"there they are. Flora and Duncan. 'Tis true. And what of it?"

Gilbert had strength, and he had Whig thoughts, though he had never taken sides, and it made Duncan uncomfortable. Gilbert seemed to bulk large in the room and share domination with Flora.

Mary pointed accusingly at Flora. "She would make me marry," —and she pointed now at Duncan—"him!"

"So! Ho, ho!" Gilbert's gray old face seemed to writhe with suppressed laughter. He spoke, and between words he took little puffs through his reed pipestem and looked down benignly upon all.

"How dare you, sir,"—his eyes twinkled at Duncan—"desire t' wed this lass?"

Duncan was resentful at the interruption, but he smiled grimly back at Gilbert.

Old Gilbert crooked his forefinger and lifted Mary's chin and looked into her face. He continued to look, though he spoke to Duncan. "Still, perhaps," he jibed him, "though auld and gray, I can understand. Beautiful brown hair,"—lifting a lock of it, continuing his wordy rambling—"cheeks like Flora's, broad from bone to bone and fair, droppin' down to a bonnie chin, wi' plenty o' bone in it and plenty o' meat on the bone. Aye, Duncan, ye had the sense to know a good lass when ye saw her—see? A sonsie mou', easy tae smile, like Flora's, but hard like knots at will. Aye, Duncan, ye were quick t' see. Eyes, light brown, mixed wi' green—eyes to hauld back and resist until they be wrung out, or t' give so bountifully as t' make a man humble that he has so little to give in return. Aye, Duncan—ye were quick t' see—but are ye the man to cope wi' them eyes?"

Duncan sprang to his feet and waited until he could think how to upbraid Gilbert. The old man had made bad matters worse.

Mary, too, was resentful. "I begged ye f'r help," she wailed, "and ye but make jokes!"

Flora's mouth twitched, for she was angry and she held back only for courtesy.

Gilbert's eyes never ceased to twinkle. "Now," he said, "I hae made all o' ye mad at me. What a doited auld fool I am! I maun hae taken on some o' these insane American attitudes."

But while Gilbert rambled on and his dignified old eyes twinkled, he must have been thinking quite straightly.

"I fear," Flora sighed, "ye have compounded a difficult situation into one more so."

Gilbert laughed and spoke crisply, to Flora and to Duncan: "Ye both were i' the wrong. See y'rsel', Flora, thirty years ago, and ye wi' know ye canna force Mary to do aught. Could all the auld Geordie's might force ye to reveal a single guilty Hielander's identity? Na! Neither can ye force Mary. She has in her what ye have in you, and ye should be the first tae recognize it."

"Aye, but I ne'er went off on radical——"

"When the King was a Whig, Flora was a Tory, nonetheless."

Flora was on the defensive, and it was not her wont. "Gilbert, ye have utterly ruined whatever chance I may have had for settling this obstreperous girl safely. Now, how will ye make it right?"

Gilbert smiled widely. "Good tactics, lass! Good tactics! Ye have cast the responsibility on me right smartly. Still, I would hae ye know I was prepared. I wi' hae my agent in Wilmington settle wi' the sea captain, and Mary and Malcolm shall have a farm o' their own t' settle on near me and work their own destiny, payin' me as they can. I have no fear o' Mary's word when it is given freely."

Shrewd old Gilbert may have spoken advisedly, for if he had reached into Flora's grasp and snatched Mary from it, the result wouldn't have been more electrical.

"Na!" Duncan shouted. "Ye hae na the right!"

Flora, at this sudden loss of her ward by ways beyond her control, rose up, furious. But she had the good generalship to consider her words before she spoke them.

It was Mary herself who ended the scene by flying desperately into Gilbert's arms as for protection and bawling so robustly as to drown out all words.

Gilbert stroked her hair and spoke: "Duncan," and Mary whimpered soft and let him be heard, "perhaps, if wooed after the free American way, Mary might——"

"Bah!" was Duncan's ungracious answer. He strode for the door, feeling, somehow, defeated by the Whigs.

"I never want to see him again!" Mary wailed.

Flora, her fury still unvented, walked out with Duncan. When they reached the hall, she paused to speak, but closed her mouth thin-lipped and went quickly up the stairs. Duncan was glad, for now he wanted to talk to no one, not even Flora.

The wind whistled cold by the time Flora reached Cross Creek three days later. The days were still warm at noon, but the evenings were uncertain. Their chill made evening fires on the up-country hearths most welcome. Flora had proceeded leisurely from Brompton Hall to Cross Creek. Before she left, she and Mary had patched up a peace. If their parting was tempered with coolness, it was because of offended pride only, for Gilbert's generosity had relieved Flora of a duty which could have become burdensome. So, leaving Mary behind with less concern than she might have admitted to herself, Flora journeyed slowly and with growing triumph up the river. There were cousins to be seen, gifts to be received, letters from Scotland to be delivered at the log cabins and big houses along the King's Highway. Those who, from illness or age, would be unable to attend the grand reception in Cross Creek but still desired to see and know the great Flora came out to the road and waited in groups until the carriages should come.

Flora, having stopped for the night a few miles down the road at the plantation of Thomas Rutherford, came on to Cross Creek early in the afternoon of the reception. She was received in the house which had been prepared for her near the Cool Spring, and

there the people of consequence from all the surrounding country
called upon her.

As if by tacit consent no one mentioned the rising tumult among
the Whigs. It was a Scottish reunion, and nothing was permitted to
interfere with its tone. Among them were clansmen who had
fought at Culloden, who remembered the dismal count: . . .
seventeen, eighteen, nineteen—you, nineteen, sirrah, step out for
execution—one, two, three . . . seventeen, eighteen, nineteen—
you, nineteen, sirrah, step out for execution—one, two, three . . .
Even now they broke out in sweat when they thought upon the
terrible wrath of the Duke of Cumberland. They had not been
back. The whole craggy expanse of the Highlands would be but a
nightmare to see. Here in Cumberland County, ironically enough
named for the Butcher himself, they dreamed of a new Caledonia.
Now that Flora had come, the proud dream began to take on
substance. So they came eagerly to Cross Creek to do her homage.

These included both the New Scots, those who had crossed the
Atlantic in recent years, and the early-settling Old Scots. Some of
the latter, as Gilbert Johnston, had become well-to-do and had
reached out to make contact with the colonists of other sections of Carolina. The New Scots were the more clannish, having
the common cause of building up their settlements and the common touch of the Gaelic language which the Old Scots gradually
were forsaking. Therefore the newcomers, not yet willing to
throw themselves upon the bosom of the raw new country entirely
without restraint, were those who gathered more closely about
Flora MacDonald and Allan of Kingsburgh. And it was these who
gave Flora the sudden flavor of being a princess.

She was so, accompanied by her consort and retinue, that afternoon, when she went down to the commons to greet the crowd
gathered there for her and to see the games. Despite Duncan's
misgivings in Wilmington, she was more at home here in Cumberland than she had been in New Hanover's soft sand. Here the
soil had its part of hard clay, and there were rolling hills with now
and then a knoll standing above the plain. And here was no
flowing and persuasive small talk, but the blunt and crumpled
honest words of her own Scots. It were home enough.

There was a grandstand of sorts, with rough plank seats reserved for the notables, beside the road which served as a race track and an arena for the games. The gathered crowds stood beside the road or sat on wagons and carts. It was here earlier in the afternoon that the young men had run the torch relay, the race of the fiery cross, emulating the ancient runners of Scotland who called the clans to the standards. It was here that the weirdly yelling Gaels had cheered on their favorites in the ox-cart race. Just now, as the MacDonald party arrived, the horses were leaving the track after the straightaway dash. Other horses were forming two hundred yards away for the final event, the "gander snatch."

And here they came, with whoops and yells, a dozen horses in single wide-spaced file, lickety-split, hell-bent for the gander. This white fowl, much perturbed by the din, hung by its feet from a beam over the track. Its neck was greased and soaped, and its head curved out like a snake's, darting this way and that, hissing its anger at the proceeding.

The crowd yelled furiously. This was a fast event and soon over, packing its whole drama in the brief seconds it took twelve horsemen to race by.

The first horseman, a black-haired young man in red-and-yellow kilt, rose in his stirrups and snatched for the bird's head, missing it completely. The victim shipped its head out of the way like a whiplash. The crowd blasted its laughter only to jerk in its breath for the second horseman's try. And he, too, missed. Six horsemen swept by before one touched the gander, and he only with straight fingers. The effort unbalanced the rider, and he pitched from the saddle and piled up in the weeds. It was the ninth man, a little Scot with bristling beard, who finally grasped the gander around the neck, sank his thumb in, raced triumphantly away with the head high in his hand.

The horses cleared out at once, for Flora MacDonald had come and the games were over. Up the street—or road, for Cross Creek was but a·roadside river-landing village with a courthouse in the square—came a most terrible screech, when seven bagpipes strove for accord. And then they came, gallantly abreast, piping proudly, filling the whole valley with plunging, spiraling sound. Among the seven was a MacCrimmon, of the ancient family which in war after war had piped the battle tunes for the MacLeods. There were two MacArthurs, of the line which had taken a like position for the MacDonald clan. And there were others, a MacRae, a Mac-Dougall, a MacAlister and a MacNeill. They whirled to a flourish before the MacDonalds, proudly finishing the Scottish medley with a tribute to Flora's descent from the Bruce: "Hey, Tuttie Taittie!"

That night, Flora's cavalcade of triumph at an end, the leaders of the Scots met in just the sort of meeting they all had wished for since Flora had landed. The rain slashed down, wind-whipped and cold. The darkness brought a chill wail that sent the people shivering indoors. Only when the big fireplaces, armspread-wide and shoulder-high, sent their roars up to answer the gale was there comfort. Bright flames swept into the chimney throats and reflected red upon the faces of Scots who clustered to their warmth.

Their eyes were anxious and their words bulletlike, carrying the burry undertones of condemnation. Tonight the Scots were speaking their minds. Scowling, they voiced the black thoughts which scarce one had dared admit to himself. But here was counsel of their own kind. Outsiders were not present and, in the bosom of the Highlanders, one could damn whom he chose.

Duncan Stuart was amazed and dismayed at what he heard. He was not in agreement with such forecasts of disaster. True, the Tidewater Whigs had plotted plots and had held what they called congress, but this was only a high-sounding name for rabble gathering. His dread was that they would become so arrogant that His Majesty would punish them. Whigs, Duncan thought, were not dangerous, only foolish. Cornelius Harnett and John Ashe and Maurice Moore were glib-tongued, and it had been his fear that they might influence Flora MacDonald before she had time to know the new country's pitfalls. That avoided, he was only mildly concerned now. As for the Whigs and their caterwauling, that was not new. They had been in a constant bicker with the King's governors for fifty years and more. If it wasn't quit rents it was paper money, and if it wasn't paper money it was high fees, and if it wasn't high fees it was tax on tea, and if it wasn't tax on tea it was this new knickknacket they called the "Cause of Boston."

"My opinion," Duncan declared, "is that if they're let be they'll talk themsel's out and be at peace, till one can find a new thing for controversy."

Flora MacDonald, who sat across the circle from him, gave his comment close heed, gauging him as well as his words.

"I hope so, truly," she said, but with the tone and lack of response in her eye which let him know that she was more impressed with other views.

"Aye," bluff Hector MacNeill said skeptically. "'Tis an unco guid way t' see it on a cauld nicht by the ingle cheek. I hae followed the standard through the snaw and sleet, and I dinna grudge them that now hae th' task. I only wish I could see the bright side, like Duncan."

Kenneth Black had said nought but puffed his pipe and listened attentively to all that was said. He nodded when Hector ceased talking.

Allan MacDonald and Alexander MacLeod, the newcomers, too, were silent, perturbed, listening keenly. They had heard something in Scotland of the American controversies but nothing so threatening as this.

"Well, I see the time," Archibald MacDougall said bluntly, "when this whole countryside will rage in war." Archibald was younger than the old men, older than those of Duncan's age. He was calm-eyed and spoke firmly. "I hope my opinion affrights no one. I pray that my judgment is awry. But I give to these Whig leaders credit to make great trouble, and I believe His Majesty has given this colony such neglect that the rabble neither knows his power nor fears it."

"Aye!" said Hector.

"Well"—Allan MacDonald hitched his chair forward to see all who might speak—"let us assume that Archibald may be right. If so, it is important to know what the Scots will do in such an emergency. If war comes, will they follow the Whigs? Will they remain neutral? Will they join the King's standard?"

The question was electrical.

"Ah! Now ye've struck bottom!" Alexander MacAlister rose to his feet to shake a gnarled finger at Allan MacDonald. In an instant the open space before the fire was filled with glowering, shouting Scots, shaking their fingers, pounding their palms.

"Wi' th' King!" some shouted.

"We stay oot! We've had trouble eneugh!" others cried.

"The King has no right! I'm for the Whigs!" was still another note.

The contention became blacker and blacker, and actual combat threatened.

Flora gathered her skirts quickly and stepped back of the line of chairs. Her eyes brightened and snapped. Duncan could not tell from her half-smile whether she was frightened at the quarrel or pleasantly excited. He went to her and stood at her side while the old men raged.

Alexander MacAlister shouted into Allan MacDonald's face: "The King permits his hellions tae rob us! He's na fit tae be fought for!"

Alexander MacKay heard him and shouted back: "Wad ye turn traitor, too, Sandy?"

"I'd na spill one drop o' Scottish blood t' defend his thievin' scullions!" the MacAlister retorted.

"He'll hae Catholicism down on us once more!" another cried. "The Covenanters maun hold ready!"

The Reverend John MacLeod moved among them with concerned expression. Suddenly he lifted his voice: "Brethren! Let us pray!"

His incisive tones cut through the turmoil commandingly. The clansmen turned angry eyes to him and saw him standing at the hearth, his hands lifted to heaven. It was sufficient. That was a strong call. The men broke away from their disputes, though their eyes still flashed, and bowed their heads submissively.

Four did not move. Two of these were Farquard Campbell and Thomas Rutherford, their arms across each other's shoulders, shaking their fists in unison, chanting jovially: "We'll fight for the King! We'll fight for the King!" Then they saw the minister's raised hands and, sheepish, sought their places.

Two others remained oblivious of the preacher. Their faces were flushed black, and they were at the point of blows. These were Hector MacNeill and Gilbert Johnston. Hector jerked angrily at the lapels of Gilbert's jacket, and Gilbert's forearm shoved against Hector's throat. But now they, too, saw the preacher and obediently bowed their heads.

The minister prayed long and loudly. His voice, rising high at the opening of his ponderous sentences, dropped in deadening cadence that inevitably lulled the battling spirits to peace again —to drowsiness, even—before he let them go. He finally found an "amen," and they docilely returned to their seats, chastened and, mayhap, better men. At any rate they now knew how badly they were divided, and, by reason of the division, how weak. They had no common front, and it was a bitter realization.

"May I speak?"

Duncan's head sprang up. He had known that Flora had strength and leadership, but he could not reconcile it with her gentle voice. Her "May I speak?" was a new voice, quite as low, quite as womanly, but it vibrated. It had power and caught attention.

"Aye!" Kenneth Black said. "Speak, Flora."

She stepped forward modestly, pausing while everyone turned to her. "My *own* mind is that we should not discuss so profitless a subject now. We wi' talk to better benefit of things which we can judge better. In the meantime, can ye na come to see my Allan and me at our new home and there, calmly, wi' that wisdom we hae, divine the right?"

Her voice had an earnest ring and made music. Scottish faces frowned and remained scowling while all waited for someone to make answer.

"Aye, Flora! 'Tis common sense," Hector MacNeill rumbled, and all the shaggy heads nodded vigorously.

Duncan did not nod. He was in agreement, but he knew the decisions would be made, not by him, but by the elders. Instead he looked on, and thrilled to, Flora's smile. It flashed. She had the countenance of a queen. The woman had the gift to lead men gallantly.

"Aye!" shouted the Cameron. "Settle here, in town, Flora. We wi' furnish the house—ye be head o' the clans."

The Scots nodded and grunted emphatic approval.

"Na! Na!" she smiled. "We wi' hae our ain house, the same as all. But ye maun come t' see us, and we wi' take counsel the-gither."

"Aye!" they said.

If Flora felt proud of so deftly having gained the leadership of the clans, she made no sign. She sat down and listened to the men.

CHAPTER 5

IT WAS OCTOBER and the scrub-oak leaves were blood-red. For mile upon mile, from sandhill to sandhill, they flung their incarna-dine mantle upon the earth, and for this one time in their year of lowly life they took upon themselves a superlative glory. To Dun-can, seldom given to fanciful thought, they were an army of King George's redcoats filling the land, flowing down the slopes and moving up the valleys. He had been thinking in terms of armies since Flora MacDonald had arrived. She was no army, but she was the spirit of an army. The Carolina wilderness had a new meaning now. It had moved closer to the throne. And he, Duncan Stuart, stood closer to the throne. He did not stop to question that new feeling. He felt it. It was good. That was sufficient.

Mary MacLeod looked on the crimson sweep and cried: "It is like blood!" She sat her horse and looked across the river at the red slope. Her lips, responding to the thought, twitched sensi-tively.

" 'Tis like an army o' the King's soldiers," Duncan corrected her. She said nothing while he dropped to the ground and helped her to alight. He tied the horses, and they stood on the bluff looking across. The river coiled down to them, gnawed at the sandy wall and swept mistily into a long straightaway.

"Ye can see it somewhat frae here," he told her, waving his arm.

Mary had sobered much these weeks since her arrival. If her thought was different, she had not said so, but at least now she had given up the wild talk of throwing herself at the heads of eligible rice planters for hasty marriage. She was willing to wait and know more of the land.

Duncan knew that she had talked much to old Gilbert Johnston, and although he had damnably American ideas for a good Highlander, he had steady thought, too. So Mary had changed from revolt to subdued thinking, and Duncan had cause to wonder if old Gilbert hadn't quite shrewdly painted for her a new picture, with himself, Duncan, not unfavorably in it. At any rate, while she would not talk of love and marriage, she was glad when he came—and he bided his time. She was bewildered, and he could wait. For he was bewildered also.

The morning had just begun when they stood on the bluff and looked across at the glare of scrub oak on the sandy rise. Beyond, on the clay level where the stouter trees grew, there were green pines and yellow hickories and flaming sweet gums, but these were two furlongs distant and not so plain.

Mary's brown eyes played on the wild redness, roving anxiously. Duncan said nothing. It was to be her home, and she should make her own thoughts. Old Gilbert had arranged it with John Slingsby. Malcolm, her brother, had signed a paper. Today the neighbors would assemble for the house-raising. They had not come yet. The plot of ninety acres across the river was still the wilderness. Its silence throbbed, as though the silence of all time past hovered there and pulsed, almost audibly.

"Duncan"—Mary's voice was little, with a catch in it—"is it good?"

"Aye."

"Tell me again, Duncan," she turned on him searchingly, "that it is good."

"Aye," he nodded stoutly. "It is vera good."

She looked across at it once more. Her eyes were uncertain, but her voice, still tense, held true.

"Then if ye grace it wi' your approval," she acquiesced doubtfully, "it maun be vera good."

Duncan was not thinking in terms of a woman preparing to battle the deadening solitude of the woods, but in terms of the man who could shoulder his axe and march in to hack and batter it to his bidding.

"Pines," he said, "to be boxed this month for next year's virgin turpentine—enough to pay y'r whole debt, like as not. New ground to be cut and burned over for next year's corn and potatoes. Dead pine logs to be cut and split for tar burnin'. Short-leaf pine to be split for fence rails. Traps to be made for otter and mink and coon skins. Aye, Mary, 'tis vera good."

But to Mary, born and bred in a finished, if unproductive, land, the prospect was an assault upon her instincts. The wilderness was fearsome, but to violate it was waste and destruction. She liked the penetrating sweet smell of new boxed pine, but when the axes tore into the bodies of the round, stately trees, that was desecration. She heard it everywhere she went. The acrid smoke of the burning new ground was destruction. The oily, black smoke of the tar kilns choked her. The jet tar coiling angrily into the pits was escape from the despoiler. Trees crashing, twigs bending and curling in the heat, canes scorching and popping, grass withering and turning black before one's eyes, like dead black hair to be fluffed by the wind and scattered—it was all desolation and holocaust. The land was raw and bleeding and cried against the rape of steel and fire.

"Then," said Mary, "it maun be *vera* good."

They crossed the river in a boat and beached it upstream on a sandbar that jutted into the black water of a cypress-studded cove. A red-bellied bream flipped into the air and back to the water with a thundering crash, and the stillness came back, also like thunder.

They toiled up the sand and slippery wire grass. Mary searched a place where the cabin should be. She stopped where the clay level bent over the ridge to the sandy slope and was between a spreading chinquapin tree and a stout hickory. From under their branches the house would look down quite snugly upon the creeping water.

"Here"—Mary twisted her toe in the sand—"wi' be my home." But her voice was dead, and her glance was dead.

The sharp bite of axes rang in from down the river, and the people approached, making their trails as they came.

"But, Duncan," she shook her head, "I dinna understand. I dinna! Why should all these good people flock here to build for Malcolm and me?"

" 'Tis the custom," he said. "One helps the ither."

"It is good," she said. "It is *vera* good," as if making sure of something she must remember.

In an hour the ridge was full of tethered horses and oxen. Some of the people came in ox carts. Some, with long legs nearly dragging the ground, rode shaggy little banks ponies, something like the tiny Galloway nags Mary had seen. Others had horses of greater size. The women brought shrubs and cooking utensils and food and strings of red pepper and bundles of sage. The men brought tools and materials.

The women brought their gifts to Mary, more abashed than pressing. They dressed for no style. Their frocks were long and straight, some of wool, some of cotton. All were of homespun and mostly brownish. Most of the women were thin-faced and slow-moving. Some were short and fat and bustled about. Some were as nonchalant in their pregnancy as they were with their snuff brushes. Their scrutiny of Mary was as frank as their welcome.

"Fiddle-faddle!" Laurin Blue's outspoken daughter appraised her. Janie was an old maid, twenty-five at least, and could speak her mind as she wished. "As pretty and strong as she is, somebody will marry her before we can get the roof on."

The women chuckled at her, and Mary could think of nothing more than to smile.

"Damn right!" the shaggy-haired and dirty-nailed, tar-smelling old swampster, Ganny Tew, loosed gusto beyond the group. The men snickered brashly.

As if afraid that Mary might be embarrassed, Tom Hadley's sweet-faced tall daughter walked before her and nervously thrust out a package of nails. "Pa couldn't come, but he wishes you well," she said anxiously. "He burned up an old barn to get these nails for you."

Tom Brown came. He was full-bodied and energetic, with quick gray eyes and a hearty manner, often, as if to induce thought, scratching into his bristle of copper-red beard.

The men grouped around him as their natural leader. They wore knee-length buckskin or homespun breeches. Some were bold and outchested, with hard voices through their black beards, but most were gangling and soft-speaking. They murmured monosyllables when facial expressions and eye-talking wouldn't do. Some, be-

ing well aware of the prevalence of the intermittent fever and
bloody flux, and knowing full well that too much bathing tended
to bring on these and other ails and distempers, showed evidence
of their commendable caution. Some, of course, were square-
shouldered and stout, with the daring to be clean, but most of
them were thin and slow and, while lacking the power and thrust
of the Highlanders, had the air of being tremendously tenuous.

For all their slowness, under Tom Brown's voice, which they
followed without question, materials soon began to flow in from
the woods, and the cream-white walls grew up stout and true,
higher than their heads.

As the day wore on, the long-legged ones became less taciturn.
They never seemed to tire. Now and then one would make a passing remark to Mary.

"We'uns hopes you'uns will jine wid us," smiling, black-haired
William Bratcher murmured surreptitiously, pleading with his
eyes.

Mary did not understand, but nodded and smiled. Her wonder
of the day was at this strange, quiet tribe which gathered from so
far afield in the swamps merely to be kind.

"Shut up, Bill," Tom Brown laughed. "None of that!"

"Na!" Duncan joined him. "None o' that damnable Whig
doctrine!"

"Whig doctrine?" Mary asked eagerly, turning to William. "Tell
me about it!"

But Bill only rolled his eyes toward Brown and Duncan and
shook his head. "Ask them," he lifted a falsetto voice almost to a
shriek. "All I know is we ain't gwine to stand for no more o' the
King's hellishness."

And Bill, who had said too much and got himself in a situation,
rushed off worriedly to tote another log.

The star performer of the day was scragged old Ganny Tew.
With Gillie Black to do his tromplin' in the clay pit, he made the
splint-and-daub chimney of sticks and clay batter. As rapidly as
the walls went up, the old man's masterpiece climbed beside it.
When the roof went on, his chimney was done, leaning to the
house like an ungainly wet yellow worm clutching there and looking over the ridgepole.

"It ain't perty," Ganny lamented, looking at it. "Don't know as I ever seed a perty clay chimbly."

Then, as his climactic achievement, Ganny made the pot crane. It was a bent iron rod hung in staples in the chimney jamb—the ingle cheek, Mary called it—so that the pots could be swung into and out of the fire.

The cabin's only pretension to luxury was the sliding glass window sash which Tom Brown had contributed. It was in the front, and one might sit before the fire and look down upon the river.

When the work was done that afternoon, the neighborfolk gathered at the door while Benny Gillespie nailed a horseshoe over it to bring good luck.

"We're glad to have you and your brother in our neighborhood, ma'am," Tom Brown said for all. "We'll be to see you and you-all come to see us. If we can help, just let us know—that right?" He turned to the crowd.

"Shore nuff!" they nodded.

Mary, standing now in her own door, built for her thus amazingly, attempted to express her thanks.

"Ye've been so good——" she began. "Ye've made me so happy——"

But she had to stop and turn against the door jamb to weep, and the men, their women following, turned away, chuckling. This was even better than a speech they couldn't remember. She was so happy she cried, was what they could tell.

Mary and Duncan sat on the pine block which served for the doorstep and watched them go. He said nothing, and she said nothing but looked and half smiled and thought her own thoughts while the carts and the ponies and the people faded into the woods whence they had come.

Mary looked up at him with a tired smile, like a bairn. He gasped and caught her, for, in one of her daffy impulses, she had flung herself backward across his lap, laughing silently. Then, feeling herself held safe, she smiled into his face slowly and serenely. He bent to kiss her, for he considered this her answer to him, and he had the sudden urge to squeeze her and kiss her until she went limp.

But she held him away. "Na!" she rebuked him sharply. "Be still. I winna be kissed. I wi' be held in y'r arms gently—can ye na see?"

"I see I canna comprehend ye, ever, at all," he grumbled.

He looked into her face hungrily. The thin, twitching corner of her lips fascinated him. He couldn't take his eyes from the spot. Her eyes roved slowly over his face, almost casually. She lifted her hand and fingered a low-hanging lock of his bright hair, and her hand fell back to her breast. Her eyes strayed out to the sky, seemed to listen, and came to rest on the red leaves.

"Ye told me," she said, although not exactly to him, "that all the dreariness someday would sing a sweet melody o' peace to me."

"Aye."

"I didna believe it. 'Twas too drear. Then to the dreariness came destruction and harsh smells and ashes. I thought this morning I couldna stand it."

"Aye?"

"But today the new land so sang to me. I walked away frae the people to consider their goodness—and then I heard the song in the pines and the melancholy sweet silence frae one hill to anither. It seems—— Duncan, are ye laughing at me?"

"Na, lass."

"The new land, I tho't, wept sore because it was wounded and bleeding frae all this crash and slash and flame—a' this man-made outrage."

"Aye?"

"Aye, Duncan, and I was wrong. The new land is like a great fruitful woman. She wants to be ravished by men. She thrills to't, because she is lush wi' livin' and she loves to be raped so that she can gi' birth to every kind o' life that mankind can beget on her. And she takes the pains o't most gladly."

"Ay-y-y-e?"

"Aye. But all her offspring must be freeborn. That is why the puny little King on his throne must cease his presumption o' keeping so grand a land in slavery. The land wi' laugh at him and throw him off."

"Mary!"

But Mary was thinking and not listening, looking into his face.

"I am like this America. I long to bear childer—many childer. Braw, sonsie, free childer."

"Mary!" Duncan was ardent, pleading. She looked at him absently and shook her head, dismissing a thought.

"Na. My bairns maun be freeborn. Ye would enslave them to the King. Na, Duncan." She got up and walked away from him as carelessly as though he had no passion to burn.

Duncan's tar ran freely that October and November, and his stout house progressed faster than ever. He had a new zeal, flamed by an inner frenzy that would not let him rest. When he sat down to consider these agitating thoughts in calm, he could explain them to his mind quite satisfyingly, but even as he pondered, his frenzied spirit drove him on to new apprehensions. The Whig uprising, he assured himself, would pass off as others had done, and he had no cause to worry, but his frantic ill-bodings swept him on to finish his house and expand his plantation before ominous happenings arose to blast his dream.

Mary, too, was tantalizing. After she had capriciously thrown herself across his lap to smile into his face and set his heart on fire, she had thwarted his longing and put him mixtie-maxtie with a cheery, sisterly friendship. She was as constant and as unwarm and as appealing as an Indian-summer breeze, and he went miserably to the MacLeod new cabin often only because he was more miserable away.

So he found outlet for his pent-up feelings in action, in his cooper shop and high in the hewn joists and rafters of his growing house. He bored holes from timber to timber and sealed the joints with hickory pins sent home with driving blows.

Thus he was now, this early December day near sunset, pinning pine rafter to cypress beam, and he paused to listen. He did not smile but frowned, for he was in the mood to frown, whereas always, when the folk up and down the Cape Fear heard the faraway blast of Angus MacCooish's bagpipe, they smiled.

The bristling little Gaelic-speaker roamed the valley, almost a hermit, and took no companionship but his beloved instrument. His blasts could be heard from Tidewater to Deep River, always beyond the woods, always, somehow, appropriate. Boys sometimes chased him and caught him and never after took pride in it, for back of the brassy bristle of his face were the pleading, simple eyes of one afraid of his own kind. Some thought he was daft, but none knew, for he could speak nought but Gaelic and he kept silent when a Gael-speaker questioned him. Some said he had been a boy piper at the slaughter of the Scots at Culloden and ever after was daft, but none knew that either.

This time he was far toward the river from Duncan, and he played "The Campbells Are Coming!" and that meant to Duncan that somebody was on the road, somewhere, on some road, and inspired Angus to music. Also that Angus did not like the wayfarer he saw, for the MacCooish belonged to a sept of the Mac-Donald clan and shared the MacDonald dislike for the Campbells. Angus saw a Whig, no doubt. Duncan's heart sank. What if it were Martha McGee coming back? So he frowned, for he had worriments of his own and was in no mood to take on Angus MacCooish's.

He climbed down from the scaffold to join Gillie Black and do the evening's chores, and as he reached the ground two horsemen rode up under the trees.

"Cornelius Harnett!" Duncan cried in welcome, and less heartily: "Robert Howe!"

"So-o-o-o!" Harnett looked up in surprise. "And this is your house! A fine, big house, lad!"

"Na sae big," Duncan deprecated it. "Welcome to't, anyway."

"Duncan plans a family, you can see that," Howe smiled, and Duncan failed to like the remark.

"It will be a goodly shelter soon," Harnett said quickly, searching Duncan's face, "for a fine, beautiful Mistress Stuart, I'm thinking."

Duncan answered Harnett but not Howe: "God grant."

"Aye. Amen."

"Not the lovely MacLeod girl, I hope," Howe bantered him. Harnett was swinging from his saddle and looked a warning at his companion.

"An it concerned ye, Robert Howe," Duncan began to bristle, "I'd answer y'r question."

Cornelius laughed shortly and good-naturedly as though it

were all a joke and now they would talk of something else. But Howe persisted.

"I had understood," he said to Duncan, "that Miss MacLeod had removed herself from your regard by becoming a Whig. If I am wrong, then I have come a long way on a fool's errand."

They were walking down the path to the creek, toward Duncan's cabin and the barn. Duncan stopped and faced Howe and looked at him a long moment. His lips twitched as if searching for the right words. He had the sudden urge to grip Robert Howe's throat and knew that was wrong. He said:

"I wi' give ye the answer to that at the cabin."

They paused at the creek for the horses to drink and passed on up the slope to the cabin. Duncan walked ahead, leaving Cornelius and Robert speaking so low that he could not hear what they said. Inside, he snatched his father's broadsword from the pegs on which Martha McGee had laid it and coldly went out to meet Howe.

"Duncan!" Cornelius sprang ahead to stop the slaughter, but Howe did not change his pace or indicate that he saw the weapon until he reached Duncan and stopped.

Duncan stuck the sword in the sand between them. It stood there as high as their waists. They faced each other across its hilt. Duncan did not refer to it.

"Robert Howe,"—Duncan felt his heat rising and determined to hold cool—" 'tis well that we hae an understanding—now. The lass ye mentioned is na betrothed to me. Also, she displays Whig leanin's, which is neither my concern nor yours. All I say is that she is a Scottish lass, not long in America, and is not acquaint wi' the ways o' the rakehells o' the Tidewater. If ye take unfair advantage o' her, ye must answer to me. That is a' I hae to say."

Bob Howe's thin skin flushed deep red. He stared open-eyed. He sputtered. Out here in the wilderness he was unable to turn words as swiftly and smoothly as in Mrs Cobham's drawing room. He was not dealing with an uncertain youngster who was afraid of upsetting a chair, but with one who was strong and held himself calm and spoke in deep earnest.

"Why—you—you——" he sputtered. "It's an insult! An insult, sir! You shall answer!"

"As ye will, Bob Howe. 'Tis foolish, but we'll fight when ye wish. I hae the choice and I'll take broadswords."

"Bah! I wouldn't fight with such barbaric——"

Cornelius Harnett's laugh was like silver. His hands on his hips, he bent his knees and moved up and down in his merriment.

"Ah, Bob!" he moaned. "You fool! You never can see beyond the point of your own nose. And you might have seen a mile away."

"But," Bob stormed, "he will not fight like a gentleman but——"

"I'll fight like better gentlemen than e'er condescended to the likes o' you."

Cornelius, still chuckling, stepped in and grasped Howe's arm.

"Hush! Hush, the both of you gamecocks! Come, Bob—I must speak with you."

Cornelius jerked the reluctant Howe off balance and led him some distance away. There, with no pretense of jocularity, he spoke severely, shaking his finger in Howe's face. Finally Bob Howe nodded and, without more ado and without the grace to look at Duncan again, pulled into his saddle and rode back the way he had come.

Cornelius walked back to Duncan, chuckling, making it appear that Duncan had utterly routed the romantic Howe.

"I told him not to come," Cornelius said. "I told him the Highlanders would stand for no philandering, that he would only increase their suspicion of the Patriots and make bad matters worse —but he insists that his intentions were honorable."

"Weel," Duncan half smiled, "honorable or not, I'll na have him competing wi' me on my own sandhills."

"I knew it! I knew it!" and Cornelius laughed again, shoving Duncan's shoulder, as though the two of them enjoyed a huge, humorous secret.

Cornelius Harnett was a bonnie companion. He went with Duncan about the business of feeding the stock, and they were in high good cheer, as though, together, they had won a battle. For all his wealth, Cornelius loved common ways. He shucked the corn for his own horse and threw the shucks among the fodder. He always did say, he told Duncan, that there was more strength in shucks than in the fodder, but it took a horse with extra-sound teeth to eat them.

They were through now except for calling the unfattening hogs from the swamp for their nightly nubbins. They strolled out by the tar kilns beyond the cooper shop, to stand on the knoll and whoop for the pigs. Cornelius was telling of the year's rice crop, and how great was the demand for the seed from the Cape Fear's golden rice. But Duncan was not paying much attention. He was thinking of something else. He was curious.

"Cornelius," he said slowly, "when ye wished me a bonnie wife as ye came in, I said 'God grant,' and ye said 'Amen.'"

Cornelius was on his knees at the swamp edge tickling a Venus's-flytrap with a blade of grass to make it close. He said nothing until the green flaps swung to, like eyelids with lashes.

"I always thought," Cornelius mused, "that Nature played us a dirty trick there—a greedy trick. Think of a vegetable eating an animal!" He twisted his mouth in whimsical distaste and leaned over to uproot another swamp plant.

"And here's another, the devil's pitcher!" He turned the slender, trumpetlike thing of grace upside down and shook out the dead bugs which had been trapped and drained of their juices. "The dear Dame," he complained, "might be content to wait until we breathing things are dead before claiming us for food." Then, holding the greenish yellow vase in his fingers to admire it, he said: "Aye, Duncan. I said 'Amen.' I say it again."

"But they say," Duncan protested, "that ye are an infidel. How then, when I speak in reverence o' my God, can ye say 'Amen'?"

"Don't let that trouble you, my friend." Cornelius smiled quietly and looked across the swamp as if shaping his mind.

"It means more than just the feelin's o' y'r heart, Cornelius, else I wouldna comment on't. Ye ken what our own Jamie Mac-Pherson hath said: 'Anarchy is hatred o' human authority, atheism o' divine authority, and the two are parts o' the same.' If ye Whigs are——"

"Ah! I see! You can't condemn us utterly of anarchy, so you search for more evidence. 'Tis more than I hoped!"

"Weel—na."

Harnett, who was smiling, now became solemn. He waved the devil's pitcher to the west. "There is the sunset—the gloamin'-shot, you call it most engagingly—with its purple and gold and infinite

splendor. Can a man make one? No, Duncan. His best is but a
daub. Now look over your own swamp—can a man make a blue
shadow on a swamp? Or can he make the pines whisper or a song
that the wind and the trees sing together? Or can a man make the
evening birds wing for the swamp? Or can he make eternal silences in the wilderness to throb and echo the music of the
spheres? Can a man see and hear these things and then arrogantly
say: 'There is no God'?"

"But they ca' ye an infidel." Duncan was perplexed. "Ye hae no
talk o' an infidel."

"They call me an infidel,"—Harnett shrugged and twirled his
pitcher—"because certain little men like me—as right as I and as
wrong as I, and a damned sight grimmer—insist on making God in
their image and I will not worship that kind of God. They find
Him in old dusty books, while I——" Cornelius paused and
turned to Duncan with a quizzical smile. "But what merits all
this? What matters it if I'm an anarchist to the King and an
infidel to the Pharisees? A man must seek his God as he will, and
I would not bend you to my way. All I say is, never worship against
your conscience, and my life is yours on call should you be forced."

Duncan frowned mightily. "Weren't ye so damnably against the
precepts," he said, "one might e'en give heed to ye."

"Harken, Duncan!" Cornelius cried jovially. "In my desk at
home is an epitaph which I have copied for my headstone. It goes
like this:

"*Slave to no sect, he took no private road,
But looked through Nature up to Nature's God.*

"When you have split my skull, by the King's command, as you
once promised, will you see to it that they inscribe that on my
stone?"

"Aye," Duncan promised seriously, and then divined that he
was being laughed with, and at, and chuckled sheepishly.

Cornelius threw the pitcher to the ground and grumbled with
exasperated good humor: "Why can't the Highlanders get it—
why can't they *want* to be free?"

"Ye mean, why don't they wish t' rebel on their king?"

"That's one way of saying it."

"Ye ca' my hogs, and I'll show ye."

"Call your hogs? I don't——"

"Just ca' them. They're out there in the swamp."

Cornelius chuckled and laughed aloud. He raised his voice high on the crisp December air: "Gee-wo-o-o-o-pe! Gee-wo-o-o-o-o-o-o-ope!"

He paused and listened. There was no answering crash in the brush. He shook his head and called again: "Gee-wo-o-o-o-o-o-o-o-o-o-ope! Gee-wo-o-o-o-o-o-ope!"

They were quiet again and still the swamp was undisturbed. Duncan laughed uproariously. "Whig hogs, perhaps, would heed ye, but, Cornelius, ye hae na the voice for Loyal hogs. Now listen." He put his hands to his mouth, and his call went out high and searching: "Pig-oo-oo-oo-oo-ooie! Pi-goo-oo-oo-oo-ooie!"

And not fifty feet from them came a hungry squeal and a mad rush through the bushes. From a dozen different directions the swamp spouted grunts and squeals, and those farthest were the maddest and most anxious.

Duncan laughed and Cornelius chuckled.

"Same way," Duncan said. "Y'r call has no meanin' for the Loyal."

They left the ravenous razorbacks for Gillie to feed and went to the cabin. They took down the demijohn from the shelf and poured drinks. They cooked supper together, Cornelius drinking his coffee from an earthen bowl with the same ease as from the fine china at home. He still had given no reason for his visit and, as they walked to the tar kiln to relieve Gillie, Duncan wondered why he had come.

The wind grew colder as the darkness clamped down, and they sat on a log in the brush shelter, warmed by the heat of the kiln. The fire crackled and hissed, and now and then the wind whipped puffs of oily smoke their way to make them cough and their eyes to smart.

Duncan went to the cooper shop and came back with a short length of hickory log the size of his arm. With a handaxe he split it, and in the lengthwise hole which had been bored through the wood lay the stuffed golden vein of tobacco which had cured from last year. In comfort and contentment they sliced the leaves and filled their pipes and smoked in silence.

"I came," Cornelius said, "for a great favor."

"Aye? Then, 'tis granted." But, hastily, because Duncan was always on guard against Whig traps, he added: "If it's in reason."

" 'Tis this: For a better reception than if I went alone, I want you to go with me to Flora MacDonald."

"Hah?" Duncan nearly snarled and toned his voice with a smile.

"Yes, and I'm willing to make it right with you by returning the favor."

"Ye? Favor me? What can ye do for me?"

"Well, for one thing"—Cornelius smiled and pulled his nose— "I can advise Martha McGee that you are not for her, and save you a problem."

"Martha? Hell, Cornelius, what do you know about that?" Duncan laughed immoderately.

"Plenty. Ah, Martha is a great lass—a natural rebel! A regular female swashbuckler, with her guns and all. Duncan, if she lets her liking for you ripen into love, look out, lad!"

"Aye!" Duncan said, disturbed. "I've been afeared o' that."

"These widows——"

"Aye. I been thinkin' o' that. Moreo'er, her bein' so wild and grand a woman, wi' a' that land and a', she's nigh o'erpowerin' to a man. If a man didna watch sharp wi' her—losh!—his conscience would go up in smoke and he'd be sold out to the Whigs for a mess o' love!"

"Aye!" Cornelius laughed. "Well, she takes my advice. I can handle that for you. I can do more for you—something you want more than you fear Martha."

"And what would that be?"

"I can persuade Mary MacLeod, perhaps, that her true place is with her kind."

"Ye mean," Duncan turned to glare into Cornelius' eyes, "ye would advise her to be Loyal?"

"Exactly. If the Highlanders go Loyal. I would advise you the same."

"Great God!" Duncan swore in disbelief. He picked up a small pine knot out of the sand and sent it spinning deep into the fire.

"Na!" This was not right. It was out of Cornelius' province. Must he beg the Whigs for his woman? "Na. Handle Martha if ye will. 'Twas a gift frae the Whigs I didna seek in the first place. But, Mary—I'll do my own winning, and I'll make no trade wi' ye about it. What do ye want o' Flora? Treason?"

"No-o-o-o! No. I want to beg her to be neutral."

"Na! Ye would blind her wi' your blandishments, and the poor woman might be drawn into greater trouble wi' the Crown than she had in the 'Forty-five.''

Cornelius chuckled. "You flatter me! I couldn't bend that lady's will. She is able. She is wise. You don't believe I could, really—I, only of Irish blood; she, Scottish?"

Duncan scratched his neck thoughtfully. "That's true," he agreed. "I wi' go."

Cornelius Harnett smiled in urbane triumph, and they talked of other things.

Flora MacDonald received them in the quietness of a snowy December Sunday afternoon. She was domiciled long white miles northwest of Cross Creek on a plantation called Cameron Hill. It happened that she was alone with the servants when Duncan and Cornelius came out of the gentle storm. A Scottish woman took their cloaks, being careful not to scatter snow on the rug. Flora sat meditatively before the fireplace, the Bible in her lap. Duncan felt her serenity even before she spoke.

"I wished someone might come," she smiled to them, "to relieve the lashings of my conscience. Have seats in the inglenook, you must be near frozen."

The two of them bent over the fire eagerly, extending their aching fingers.

"I am amazed, madam," Cornelius, chilled but gallant, turned to say, "that you should know such pangs. They should be held for those of us who deserve the punishment."

"I'm afraid I must insist on admittance to your circle, then," she laughed, "for I am constantly tormented. Now, this morning, I looked out upon the snow, and all kinds of reasons flooded my mind why I need not attend worship at Barbecue Kirk and hear the Reverend John MacLeod preach. It was snowing. Allan and the boys were away on a journey, and I thought I might become snowbound and great inconvenience come. So, I gave up the kirk, only to feel that had I really tried I could have gone. The good Lord will forgive me, I know, but it were so much better not to test His indulgence so continually. Now, had I——"

"Your husband is not at home, then?" Harnett led the conversation away from the lady's conscience.

"No. He is with Mr Caleb Touchstone down on Drowning Creek, not far from the Kenneth Blacks, Duncan, dickering for a farm."

"It is good Scot country," Duncan approved it.

"If we take title we shall call it Killiegrey."

The fire crackled, the hall clock knocked out its hollow rhythm, the snow feathered on the window sash. A servant brought a bowl of toddy, and Duncan soon had an inner glow that was as cheerfully melancholy as that of the Sunday-afternoon fire. He lounged on the high-backed bench at one side of the hearth and Cornelius on the other. Flora sat directly in front, and the fire lighted the blue in her eyes and put little twinkling gleams on her teeth as she talked. She so adroitly included him in all that was said that it was a long time before Duncan realized that she and Cornelius had been discussing Bonnie Prince Charlie without his having said a word.

"Aweel!" Flora sighed a smile. "I long ago gave up protesting the tradition. The poets and the story-makers made quite a beautiful romance of it. I hesitate to say much for fear I would disturb their art. Even yet it seems to me that they speak of some other Flora MacDonald and some other Young Chevalier."

"Oh, my dear lady!" Cornelius' hands waved, and his eyes shone in contradiction. "You are far too modest. The established history is too clear—the King's soldiers threatening at every step—the darkness—the superb intrigues from clan to clan—the storm on the Minch—your marvelous strategy at Monkstadt House and at Kingsburgh——"

"Dear, dear, dear!" Flora laughed gustily. "You are about to convince me after all these years that it was as romantic as the poets said."

She liked it. Duncan sensed that. So did Cornelius, and he, too, was enjoying his part of it.

Cornelius slapped his leg and laughed delightedly, and said: "I'd give a hair ribbon to have seen the yellow-headed young prince creeping over the Skye bogs, disguised as the spinning maid."

Flora laughed, too. "I can at least take credit for the maid's frock," she said. "The Prince balked most obdurately in putting it on, chiefly, I think, because we laughed so." She sighed and, to Duncan, for very little it could have been a sob. "We shouldna laugh," she said, her pensive smile barely holding. "He was our own prince, and he fought brashly against o'erpowerin' forces for our olden glories. He is the last o' the Stuarts."

Duncan sighed, and Cornelius quickly turned the conversation away. Flora smoothed the white sheet, wrapped in black silk, in her lap. It was the sheet under which the bitch-fou drunk prince had slept in Kingsburgh Palace the night after he had escaped. Flora held it as a treasure and had decreed that she should be wound and buried in it. Duncan disliked to look at it because it made him think of death. He preferred to look at the silver which the lords and ladies of London had showered upon her after her imprisonment. He especially liked the pitcher with the line of silver globules on its handle. It was on the table beside the window. He could see it from where he sat.

"I should think," Cornelius said slowly, as if speaking dangerously, "that after the King captured you and imprisoned you, and so ruthlessly murdered so many of your friends and kin, even yet the name of the House of Hanover would be forbidding."

"I was afraid," a sudden cooling change coming upon her, "that you came to say that."

She arose and held the sheet in her arms as though it were a baby. She left the room to put it up, and Cornelius looked into the fire, frowning. It came to Duncan that Flora had known all the while what he only now realized, that Cornelius had been attempting to inveigle her against the Crown through her deep sentiments. Wherefore he glowered upon Cornelius and rued the hour that had induced him to travel with him. Well, from now on he would have a part in what was said.

But when Flora came back she was smiling brightly and seemed to take as a joke what Cornelius had attempted.

"Ye're a most circumfluent advocate, Sir Cornelius," she upbraided him, and Cornelius had the good grace to smile guiltily and make no protest. "We shall get to the point sooner by being direct."

Cornelius shrugged and seemed to welcome that approach, too. Perhaps he had sensed long before that Flora was not to be swayed by feminine heart throbs. "But I swear," he said boldly, "I can't see why you stick to the House that has throttled your land and banished you, from the home you love, to this"—he waved his hand to the blanketed scene outside—"this white wilderness. It's a damnable injustice for gentle people to be uprooted at the peak of life and made to pioneer!"

Whether Cornelius meant it or not, it convinced Duncan. "Aye!" he said loudly, breaking into the conversation. " 'Tis God's truth! But, ne'er mind—we'll build a Hielands on the Cape Fear, for Flora, to exceed the glories o' Somerled."

Flora smiled at him, but when she spoke she answered Cornelius. "Isn't it sufficient," she said, "that we—do stick?"

"It has to be. I only wondered why. Your true sympathy was revealed when you aided the Prince against the Crown. You were imprisoned, your land ravaged, your people butchered, your clans scattered, your feudal manner of living destroyed, your proud people put under the rule of merchants and money-makers. And still you meekly submit, though the same House attempts to stifle the ancient liberties in the new land. I do not understand it, madam. Never was true revolution better known than in Scotland."

Duncan sat upright, burning to protest, but Flora merely smiled. "You have said much, but you overlook much. So few do understand." Flora was calm. Her tone was rich and unruffled. For all his speaking, Cornelius had made no dent in her defense. He got up and stood with his hands in his pockets. He put his foot on the bench and rested an arm on his knee. He looked at her intently, his racing brain eager for another thrust. But Flora spoke yet.

"It is true," she said evenly, "that the House of Hanover wears the Crown. For how long, one cannot say. But the Crown is Scottish, it was taken to London by the Stuarts. In the Coronation Chair is the Stone of Scone, and we have—and love—the tradition that where the Stone is, there Scottish princes shall rule. There are other bonds, but these considerations make them doubly strong."

Cornelius opened his mouth to speak and slowly closed it.

Flora laughed joyously. "You were about to say, I doubt not, that you cannot answer mysticism and unreason with logic. You would say, I think, that the Crown is his who wears it, and that the traditions of an old stone are no more than old wives' tales. Perhaps. For all the vaunted common sense of the Hielands and the Lowlands, I mistrust we are often led astray by sentiment. The fact that we love it makes it all the more devastating."

Cornelius, still pondering his way out of this blind alley, tapped his clay pipe against a chimney brick and filled it with tobacco. From a triangular basket hanging at the mantel he took a wooden splint, lighted it at the fire and puffed vigorously. Flora watched him in quiet amusement.

"What you really are saying, of course," Cornelius reasoned slowly, "is that the Highlanders have the hope—at least the instinct—to restore the Stuarts—or, anyway, the glory of the old clan system."

"Aye!" said Duncan.

"I haven't said so," Flora said, and Duncan's chin dropped.

"No. Nevertheless, let me assume the treason. So, then, if the American disaffection should become extreme, Scots in this country might see a danger of being cut off forever from even a chance of restoring the Stuarts. Could one see it that way?"

"Yes, one might see it that way," Flora said, not committing herself.

"Now let me suggest," Cornelius continued, "admitting all that to be true, in a land that is free, where there are no overlords and subsidized merchants to prey on the people, one, conceivably, might manage without a crown at all."

"Please! Please, Mr Harnett! I do not wish to be impolite, but I cannot listen. Your suggestion smacks too strongly of sedition."

"Then, of course, forgive me," Cornelius said, not very contritely. "My fealty goes only so far as the Crown respects my rights and gives me protection. It has failed in both, and I hold myself to no obligation."

"I fear," said Flora, "you leave us little to discuss."

"Ah!" Cornelius smiled. "We've seen but the one side of it. It cannot hurt you to receive information from the enemy. You may even pass it on to the King, if you like."

She smiled. They held each other in mutual respect.

"I have no will to bear oppressive tidings, merely as such," Cornelius said solemnly. "But you may as well know. The uprising daily becomes more and more ominous. I was in the North in the summer and again in the autumn and, madam, I am aghast at what I know to be brewing. Things are equally portentous in our own province. Steel our spirits as we will to a hope of peace, there is bound to be a time of blood and terror before the right shall triumph."

Flora grasped her hands in her lap and looked into the fire without answer.

Cornelius continued: "In our own province we are quite prepared. Within a week we can put six thousand men under arms, and within a month, ten thousand."

"Weel," Duncan said calmly, "e'en so, it wouldna take long to get three thousand braw Hielanders out wi' their broadswords—and then where would your donsie little Whigs be?"

Cornelius burst into a peal of sudden laughter and turned back seriously to Flora. She had not smiled, but looked into the fire. "We do not ask you to join us," he persisted, "only that you take the position that this is not your quarrel, that you will have none of it. Let the Scots stay in their own fields, attend to their own business, stay out of trouble."

"Aye," said Flora, for the first time looking disturbed. She had her little round locket in her fingers, playing with it nervously. "That seems braw and sonsie. I cherish the wish that it might be so. War is most horrible, and I have a husband and two sons in America, a son-in-law and much kin. It is a tragedy I would—and will—avoid, if in honor it may be."

"Then," Cornelius spoke brightly, in sudden hope, "I pray you give no attention to the harpings of the Crown's Governor Josiah Martin, who moves heaven and earth to involve the Highland——"

"I have not seen or heard from Governor Martin. Did you——"

"Mrs MacDonald!" Cornelius suddenly was before her, impetuously, his face strained with his appeal. "I love the Cape Fear

Highlanders. I love their young men. I pray you—I beseech you—help me save the blood and the lives of such lads as our own Duncan Stuart!" He ended his dramatic thrust standing, his finger pointing to where Duncan sat.

Flora did not move, except that her eyes turned to Cornelius in torture. She looked back to the fire. She did not raise her voice, and her monotonous tones fell dead before her lips.

"Did you e'er hear our oath?" The way she spoke made Duncan wince.

"I have not!" Cornelius spoke impatiently, as though he had delivered the winning stroke only to have it brushed aside.

"We seldom speak of it, e'en among ourselves," Flora said in the same pained tone. "It haunts us and gives us to think o' terror. I wi' repeat it, for your better understanding o' the Hielanders. Ye will take heed that when the oath was administered after the 'Forty-five, the whole issue of loyalty to Hanover was bound up in the royal decree that the Hielanders should give up their kilts and tartans. So when one swore to give up arms and the garb, it was implicit that he should be loyal to the Crown, and so understood. Since that time the kilts and arms have come back by tacit consent, but the most horrible implications o' the oath are with us still."

Flora closed her eyes and leaned back, her face paler than before. Duncan and Cornelius watched her in silence. She repeated:

" 'I, ——— MacDonald, do swear, as I shall answer to God at the Great Day of Judgment, I have not nor shall have in my possession any gun, pistol or arm whatsoever, and never use tartan plaid or any part of the Highland garb; and if I do so may I be cursed in my undertakings, family and property; may I never see my wife and children, father, mother or relation; may I be killed in battle as a coward, and lie without Christian burial, in a strange land, far from the graves of my forefathers and kindred—may all this come across me if I break my oath.' "

Flora opened her eyes with a little tremor, as though she came from under a spell. She looked into the fire a moment and gained better possession of herself.

"That is the oath, Mr Harnett. It was constructed by some genius of subtlety who knew how to sink barbs into the Scottish soul where it was tenderest. Superstition. Fear of Heaven. Dread of the unknown. Love of family. Sacredness of the oath. You must have a strong pull, almost to the death, to drag a true Hielander from these clutches."

Harnett compressed his lips, his eyes holding strong on hers. "Then," he said disappointedly, "there is nothing I can offer—no argument—no inducement——"

"If you were thinking of offering a bribe," Flora said, "no."

"I hadn't that in mind."

"Thank you for that. Your weakness, I think, is that you have nothing to offer. Scots love a great and mighty chief, and to ring around him. Hielanders have fought always for the Hielands, and though separated from them, as they now are, their instinct is to fight back toward them. In addition is their oath, unwelcome as it is. Every tie that binds them draws them against you. Your whole movement heads toward open rebellion and war for independence. E'en you win, what have you? No one knows. The Hielanders, especially those who speak only the Gaelic, have a terror of the unrevealed, and you invite them on an unknown and uncharted adventure. When the King calls his Loyalists to arms, what appeal have you to resist the call? None, I think. Still—I give you no answer. I merely show you the trend of the minds of those who have counseled wi' me."

For a while no one spoke. The snow still fell like feathers across the open spaces. Cornelius looked at Duncan and sighed. He said they must be going if they were to make Cross Creek that night.

CHAPTER 6

JUNE 1775 found the Scot country perturbed. As Cornelius Harnett had foreseen, the winter had brought confusion and added bitterness to it. Duncan, in the lush smells of spring, remembered yet that day in December when he had parted with Cornelius at Elizabethtown. The Tidewater man, his head heavy with the sureness of Highland loyalism, had ridden depressed down the highway toward Wilmington, and Duncan had sat his horse and looked after him with a strange feeling of loss—and of farewell.

After that the reports of open rebellion had begun to flow in. The Whigs had grown bold. They had forgotten the King's might and become arrogant. They had formed so-called Committees of Safety in the counties, and these members, chosen from among the most consummate, had presumed to impose insolent decrees upon the inhabitants. "The Cause of Boston is the Cause of All!" they had cried. They had levied upon the planters, even the Tories, for hams and corn and potatoes to ship to the contentious Whigs of Massachusetts. In their arrogated authority they had gathered the rabble in drinking bouts to march and drill. They had sent squads of military to the farms to intimidate the people and impress them into the damnable Whig cause. One such squad had come to Duncan and he had scattered them pell-mell in four directions with a grubbing hoe. He had not been molested after that, although he had heard mutterings. He had paid no attention to these, for other, more important considerations had kept him moody and morose.

He no longer went to Mary MacLeod's cabin, and for very good reasons. She had never changed her course of amiable friendship, but she was now so much the Whig that she spiced all her conversation with rebellious boastings, and there was no pleasure in her. She declared that only now, for the first time in her life, she knew what it was to live gallantly, and all her brother Malcolm's fulminations could not change her.

For instance, there was the unspeakable affair at New Bern, where the Assembly had been convened by Governor Martin to attend to the King's business. Farquard Campbell had been there, and Thomas Rutherford, and James White, of Bladen, and the whole state representation. As rapidly as the governor had turned his back, the irresponsible ingrates by parliamentary bastardy had formed themselves into a congress of sedition and made speeches and adopted resolutions insulting to the Crown. No wonder Governor Martin, humiliated beyond endurance, had voiced his mighty wrath and dismissed the Assembly. Mary had gloried in the reports of it most irksomely, and he had not gone back for a week.

Hard on that had come the King's most gracious offer to the
two colonies of North Carolina and New York to lift the embargo, so far as they were concerned. It was ironically just, Duncan thought, for if North Carolina chose to be peaceful and
obedient, which was her high duty, then she would quickly grow
rich at the expense of the obstreperous other colonies. But would
the representatives accept the offer? No! They had spurned it,
and Mary had gloated over such illicit patriotism.

Then, in May, had come the crowning indignity in Wilmington.
John Ashe and his rabble had hauled up the inoffensive Dr Cobham
and with him the fair-minded Tidewater merchant, John Slingsby,
who owned land in Bladen, and demanded that they sign the
Whig Association paper. Quite properly they had refused, and
would have suffered some bizarre penalty, such as being put in
the stocks, or dipped like a woman in the ducking stool, except
that indignation, even among the better Whigs, had prevented
it for some more subtle attack. At any rate, a week later, to their
disgrace, both men had taken the detestable Whig oath. Duncan
had been outraged and had rushed over the sandhills to report
to Malcolm and declare his indignation. But Mary had been in
high glee and had danced around the room most unseemly.

Just later, according to the tale which Duncan had heard at
the Elizabethtown store, his old friend Cornelius Harnett had
engaged in a process of high treason, an inciting to riot, no less. On
a Monday in May a courier had sped in from the North, bringing
news that the Whigs had been fired on by the British in Lexing-
ton, Massachusetts. Galloping messengers had brought the tidings
south by night and by day, and Harnett had received it and copied
it and sped it on to South Carolina, with an added: "For God's
sake make haste!"

Then Harnett, who now was chief of the King's enemies, had
spread the news like wildfire all over North Carolina, sweeping
excitement to the farthest corners. One backwoods community
of Ulster Scots, Mecklenburg, arrant Whigs almost to the man,
had forgotten its duty to a long-suffering King and proclaimed its
independence. Mary had been so excitedly gleeful that Malcolm
had threatened to punish her, and Duncan had wished to God he
would.

The Scottish Highland country felt the impact of these things but set up a wall of stubborn disregard. The word from Flora MacDonald was that none was to yield to the turmoil but should stand steady until the right should be known. But Duncan was near the line where the Welsh and the Irish and the Swiss and the English Whigs sounded their rabblish harpings, and he could not remain entirely out of it. Where other Scots never had to listen he was forced to know that John Ashe and "Mad Jimmie" Moore were scouring the Tidewater country for political support. They were in a most damnable contest. Both, ludicrously, demanded to be commander in chief of the ragtag-and-bobtail army, which drank itself to arrogance on field days. Ashe already had mortgaged his plantation to pay his rabble, and Moore's followers were moving heaven and earth. It wouldn't have mattered, except that the contest stirred the nobodies through the province. Mary thought it not beneath her to sing their praises.

In Bladen the four Thomases—Brown, Hadley, Owen and Robeson—were the high priests of sedition, riding at night, secretly, holding field days in the lower precincts, away from the Scots. They took care, Duncan noted in satisfaction, not to cause the Highland swords to clank. And it was well, he soothed his distemper, for when the clans unsheathed their broadswords upon the Whigs the battle would be short and terrible: a yell, a rush, a splash of blood and a buckle of bone. It had been that way since the times of the ancient chiefs. Pray God the damned Whigs might see they were still preserved only because a generous king forbade to give his anger rein. Duncan had no wish to fight. He yearned to build his house and till his fields. His plan of life was straight and sound, gauged true to his God in heaven, to his king on the throne, to his governor in New Bern, to his corn rows and his pine trees, to his mansion and to his brown-eyed Mary, to his bairns and his slaves. He did not want to fight, but his gorge rose at this constant, growing threat.

The hell of it, adding sting to the pain, was Mary's gleeful Whiggishness. She called herself a Patriot. She called him a Tory, which he was, but "Loyalist" sounded better. She jibed him over the bungling of the British government and twitted him on what she called Patriot victories. She gloried in the audacities of the rebels. He could not sit with her without angry disputation and, she being quick-tongued, their arguments always ended in the semblance of her having triumphed. It became unbearable, though it did not change his plan, and he did not go to the MacLeod cabin any more.

That June Tuesday was mill day when he, having been to mill, rode by Elizabethtown to see what the Whig smugglers were paying for turpentine. The still was in full blast. The weather was hot, and the yard was full of barrels. The spirits, condensed in the worm in the great tank, ran out the low end in a thin clear stream. The hard, turpentine-soaked sand under Donald Bane's feet was softening in the sun. Nags tied under the trees looked at Donald Bane and whinnied. A dutiful horse, he did not answer.

On the store porch a group of neighborhood men sat in lazy talk. Others, over in the shade of the warehouse, were pitching horseshoes. Those at the store discussed the whirling events of the time in lofty nonpartisanship. Few, these days, unless in groups of their kind, had the temerity to boast openly their cause, whether Whig or Tory. Duncan saw old Tom Hadley sitting there, on the floor, leaning against the post, scratching in his gray beard, and had a sudden bristling ire at his old Whig friend. It was such men as Tom Hadley who were causing all the tumult.

Duncan reined Donald Bane over to sit and listen. Old Theet Sells was there, taciturn and interested. And Arn, his son, and Duncan wondered if Arn's wife had had her baby yet. Pete Arabell, the loud-mouth from Upper Carver's Creek, whittled a stick and told a tale of cockfighting. A man from Slingsby's farm and two boys from the Waddell place swung their feet from the edge. Old Tom, usually talkative, today was as taciturn as Theet Sells, and Duncan wondered why. Young John Hadley held his knees in his arms and glowered at his feet. Other horses were at ease, but John's stood saddled and ready.

"Hi, Dunk!" Pete greeted him loudly.

Duncan nodded to all. "How're the folks?" he inquired, still wondering about John Hadley's horse.

"Peart," old Tom said, offhandedly.

"Middlin' tol'able," Theet Sells admitted.

"I was better, but I got over it, thank the Lord," Arabell haw-hawed. The others were content to let the oldsters speak.

"Hey, Dunk," Arabell demanded, "what's this about the Whigs runnin' the governor outa New Bern?"

Old Tom Hadley turned on Pete fiercely before Duncan could answer. "Oh, shut up, fool!"

"Eh?" Duncan thrust in. "I know nothing. What of it?"

Pete shrugged and kept silent.

"We don't know," Hadley said. "You can hear anything these days."

Old Tom looked at Duncan, and Duncan returned the gaze, each sharply estimating the other.

"D'ye put dependence in what ye heard, Mr Hadley?"

"Don't know, Duncan—don't know's I do, don't know's I don't."

"If the governor left, where did he go—did ye hear that?"

"No, I didn't hear that."

Duncan's indignation rose, and he was minded to blast and flay into this knot o' Whigs until he learned the truth about the governor. There had to be a break sooner or later, and, by God, now was as good as any other time.

Old Tom looked him over in shrewd speculation. He extended his stockinged legs to the ground and nodded away from the crowd. "Got sump'n I want to ask you, Dunk."

They went out to a tree, beyond earshot, to stand in the shade. Duncan dropped from the saddle and rested his arm across it. Donald Bane pricked his bay ears up the road, shook his skin, and eased his left hind foot for rest. Old Tom rested a gnarled hand on the pommel and looked at Duncan squarely.

Duncan said bluntly: "If ye plan t' inveigle me into y'r Whig schemes, then don't!"

But old Tom was looking at him with the same hurt in his eyes that Duncan had had in his heart when he had watched Cornelius Harnett riding away.

"We been friends a long time, Duncan," he said softly.

"Aye, Mr Tom. 'Tis true."

"A long time, says you. Why, boy, I was your friend before

you could reach up and tetch a snake's belly. I thought a sight of yo' li'l broke-up daddy, and you don't hardly remember him. Yes, we been friends."

Old Tom scratched into his beard and wrestled with his thoughts, trying to strike a key. "I don't know what's comin'," he sighed. "You don't, neither. I feel it in my bones, though, Dunk, that this country's bound to be tore up."

"I hope y're wrong, Mr Tom."

"I do, too. Before my God, Dunk, I hope I am. Now, take the Scotch. I know them, if anybody does—and sometimes I think nobody does. Tom Brown thinks the Scotch are going to stay clear. But I know the Scotch. They are oathbound, and if there is anything stuck tighter than an oathbound Scot I don't know what it is. Ye'll all be in, and that's the hell of it.

"Now I can see, Dunk," old Tom waved his hand widely, changing the course of his thoughts, "how, if you all was followin' your own intrust, you could see the thing like me. 'Treat me right and I'll treat you right,' that's my style, be you king or nigger slave. If the damn King wants to talk sensible, then I want to talk sensible, but if he wants to gouge my eye, then I want to gouge his eye. And it looks like that's the only way we'll have it, and we're just about in for the damnedest eye-gouging the world ever saw.

"Now, where does that git us? I dunno. Now, look. Here we are, about to buck the King. Maybe we bluff him down or maybe we don't. Or maybe we fight it out with guns and swords. It's all the same. It is a fight, and we win or he wins. Maybe he wins— what'll he do? Chop us to pieces and throw us to the hawgs, like Butcher Cumberland did the clans? Maybe. Like as not. It's a chance we take. But I don't think much about that, Dunk, because, by God, he can't do it. The King's started something he can't finish.

"But what gits me—maybe we win. Then what? You say—no, I don't mean you personally, Dunk, but a Whig. A Whig would say, 'Shucks, that's easy—we'll just go on like we been goin' on, except the King will reckernize our rights,' says he. And that's all *he* knows. But *I* know better."

Duncan held still with what patience he could. He was trying to think.

"You take the Cape Fear out there. She's runnin' free, but dam it up, and what you got? Still water. Cert'ny. Well, that's what we got now—still water, dammed up behind the King. And still water always pushes, always downhill.

"All right. Break the dam. Can you ever get that water behind the dam again? Answer me that. Cert'ny not. It'll go bustin' outa there, rippin' up hell as it goes."

Duncan slapped a mosquito and grimaced. Something back of all this harangue alarmed him. Old Tom kept it up persistently.

"Then what have you got? Runnin' water. Yes, sir. Rootin' up trees, gashin' new gullies, tearin' up barns, drownin' the livin' and washin' up the dead—floodin' the country!

"All right! All right!" Old Tom stood back to flatten his hands wide, to show the vast extent of the flood. "What you goin' to do with all that water? Let it back into the swamps and pocosins and stagnate? I mean, are we goin' to have tribes like the Injuns? We goin' to have a new king? Or just pick a man one year to run the government and kick him out the next? What you goin' to do?"

Duncan's impatience surged. Some Whig scheme was afoot, and he had muddled into it and become a stumbling block. He couldn't figure old Tom's purpose, this palaver—as true as it might be. Old Tom was his friend, he knew that; but he was a shrewd old schemer, too.

"What about Governor Martin?" Duncan asked abruptly.

Old Tom spat disgustedly on the sand. "That damn Arabell!"

"Did the Whigs really try to capture him?"

"I don't know."

"But don't they know they'd only hae the King's troops down on 'em?" he demanded.

"I'd thought about that."

"E'en," Duncan protested, as though they braved the uttermost calamity, "the Hielanders?"

"I'd thought about that, too."

"Where did the governor go—to sea?"

"Reckon not. I dunno. Maybe so. I spect he did." Old Tom didn't want to talk about it.

"It's treason!"

"Well—whatever you call it. Now, about this business of a revolution—a new government . . ."

But Duncan was giving him no attention. A startling new thought was blazing in his mind. He had to get away and think about it, quickly. The meaning of John Hadley's saddled horse came clear.

"Don't you worry, Mr Tom." He slapped his old friend on the shoulder and took time to grin. If Hadley could dissemble, so could he. "The dam wi' hold," Duncan assured him, putting his foot in the stirrup.

"Wait! What's your hurry? I want to talk——"

"I got too much virgin to dip to waste time gabbin' politics," Duncan laughed. He rode toward the ferry, toward home, leaving old Tom standing there calling him back.

Duncan trotted slowly until the trees hid him. Then he turned swiftly into the woods and rode up the river. He knew now. The thing made sense. The King's governor had been driven out of New Bern, but the Whigs did not know where he had gone. Whatever route he had taken, he surely would go to the mouth of the Cape Fear and take the protection of Fort Johnston and the King's man-o'-war, *Cruzier*. He could sail there from New Bern, but it would be much wiser for him to drive to Cross Creek and then down through the Scot country. If he did that and left Cross Creek early in the morning, then it was about time for him to be approaching Elizabethtown. That explained everything. Tom Hadley was watching for him, holding John ready to ride instantly as a courier to the Whigs in Wilmington. The Whigs would march into Brunswick and capture the governor before he reached the fort.

Duncan rode the woods, wild and free, with his spirits soaring. Here, now, after all the indignities and the humiliations, was something he could do for the King. He hadn't felt so triumphant since he had laid the ridgepole on his stout house. For all the Whig cunning he would thwart their deviltry and preserve the governor—if he came this way.

Miles above Elizabethtown he hid Donald Bane in the brush and went carefully to the highway for a look. There were no recent carriage tracks, no tracks of a troop of horse. The governor had not been that way today.

He drew back into the woods where he could get a long view up the road and waited. The day was hot. He sweated, even in the shade. The wait was even more irksome because he had no idea how long he must watch, or even that the governor would come this road at all. All he knew was that Tom Hadley watched below and that he, at cross-purposes, watched here, and that Mary Mac-Leod would have a spasm if she knew of it. That was a pleasant thought. For a time he waited most energetically, but it is hard to wait with vigor, and he gave over to sitting on the sand and digging little holes with a stick.

Far up the highway a carriage drawn by four horses swung around the bend, and behind them a troop of horse galloped. Duncan was on his feet, staring. If it was the governor, he had changed horses since he had left Cross Creek. The animals were fresh and lively, and that was good. Duncan waited in the brush, and when they neared he stepped to the road and held up his hand for them to stop. The driver, a Scot, drew rein with one hand and held his other on a rifle. The six Highlanders behind drew close to the carriage alertly. One man rode in the carriage. He wore a black silk hat and peered out the window.

"What is it, my man?" he asked sharply.

"I wait here for Governor Josiah Martin," Duncan said.

"So? Who are you?" The voice was testy and impatient, and Duncan felt his glowing purposes cooling.

"It doesna concern ye, unless ye be Governor Josiah Martin," he answered quietly.

The Scots in the rear seemed to understand Duncan's resentment. One of them pointed to the carriage and nodded, and Duncan went to the governor without more ado.

"Are you a Scot?" the passenger asked nervously.

"Aye. Name o' Duncan Stuart."

Martin opened the door and stepped out, throwing a pistol back to the seat.

He was dressed in broadcloth, but his white stock was dusty and crushed with the day's travel. The hat made him look taller than he was. He was thin and pale, with deep creases at the corners of his mouth, as though he had chronic illness. His eyes were darkened and sullen with weariness and worry.

"One never knows, these days, to trust his best friend, even," Martin said ungraciously. "The damned Whigs are around like fleas in the sheets. Are you a Whig?"

"Na. I am Loyal."

"How do I know that?"

Duncan flushed. The Scots in the rear shook their heads for him to be discreet. But his lip curled nevertheless. Was this his reward for saving the governor from a trap?

"Ye hae my word, sir, and since that is na sufficient, I bid ye good day."

Duncan turned to leave, but Josiah Martin, the testy, showed that he had deeper qualities as well.

"Hold! Hold!" he laughed and strode in front of Duncan. "Forgive me. I lately have been played so false by spurious friends that I am suspicious and my good judgment is gone. You are one of His Majesty's most loyal subjects, I have no doubt. Now tell me what message you have."

Duncan's anger did not go quickly. His face was flushed still, and he looked half smiling, half frowning at the mounted men. "Aye," he said slowly. "Your Excellency's journey down this road is suspected by the Whigs. They have out-watchers at Elizabethtown to detect if ye shall pass."

"So?" Josiah Martin visibly was anxious. A cloud, darker than that which originally rested upon it, passed over his face. "Come, gentlemen!" He waved his hand nervously to the Scots. "Gather closer and hear—and give me your counsel."

The Scots dropped to the ground and held their horses' reins over their shoulders, making a group.

"And what—what—what will they do at Elizabethtown, do you think?" Martin asked Duncan.

"I am na privy to their plans, but I suspect they would send a courier ahead to notify John Ashe, that he may intercept ye."

"Yes." The governor pondered what Duncan had said. "Yes, I think you are right."

Martin threw back his thin shoulders and, with the gesture, dismissed any semblance of fear. Duncan had better respect for him.

"Very well. Gentlemen!"

The seven men gave him heed, and he spoke:

"You have heard what Duncan Stuart has said. Now let us make our plans. I need not tell you that it would be disastrous to my promise to the King to quell this uprising if the Whigs should take me in custody."

"Aye," said one of the Cross Creek men, "but your custody would be short, ere we of the Hielands relieved ye and left broken skulls in our wake."

"Yes, yes. No doubt. But before that need, we must avoid them if we can. What do you propose?"

"Gie us our broadswords," one said, "and we'll cut a swath through the rabble wide eneugh for your coach to go in a gallop."

"You are seven," Martin said, "and good for thrice your number."

"Ten times," the first speaker corrected him quietly.

"Even so," the governor agreed, "but I am told that this Ashe commanded five hundred men less than a month ago. Gentlemen, by all means I must reach the fort safely. Have you any other suggestion?"

Duncan had said nothing while the others talked. "I propose this," he now offered. "I thought on it while I waited for ye. Drive down the road here," pointing down a woods trail, "and frae one trail to anither, which I can show ye, circle back of Elizabethtown and come again to the highway beyond."

Martin's eyes became hopeful, but he tested Duncan's plan step by step, criticizing it, and then accepted it wholly.

"The only alternative I see," he said, "is to camp here in the Scot country and summon a force large enough to drive through to the coast. But that would take time, it might bring on an engagement, and the time for that, gentlemen, is not ripe. When we start the process of stamping out the rebellion, we must be better prepared. We will dash for it by this side road."

"I will go wi' ye all the way, if ye consider it desirable," Duncan offered.

"No," said Martin. "If the plan succeeds at all it will be by reason of celerity and not by strength. By your plan we will be in the fort before the alarm is given. I thank you, but you'll have no need of leaving your work. When I need you I shall send for you —and, depend upon it, you shall not have long to wait."

It was near night, miles below the store, when Duncan Stuart lifted his hand in salute and Josiah Martin cried out his thanks and sped down the highroad toward Fort Johnston. Three of the Highlanders galloped in front, three behind. Old Tom Hadley, no doubt, still was watchfully loafing at the store front in Elizabethtown.

Twilight was upon the land when he reached home with his bag of meal. Gillie Black looked at him inquiringly, but Duncan, with a strange new feeling of pride in his chest, explained cryptically: "I hae been on the *King's* business."

Duncan had no thought to rest or to eat. He stabled Donald Bane and soon was on his way across the woods. He wanted to see Mary. He wished to make payment for her jibes. He wanted to boast, now that Martin was safely away, how he had outwitted the Whigs. His long strides took him over the sand, and he smiled more than once when he considered how he should say it to her.

But, curiously, his sense of revenge lifted as smoke in the wind when he approached the cabin. She was boiling haggis. He detected the odor long before he reached the door, and his hunger rose mighty and compelling. War or no war, Whigs or no Whigs, what Highlander "looks down wi' sneering, scornfu' view on sic a dinner"?

Lamb liver, and lungs, and heart, with onions and oatmeal, boiled in a lamb's stomach, served in the tradition of Scotland! Duncan gave himself over to it like a rail splitter.

Mary set the platter on the little table between Duncan and Malcolm and wailed: "What a waste! Good haggis and nane t' eat it but a pair o' wranglin' Tories!"

But she was happy. Her brown eyes watched them and smiled. She needed no spoken compliments, only their eager looks, to take that satisfaction which comes to her who boils haggis for a Scot.

"Y'r pupils takin' to book learnin'?" Duncan asked Malcolm between mouthfuls.

"But poorly," Malcolm lamented. "They hae the o'erpowerin'

desire tae fish and roam the woods and pick huckleberries. I hae gi'en up teachin' them the English o' Caesar's Gallic Wars—I just gie it to them by rote i' the Latin, hopin' that through one o' God's mysteries they absorb some part o't."

"More haggis, Duncan?" Mary tempted him.

"Aye, bethankit!"

After supper Mary displayed the new shuck-bottomed chair she had made and showed Duncan the two new gifts which had come to her from her new friends in the swamps. One was a mad-stone, to cure the bites of snakes and of mad dogs, and the other was the large wing bone of a fighting cock, to ward off the yellow fever.

"Aye," Duncan approved. "One shouldna be wi'out them."

After that he and Mary went down to the spring. By now she knew the path, every root and turn in it, and went lightly along while he stumbled after her with the bucket.

Mary was in subdued mood tonight, sweeter than common. He'd rather make love to her than boast of his triumph. After that haggis, especially. She spoke first.

"It is a drear time, Duncan," she said anxiously. "It is ominous. It is i' the air. I feel it. More and more, all the time, it creeps on like a black fog frae the swamp."

"Aye," he said stoutly, dipping the water. "Some o' y'r donsie Whig friends will be hurt before it's o'er, I'm thinking."

"Aye. Whigs and all, I fear."

"Did ye hear about 'em chasin' Governor Martin out o' New Bern?" he asked indignantly. She said nothing.

"Aye. He escaped t' Cross Creek and, today, down the King's Highway t' Fort Johnston."

"Oh!"

" 'Tis true," and he added crushingly: "I guided him by a side road and thwarted Tom Hadley's spies!"

"*You,* Duncan!"

"Aye! 'Twas time I was doin' something f'r my king. And I'll do more yet, come the time."

"Oh, I *hope* they don't learn of this," was all she said.

"Let 'em learn! I'm proud o't."

"Yes, yes, but they may take reprisal on ye."

"Who? Whigs?" he scoffed.

Then she laughed. She laughed the more. It rang out over the swamp, and night birds answered.

"What's funny?"

"I was just thinking," she said between peals, "how ludicrous it was f'r His Majesty's proud governor to be running through the land like a rabbit frae the hounds!"

Duncan did not stay long. One could talk to no satisfaction wi' such a woman.

The governor's escape into Fort Johnston came to be a seven days' wonder along the King's Highway. The Whigs had had him trapped, and had known it, and, yet, the next they had heard of him he was safely inside the fort and making great plans to take the war to them. Duncan's satisfaction, denied him by Mary, came from the dark looks of the Whigs who flattered him with their suspicions.

His news, now, was that the Tidewater soldier bands tended to march and countermarch in the territory between the fort and the up country and, so, prevent the governor from sending messages to his friends in the interior. The Whigs stormed and thundered at a proclamation which Martin had issued, denouncing the Committees of Safety, and swore that no Tory should go through their lines.

Duncan, that Saturday afternoon, July 15, more than a month later, sat in his cooper shop to escape a thunder shower. The rain had ceased, and the air was fresh and sweet. The black cloud still hung to the south, flashing and rumbling. He was proud of the escapade, but the following events worried him. No word had come from Flora MacDonald. The governor and the Whigs were rapidly raising an issue which surely must force armed conflict. Duncan was against the Whigs with every pulse of his soul; still, yet, he had no bitterness against the individuals. He had no desire to slay his neighbors. Outwitting them was one thing, and drawing blood another. He knew how the Highland sympathies lay; he did not know what the Highlanders would do. He wasn't ready for a decision, and it troubled him that it might be forced at any time.

He was in this disturbed state when a soldierly young Englishman, dripping wet, came from the woods and handed him a note. The letter was addressed to no one and bore no name except that of the signer. It read:

"Please report to me at once. Jo. Martin."

The young man saluted and left him standing there, grimly, the note in his hands.

Gillie Black, his face buried in a huge quarter of a watermelon, looked up curiously. Duncan walked out on the wet sand, thinking, tearing the note to tiny bits and dropping the pieces along the ground. He came back, his chest full, striving to speak calmly. He told Gillie:

"Ye wi' take charge until I return. Scrape the ticks daily frae the oxen. Hoe, Monday, the beans and the peas and the kale in the kitchen garden, and should it rain after ye hoe and the grass take root again, then hoe Tuesday also. Ither things ye ken well enough to do, and take note that I shall flog ye when I return if they are not done. Now ye shall saddle Donald Bane and put feed in bags for two days' journey."

The decision having been forced upon him, Duncan set out with a greater feeling of ease, even of relief. If the governor needed him as a guard, that was nothing less than the duty of any loyal subject. He had no fear of the Whigs. Donald Bane was young and fleet of foot and sound of wind. Nor did Duncan expect danger of being intercepted until the second day, down in the Brunswick area. With his knowledge of traveling the swamps, he had no fear of being stopped even then. So, kilted in the tartan of the Stuarts, he rode away, with something of the consciously foolish soaring spirit of knight errantry.

He rode all that afternoon and far into the night, when, Donald Bane becoming weary, he camped in the shielding pines of an old field.

He was wary, for now he was in the territory where the Whigs were most active. That, perhaps, was why he so lightly slept and awoke near daylight to the faint pad-pad of marching men distantly across the field. Alarmed, leaving Donald Bane tied, he ran down to see what he might. He saw and stared, for the Whig company of fifty men or more was equipped for battle, not merely for drilling. The soldiers were on a road which led toward the town of Brunswick, they marched briskly, and soon they were out of sight.

Duncan pushed on rapidly that day, avoiding houses and bridges. It was almost night again when he pressed down the interminably long straight road which led to Fort Johnston, impatient with his tidings. The fort was strangely quiet when he arrived. The great soft blocks of shell rock, set like tremendous bricks in thick, high walls, cast foreboding shadows. Where there should have been the bustle of military men and the shrill of bugles, the high sharp commands of Captain Collett and his officers, there was but deep stillness and twilight.

Across the sand and out in the harbor the warship *Cruzier* was at anchor, an ancient vessel and well barnacled, but a fortress in herself. The ship, too, seemed strangely alone and lonely. The house of Captain Collett, the commander, across the area, was dark and silent.

"An' wat'll ye 'ave, me man?" The inquiry came from behind, and a little English cockney, in uniform breeches and shirt, walked up to him through the sand.

"I hae come in answer to Governor Martin's summons."

"Ah then, ye'll go to the ship. Ye hail, they answer, ye give yer naime, and they come for ye in a boat."

"But the fort? I thought——"

"Aye, they've deserted the fort an' left me here to hould it—as if I could!"

"Abandoned the fort?" Duncan asked blankly.

"They've orl gone to the ship—the gov'nor, the orficers, the cannon, the soldiers, and precious few av them there were left after the desertions—and they left me here, a stableman, to meet the enemy and, I presume, repel them by throwing 'osses at them."

"Then I must hasten to the governor. Where shall I put my horse?"

"You can put him in the stable with Captain Collett's horses, but if the Whigs should come and taike the 'osses I carn't be responsible for yours."

"Then I wi' hide my nag in yon thicket beyond the dune."

It was a gloomy path that Duncan followed around the long line of the fort. The great blocks of masonry were weathered and wind-eaten. Along the whole foot of the wall was a trail of particles which had fallen to the ground. He had heard it said that, every time a cannon was fired in the fort, sections of the wall broke away, and now he believed it. He felt shame that King George maintained such shoddiness to uphold his dignity in Carolina. No wonder the Whigs had become insolent. No wonder they felt capable of storming it.

The *Cruzier* was a big, shadowy mass in the night when he climbed aboard. His first impression was that it, too, had been deserted, and then in the dim light of a lantern he saw half a dozen soldiers loafing in the bows. He was shown back to one of the cabins. In it, in his shirt sleeves, perspiring freely in the summer night's heat, Governor Martin sat at a desk. A pale-faced young secretary stood at the end of the desk holding a sheaf of papers. From up a companionway came a sudden burst of laughter, as though some gentlemen were enjoying their cups.

As Duncan stood in the door, Martin looked up absently from his work and frowned. He was quite as sallow-cheeked as when Duncan had seen him more than a month before, but his eyes, still hot and sullen, were not so wearied. He was more alert.

"Oh!" he exclaimed, rising. "Duncan Stuart, of Bladen!" and walked around the desk to shake hands. "I'm afraid I called you down on a fool's errand. We'll speak of that later."

"The Whigs mobilized today to take the fort!" Duncan felt too dramatic and blushed.

The secretary frowned petulantly at the interruption. Martin shook his head and laughed.

"Oh, they do that every day. Let me read this last letter again before it is sealed—we hope for a packet ship tonight," he explained. "Then we shall talk. I'll read the letter aloud. You'll be interested."

Martin sat down again and held the letter to the light. "It is to Lord Dartmouth," he said. "No doubt you've heard General Gage's proclamation of amnesty in Boston, but proscribing John Hancock and Samuel Adams. Listen."

Martin read his own letter with relish, as though its heavy phrases themselves carried punishment to his hated enemies:

" 'Hearing of a proclamation of the King, proscribing John Hancock and Samuel Adams of the Massachusetts Bay, and seeing clearly that further proscriptions will be necessary before government can be settled again upon sure foundations in America, I hold it my indispensable duty to mention to Your Lordship Cornelius Harnett, John Ashe, Robert Howes and Abner Nash, as persons who have marked themselves out as proper objects for such distinction in this colony by their unremitted labors to promote sedition and rebellion here from the beginnings of the discontents in America to this time, that they stand foremost among the patrons of revolt and anarchy.' "

Martin twisted the corner of his mouth and nodded his head, and mouthed the phrase again: " '. . . They stand foremost among the patrons of revolt and anarchy.' "

He handed the paper to the secretary with a flourish, as though giving a written judgment to the hangman.

Then he looked at Duncan triumphantly. Duncan, still feeling the dramatic fool, and feeling, too, that Martin took the danger too lightly, strained for a response.

"What's to be done with them?"

"Ah-h-h!" Martin said. "When the rest of the rebels have knelt before me to accept the King's gracious pardon, these—these four —will be led away to meet the fate of those who stir up sedition."

Josiah Martin's eyes gleamed through narrowed lids, enjoying the picture, in advance, of the traducers of his dignity being led out to the slaughter.

"What can I do for the King?" Duncan asked abruptly.

Josiah Martin sighed and compressed his lips, as though reluctantly giving up the thought.

"I'm afraid it is too late," he said. "I sent for you to commission you to organize a company of Highlanders to stand by with me at the fort. But the fort isn't worth defending. I abandoned it when I heard the Whigs were rendezvousing for their assault."

"Then ye know the Whigs plan to come?" Duncan was relieved.

"Who knows? They meet, they carouse, they march and countermarch, they make loud talk about capturing me, and then they go home. If they were of the army, as I am, then one might gauge their purposes. But they are but rabble, spurred on by evil connivings. Here," reaching for a paper, "is what I wrote His Lordship:

" 'I daily see indignantly the sacred majesty of my Royal Master insulted, the rights of his Crown denied and violated, his government set at naught and trampled upon, his servants of highest dignity reviled, traduced, abused, the rights of his subjects destroyed by the most arbitrary usurpations, and the whole constitution unhinged and prostrate, and I live, alas! ingloriously only to deplore it.' "

"Aye," Duncan said solemnly.

"It is a good letter, don't you think?"

"Aye."

"I think so, too. '. . . And I live, alas! ingloriously only to deplore it.' "

"I hae thought they would tire o' their foolishness and quit."

"His Majesty has entertained that error, also. No, they will not quit. They have tasted victory, though it has been the empty triumph of the Crown's tolerance. Now they must be crushed."

"But how?" Duncan asked, dreading to hear the answer.

"I have written a letter on that," Martin said, as though the letter had settled the matter. "I have conceived a plan which would restore all the colonies to His Majesty's profound obedience. I shall explain it to you. North Carolina would be the scene of the campaign. I have asked for the restoration of my lieutenant colonelcy and authority to organize the Cape Fear Highlanders—they should number from three thousand to five thousand prime young men. We could double the number if we wished. I recommended that John Stuart, who has a special facility for that kind of business, be kept among the Indians of the mountains and enflame them against the Whigs with promises of money and booty. That would result in murder and rape, which is beyond my desire, but Indian warfare is of a type all its own, and I cannot control it. Then I asked for several regiments of trained soldiers from England, and a fleet to preserve our base here at the mouth of the Cape Fear.

"Do you see it now? The plan is ideal. We shall organize the

Highlanders. They will march here to join the regulars. We march up the state, subduing it as we go, meeting the Indians and the backwoods Loyalists somewhere in the foothills. We shall sweep North Carolina from east to west, separate North from South, and break the back of the revolution. The colonies to the south should subside without further ado. Our army then would march northward as long as might be necessary to overawe the obstreperous. After that we merely would have the task of arresting the ringleaders and shooting them. Peace should return to the provinces quickly when we are prepared. And then—back to New Bern! In the meantime my plan is to give the damned Whigs free reign, so that there will be full justification for a merciless campaign."

Duncan remained open-mouthed. He had thought vaguely of war and of the ensuing suffering, but now Martin had brought him a terrible picture of Whig women—women like Mary MacLeod—writhing at a stake while painted Indians shrieked and danced and threw more wood and straw on the fire. He saw old Tom Hadley and his sons running through the swamps, with the British soldiers surrounding them and shooting them down. He saw Cornelius Harnett standing condemned for rebellion. He winced. The soldier across the table coldly laying out his line of march, and estimating the number of North Carolinians who would fall dead before him, left Duncan suddenly numb. This governor was making plans to have him, Duncan, kill his own neighbors. The thought gave him a chill in the belly.

"That plan of campaign," said Martin, "would wipe out this damnable uproar."

Duncan spoke dully: "Aye."

"It contemplates that the Highlanders will co-operate in good spirit."

Duncan said nothing. Martin looked at him sharply.

"I shall depend upon you, personally, to help put it through."

Duncan still said nothing.

"Can I?" Martin demanded.

"If the King commands," Duncan said, as if in a trance.

Josiah Martin, who had watched him keenly, smiled in new ease and walked around the desk to slap him on the shoulder—an act of unusual demonstration for him.

"That's the spirit! Now, let's have a drink with the gentlemen and then, dinner."

Another gust of laughter from below guided them to the saloon. Duncan was surprised. Forty men, at least, were seated, drinking. He knew many of them. John Rutherford, John Slingsby, Colonel James Cotten, of Anson, one of the younger MacDougalls, and, of all people, Farquard Campbell. Duncan looked at him pointedly, for Farquard no longer ago than spring had voted in the bastard Assembly to castigate Thomas MacKnight for not upholding the Whig Association paper. Beyond them stood young Alexander MacDonald, Flora's son.

"Now let the damned Whigs come!" the rosy drunk young Mac-Dougall declared jovially as a greeting. "Duncan Stuart is with us."

"With you, when the King commands," Duncan said. He clung to that thin distinction desperately.

They had a roistering July night on the *Cruzier*. Nobody got very drunk, but they all carried enough liquor to make them feel equal to meeting many times their number in Whigs. There weren't enough cabins to accommodate all the guests. Duncan slept on the open deck on his tartan and was none the worse for it. No one gave thought to the attack of the Whigs. That had been in the air for a month, and nothing had happened. There was no more reason to expect them tonight than another, and in any case it was safe aboard the ship.

Duncan was soon asleep. He had drunk little, but he had been in the saddle all day and he had eaten heartily. The deck was hard, but sleep nevertheless came as a blessing.

He was awake all too soon. He came from sleep almost in pain. The sun was rising, and the light was in his eyes.

"I tho't that was west," he said to himself dazedly.

Someone yelled: "The fort's afire! The fort's afire!"

The alarm rang through the ship. Men thumped on deck, running. Flames reached up from behind the fort wall and wriggled like great bright yellow snakes against the sky.

"Gur-r-r-reat God!" Duncan gasped. The Whigs *had* come. He gazed stupidly, awed by their audacity.

The fire began to roll and pop, and shoved great loads of smoke before its climbing blaze. Its roar was like a faraway waterfall.

Governor Martin came to the deck buttoning his trousers, swearing like a maniac. "They can't do that! The damned skunks! The anarchists! The bastards!" But he said nothing of firing on the Whigs.

"Might as well not swear if we're not going to do anything," Duncan thought.

The Whigs were too far away to be heard, except for their yells. Dozens could be seen, and these were doubtless but the fringe of hundreds. They were in no order, just a yelling maniacal rabble making the night hideous. Duncan saw three men dashing across the areaway toward Captain Collett's house. The head man bore a torch, a bit of pale light against the holocaust. The stableman, the little cockney whom Duncan had seen the afternoon before, came running out with a club, defending the house. The three men surrounded him and danced around playfully, and then they dived in and bore him to the ground.

In the murky light men were seizing Collett's horses—Collett the hated, the cruel, the instigator of Negro rebellion. The Whigs were taking their revenge. He was in New York at the moment, but the rabble treated him none the easier for that. The man with the torch must have spread tar on the house, for almost instantly the flame began to climb up the front wall, giving a second light to compete with the roaring, tumbling mountain of flame over the fort.

The light glared in the areaway. The heat must not have focused there, even though the warmth of the blaze was felt faintly as far away as the ship. The light was so bright that the little drama of the stableman could be followed perfectly. They, a half dozen or more, were tearing his clothes from him. He stood there whitely naked for a flash, and then he began to melt in thin air. They were tarring him with a brush. Their yells of laughter could be heard all the way to the *Cruzier*. Then, against the dark background, he vanished. Suddenly he came to life again. This time he was white all over. Feathers. He was fuzzy with white feathers from his ankles to his head. Then he started running, and they stood and laughed, throwing their hands up and then resting them on their knees, while the fuzzy white figure sped over the sand.

By now a half-dozen fires were in full blaze: the corn cribs, the hay barn, the smokehouse, the tenant houses, the carriage house.

Duncan thought he recognized two figures. One of them walked like Cornelius Harnett. The other surely was John Ashe. As the fire reached its peak, the rebels faded more and more into the woods to escape its heat. Finally there was a long rolling, jeering yell from beyond the fort, and no more was seen of them.

Governor Martin stood at the rail, looking, his face working, refusing to answer questions, his fury beyond expression. Duncan remembered the words of his letter: " . . . patrons of revolt and anarchy."

Now it was daylight. Those on board gathered around Governor Martin in council. The foolhardy were for dashing after the Whigs and engaging them, but the wiser ones merely smiled at so vain an enterprise. The time, Martin said, was not ripe. There was nothing to do except swallow the humiliation and remember it for revenge.

Seeing no point in cooping himself in the impregnable ship for an indefinite and profitless stay, Duncan prepared to return to Bladen and wait there until he should be called. He rode between the black and gray heaps of ashes, the smoke stifling him. The Collett chimneys rose from the smoke and needled above the withered trees. Wrath at the Whigs swelled in him, all the more because he could do nothing.

That was Wednesday, July 19. Duncan willed to remember that. It was a day of historic wantonness.

He saw many Whigs on the road that day. They were smoked as though they had been burning tar. They spoke with audacious good humor. They asked no questions, volunteered no information.

It was Thursday afternoon late when Duncan reached home. Gillie Black met him down the road, running.

"Two mens waitin' fuh you," he said excitedly.

"What sort of men?"

"Dey wears li'l gal frocks, like you'n."

"Scots, eh? And did you hoe as I told you?"

Donald MacDonald and Donald MacLeod sat and waited for Duncan. They eyed him closely as he rode to them. MacDonald was florid, with keen blue eyes, with broad shoulders and of middle height. He was fifty years old—older perhaps. MacLeod was thinner, younger, with a mixture of daring and caution in his eyes. They wore the same tartan design, as though they were soldiers of the same regiment.

Donald MacDonald spoke first. It was a thrusting voice, one of command. Duncan recognized him for an army officer before he knew his name.

CHAPTER 7

Donald MacDonald and Donald MacLeod were strange visitors. They said they had fought for the British in the Battle of Bunker Hill. Duncan asked what battle that was, and they said it was fought a month before near Boston, when the rabble twice repulsed the British before they could be overcome.

"Could they fight?" Duncan asked incredulously.

"Aye," said Donald MacDonald. "They could fight."

"But there were no Scots against them," Duncan stated.

"Weel—some." MacDonald and MacLeod smiled, not proudly.

Now, said MacDonald, they had come to the Cape Fear to settle among the Highlanders and become attached to the soil.

"But ye hae no appearance o' farm folk," Duncan said dubiously.

Donald MacLeod chuckled. "We'll farm," he said.

Donald MacDonald looked at Duncan closely, observing his tones. "Ye were na born in Scotland," he said.

"My father came to this country soon after the 'Forty-five."

"Aye—the 'Forty-five." A shade of pain passed over Donald MacDonald's face. "I fought at Culloden."

Duncan was silent. It was not good to ask a MacDonald on which side he fought on the Drummossie Moor. He would say if he wished it known.

"I hae just returned frae Fort Johnston," Duncan said. "The Whigs burned it yesterday morning."

The two Scots came up alert. They looked at each other long and cautiously, and then turned back to Duncan.

"Tell us about it," MacDonald said.

"I winna tell ye."

"And why?" MacDonald growled, and his broad shoulders swung to Duncan.

"Weel—if I offend ye it is without intent. Ye ask questions about the King's business, but ye conceal y'r purposes in the province. Ye may be spies."

Donald MacLeod chewed a straw, splitting it with his displayed teeth, smiling curiously.

Donald MacDonald flushed deep, and demanded: "Take care, my man!" Then he laughed and shrugged. He looked a question at his companion.

"We've got to talk with someone," MacLeod agreed.

"True."

MacLeod asked Duncan: "Are you for the King?"

"That's a fair question. I'm for the King, and anyone may know it by asking."

"Could you keep silent on certain information we might give you?"

"Aye."

"Then, we are the King's servants. We are sent to look through the Cape Fear country and report what we find."

"Aye?"

"Sir Henry Clinton wishes to know if the Scots are, indeed, as loyal as Governor Martin estimates."

"Ye'll find some Whigs among the Scots. The Old Scots maistly. The great bulk o' the Scots are Loyal. The newcomers are Loyal to a man." Duncan thought of Mary MacLeod and added, "Amaist."

"Yes, yes. But we wish to be more specific. How about yourself? Would you respond if called to the King's standard?"

"Weel—now. If Governor Martin called me out, no. If you called me out, or Sir Henry Clinton called me out, no. But if the King expressly commanded it, and if the Cape Fear Hielanders marched out, aye. What else could I do?"

"Humph!" Donald MacDonald gave thought. "I guess that's a good enough answer. Now, will you say what happened at Fort Johnston?"

Duncan told them about Governor Martin's removal to the ship and the salvaging of the cannon, of the fire in the night and the destruction of Captain Collett's property. He told of seeing the Whigs in great numbers in the light of the fire and of their tarring and feathering the stableman.

"Recognize any of them?" MacDonald asked.

"John Ashe, for one," and had the impulse to conceal the name of Cornelius Harnett. Then he said: "And Cornelius Harnett."

"Harnett. We've heard of him. We'll have him up by the heels before this is over."

"Ye speak as though the war had already started."

"It has, but you're the only one on the Cape Fear that knows it. So be discreet. Tell no one. Not even your wife."

"I hae no wife."

"So much the better." Donald MacDonald looked on Duncan with a slow smile, as a father might look on a well-favored son. "Ye'll make a gr-rand soldier, my lad."

Duncan worked furiously those hot weeks in July and August. He and Gillie dipped and chipped turpentine trees, which was the accepted task of four men, and they laid out those big tasks because they could do the work of four. They had more trees to the stand, bigger buckets. They plunged through the lofty pines, gouging the clinging sap from the boxes like men possessed. This task had to be done tonight, so that tomorrow Duncan could go to Killiegrey to the clan council and Gillie, yet unaware of it, could hack his way alone through another task and drag new slots in the box faces so that new turpentine would run before the summer heat grew cool.

Thomas Brown rode to him through the woods. He rode a sleek, spirited horse that trotted as easily on the wire grass as on a highway. The nag was a light sorrel, almost the color of Tom Brown's beard. And as fleet as Donald Bane. Duncan wondered if, now, he and Tom Brown ever could have the horse race they had planned.

"Keep on working," Brown greeted him cordially. He smiled as at a secret thought. "I'll ride and talk as you work."

"All right, Tom Brown. That's good. I've got to finish before dark."

"I've got something to say to you—something to your advantage —and because we've been friends so long and all, I hope——"

"Aye." Duncan's lip twisted at the irony of it. "That's what Tom Hadley said to me, also. Friends!"

Tom Brown laughed loud. The sound echoed in the pines. 'Twas the hell of it. You couldn't pin Tom Brown down. He laughed. He'd laugh in your face, were you slashing down on him wi' y'r broadsword.

"These Scotch army officers," Brown continued, "are going through the Tories, stirring them up. We're friends—better friends than you will admit—you and me—and I want to save you trouble."

Duncan, suddenly irate, thumped his turpentine bucket to the ground and faced him. Tom Brown drew his rein, and the horse curveted lightly and snorted at the lack of action. "Whoa, Jess!" Brown lifted his leg over the saddle and stood before Duncan.

"Be ye such damned good friends," Duncan told him bluntly, "then 'twould please me f'r ye to be less diligent in trying to tear up everything I stand for! Why don't ye let well enough alone?"

Brown chuckled. Damn a man who could laugh at death and, worse yet, at life. "That's what I want to talk about."

"Weel—talk."

"I'm warning you, Duncan—as a friend, and don't forget that. We're not going to brook this new move by the King. We've stood enough. If the Scotch Highlanders can't see the thing with the good sense of the Scotch Irish of the backwoods, then they'll have to take the consequences."

"Aye. They can take any consequences ye can visit upon 'em. And don't forget the consequences to y'rsel'."

Brown laughed that off. "You've got a lot to lose. I'm trying to tell you how to keep it. Your land, your plans, your house—your grand lassie!"

Duncan frowned and shook his head impatiently. Mary was not Tom Brown's business.

"I'll na be a renegade t' my kind, though I lose my neck."

"Oh, I know that!" Tom Brown moved up and clapped his hand

on Duncan's shoulder. "We're talking straight, but we are still friends—see? Now listen. I've got Scotch blood in me, too, just like you. Not all Scotch, but I know how you feel. I'm telling you that if the Highlanders march for the King, and you march with them, you desert your true cause!"

"Na!"

"You think, lad, that your heart's in the Highlands, like the song says. But you belong in the ranks o' free men, in a free country, where you can be strong for yourself, and build for yourself, and be your own king. We're starting a new race o' men. You belong —and I'm offering you a place without fighting for it."

"Like Gilbert Johnston!" Duncan answered him disdainfully.

"Like Gilbert Johnston. The man's got sense."

" 'Tis no inducement—a chance not to fight when my king calls. Ye'd make me a sorry spectacle."

"I'm telling you, Duncan, we're breaking away from the old way. Come along with us."

"Na. I'll na rebel on my king. If he calls and the Hielanders respond, then I'll march on ye—though I hae no wish for it."

Tom Brown laughed again. "Chop us through, from gill to gut, eh?"

"I'll follow my chief and obey his commands."

Tom chuckled and shrugged. "Well, I might have known better. Tom Hadley said it was no use, and he was right. I'm sorry, Duncan—but it is good night for your property and your prospects. You'll be like a suck-egg dog in these parts, when we win."

"Aye. When ye win."

Tom, still laughing, his leather creaking, pulled back into the saddle. He drew the horse around and extended his hand. "Friends?" He smiled.

Duncan felt a quick impulse, a kind of ripping inside. He grasped Tom Brown's hand. "Aye. Friends."

The horse gathered his feet, quivered and dashed through the pines. Half a furlong away Tom Brown turned, raised his hand and waved it, as though that were farewell.

Duncan shook his head. Tom Brown was a dangerous man and a bonnie friend. 'Twere a distress of soul for him to dash headlong into the disaster that must crush him.

"Get to work!" he yelled to Gillie Black. This stand had to be finished by night. The clan leaders met at Flora MacDonald's at Killiegrey the second day hence, and he must go. It was there they would give Donald MacDonald their answer for the King. Duncan was ready. The Crown had delayed too long and must move drastically if there was to be strong government in Carolina.

Duncan slept fitfully. He was tired, but his mind could not rest. When he dozed to sleep, troubled dreams of Mary threw him awake again. Menacing cloudlike figures rose and twisted upon the firmament of his dreams, and he was in torture. In his waking moments he was no less tortured by the resistlessly approaching time when he must face the things now vague and ominous. It was well enough to say that he would obey the King's command. Well, he would. Of course. But there were things to dread about it—when he fought for the King he would be against Mary. When he fought for the Hanovers he must fight against his old friends. He would bear the broadsword his father had brought from Scotland. That steel had split Hanover skulls. When Duncan wielded that sword he would heave it for the family that had cut his own father down. He could take no pleasure in killing Tom Hadley for the smile of a Hanover prince. Of more immediate pain was the thought of the fanatical Malcolm MacLeod haranguing and harassing Mary. Mary thought wrong, but, by God, she had the right to think wrong if she wished.

Duncan tossed on his bunk and groaned and cursed, and Gillie Black came to the door and asked:

"Sick, Mas' Dunk?"

Duncan swore at him and took relief from it. Daylight would come soon, and there was no gladness in the sunrise. It meant the time was one day nearer when, like tearing his arm out, he must walk to the right or the left. Then he went to sleep.

Gillie Black waked him, shaking his foot.

"Ge' up, ge' up, Mas' Dunk. Us got t' chip teppentine!"

"To hell with turpentine." He leaped out of bed. His mind was clear and he was eager. If the damned Whigs would not leave well enough alone, it was time to force them. He would go to Killiegrey and vote to mobilize. "You chip it. I'm going off."

He ran down to the creek, shucking his shirt as he ran, and

plunged in. He lathered with homemade soap that stung every brier scratch on him and left his skin shining. He came back naked and dripping, reaching for the towel that hung at the corner of the cabin.

"Ain' gwine chip no teppentine?" Gillie wondered, worried.

Duncan donned his clean undershirt and reached for his dress kilt and his bonnet. Today was a great day. He would end the uncertainty. He would counsel with Flora about Mary, and the clans would decide about the Whigs.

Flora MacDonald had strong counsel. He found her at Killiegrey. It was not snowing this time, in late August. Things were green. Cotton bolls hung heavy in the fields, and corn ears stood proudly on the stalks. Watermelons humped up in the grass with wriggling green stripes showing through. Harvest time was not yet, and the people had time to move about. He had met them on the roads. Their faces were grim. They talked little. Some had fear in their eyes. Some quarreled and fought about war.

There were no Negro slaves to come running when he rode up to Killiegrey. There were Scots working in the fields, Gaelic-speakers. There were women washing clothes in the back yard. The house was big enough, but it was not as palatial as those down the river, not as fine as some of those near Cross Creek. That was not good, for Flora MacDonald should have the finest.

She came to him herself, out the front door. She recognized him as he tied his horse, and came. As before, she was serene, maternal, making him feel the lad.

"Ye hae the lines o' saire pain in your face, Doon-kan," she said kindly. Her smile was rich, and her voice was musical and soothing.

"Aye. I hae stabs i' my heart, Flora MacDonald."

"Ye are weary. Ye shall refresh yoursel' and we shall talk."

"But I came all this way to see ye, and I must talk now."

She put her hand on his arm and walked through the cape jasmines to the porch.

"I hae told ye tae refresh y'rsel', Duncan Stuart," she laughed. "And refresh y'rsel' ye shall."

"Aye." He had no way of combating Flora MacDonald's will.

She exerted mastery beyond his ken. She confused him and put thoughts in his mind which were not his. She was a wonderful woman. Quite willingly he put aside his urgent desire to unburden his spirit and followed her with no protest. Her mere presence eased him.

She led him to the shaded back porch for a drink of water from a fresh-drawn bucket. He washed his face and hands in a wooden basin and threw the water to the ground, scattering the chickens which clucked in the shade. Flora MacDonald handed him a towel. The smoke from the washpots came thinly to his nostrils and was not odious. A woman punched the boiling clothes with a stick. It was cool here. The shade of the trees made the light soft. It was peaceful and homelike. He was tired, and now he knew it.

"You sit here,"—she waved to a large rocking chair. "Close y'r eyes, while I hae Sandy to see to y'r horse."

"Na. I wi' see to my horse."

"No. You sit there." It was as though she had asked a favor. It was bonnie here, and he was drowsy.

When he awoke, Flora MacDonald was sitting opposite him, knitting. He opened his eyes and blinked, and she smiled at him.

"I hae enjoyed sitting here and seeing you so sweetly resting," she said. "It was like seeing the Bonnie Prince again, ye are so like him."

"I? Like him? Ye said that once, but I tho't ye joked me."

"Na, Doon-kan," she sighed. "Ye are much like him. I spied the resemblance when I first saw ye on the ship."

"Weel!" he said, not knowing what to say.

"Wi' that resemblance," she said, tossing her head, "I expect much frae ye as I may need ye."

"I wish I had ways to serve ye," he said simply.

She rang a little bell from her lap, and a woman brought tea.

"Ye see, we are not so Americanized yet as to do wi'out tea," she smiled.

"Whigized, you mean," Duncan grumbled.

She took the subject from that quarter and spoke of their new home. It had a mill down on the creek. Allan had bought a near-by farm and settled the indentured servants on it, planning for them to buy it for themselves when they had worked out their time.

They were getting some fruit, apples, grapes. Allan had great hopes of building a fine farm and a mansion, but as for herself she was satisfied.

"Old ladies," she said, "are not so ambitious."

"Old ladies!" Duncan scoffed loyally.

"I had ambitions once. I seldom think of them now. When I see you, you stir up memories unaccountably. When I went to London and the lords and ladies were so kind, wi' the Prince of Wales, the present Geordie's father, so solicitous, I had the aspiration then to live that kind of life—fine carriages, fine clothes, fine ways, takin' pleasure in endless romance. But I ne'er could make it fit in wi' Allan's style of life. I had to choose between that and Allan— and havin' much of Scottish common sense in my make-up, I chose Allan instead of ambition. I would do the same again. And now Allan is about to outstrip me in ambition—he wants to build fine things and be the laird again as his father was in Kingsburgh. Well—as Allan does, so do I. But I do hope the laddie doesna wear himself away wi' too much ambition. When one is fifty-two it is na long until one is old."

"I want counsel about Mary," Donald interposed. It would not be long until the clansmen came. He wanted to talk to Flora before they arrived.

"Aye, Mary," Flora dreamed. "Mary is fortunate. I thought ye would be coming to see me about her ere long. Is she still the whimsical little Whig?" She smiled indulgently, but her eyes narrowed as she studied him.

"Aye. She says that America is a grand country and free, and those who live in it must be free, and that it canna be bound under one man, though he be king."

"Then she is a Whig," Flora said, as if making a note.

"Malcolm browbeats her unmerciful, but she willna change her opinion. I have tho't to give Malcolm a clout f'r his mistreatment o' her—but I hae no right. What must I do?"

"And so ye came to me f'r advice?" The thought pleased her.

"Aye."

"So did Old Kenneth Black and Hector MacNeill and Gilbert Johnston. Tom Rutherford did not, and Farquard Campbell did not. Many young people have. I shall say to you what I said to them. It is not about Mary MacLeod, but it takes precedence o'er her. When ye settle one question ye settle both."

Duncan Stuart frowned. There might be things which took precedence over Mary, but he did not know what they were.

"Na," he said. "We shall settle that question first."

"Listen to me, Duncan Stuart. Ye're a good lad and a braw lad. Ye hae lived wild and free, and only recently hae ye come to face life's mockeries. I wi' speak to ye and say those things y'r ain mither would hae said."

"I do na regard ye as a foster mither," half seriously, half jokingly, "but as a lass denied me f'r Stuart Hall."

Flora flushed and laughed. "You're sweet. Anyway, I was about to say there comes times with all of us when we do not give attention to oursel's but to the common good."

"Aye. That's what the Whigs say, too."

"Well—so they may. 'Tis neither here nor there. When I was in London I took my oath. The keeping of it is as dear to me as life. Y'r ain father, who stood between a doomed nineteenth and a doomed nineteenth in the slaughter line, took his oath. But, Duncan, ne'er forget," and Flora MacDonald's voice dropped to a whisper, "the words of the oath were for loyalty to Hanover, but the acceptance of them in true Scottish hearts was for loyalty to the Crown—and the Crown rightfully belongs to the Hielands. When we march we follow the wraiths o' Somerled and Douglas and Bruce—not Geordie. Your friend Harnett divined that."

Duncan was leaning forward, breathing quickly.

"Aye!" he said aloud. "That is the tho't that bewilders me. I feel a loyalty. I hae said it was f'r the King, but I knew in my soul that it was something else."

"Well, that's what it is, Doon-kan, and when ye hae that heartbeat, then ye know that every true Scot has the same throb. They may not say it. They may, e'en, not know it. But it is the inner call o' auld Caledonia, holding them yet."

"Aye."

"Yes," Flora whispered. Her eyes were misty, and Duncan had a gripping in his throat.

"That is why we canna join wi' the Whigs. That is why we canna, as y'r good friend Harnett wished, remain aloof. We follow the Crown, though the Hanovers be its spokesmen. It is the oath of the Scots, and their destiny."

"Aye," Duncan said solemnly.

"So," she sighed, "when ye see that question fair, y'r decision is made—was made long ago. It is nought f'r you to decide. Y'r ancient fathers did the deciding. To you, it is a command."

"So it is."

"Then, as between you and Mary MacLeod, the decision is for her, not you. If she be loyal, she wi' come to you. If she turn traitor——"

"Na! Mary is no traitress. Ye shall na say that!"

Flora MacDonald looked straight into his gaze. In her calm gentleness was a deep firmness, just as calm. "Doon-kan, when ye're truly loyal, such questions become very simple."

"But Mary is good, despite her flighty way. It is na in her to engage in deceit against her conscience. I hae said the same thing o' you. She is no traitress when she is moved by a spirit of righteousness."

Duncan's yellow eyebrows fell more over his eyes, for Flora MacDonald's voice now sounded a note more compelling: "What else then can ye ca' a subject o' the King who turns against him!"

Duncan looked uncomfortably away, out in the yard at the woman punching clothes in the pot. Flora MacDonald almost was accusing him of leaning toward sedition himself.

"Flora MacDonald," he said, "ye hae confused my way o' thinkin'. I hae the feeling that Mary is good and——"

"That is just it, Duncan! Else why should I add to y'r pains when I hae such a regard for ye? When I see you blinded it is but kindliness to guide you from a pitfall."

"But she *is* good. I hae no gratitude for statements that she is na!"

Flora's insistence tempered to a gentle smile. "I know, Duncan. I know. Let us speak no more of it for the present. I hae no office to change y'r mind, only to bring ye to face y'r facts. Everyone has his miseries, and none can help much."

Duncan looked at her quickly, moved somewhat by suspicion, for Flora MacDonald's voice carried a little ring of triumph, though she smiled most benignly. And well she might have, for now Duncan frowned and considered in his mind two figures set opposite each another. One was Mary MacLeod, whose brown eyes of slow fire held him and challenged him and reproached him. The other figure was that of his king—a stately figure without a face, a glittering crown upon his head and his body garbed in the richness of gold cloth and purple silk.

"Ye hae not helped me, Flora MacDonald," Duncan complained without bitterness. "Ye hae proposed me a question which has but one answer, and that maist hard—if I be willing to make it."

"Ye will," she said confidently.

"Aye," was Duncan's glum assent.

Flora MacDonald smiled in sympathy. She now had closed that well of vigor which could open at her command, and she again was the woman of compassion. "There wi' be those here tonight who will clear y'r mind the more. It was just such a time o' hard decisions, Duncan, when the Young Chevalier came to the Western Isles and ca'ed to the MacDonalds and the MacLeods and the Campbells and the MacKenzies to rally to his standard. 'Twas a hard time, and wae's me, Duncan, that I hae to go through it again. I couldna face it, believe me, but for the sense o' bein' i' the right."

"Aye, Flora."

She walked away from him into the dining room and out it over a covered runway into the set-apart kitchen. Duncan thought, and knew he was wrong, that as she walked her firm shoulders slumped a bit and her eyes went desperately heavenward. Then she straightened and went in briskly short steps about her business.

"We'll forget all that!" Donald MacDonald said peremptorily. He sat at Allan MacDonald's right at the supper table. "Nothing came out of Culloden to concern us now—except the oath!"

He looked, perhaps a bit defiantly, at Allan, who was in the King's army at the time of the Rebellion but not at Culloden; and at Hector MacNeill, who was at Culloden for the Prince and in the King's army later; and at Flora, who helped the Prince escape, and at Duncan Ray and Archibald MacDougall and Farquard Campbell and Alexander MacLeod, Flora's son-in-law, and the younger men. His eyes lingered for a moment on Duncan. Those at the table looked back at him with pinched lips, for the subject of Scottish dominion over Great Britain was dear to their hearts.

"We hae too many varying opinions about that," he said, "and it is time now to give undivided loyalty to the Crown."

"Aye!" said Farquard Campbell.

"Weel—I wi' question ye about that," Donald MacDonald said boldly. "Were ye not in the autocratic convention of the Whigs which censured our good countryman, MacKnight, for daring to stand up for Loyalty? Did ye not vote to condemn him?"

All eyes turned on Farquard Campbell, some of them gleaming their condemnation, for Farquard's turncoat vote had been talked on the Cape Fear from headspring to Tidewater. But if they expected him to cringe in their stares they were disappointed. His clear pink skin colored not one whit the pinker.

"Aye!" he laughed delightedly. He buttered a roll and ate a crunchy mouthful with relish. "Aye—I voted against him, and so did Tom Rutherford, there. We made it up in advance. It was no surprise to Thomas MacKnight. So—what's hurt? It gained us the confidence of all the Whigs—put us in position to serve the King more greatly than our vote would have helped him. Am I to be castigated for that?"

"It does not look good," Donald MacDonald replied.

Farquard Campbell shrugged elaborately, still smiling. "Weel— I still hae the confidence o' the Whigs. I can go tae them if ye dinna want me."

Duncan felt the chill of suspicion relaxing all around the table. Farquard was too frank, too hugely pleased with his own trickery, to be doubted seriously.

"Oh, I am sure," Flora laughed easily, "that Mr Campbell is quite as Loyal as any of us. We have to make allowances for his extraordinary temperament."

She touched a bell, and a Scotswoman came in and began to clear the plates, and another brought in pie on smaller plates. Flora whispered to this one, and soon the servants, eight of them, field hands and all, filed in and lined up against the wall. Flora spoke to them rapidly in Gaelic, and they nodded silently.

No one raised an eyebrow. Servant folk of the strain to spurn the King's offer of £30,000 for the betrayal of Bonnie Prince Charlie were to be trusted to the uttermost.

"Of course everyone at the table, too, understands," Flora said, "that no word spoken here is to be repeated outside."

Several nodded, and Hector MacNeill took that as the signal that the discussion was open. He was somewhat like Donald Mac-Donald, with the bluff military air. He had seen much of army life.

"Weel," he said to Donald MacDonald, sitting back deliberately and taking out his pipe and tobacco pouch. Others did likewise, and a servant brought a lighted candle. "I take it we are ready. What does the King offer?"

"Ah!" protested young Dushee Shaw of the dark eyes and handsome brow. Flora MacDonald, too, frowned at the plain suggestion that the Scots were offering their services for sale.

"Weel," Hector said, turning his deliberate look and slow smile on Dushee, "the question has nought to do wi' our high purposes and patriotism. But when ye hae served y'r king in the army as long as hae I, ye'll find it best to hae a clear understandin' e'en wi' a king. It's y'r *life* ye put at stake, laddie, and for that the King has an obligation to make the best compensation he can—and the best is little eneugh."

"But the King," said Flora, "surely wi' na be inclined to haggle and drive bargains."

"That he will," Hector said grimly.

Donald MacDonald and Donald MacLeod, the newcomers, had turned on each other's shoulder to whisper. Allan MacDonald sat at the head of the table turning a water glass, as though indifferent. He had said little through the meal. Now he passed a knowing glance at Flora at the other end of the table. Alexander MacLeod, their son-in-law, an army man, too, seemed to be privy to their unspoken conversation. There was a tenseness which all felt, but which all did not understand.

Donald MacDonald and Donald MacLeod were having trouble reaching an agreement. Their faces were flushed, and each was protesting to the other. Then, doubtfully, they straightened in their seats.

"Officers and privates," Donald MacDonald said bluntly, "get full regular-army pay. Those designated as recruiting officers get commissions, with the rank of captain, when their companies are at war strength. We will name the colonels."

"'Tis not eneugh," Hector MacNeill said flatly. "We spend six months mobilizing and two months campaigning and come back home wi' not eneugh in our pockets to buy horse feed."

Donald MacDonald looked at him hotly, but said nothing. He turned to the others at the table. "That is the King's offer," he said. No one answered him.

Dushee Shaw spoke up: "I ask nought except what the King in his graciousness chooses to give."

"'Tis fair enough," Duncan agreed. "I am ready."

"Aye," said Donald MacDonald absently. He looked up and down the table, for here was to be the important decision. If these older Scots refused him, recruiting would fall away to nothing. He could raise the King's standard and command them to the colors, but he would do no more than force these pillar Scots over to the Whigs and the bulk of the others with them.

"Of course," he said when he had waited and the silence had become painful, "I suppose you understand that lands will be forfeited to the Crown and ye, if ye have joined the King's colors, wi' be permitted to buy them in for a few pence tax when we hae peace again."

"No!" said Hector MacNeill. "We didna understand that, and ye were a long time saying it."

"Weel, I hae said it now."

"Officers and men to share according to their rank?"

"Aye." Donald MacDonald twisted his mouth in displeasure. This might raise the cry of looting and make Whig subjugation that much nastier. But better that than lose the Highlanders.

That broke the dam, and the questions flooded down upon Donald MacDonald. Now he was the clan chief, giving orders, putting his army in array. He had been accepted. No one was afraid to question him, even to argue with him, but his final word was law.

The servants questioned him as sharply as any. "Gin I get a farm," asked one, "can I sell it and pay my indenture debt to Allan of Killiegrey and go free?"

"Aye," said Donald MacDonald.

"Even better," said Allan. "Serve the campaign in my company and ye shall be free anyway."

"Losh!" whispered the man, amazed, and his staring wife turned on his shoulder, to cling to him and weep.

"Who's to command the expedition?" Duncan Stuart broke in. "When I was at the burning of Fort Johnston in July, Governor Martin told me that he was to take back his commission as lieutenant colonel and command the Hielanders himsel'."

Donald MacDonald smiled and shrugged. "Can ye imagine the Hielanders following an Antiguan?" he asked. "Na. Martin does not know it, and none must tell him, but I hae the commission in my pocket now. Until I show it, I am only a major and Martin hopefully awaits his high rank. When I raise the King's standard at Martin's orders, then I shall proclaim my commission. By that time his disappointment can do no damage. But let no one whisper this until I say."

"But what is the plan of campaign?" Hector MacNeill asked.

"Martin's plan. It is good. The Hielanders march to the sea and join the regiments from Britain. From there, protected by the fleet at the mouth of the Cape Fear, we march west through the Whig country, subduing them as we go, until we meet Stuart's Indians raping and burning their way east. If the revolution has not broken by that time, we continue north and south until it has broken. The plan is simple and good."

"What will ye do to the Whigs?"

"Everyone that shows fight will be cut down, and the more the better. The ringleaders will go to the firing squad. The rest, according to their offenses, will be pardoned, paroled or imprisoned."

Names were running through Duncan Stuart's mind—Cornelius Harnett, John Ashe, John Sampson, Tom Hadley, Tom Owen, Tom Brown, Tom Robeson. He thought of Tom Brown facing a firing squad and laughing at those who shot. He thought of Mary MacLeod and thanked God that Malcolm was head of the house and was Loyal. The professional tones of the soldiers somehow numbed him. When they spoke of cutting the Whig leaders to pieces, they referred to units of opposition, but to him they referred to human beings he knew and loved.

The talk wore on and on. Duncan Stuart grew weary of it. He

was willing to serve the King. It was instilled in him. It was a glorious enterprise, calling out his best impulses. It had glamor and the dash of high sacrifice. But this talk of how much for a horse, and what allowance for feed furnished, and what about shoes and supplies—all this had no appeal for him.

The men got up from the table and walked about the room, talking. Sometimes several of them shouted at once. Duncan thought that as soon as his horse rested he would go home. He stepped through the back door to walk on the porch. The air seemed clearer there. Once more, as on the ship, he had a feeling of disgust. Did they think, perchance, that the Crown would swindle them? And if they received nothing, even, should a loyal subject stop and question the high motives of His Majesty? And Farquard Campbell—who knew to trust him?

September came again. Flora MacDonald had been in Carolina a year. October came again. The scrub oaks once more were blood-red. December came, and with it sleet and rain and snow. Duncan waited. He was not one designated to mobilize and drill companies of clansmen, and he had little part in that enterprise. He had not enrolled for the King to recruit soldiers for the March Out, to make speeches, to organize dances, to talk back to the Whigs who tried to resist the mobilization. He had enlisted to fight, and he stayed home to be called when the King's standard should be raised.

He heard about these things. He was told tales of Flora Mac-Donald riding her white horse through the settlements, rousing the Scots to fervid patriotism. He heard Angus MacCooish's lonely bagpipe across the woods, bleating the stout Scottish tunes of marching and of war. Word came to him of the clan gatherings, of how brother fought brother. Staying out of it the best he could, he knew of how Scottish flesh finally tore asunder on the Cape Fear, leaving two groups filled with fury and hate. If his face became thinner and harder, and if the lines sank deeper, he gave that no consideration. He waited. General Donald MacDonald would call him when the day came.

CHAPTER 8

General Donald MacDonald sent out no fiery cross to call the clans. No gasping, run-winded Highland lad sped through the pine barrens and pocosins with smoke streaming behind him to hand it to yet another, that the Highlanders might know to seize their broadswords and march. Notice had been given in advance, and even ahead of February 15 the companies began to arrive in Cross Creek. The orders were to march, and so had gone all uncertainty.

From out of the woods and swamps the companies came in gallant stride. Untrained captains strove mightily to maintain the military air among their untrained troops. Some of them marched in step, but where is the clansman that sees the point in parade finesse? "Gie me ma braidsword and ma enemy," was their plea. And so they came, boldly, their kilts flapping before driving knees. Screaming bagpipes heralded their coming, and growling, deep-throated cheers welcomed them.

At headquarters, up the hill from the river, General MacDonald sat behind a pine-plank desk and alternately shook his head in repressed rage and smiled broadly and patted backs and spoke soothing words. Duncan Stuart, just up from Bladen, stood dismayed in the door. Hell was loose in the camp, and the first casualties were from wounded pride. The MacDonalds demanded the post of preference. So did the Campbells. So did the MacLeods. So did the MacLeans. So did all the Macs out of Scotland. For what, they each demanded, did their fathers build the bonniest and the brawest clan in Scotland? To take second place? Na!

"Donald MacLeod," said General MacDonald fiercely, "ye are my colonel and ye will tak my orders. An' gie me no back talk."

"Aye, sir," answered Donald MacLeod. He had given no back talk, and he had demanded nothing. He was a regular-army man on duty, and he had no preferences. But it eased Donald Mac-Donald's harried spirits to have someone he could berate safely.

"Then," he said, "ye will take command o' the Regulators, the back-country Loyalists, who hae no pride o' clanship. Ye, always, wi'out exception, bring up the rear. That's that, and now we will sort out the clans."

But before he could appease the MacDougalls and the Gillespies a Regulator captain, named Lowe, was shown in. Captain John "Scalpie" Campbell and Duncan MacRae and Murdoch MacRae and Colonel James Cotten, of Anson, glowered over the desk and thumped it with their fists.

"I tell ye," Cotten raged, "two o' my companies went home, and it's not in me to blame 'em! For what service do you want us, to be batmen? Shall the other companies take the glory and leave us the drudgery? No! No! We'll join the Whigs first."

General MacDonald signed papers evenly. If he heard he made no sign. The argument was between the Scots standing there.

"Well, go wi' th' damn Whigs, then!" John "Scalpie" Campbell roared. "If I'm to lead the strong squad in the advance, as bonnie a crew o' brawn and bone as the MacRae e'er assembled, then I want none o' y'r weasling, hoodock ill-willies i' my support. Gie me men, *men,* tae back me up!"

Donald MacDonald, sudden exasperation clouding his face, himself pounded the desk. "Peace!" he thundered. "For God's sake stop the commotion long enough for me to talk wi' this man! Get out! Get out!"

They scarcely noticed him but, anyway, moved their argument near the door.

"Your name is Lowe," MacDonald said to the militiaman who sent frightened glances at him and at the quarrelsome clansmen. "You are one of the Regulators from Chatham. What do you want?"

"I—uh—we—that is—we killed a man."

"How?"

"He was a Whig. His name was Dent. One of our men shot him. He—he—he——"

"Stop stuttering. Why was he shot?"

"He—he—he—tried to stop us in the road! So one man shot him. I—I—I—didn't tell him to shoot. But he kept coming, kept coming, he said he was going to break up that damn Tory parade, and I didn't know what to do. So a man shot, and this fellow Dent kind of buckled at the knees and looked right straight at me—just like this. I didn't want him killed, mister, but I reckon he oughtn't to ha' tried to stop us. He just sort of buckled at the——"

"That's enough. Report this to Colonel Donald MacLeod, who commands the Regulators. Have him inspect your company, also."

Duncan stood in the door and listened. He had just come through the milling soldiers out on the street. Leggett from Bladen was there with his men. Leggett had asked him to join his company, but Duncan had heard of another company he wished to join—a vanguard of big Scots. Ah, that was to his likin'. Big, brawny, braw sojers, out in front.

The way cleared, and he stood before General MacDonald. The harassed officer looked up, frowning, recognized him and smiled.

"I thought you'd be here," MacDonald said. "What do you want —to lead the march? Everyone else does."

"Aye."

Duncan's solemn assurance broke the general's mood, and he leaned on the desk and laughed, hammering it again with his fist. "Damned if he don't! Damned if he don't, too! Everyone does, and so does he! Say," MacDonald demanded, "how do you think everybody can lead this parade?"

"I dinna ken," Duncan admitted. "I am not concerned. I only seek what rightfu'y belongs to the Stuarts."

"Weel," said MacDonald, still smiling, "I think ye'll probably hae y'r desire. Captain Campbell!" he bawled.

Campbell dropped his argument with Cotten and came over. "Here," said General MacDonald, "is another who wants to be in the vanguard. Hae ye room?"

"Aye!" said Campbell, pleased, stepping back to eye Duncan's stature. Campbell was as big and as braw as Duncan. "Ay-y-y-ye! And as many more like him as ye can get!"

"Weel—keep y'r eye on 'im. He also has th' desire tae fight the war by hi'sel'."

For three days Duncan Stuart remained in Cross Creek in a monotony of marching and countermarching, the growl of men and the rhythmic beat of shoes on soil. The sharp commands of officers trying by their own fierceness to overcome their ineptitude grew as common as the dust on the streets and on clothes and on the leaves which had fallen to the ground these three months ago.

The little town was literally overrun. The streets between the few houses were packed with soldiers coming and going to their camps all around the town. Some wore kilts and spoke Gaelic. Most of the others wore kilts but spoke English. The Regulators wore homespun clothes. Some of them wore leather breeches, and the bagpipes day and night played "Leather Breeches." The Scots of the vanguard carried broadswords proudly, and some awkwardly. Some of the houses were closed tight. Duncan wondered about that.

"Why are so many houses closed?" he asked Reverend John Bethune, the chaplain. The young Presbyterian preacher had not been in the country long, but he knew Cross Creek. "Ither houses are wide open wi' sojers comin' and goin' and findin' the lassies most sympathetic."

"Aye," said the chaplain. "'Tis the Whigs. They couldna stand the sight of sae much loyalty."

They stood in front of Lewis Bowell's bakery, and the round young German was beaming with new prosperity.

"Py Gott!" he declared for all to hear. "America, hoes fine contree!"

Duncan shouldered his way up the hill from Campbelltown on the riverbank to Cross Creek courthouse, a crowded half-mile. Many women were in the jostling throng. They wore their good brown homespun frocks and needed no coats though the February weather was cold. Many of them wore woolen scarfs over their heads, especially mothers who looked anxiously after their daughters. Girls wore lighter dresses, brighter-colored, and some wore no hats, leaving their brown and yellow tresses bare to the wind. It was all too easy, Duncan found, to have a sonsie, excited Scottish lass hanging to one's arm.

"Duncan!" One grasped his arm now, looked up at him beseechingly.

Her brown homespun dress was much like the others. Her bonnet covered her head. Nothing showed but her eyes and cold-pinched pink face and a bit of her throat. They stood under a great tree beside the main street.

"Mary!" he cried, bending to her. Then, with a sudden rush of derision for her Whig jibes, he straightened and boasted: "Ye'll na be sae disdainfu' now—hah?"

"It's Malcolm," she ignored his boast. "He wi' na stay home. He rashly wants to fight for the Crown. He wi' na listen to me. And Doon-kan, ye know as well as I that Malcolm is no fit subject for the army!"

"Di' he leave ye all alone?"

"Aye, but no matter. I hae secured Minnie Meacham tae live wi' me. I am a'right—but it's Malcolm, Duncan! He wi' get hurt! He is na strong like y'rsel'. He is awkward and absent-minded. He should stay home and teach the childer while ye ithers fight th' war. Oh," she wailed, "why does there have to be a war?"

"Ne'er fear! Ne'er fear!" He patted her shoulder. It was the first time he had talked with her since he had discussed her with Flora MacDonald, and, seeing her again, he had a mean feeling of disloyalty. "Let Malcolm be. Let him march a day or twa, and I ween his patriotic impulses wi' gie way to sore feet. He wi' be home again wi'out damage."

"Oh, but you don't know Malcolm! He is that stubborn."

"Weel—since ye have a woman to be wi' ye at home, let him march. He'll bungle into things, no doubt, and scrape his shins on the wagon tongues and the like, but he'll take pride in servin' his king. 'Twill do no harm."

She whispered: "But he may get shot. He is all I hae, Doon-kan!"

"Shot! Ho, ho, ho, ho!"

"Laugh if ye wi', but Malcolm is one o' the unfortunate. He would be one o' the first."

"Now, Mary!" Duncan chided her. "I wager no one gets shot."

"I would be sae alone!"

"But I tell ye, no one wi' get shot. I hae talked to the general. He says there'll be no battle for weeks, if then. By that time Malcolm'll be well out o' it and safely home."

"But there wi', Duncan! There wi'! The Whigs are marching night and day. Ye'll ne'er get to Brunswick wi'out a battle."

"But, Mary, listen and take heart. The general says he wants no battle. He says 'tis na th' time tae fight. We go t' the coast, we join wi' the regulars. We wi' hae cannon then, and tents, and seven

regiments o' the best sojers i' th' world—as good amaist as our
own Cape Fear Hielanders. The Whigs then wi' see their deluded
foolishness and scatter in the night. There'll na be a shot fired,
I'm tellin' ye."

"Doon-kan! Doon-kan!" She grasped his arm and stared into
his eyes as though trying to force her thought into his mind. "Ye
dinna ken! Ye dinna! Ye scorn the Whigs, but ye delude y'rsel'."

"Weel, let 'em impede us, gin they be so brash. There be men in
the camp who would wait no longer to start the slaughter. Donald
MacDonald knows best, and he restrains them. But I consider it
all idle talk. The Whig rabble wi' na show itsel' to our front."

"It is na a Whig rabble, I'm tellin' ye!" Mary's pride in the
Whigs gave way to her fears for her loved ones, and she shook
Duncan's arm again, trying to make him understand. "They are
led by able and brave men, and they are determined that ye shall
na reach the coast!"

"Ah! Give y'rsel' no fears, Mary. Ye hae been misled by y'r o'er-
brash friends. Give y'rsel' no worry about Malcolm."

She looked to the ground. "'Tis na alone Malcolm," she whispered. Then she gasped and ran quickly away from him, and a
crowd of Regulators separated them.

"Mary!" He leaped after her, but the rabble blocked him until
he lost sight of her in the mob.

Duncan would have followed yet if he hadn't become engaged
suddenly in another matter. A gawky Scottish lad, about fourteen
years old, gaped his way through the crowd, carrying a gun. His
handling was much in the same careless way that he would have
gone through the woods for a wild turkey. The consequence was
that the stock went through the legs of a shortish backwoodsman,
who tripped and fell with a cry of fury, and the crowd swung
around to look. Springing up, the backwoodsman leaped on the
boy and struck him down. Not content, he lifted his foot to kick
him in the ribs.

This happened immediately in front of Duncan. His first reaction was to let the lad take a drubbing for his lackadaisical way,
but the backwoodsman was too cruel. Grunting his contempt,
Duncan swooped down, grasped the upraised foot and sent the
man sprawling halfway across the street.

They rose from the dirt together, the man and the boy, the lad, now having a champion, screaming his jittery derision of his enemy.

No word had been said, and none was said now. The man fairly bounced from the ground, and before Duncan was set for a fight, plunged upon him, screaming like an animal. Duncan, unbalanced, went over, sitting down. But when his hands reached the ground he defended himself with his feet. He kicked the man back out into the street. Then both rushed at each other on an even footing.

The backwoodsman had lost his hat, revealing a flaming red silk skullcap. He somehow was familiar. He came with greater caution now, though with undiminished rage. Duncan, too, had realized that though his adversary was only a middle-sized man he had uncommon strength.

The fight packed the street from all directions. Fights among the soldiers were not unusual, but this was better than most.

"Hold, man!" Duncan demanded. "I dinna wish to hurt ye."

But the backwoodsman only screamed insanely again and leaped. Duncan was much taller. He stooped and rose, with the heel of his palm shoving out. It caught the man's head while he was yet in the air, spun him around and flung him to one side. The crowd yelled delightedly. Not many men were heavy enough and strong enough to do that. The little fellow was a fool for fighting such a man.

The backwoodsman was down again but undeterred. This time he snatched a dirk from his boot leg. That ended the fight, for Duncan unsheathed his broadsword and held it with both hands in chopping position.

"Gin ye come on me wi' the blade," he stated, coldly angry, "I'll lay ye in twa pieces."

That held the backwoodsman. Even a maniac would not have advanced.

"Damn Tory!" the man spat. Then he turned and searched frantically on the ground for his red silk skullcap, and Duncan stared at his head. It was bald almost to the last hair. The pate glistened with the white scars of healed sores—the sign of the nauseous tetterworm. The distemper was long gone, but Duncan had the sudden retching feeling that his hand, which had touched the head, was filthy, and he wished to wash it.

Uncrowned and exposed, the backwoodsman displayed his shame. He dived through the ring of spectators without a word and left. The fight was over. The crowd dispersed.

The boy remained, staring in shining-eyed admiration at the big golden Scot who had come to his rescue.

"Wha's y'r name, laddie?"

"Hugh MacDonald—I live over around Cross Hill. I'm a sojer."

"Na! You're no sojer. You're just a lad!"

"I am so. I'm in Cap'n John Martin's company. I rate full sojer's pay."

"Don't lie, laddie."

"'Tis so, too. Cap'n John, he came home, he told Pa to jine up and fetch me. Pa said I was too little, and Cap'n John, he said he'd have no back talk, to jine up, he had to have two more men to git his commission. Pa said he wouldn't nohow, and Cap'n John said he'd have him shot for a Whig if he didn't. So he did, and I'm a sojer, mister, like I said."

Duncan squinted and shook his head. "Who was the man that struck ye down?"

"I don't know him, much. He's an Indian trader. He brings furs from down in South Carolina on his way to Wi'm'ton. His name is Fanning—David Fanning."

"Oh." Duncan suddenly remembered where he had seen him before—on the docks in Wilmington the night Flora MacDonald arrived. Fanning had a hickory club and whacked at things.

"He must be a Whig."

"He's got that name," the boy said.

Duncan strode away, searching for Mary, suddenly weary of this whole proceeding—the constant bickering, the fights, the wind-whipped dust, the delays, the too great patience of General Mac-Donald, who always was at the center of contention. This might be serving his king, but Duncan's sudden urgent preference was to build his stout house and tend his pine and burn his tar. Gillie Black was there, faithfully. Donald Bane was in the stable. The oxen were in the canebrake in the swamp. Duncan wanted to be there, too.

Here it was Saturday, the seventeenth, when the call to arms distinctly said that the Highlanders were to march to the coast on Thursday, the fifteenth. Yet they still milled around Cross Creek, not half organized. It was not yet known in what positions the divisions would march. All knew now that four divisions were set up, the Cumberland Militia, the Anson Highlanders, Cotten's Brigade and Donald MacLeod's Regulators. Yet all companies did not know to what divisions they would be assigned. There was a great discord. Scots stood around in dour groups, each according to his clan or friendships. Many of them marched between headquarters and Allan MacDonald's camp—a house, really. Someone said that Flora had come that day, hoping to assuage the high feeling. Duncan had not seen her. He went to the house. Flora was not there. Neither was Mary. Flora must know Mary's distress and be kind to her.

The bickering had become so general that hundreds of the Loyalists marched out of town, sometimes by whole companies. One reason they gave was that Governor Martin had promised that a regiment of British soldiers would be at Cross Creek to protect their mobilization and march with them to the coast. There were no British soldiers in Cross Creek, and it was rumored that there were not any on the Tidewater.

"When we git down there in the Whig country," one Regulator told his fellows, "they'll pick us off one at a time from behind trees—they'll kill every damn one of us."

"Mout," one agreed.

"And not a redcoat this side o' New York."

"Mout."

"You c'n do as you please—I'm gwine home. They done fooled me."

"I'm gwine, too."

Another one said: "They done promised me double pay and double honors and double loot, but I'm gwine home—double-quick."

And leave they did, eight of them, picking up their bags and rifles and walking away, their captain standing by, pleading helplessly.

Over at headquarters Donald MacDonald was speaking with

measured earnestness to a circle of his leaders. Duncan came in and stood there, listening. No one told him to go, and what they said held him. In the circle were Allan MacDonald, Alexander MacLeod, Hector MacNeill, Scalpie Campbell, Colonel MacLean and, listening but taking no part in what was said, Donald MacLeod. General Donald MacDonald was slapping his palm in slow rhythm as he talked.

"Ye Scots make fools o' y'rsel's! We're in no position to march to the coast now—not for three days yet, at the least. We'd be like a straggling band o' gypsies gangin' through the woods. We've lost time, valuable time. We should hae been gone two days ago. And what's happened since? The Whigs hae camped on Rockfish, only eight miles away, blocking our road. They are in strong position. They are bold men. In a fair fight we could defeat them wi' half their number. We hae thrice their number, but we are in desperate danger if they should attack."

No one answered. Donald MacDonald walked a slow circle behind his desk and renewed the attack:

"We hae three thousand men today. Yesterday we had five hundred more. Tomorrow we wi' hae less than today, for they leave faster than they come in. I hae ne'er i' a' my life been in a scene o' such confusion. Now, I hae this to say, ye Scots shall cease y'r bickering and take such assignment as is given ye or I shall make full report tae Lord Cornwallis on y'r extraordinary behavior. That should take complete care o' y'r future welfare i' the army. We are in such dire shape this minute that if this so-called 'Mad Jimmie' Moore should lead a determined charge upon us he would scatter us like birds, and it is all your fault. That, gentlemen, is the situation. Now—speak for y'rsel's!"

Farquard Campbell was the first apparently to catch the full import of what had been said. He saluted with a military flourish. "General MacDonald," he said, "I am at your command!"

The others frowned on him, as a deserter to their hard-fought, if vague, cause. But Farquard Campbell was a wealthy man and influential, and he had quicker wit than most.

"Aye," they nodded in assent, following his lead.

"Now, listen," said General MacDonald crisply. "It is all poppycock, expecting the British regiment to meet us here. They are not coming. I've a courier from the governor. The Lord knows how he got through the Whigs. The governor says that he is expecting the British ships daily. He anticipates that they will arrive before we reach the Tidewater. But they are not here yet. That is important, but it need make no change in our plans.

"Now, I hae no intention of engaging the Whig bands in battle before we join Lord Cornwallis. The Crown's strategy is to show a great force and intimidate them. If they will not be intimidated, then we will be in position to drive through them in such superior numbers that they will not impede us at all.

"That is what I wished to tell you. I am expecting you gentlemen to drill your companies, develop your discipline, and be ready to march when I give the order. In the meantime I will engage the rebels in correspondence, giving them the opportunity to depart, or to take the oath, or what they will, but I will keep them still, at least. Then, when we are ready, if they still are at Rockfish, we will find a way around them and drive for the coast, leaving them behind."

"Aye," said Farquard Campbell. "I will show you a road east of the river which will avoid them."

Colonel MacLean, Governor Martin's confidante, shook his head. "I do not like it," he protested. "It smacks too much o' retreating from the rabble."

"It is best, despite how it smacks," Colonel Donald MacLeod spoke for the first time, "tae get this disorganized force tae the sea, and stiffen 'em among trained soldiers."

"Our soldiers are as good as theirs and a damn sight better," MacLean retorted. "Unless," he suggested with insinuation almost too bold, "our officers be timorous."

Colonel MacLeod cut him through with a glance but made no answer.

"Gentlemen!" General MacDonald hushed them. He handed a letter to a courier named Morrison but kept a stern eye on the officers.

"All I hae tae say," Scalpie Campbell said, his great shoulders thrusting forward, "is that my men are ready to march wi' ten minutes' notice. Be it marchin' through Whigs or marchin' through scrub oaks, we don't give a damn!"

Duncan Stuart slept in his plaid that night, but not easily. He hadn't found Mary. He hadn't found Flora. And all this was not what he had anticipated. He had dreamed all his life of serving his king. Now, serving him, he was in the middle of violent and senseless quarrels, the contention of false pride and the insolence of new-made authority. He wondered whether Gillie Black, as faithful as he was, would think to water Donald Bane regularly twice each day. He thought of the Whigs marching up the King's Highway from Wilmington, and wondered if they were strict not to molest anyone's property. He wondered if Mary had returned home. He wondered if she had seen Flora MacDonald and what Flora had said to her. He wondered where Malcolm MacLeod had billeted himself. He must look for him tomorrow. He must see Flora MacDonald. He must help her bring order out of the ceaseless bickerings. He wondered where Cornelius Harnett was and if James Moore and the big Alexander Lillington would be senseless enough to show fight. The companies might be disorganized, but the Hielanders in the front company could disperse all the Whigs in Carolina.

It was dark yet the next morning when Duncan was awakened by the shrilling blast of the bagpipe before his camp, playing the "MacRae's March." The advance guard had started with the Mac-Raes, but many of them had been taken out, and other, stronger men had been added. The guard consisted of the strong men of many clans, but no point had been made of continuing the MacRae sponsorship. Duncan opened his eyes and looked out from the shed under which he slept. The silvery glisten of frost was on the leaves, and the stars gleamed cold. Men were stamping around the lot, breaking the frozen crust of ground, grumbling at the sharp chill. Their breaths made puffs of gray fog lighted by the camp-fires. Women faded into the darkness like wraiths, on the way to town.

Duncan threw back his plaid. He rubbed his bare calf, and the hairs on his leg bristled as the sudden cold whipped up the goose bumps. "Gang awa'!" he yelled derisively after the women, but in the noise of the piper his voice was no more than the other bang and clatter of the awakening camp. Duncan was soon up, with his tartan across his shoulder.

The men stood in groups around the fires and drank coffee and ate fried bacon and bread.

" 'Tis na sojerly," Scalpie Campbell commented, "but we'll be better equipped when we join the British. We're na sojers, anyway, but fighters."

Scalpie was a braw Scot with no feeling of superiority. He was the officer only when duty made it so. Like all the others of the advance guard which General MacDonald had set up in lieu of artillery, he considered the spearhead of the Highlanders as the whole army. Being at the front, and composed of men of many clans, Campbell's Highlanders, of course, shared none of the discontent which rankled in the other companies. They were at the front. The fight was about who should head the front line center and right and left.

"We," he said, "wi' hae more o' the bangin' an' smashin' wi' the handspikes today."

Duncan shrugged. He was tired of it—this dividing into teams and whaling away with a hickory stick at another clansman with a hickory stick. That was their training to meet with broadswords Whigs who might have bayonets. Their swords remained in camp for fear of breakage in the practice.

"Whaup!" Scalpie Campbell shouted when breakfast was over. It was an order, and it sounded like that, but Duncan had never been able to understand the words. He knew it was time to fall in, and he took his place. The men came yelling from the fires, and one shouted: *"Sgur Urain!"* It was the name of a mountain in Kintail and was the MacRae battle cry. From the end of the line, nearly a hundred men away, came another, a screeching: *"Dh'aindeoin co theireadh e!"*

"That's the MacDonald of Clanranald," Duncan said to a Mac-Dougall standing next to him. "I ken that, but what's it say?"

"It means: 'Gainsay who dare!' " the MacDougall burred, disdainfully, "and has a sharp edge out f'r friend and foe alike. Now, the MacDougall has a better one: *'Buaidh no bas!'* which means: 'Victory or death!' "

"Aye," said Duncan, " 'tis good f'r them that need to be spurred on. The Stuarts need only: *'Creag-an-sgairbh!*—The Cormorants' Rock!' I saw that when I was a lad."

But the MacDougall had no relish for Duncan's unconscious belittling and turned away. The company fell in by twos and marched to the woods.

It was Sunday. The sun came up, first chill upon a frosted world, and then warmly as it lifted the frost in white vapor. The men found their hickory pikes where they had dropped them the day before. They were in a little field, with persimmon trees standing stiffly here and there. The corn ridges had been stamped flat with the mock battles of the previous days.

The men broke what loose formation they had, found their pikes, wiped off the bristling frost and gathered again.

"Remember now," Scalpie Campbell told them, "when ye grasp y'r blades ye hae the strength o' a thousand years o' Scots i' y'r arms. Men like ye, wi' their twa hands swingin' braidswords, hae kept the invader out o' Caledonia since the beginnin' o' time. And they hae fought giants, too. Ye can fight as well as they, for now ye are trained. Puny Whigs canna buck ye. Remember, once for all, when ye swing, split y'r man and be done wi' him. Wark!"

Duncan glowed in the warmth of such talk. It was like the things he had dreamed of. He did wonder, at times, what might be if the Whigs opened fire with their rifles before the Scots could be upon them with their broadswords, but that was a matter for the officers to prevent.

He grasped his pike with both hands as he later would grasp his sword and marched out on the field. Sandy MacCallum faced him. Sandy was black-browed and big, with arms as stout as Donald Bane's foreleg.

"Ye be my Whig," Duncan said, feeling his stick. "Then I'll be yours. And take caution, Sandy—I'm out to split y'r pate."

Scalpie Campbell's big voice boomed from somewhere: "Whaup!" and a sudden clash and clatter and a turmoil of yells shattered the quiet. Shouts and curses rose above the whacking wood. A hundred Scots, their kilts flicking out like the short skirts of so many little girls, jumped and swung, and their white hickory sticks flashed over their heads and smashed down.

Sandy MacCallum was a strong man. Duncan's tough hickory bent a dozen times upon Sandy's "gun," held with both arms above his head.

"Hah!" Sandy jibed him. "Hah!"

"I'll sit ye on y'r butt gin I whang a' day!" Duncan shouted and with a mighty heave did just that. Sandy sat down with an "Oof!" No one heard, for the field thundered and clattered. Scalpie Campbell charged in between the battling clansmen. He swore. He pleaded. He urged them on, as, soon, he might have to do in actual combat.

Duncan leaped forward and went through the motions of laying open Sandy's belly. Then, amicably enough, they went to the edge of the field to drink a dipper of whisky from a bucket.

After an hour of it the men were perspiring. Their shirts lined the edge of the field.

" 'Tis like unto the Battle o' the Shirts," smiled a man standing beside the whisky bucket.

"Shirts?" Duncan inquired, looking at him over the dipper. "Oh," he said, apologetically. "Young Preacher Bethune!" He handed over his drink for the minister to take precedence. The preacher downed it without ado, filled the dipper again and gave it back to Duncan. Duncan thought him quite braw and dapper in his clergy kilt of blue and black.

"Yes," he said, "the battle of Loch Lochy between the ancient Frasers and the MacDonalds. They wrought so manfully and got so hot they flung off their shirts and the field was littered with them. When the fight had ended, only eight MacDonalds and five Frasers were left alive. 'Twas called the Battle o' the Shirts."

Duncan and Sandy nodded their heads, as though they had learned something. The young preacher—he was not as old as Duncan, and Duncan was barely twenty-five—said in quiet authority:

"Ye wi' ca' Captain Campbell, gin he can cease that awfu' swearin', and we wi' hae service."

Thus, on that Sunday morning, while beyond the Yadkin in the foothills the Presbyterian ministers among the Ulster Scots called down maledictions upon the tyrannical Crown, the youthful Presbyterian Reverend John Bethune wrestled with the Almighty to preserve the land from the Whigs.

In a short talk after the prayer Preacher Bethune gave them solemn thoughts.

"I bring ye no news," he said, "when I say that the rebels who ca' themselves Patriots grow strong to the east of us, and no more than eight miles away more than a thousand of them lie entrenched to obstruct our passage down to join His Majesty's forces. The wise and resourceful General MacDonald seeks to avoid conflict now, and if it be God's will, there will be no battle. But, if God should so direct our destiny as to bring on at once the perilous ordeal, then remember ye fight with the God of Abraham, of Isaac and of Jacob lending strength to your arms. And remember, too, that when battle comes, whenever God in His wisdom decrees, I will be in the midst of you as the battle sways, lifting my voice to Jehovah, asking Him to take His eye not once from any one of you, that ye be not afraid. In the name of God I say it, and so be it. Amen."

"Amen!" said the soldiers. "Amen!" said Duncan, but he frowned as he raised up from his knees, lifting himself by his staff. Preacher Bethune had given him a picture of the Almighty sitting in heaven in all majesty, thrusting His finger here and there as the battle raged to still this Whig or that Whig who might threaten one of His elect among the clansmen. It struck Duncan as very good, but not exactly fair to the Whigs. The Highlanders, he thought and dared not say, could cut the Whigs to pieces even if God stayed out of it. The preacher had given him a new, somewhat aghast, conception of the Almighty's power, and thought what a weak, impersonal God, who loved beauty and peace and the wind in the trees, Cornelius Harnett envisioned. Duncan shook his head doubtfully. He wondered if the mighty God of Abraham would heed so young a preacher as Bethune.

The advance guard, with many bruised spots on their shoulders and even more battered fingers and thumbs, went back to camp like woodsmen returning from the forest.

They had midday dinner at the camp, and from a dozen hills came the shouts of other clansmen and Regulators eating and preparing for the afternoon drill. And, drilling, they spent Sunday afternoon, up the slopes and down the valleys and through the brush, never far from camp, never in it, all companies separate from each other. Duncan came to hate the ever-swinging, never-ceasing driving of the indefatigable Captain Campbell who led them on. But through his hate also thrived a lusty confidence and a grudging admiration. Scalpie Campbell would be the one first to smite the enemy, and he, Duncan, would be damned if he wasn't there, shoulder to shoulder, with him.

A new, strident note belched from the bagpipe at dawn the next morning. Duncan jumped erect from his plaid before he was quite awake. Again he saw the wraithlike women fading into the night and shouted after them.

"Whaup!" John Scalpie Campbell was among the sleepers, adding his voice to the terrible screech. Breakfast was ready, and the men drank their coffee and ate their bread and meat while learning that the whole army had been called to march.

"I dinna ken! I dinna ken!" Scalpie told all who asked him. "All I hae been told is to prepare to march."

"Are th' Whigs comin'?" a MacAlister asked.

"I dinna ken, I told ye."

Another strode up to join the questioners: "Wi' we smash the Whigs today?"

"I dinna ken, I'm sayin'! Get y'r swords and all y'r equipment f'r marchin'. We may not be back till the war's over."

Now, instead of hickory sticks, they swung broadswords proudly at their sides. They had rifles in their hands—rifles to shoot at the enemy, to throw to the ground and rush on with broadswords raised. They had pistols for their belts and dirks for their stockings. And powder horns for their shoulders and shotbags for their sporrans. They lined up in double file and, for the first time, they felt like real soldiers. One cried: *"Cruachan!"*

They stood at the foot of Haymount. The piper struck up the rolling marching tune "The Campbells Are Coming!" and John Scalpie Campbell shouted "Whaup!" and led the way down the road toward the river, the company following smartly.

At the crossroads everything was rumble and dust and confusion, but orderly nevertheless. The royal standard stood proudly on its platform and moved in the wind which breezed to the rising sun. Around it pounded the feet of companies of soldiers up or down the road to take their places in line.

Allan MacDonald, no longer the wishfully thinking master of Killiegrey, but the smart, handsome army officer, met Scalpie

Campbell and ordered him to hold his place at the roadside until the line should be formed, then to march to the head of the column and take his place. Duncan looked for Flora, but he could not see her. Down the north-south road he heard shouting and wondered if she was there. Allan saw him in line, spoke to Scalpie Campbell and came to him.

Duncan stepped out to meet him. Allan came as a friend, placing both hands on Duncan's shoulders. He looked almost pleadingly from worried eyes and spoke in a low tone:

" 'Tis a great favor I'm asking, Duncan. I have my duties, and I cannot take the time. Flora is here. She and General MacDonald and the governor's representative and the colonels are under the great tree down the road. They will review the line from that point. Now—Flora came to inspirit the soldiers. We needed her, and she did great good. She sang Scottish songs and spoke to them in Gaelic, and they almost worshiped her. They go off today with their hearts singing of Auld Scotland. But, having come, she is o'erenthusiastic. She did not sleep at all last night. You may not know, but she is in tender health. I fear for what may happen if she does not return to Killiegrey for rest. The trouble is, she wants to accompany the troops to the sea. She must not, Duncan. I hae told her, but that does not mean that she will heed me."

"Aye," said Duncan uncomfortably, wondering how he could do aught.

"So now," said Allan, "I hae received permission for you to stand by her as a bodyguard while the troops pass. After that, if she shows a disposition to ride after the troops, you, if there is any way in God Almighty's name that you can, shall prevent it."

"Aye. I wi', gladly. But I am like a child with her. I promise nothing."

"Good enough."

When the march began, the bagpipes beyond the trees shrieked like a coiling snake of sound, breaking on the crackling air as far back as forty howling bagpipes in line might be heard. They were around the curve of the road and couldn't be seen, but their strident, ear-shredding skirls blasted through the trees like something alive and plunging.

Duncan ran up under the great tree to stand beside Flora's white horse when the army came through. She, with the officers grouped beyond her, sat and waited. The nag, with high and restive head, stamped in excitement. Flora was as high-headed as her horse, tingling tense with the exaltation of the moment. Her blue eyes gleamed with the drive of her spirit, but her soft-firm face otherwise was rounded passiveness. She held her horse taut and held herself taut. She was in a draping black silk skirt, with the black, red and green of the MacDonald tartan across her shoulder.

Duncan was entranced. No wonder the men yesterday had almost worshiped the sight of Flora MacDonald. General MacDonald sitting there on his horse was a good soldier, a man of method and courage, his face calm, his outlook on a task to be done, but Flora MacDonald would have made a greater general. She had the fire and lift to transform even a mediocre army into an avalanche of fighting maniacs. She could have led them to thundering victory or to glorious disaster.

Flora did not see Duncan when he came. She, doubtless, would not have noticed even Allan, her husband. Duncan was unaccountably glad that Allan was not there, for this was Flora's own moment, and Allan had no part in it. Flora was the darling of the clansmen, their own, and Allan would have broken the illusion. Perhaps he sensed that and did not come.

Just then, a stone's throw away, the advance guard thrust around the bend, marching gallantly. Two pipers played "Bruce's March," and Captain Scalpie Campbell, in the green, black and yellow checks of the Campbell of Breadalbane reflecting the morning sun, stepped in view with the sureness of leadership. Flapping to the music were kilts of many colors, the green and red of the Cummings, the red, black and white of the Cunninghams, the black, red and yellow of the MacQueens, the scarlet and blue of the MacGregors, the green and black of the ancient MacCallums, the flaming red of the Frasers, and the brick-red of the Camerons, and the green, black and red of the MacDougalls.

The company's feet thudded rhythmically in time to the brisk march, and Flora's horse trembled and trampled as the bagpipes shrieked. Duncan placed his hand on the bridle, but Flora seemed to notice nothing but the troops, with their swords swinging and rifles loosely across their shoulders.

Suddenly, so quickly that the silence was louder than its shrill notes, the music stopped and Captain Campbell saluted Flora, and she saluted them.

"Fionnaghal! Fionnaghal!" the men shouted her Gaelic name. "Fionnaghal!"

She laughed happily, a deep laugh from her lungs, not the musical little laugh which Duncan had heard in the parlor. "Fionnaghal!" the men roared, and her laugh was in tune to the roar of warriors.

The strong, musical timbre of her voice carried soundly over the thumping of their feet. "Sons of the Gael! Shoulders thegither!"

Someone in the company struck the tune, and all sang:

> *"An' Charlie, he's my darlin',*
> *My darlin', my darlin',*
> *Charlie, he's my darlin',*
> *The Young Chevalier!"*

Flora laughed and waved them on. The next company was rounding the bend, and the pipers suddenly switched to the Charlie song and the men came up shouting.

This company was Scottish, too, but not more than half wore tartans. Many of them wore brown woolen homespun breeches, dyed in black walnut juice, with cotton homespun shirts and blue homespun coats. Those without kilts wore red hatbands or red strips of cloth on their hats.

"A Douglas! A Douglas!" Flora shouted when they saluted, giving the battle cry of a gray-kilted little man. His face blazed bright through his brown whiskers, and in a shrill cry he returned the battle cry of the MacDonalds of Clanranald: *"Dh'aindeoin co theireadh e!"*

"Fionnaghal!" the men shouted, while those who did not know Gaelic, or were trying to forget it, shouted: "Flora MacDonald! Flora! Flora!"

A third company swung around the bend, its gallant piper playing the "MacLean's March," and many of the company wore the light red and green plaid of the clan. "Another for Hector!" they shouted for Flora, and she translated the ancient battle cry back to them in Gaelic: *"Fear eile airson Eachainn!"* which pleased them mightily. For a MacClaren she cried: *"Creag an Turic!"* and, then, her arm held high, "Sons of the Gael—shoulders thegither!"

In mad enthusiasm they shouted back: "Flora! Fionnaghal! Flora!" and saluted General MacDonald and marched on.

And so continued the Highland march out, company after company, their bagpipes screaming, their feet thumping, with Flora on her white horse singing out their battle cries, cheering them on to the glory of their sires.

Now was a MacLeod to be recognized, now a Shaw, now a Ross or a Scott or a Fletcher, here a Ramsay, now an Ogilvie. Once a MacKenzie shouted to her, but Flora pretended not to hear. The MacDonalds had not forgotten, from ancient times, the MacKenzie who had sent back the one-eyed wife he had got from the MacDonalds, sent her back on a one-eyed horse, led by a one-eyed groom, followed by a one-eyed dog to be her shame.

In one of the companies was Alexander, her son, and he raised his arm to her. She shouted to him the old battle cry.

Then the wagon train rumbled by, and then came the up-country Loyalists. Regulators, they were called, two or three hundred strong. General MacDonald saluted Flora and joined the column.

And, so, slowly the weaving line crept down the road, melting into its own cloud of dust. The Highlanders had marched out.

Duncan Stuart stood holding the bridle, his eyes straining after the clansmen. Something new hammered in his breast. Something bold and yearning, as though a thousand ancestors thundered commands.

He looked up at Flora. "Fionnaghal!" he whispered. Then he stared incredulously. He had expected to see her still erect, looking with the eyes of an eagle. Instead she was weeping.

"Oh, Doon-kan! Doon-kan!" she wailed. "What hae I done?" She took it for granted that he would be there. He stepped back, and she placed her hand on his shoulder. "Am I in the right?"

She was all woman again, feminine, her soft mouth curved, her round chin trembling, her eyes misted with tears, thinking of the murder of battle.

"Aye," Duncan said stoutly. "You're right, Flora MacDonald!"

"Pray God I may be," she said.

"Ye wi' be gangin' home, now?" he asked.

She nodded.

"Wi' ye do a thing f'r me?" he urged her.

"Aye, Doon-kan," giving a fondling push to his bonnet. "Of course—Young Chevalier!"

"I dinna ken f'r how long we'll be gone. Malcolm MacLeod is wi' us. I wi' see to him. And, Flora, ye wi' see to Mary—for me?"

"Mary MacLeod!" Flora's sudden sharpness cut him. "Mary, the Whig!" Her mouth curled. "No, Duncan. I wouldna care to. I broke wi' Mary yestreen."

"What?" Duncan squared around to face her.

"Yes, I told her in public I wouldna see her again. I did it tae drive her frae the clans."

"But, Flora!" Duncan fairly shouted. "Ye canna do't! Ye canna! What matters it what she thinks? She's our own kin'. I love her, and ye canna set her adrift in times like these!"

"She's a Whig, Duncan. Ye hae just seen my husband march away, and my son. And ye, y'rsel'. And Anne's husband. I winna harbor any woman who comforts and befriends those who wad kill my loved ones. My bitterness is greater upon her than upon the Whigs, who, to say the least, hae not betrayed my heart."

His anger was surging beyond control. "Weel, ye are betrayin' *my* heart, Flora MacDonald!"

"Y'r heart shouldna be tender on such an ungratefu' hissie!"

"I didna ken ye could be sae ruthless, Flora MacDonald! What became of her?"

"Oh, I dinna ken. She went away alone, tae her home among the Whigs, I hae no doubt. I would hae nought to do wi' her, and she went. I repent that I brought her to this land. Now, Duncan, hae nae more tae say about this, but join y'r company and serve y'r king faithfully."

"Flora MacDonald——" Duncan's face was white, and his yellow hair trembled. His eyes flamed wild. He shouted: "Damn the King!"

He swung away from her with a jerk, not after the disappearing column. He ran toward the river. For a boat. He was on his way to Elizabethtown.

As he turned the bend in the road, Flora MacDonald sat still on her white horse, her shoulders rounded, her eyes raised as though, in anguish, searching heaven for the right.

CHAPTER 9

It was twilight when Duncan beached his sharp-ended cypress boat on the little strand down the hill from Mary MacLeod's cabin that evening. His arms were stiff, and his shoulders were numb with the paddling, but he had made fast time. Rain far up the river had given him flood speed, and thoughts of Mary had given him strength. There was a dim light through the window, through the glass window that Thomas Brown had contributed to the house-raising. He gathered up his rifle and his broadsword and strode wearily up the hill, dragging his feet through the wire grass. Then he stood on the little porch.

"Mary!" he called. He had given no thought to what he should say. He wanted to see her and know that she was safe. That was all.

The door opened, and Mary's neat little figure stood in it. Behind her a taller, washed-out, pale-eyed woman, with a snuff brush in her mouth, peered over her head.

"Doon-kan!" Mary cried, alarmed, holding out her hands.

"Laws ha' massy!" Minnie Meacham crooned dismally, as though all this were beyond her and she were helpless. "He clatters like a bag o' plow p'ints!"

Mary and Duncan stood and held each other wordlessly, each searching the other's eyes for a message. Anxiety gave way to peace, and they smiled.

"Come in, Doon-kan," she said, her joy beginning to gurgle. "Come in and warm y'rsel', y'r hands are sae *cauld.*"

She tugged at his hands, and he entered the house, going to the fire. He stood his rifle in the corner and took off his broadsword sheath and laid it on the floor. Mary picked it up and moved it over against the wall. "Ugh!" she shuddered, half seriously.

"I saw Flora MacDonald this morning."

Mary walked a step or two toward him, searching his eyes. Then she nodded and looked troubled. "That is why you came," she stated, as though answering a question she had asked herself. "We must hurry supper, Minnie, the man's half starved—can ye na *see?*"

Duncan started and laughed. "I was wonderin' why I was sae weak. I forgot to eat."

"Laws ha' massy!" said Minnie. "Ain't it lucky we roasted all them 'taters today. It takes plenty to fill up a empty Scotchman."

His own cabin was smaller than this, but Duncan felt large and ungainly. The chairs were small, and he seemed to sprawl all over the place as the two women hurried food from the fireplace to the table.

"I see old Ganny Tew's pot sling is working fine," Duncan said, working it with his hands. "Yes, sir, it works all right."

But all this was mere surface talk. Duncan and Mary had much to say to each other. They would say it later. Duncan was contented. He was with Mary, and she was faring well. Mary's eyes slowly took on concern as she thought of things of which she did not speak.

"When wi' the battle be?" Mary asked. They were sitting at the table, and she poured his coffee.

"Battle? What battle? There'll be no battle."

"I know ye said that, in Cross Creek. But ye are deluded, Duncan. The Patriots wi' na give an inch."

"Don't ca' them Patriots. They are Whigs."

"Aye," she lifted her head. " 'Whig' is good eneugh."

"General MacDonald marched toward them. If they scatter, he wi' go down the ither side o' the river. If they do not, he wi' come down this side. He wi' na waste powder on them."

"How comes it ye could leave at so uncertain a moment?"

"I just came. It was na so uncertain. Moreover, I told Flora MacDonald damned be the King, that I wouldna serve him."

"Oh, Duncan!"

"Aye, my wrath was upon her for what she said to you, and I left. I hae na considered since whether I was right or wrong."

Minnie Meacham let her discretion overcome her curiosity for once. "I reckon you folks want to talk personal, so I'll go to the spring for a bucket of water." They didn't hear her.

"But, Duncan—ye canna!"

"But I *hae!*"

"See, Duncan," she said earnestly. "Ye are na in the army servin' Flora MacDonald. Whatever she does or says to me is na the question. She thinks she is in the right, so let her go her way. She canna hurt me. There's a bright day comin', Duncan, for my happiness, and what grieves me is that my happiness must bring her low. She is na in the right and canna understand. This land is grand and unbound and has the right to be free, but she canna see that. She is blinded to't. So are ye. If Heaven could put it in y'r heart to see as I see, I would be so happy. But ye canna, and I wi' na hae ye slighting what ye conceive to be y'r duty on account o' me. Ye canna, Duncan. Ye maun go back and fight f'r y'r sense o' *right*."

"I wi' na fight for them that set ye adrift."

"But ye are *na* fighting for them. Ye are fighting for the Crown, and y'r honor binds ye."

"Aye—the oath," Duncan sighed. In the back of his mind he had known all the while it would be this way.

"Gin I loved ye less, Duncan, I would na talk so."

"But the same tie that binds me binds ye."

"Na. I rebel because I consider it right tae rebel. Ye canna because ye consider it wrong."

"Ye are right, Mary. Strange it is that Flora MacDonald drives me out o' the King's army and ye drive me back in again."

Duncan walked home slowly that night. He went by the framing of his stout house. It gave him satisfaction to grasp the timbers and feel them solid in his touch. Through them he could see the stars shining. Over the creek he heard Donald Bane stamping in his stall. He went that way and took the horse out in the darkness and ran his hands over him to see that he had been rubbed properly. He sank his hands in the feedbox to see that the nag had not been chewing the cobs, had been getting enough to eat. He woke Gillie Black, who was not much surprised. Duncan these months came and went at strange times.

"Ye hae been eatin' bread and greens, as I told ye, or hae ye been eatin' meat alone as ye are wont to do?"

"Grass, Mas' Dunk—plenty o' grass, jes lak you said," Gillie smiled.

"I suspect ye lie, but ye still look hearty, so it is well."

Duncan went to bed and with a fine, serene content upon him went to sleep. The mobilization so far had meant little to him—marching, drilling, talk. In the background the Whigs scuttled through, indefinitely going places, marching, drilling, talking. Mostly talking. The Scots would march to the sea. They would join Cornwallis, and the whole crisis would fade out. He would be burning tar again in three weeks. It seemed senseless to lose the three weeks from work.

In this mood on Wednesday noon he concealed himself in the gallberry bushes on a bluff and watched the river, to see a strange sight—a little army of Whigs paddling madly down the stream. They had sixty or seventy boats. They were like a raft of things alive, holding close together.

Alexander Lillington sprawled hugely in one boat that four men paddled. John Ashe was in another. They were in no order, merely a conglomeration of paddle boats with two hundred paddles, perhaps three hundred, flashing in the sun and splashing in the water.

Duncan grinned and shook his head. It was a queer war. Mac-Donald's army raced down this side of the river and Moore's the other. Lillington's "navy" paddled desperately between. The one that got there first, he reckoned, would win a prize. That was a joke. He laughed aloud. It was a monstrous, curious war.

Early Friday morning Duncan stood impatient among the fog-dimmed pines on a sand ridge. He was near South River, to the east. He wore his sword and carried his rifle. He had marched since midnight to join MacDonald. Now he was ready to go. Even eager. His mind was clear on it. The muffled noise which rumbled through the mist from up the trail heralded the Scots. But for the fog on the lowlands, he could see them now. He listened, instead. Presently they would wind out of the veil at the foot of the ridge, curve back into it again.

The sun put a ghostly glamor on them when they came near
enough to be seen. As though awaiting the moment, the vanguard's pipers blasted. It was a weird thing out there on the gray
flatlands. The flapping kilts, colorless shadows at first, became red
and green and yellow. The guns swayed on broad shoulders. The
swords swung like pendulums. The men looked ahead and
marched. At their head, driving doggedly, was Scalpie Campbell.
Duncan suddenly was not only dutiful: he was proud. It was a
grand company, Scots all, his company, marching for the Crown.
He ran down the hill and took his place in line.

They marched that day over interminable sandhills. They
crossed South River in the morning. They cut new roads here and
there to save distance on their way to Black River. Duncan first
gave attention to the new country, sandhills, swamps, creeks in
white sand beds, creeks in black mud beds, the tall, gently blowing
pines, the bullet-colored trunks of the bare-branched scrub oaks.
Then, eventually, it all became the same. He no longer cared. It
was just a march. At times they would stop and rest. Then they
would march again. Then it was late afternoon, and they were at
Black River. There was no bridge. Only a flat, half sunk in the
water.

They marched into a field, knee-high in dead grass, and broke
ranks. Other companies came up behind them. Fires started. The
wagons rolled up. General Donald MacDonald and Alexander
MacLeod and James Cotten and Allan MacDonald came in, riding
horses. General MacDonald was tired and pale. He rode down to
the narrow river and looked at the flat. Duncan and his mates
gathered timber and made three fires. He stood at one and waited
for supper. Scalpie Campbell came and stood beside him, smiled
curiously.

"Glad tae hae ye back," Scalpie said.

"I had to go," Duncan said. "I knew there'd be no battle at
Rockfish."

"Aye. All o' us kenned that."

Scalpie Campbell was a bonnie fellow. He had no thought that
Duncan had left to escape a fight. "Else ye'd ha' stayed," Scalpie
said.

"Aye. I'd sock the man who said not."

"Weel, there's a lot o' such talk in the line, I'm sorry tae say. The colonels and the majors are bitter."

"Aye?"

"Aye. The MacLean and ithers are most contemptuous o' General MacDonald's determination tae avoid the Whigs. He crossed the river above Rockfish to avoid Moore. He intended to recross at Elizabethtown, but the big fellow Lillington and his boatmen outstripped us, and Moore was just behind. That was twice. Then we headed for Corbett's Ferry, straight down our side o' the river and a little march across, but then we learned that troops from New Bern, under Caswell, held that. Not many, 'tis true, but General MacDonald wants nae fight at all. He has escaped three fights, and it may be that we wi' skin through, like hounds runnin' frae rabbits, and finally join Cornwallis without nickin' a Whig's hide. Perhaps it is wiser. I dinna gainsay it. But I hae na likin' f'r this seemin' retreat."

"Aye," said Duncan. "I saw Lillington scootin' down the river. They made talk o' going to Corbett's Ferry."

"Weel, they'll abandon that when they know we're crossing the Black River higher up. What's the next place they can drop back to and block our way?"

"The Widow Moore's Creek Bridge, two days' march, below."

"Weel, personally I hope tae God they make a stand there and let's hae it out wi' 'em. I'm tired o' dodging. We'll hack our way through 'em like goin' through cotton stalks."

"Aye—they winna fight."

"Na."

It took half a day next morning to raise the ferryboat. After that it was quite simple to span the stream with a pontoon bridge. Then, still seventy miles from Fort Johnston, the Highlanders again took up their march.

That day they drove through more scrub oaks and live oaks and pines, and through more swamps and across more crystal-clear and inky-black streams, and over more white sandhills. They camped in another field that night, and Donald MacDonald looked still paler and still more weary. The next day was Sunday and the march was short. The soldiers rested. Reverend John Bethune preached of the God of battle. Monday morning they marched again. Now across both rivers, with nothing but creeks between them and the waiting British ships at Wilmington, the Highlanders considered that the Whig bands would not dare face them.

At midday General MacDonald slumped from his horse, too sick to go on. They took him to a farmhouse and put him to bed. The soldiers halted solemnly in the road.

The uneasy officers stood in brown concern, the same thought in the minds of all. MacLean, Governor Josiah Martin's confidante, spoke it with some acerbity:

" 'Tis most unfortunate. Here we are, two days' march from our destination. We have dodged Whigs for a week, and now our commanding officer begins to rave with the fever. It will demoralize our men. What with suspecting that their officers fear to fight and being suddenly leaderless——"

"Gentlemen!" Colonel Donald MacLeod, who had led the Regulators, strode among them with purposeful abruptness. "If I interrupt," he said with edged sarcasm to MacLean, "please forgive me." Then he turned to the group.

"I am in command—General MacDonald's orders. My first instructions are that officers shall desist from subversive comment and co-operate with me fully in accomplishing our task according to the policies laid down."

"But," said MacLean, "how can it be by General MacDonald's orders, when he was raving——"

"Silence!"

MacLeod was an old hand in the army, and he knew when to draw an issue. He took two quick steps. He stood directly in front of the governor's friend and glared into his eyes.

"Mr MacLean," he demanded, "if it is your intention to gain command of these troops, state your authority. If not, then you will obey my orders. My immediate command to you is to be silent!"

MacLean paled. He suppressed his anger and humiliation with an effort. "Aye, sir!" He saluted.

Colonel MacLeod continued: "Captain Pyle, you will detail a squad of twenty men under a sergeant as a bodyguard for General MacDonald. Include in this number anyone you may have with experience in attending the sick. Also cut out one of the wagons for

the general's use when he shall have recovered sufficiently to continue his march. Wi' a good night's rest he will o'ertake us by tomorrow noon, no doubt."

To the others MacLeod said: "To your places, gentlemen. We
will finish the day's march as planned, so that we may reach
Nigger Head Point and board the King's ships tomorrow evening.
March!"

Scalpie Campbell was standing only a few yards away from his
Highlanders. He whirled toward them. "Whaup!" he shouted, and
the line jerked into motion, their shoes sinking in the white sand.
Nearly a mile up the road the teamsters were shouting to their
horses, and the dull knock of the wagons sounded over the soft
shuffle of feet.

They were well into the Whig country now. Lanky men,
patiently bitter, sat on the porches of their cabins, long rifles across
their knees. Litters of shirt-tailed children climbed to the fodder
stacks and smokehouse roofs to stare. Up the long lanes to the big
houses saddled horses stamped at the hitching posts. Groups of
men leaned on the fences to watch the passing column. They gave
the impression that they but waited for the Tories to pass before
they themselves took to the saddle.

Still no one made an untoward move. The only sign was of defense, but there was no denying the hostility in the air. One
weathered old woman sat on her little porch behind a rail fence
and spat snuff spitefully for every company that marched before
her. There was no fear. Some of the women looked merely curious. But nowhere along the road was there even a flicker of a smile
as the Scots stamped through.

Colonel MacLeod rode up to Scalpie Campbell, at the head of
the line. "The territory," he said, "betrays its animosity. Detach
ten for an advance guard. We should take that precaution."

The first ten men moved out from the front rapidly, leaving
Duncan as one of the two front men. Scalpie looked back over
his shoulder and smiled. "Finally the Stuarts hae come to their
own!" he called, and Duncan smiled back. Scalpie was a bonnie
captain.

The scouts went faster, impressed by their new duties. They
took to the woods, and one crouched and searched ahead. It

brought a strange, unexplored feeling to Duncan. It was but a simple act of military precaution, and doubtless not necessary at all, but it was the first move he had seen which contemplated a lurking enemy. It fetched him into a mood for brooding. He had thought of an actual blood-and-bone fight with the Whigs only on the top of his mind. Now it gave him the loose let-go of helplessness to think that any tree might shield a Whig bushwhacker.

The country was flat and open. It was inexpressibly drab. It had no song of peace and cheer, such as he had promised Mary. The chill February winds flowed over the smooth needles of wire grass, comfortless. Dead limbs stood out from the pines like cold, twisted fingers of corpses. A buzzard sat on a tree, lone and hungry, to look down on the passing column. Duncan had a revolting thought of the old seer's raven which should drink three fulls of MacDonald blood.

They marched more than two hours, deep sand pulling at weary feet. The sun was in the west, and Colonel MacLeod called a halt. There was a vacant cabin. The officers took that. The men scattered to the woods for fuel. Sentries were ordered out. The afternoon waxed cold, and the fires grew big. Duncan did not share it, but the soldiers had a feeling of elation, of new enthusiasm, despite the general's sickness. This was the last camp of the march. Tomorrow, everyone said, they would be on ships, British ships, sailing down the river from Nigger Head Point to Fort Johnston. Duncan wasn't so sure. The surly Whigs on the road seemed each mile to become more furtive and sinister. Mary had said the Highlanders could not go to the coast without a battle. Perhaps they faced one now.

He threw off the unwelcome thought. He envisioned what majesty he would see at the fort Wednesday morning—imperial spars reaching to the sky, sails furled, flags flying, bugle calls, the sharp commands of army officers. And ships, ships filling the river, a hundred ships, laden with soldiers and supplies and cannon. Clinton—Parker—Cornwallis—in gold and broadcloth—the Crown's might personified. It was a cheering prospect, but his fit of brooding returned.

After supper the men lay on their tartans before the fires and rested their feet, cursing the sand for a nuisance for getting in their hair. Scalpie Campbell called Duncan to him, and they walked away from the men. Scalpie was worried.

"Did ye na say that we hae come back into the trail which crosses the Black River at Corbett's Ferry?"

"Aye."

"I hae given thought to it. If this Lillington caught word that we had dodged Corbett's Ferry, he might head for that creek bridge—whad'd ye call it?"

"Widow Moore's Creek Bridge?"

"Aye—how far from here?"

"Three miles, no doubt."

"Aye—and did ye see what I saw i' the road? Foot tracks, lots o' them?"

Duncan frowned. "Aye, I saw foot tracks—fresh tracks. I thought them to be those of the advance guard."

"Too many. Hunders o' men hae marched ahead o' us. I kept listenin' f'r the scouts tae report something, but they didna. We should take care before we march in the mornin'."

"Aye," Duncan agreed. He frowned and looked into the woods. "Aye!" he said again.

"Listen, Duncan—I hae said little tae ye o' the march, but I wish ye to know——"

An orderly came up hurriedly. "Colonel MacLeod's compliments, sir. He wants ye over to headquarters."

Scalpie threw his arm around Duncan's shoulder and drew him toward the cabin. Duncan did not question the gesture, taking it as an indication of the welcome camaraderie of Captain Campbell. Brave men have an unspoken language by which to know each other, and Campbell and Duncan Stuart had developed such a friendliness. Duncan was surprised, however, when Scalpie pushed him into the door and into the council of the officers.

"Flora MacDonald," laughed Scalpie, "says he is the spi't 'n' image o' Bonnie Prince Charlie, so I figgered he belonged in our councils."

Duncan prepared to be embarrassed by the laughter, but lost the feeling in the sudden air of gravity. The officers standing around the plank table were tense. They merely flicked glances to see who entered and turned back to Colonel Donald MacLeod.

"Now, let me repeat," MacLeod said, "for those who have just come in and for your own better enlightenment."

The top of the table had charcoal marks on it, and MacLeod was explaining: "This dot, here," pointing, "is our present camp site. This meandering line on our left is a creek, the Widow Moore's Creek, which flows from up the country, paralleling our route about a mile distant. Ahead of us it crosses our road and goes on into the Black River. From here to our bridge over the creek is a distance of three miles. Do you understand, gentlemen?"

No one spoke. The officers studied the rude black lines in silence.

"Now," MacLeod said impressively, "the Whigs are entrenched immediately beyond the bridge."

Duncan drew his breath. It was as though the colonel had given him the truth of what had haunted him in the bitter, secretive eyes of Whigs along the way.

MacLeod continued: "The creek at the bridge is about thirty feet wide and, with recent rains, probably six feet deep. That is our problem, gentlemen. General MacDonald is in no condition to counsel us. I will assume the responsibility, but I wish your suggestions."

"How many Whigs?" Old Hector MacNeill asked the question, and he was a regular-army man. So were Allan MacDonald and his son-in-law, Alexander MacLeod. Their opinion had weight. Duncan liked, and was lifted by, their direct, thrusting comment. They rallied him from his vague forebodings.

"We know," Colonel MacLeod answered Hector carefully, "that Lillington is there. He made good time in his boats. He arrived this morning or yesterday and has thrown up breastworks. He had Colonel John Ashe and a company of volunteers with him—about two hundred and fifty riflemen, I'd say. They were not encumbered with wagons and made much better time from the Upper Cape Fear than we did. They have no cannon in this contingent.

"Then, arriving just ahead of us was Colonel Richard Caswell's contingent from New Bern. They have at least one cannon. It may be one of those which Governor Martin dismantled just before he fled the mansion last summer. Caswell has approximately six hundred men. That makes, say, nine hundred in the two outfits. Then,

I'm informed, other local companies have flocked in, and these have been joined by swampmen with squirrel rifles. We have facing us, gentlemen, at the most eleven hundred men, most of them badly trained if trained at all."

"Then how many," asked Alexander MacLeod, "hae we?"

"We had more than two thousand leaving Cross Creek," Donald MacLeod said. "Our losses have been fairly constant. We have, in round numbers, fourteen hundred clansmen and two hundred and fifty to three hundred Regulators—sixteen to seventeen hundred."

"Well," Farquard Campbell asked, "what courses are open to us? What—how many different things can we do?"

"Three," said the colonel.

"Three?" demanded MacLean, the governor's friend. "I see but one."

Donald MacLeod shrugged. With his new responsibilities he could not indulge the luxury of wrath. "First," he continued, "we can hold our ground. We can camp here and wait for the British to send reinforcements, catching the rebels between us and decimate them with little loss. Thus——"

"Hold! No!" MacLean said boldly. "I may as well say now as tomorrow—gentlemen, there are no British on Tidewater. Even the old *Cruzier* was beaten back by riflemen ten days ago. No ships will meet us at Nigger Head Point. Governor Martin expects them any week, but they have not come. In the meantime the governor is in the humiliation of hiding on the old hulk, awaiting our arrival. This command is the only force in Carolina to uphold His Majesty's dignity! We must hasten to the governor, through hell or high water, for our own self-respect."

"Well—hell! Why hae ye been holding this back?" demanded Hector MacNeill.

"We've been tricked!" Farquard Campbell charged.

Donald MacLeod's knuckles bore so on the table that the bones crackled, but he forbore to vent his indignation. "I have been telling the gentlemen," he said in a low, cutting tone, "that the British would meet us there. I hope they now will understand that I was as much deceived as they.

"Now," he continued. "Second, we can deploy to the left before daylight tomorrow morning, flank the Whigs, and be below them again before they are aware. The advantage of that is that it would avoid the meeting we have so consistently prevented and would get us to the *Cruzier* without violating General MacDonald's most wise strategy. Third, we can force our way through the Whigs."

The officers looked at each other for a moment in silence. It was as though they thought rapiers and clashed suspicion with suspicion.

"For me," Scalpie Campbell said boldly, "I'm tired o' dodgin' Whigs. We've been at it f'r goin' on a week and——"

"Right!" said MacLean, smiling in triumph at Donald MacLeod. Scalpie Campbell looked at him with a frown.

"But," said Scalpie, "Colonel MacLeod is the best-equipped army man among us, and I doubt my wisdom and defer to his judgment. That is a' I hae to say."

Farquard Campbell was for the flanking movement. Hector MacNeill also was. Allan MacDonald suggested that, inasmuch as the Whigs insisted on it, they might as well be met one place as another. Alexander MacLeod agreed with him.

"Gentlemen!" said MacLean. "Are we going to make ourselves the laughingstock of the whole British Army? Here we are, with the flower of the Carolina Highlanders primed to fight, eager to fight, knowing they are in a glorious cause—and we haggle and wiggle and dodge and twist, and then let half our number of ill-equipped, untrained lowland clodhoppers throw us on our haunches. How shall we ever gain the King's favor and win promotion in his army? Gentlemen, do we tremble before the Whigs?"

MacLean looked around with a sneer. His circling eyes finally met Donald MacLeod's, and they clashed.

"Ye have left the decision to me, gentlemen." Donald MacLeod stood up, white-faced, but still gripping his anger. He spoke to all, but his eyes never left those of MacLean, and MacLean's did not waver. "We meet the Whigs at dawn. I invite Mr MacLean to stand wi' me in the battle, and we shall see where the cowardice, if any, be."

It was a dead-gray dawn that Tuesday morning. The deadness and chill of a graveyard lay on the bristling frost which hugged the limbs and the grass and made even the rich green of the bay trees gray and grisly and cold. Campbell's vanguard swung down the road to Moore's Creek, with the whole army in support. They were not cold. They had been marching an hour, and the numbness had left their fingers and their blood coursed hot and free. But they were glum—seventy-five hand-picked men to flush and flay the enemy. It was their job to smash the Whig front lines, making the way clear for the riflemen to charge in and complete the slaughter. No matter how brave, one cannot contemplate splitting his first skull without dark thought.

A full mile back in the darkness the whole column had stopped its soft padding in the sand, and each captain had addressed his company. John Scalpie Campbell had said:

"I wi' not waste time telling Hielanders what tae do in battle. Ye hae the instinct in y'r blood and bones. All I say tae ye is follow me. Gin I fa', then charge o'er my body and keep going. Wherever a Whig shows his head, split it!"

The line had surged as though lashed. It had been too dark for one man to see the face of another. There was another mile to march. In that mile black night became dark gray, and the Highland column was like a great dim shadow moving on the road. Big dark Scots, big bright Scots drove grimly, each with his picture in his mind, a Whig going down with a gritty whack.

Duncan knew the bridge, a plank span, high in the middle, ten paces across. The vanguard would go across it like a spearhead and mushroom into the Whigs up the slope.

He had a cold, retching feeling. He was not afraid. His belly just quivered. He couldn't help it. He saw Whigs lurking in the swamp shadows at the left. But they weren't Whigs. They were trees. He whispered the company's battle cry: "King George and Broadswords!" No good. He whispered the ancient cry of the Stuarts: *"Creag-an-sgairbh!"* That was better.

He had the impulse for horseplay, to tangle Sandy MacCallum on his left with his broadsword, and to bump Laughlan Bethune, in front, with the butt of his rifle. Anything. Anything but this damnable glum, cold silence, with Whig eyes peering out of the dark behind every tree. It gave him the jerks.

There was a shuffling behind him, and he turned to look. Mary's brother, Malcolm MacLeod, tall and gawky and half crazed with excitement. He shouldered his way into the line. Those before and behind cursed him under their breaths. Duncan, too, swore. Braving a reprimand, he went back.

"Get out and get back," he whispered, thumbing down the road.

"I winna!" Malcolm shrilled.

"Ye can't stay here!"

"I wi'!"

"Listen, Malcolm," Duncan protested. "I told Mary——"

"T' hell wi' ye! I know my duty. Leave me be!"

A sergeant tugged at Duncan's arm, and Scalpie Campbell looked back. He flung the sergeant's arm aside and then gave up and took his place in line. An officer, walking fast, came up from behind, brushed against him and passed on. It was Colonel Donald MacLeod. He went to Captain Campbell, and they saluted. MacLeod took the left, Campbell the right, and they marched together.

Something gallant was in it. Duncan remembered last night. MacLeod had said: "We wi' see where the cowardice, if any, be." And now, there he was, out front, sharing the danger with Scalpie Campbell. Duncan's grinding belly came still. He shoved forward eagerly. If they'd let him, he wanted to march with 'em. His will to fight flamed alive.

"Halt!" was the hushed command.

Two hundred paces ahead was the bridge. They could see the timbers faintly. The dark blotches beyond were the trees on the slope. The yawning caverns on the left were black shadows in the swamp. The silence fairly screamed its hidden menace. The breathing of the men sounded like wind. But there were no fires, no Whigs, nothing but darkness and cold and the dim white light of frost.

MacLeod and Campbell crept up the road, and the company, forgetting instructions, crept behind them. Duncan took down his rifle and dribbled powder into the pan. Others did likewise. He wanted to shoot the damned thing, according to orders, and drop it.

The officers stopped and peered in the dark. They hissed softly for silence. If Whigs hid in the brush, they were as quiet as the frost. There was no sound. The colonel and the captain crept forward again. Whigs or no Whigs, it took guts to invite bullets like that.

Then Scalpie straightened and laughed softly. "See?" he pointed. "There's their trench just beyond the bridge. Not a soul in it. They've gone!"

"Sh-h-h-h-h!" Colonel MacLeod was cautious. "Take care!"

They were at the bridge now, and Scalpie stopped and swore roundly. "They stripped the planks off!" He stepped on one of the naked, peeled-pine stringers and fell back with new oaths. "It's the slickest damned log I ever——"

But now he was giving attention to getting over. He stuck his broadsword point into the log and braced his steps against it. Mac-Leod did likewise. They warned the men behind them that the logs were slippery with soap and tallow. They could smell it now themselves. It would be slow getting over, but the Whigs had fled.

MacLeod and Campbell stepped off on the far side, and the head of the line marched up on the stringers to pick its way across. Everybody suddenly tensed. A figure dimly moved beyond the trench to call out:

"Hey, you-all! Who comes thar?"

"A friend!" answered Colonel MacLeod.

"A friend o' whose?"

"A friend of King George!"

Scalpie Campbell screamed like a preying animal: "King George and Broadswords! Highlanders, charge!"

Back in the pines a battery of bagpipes shrieked. The Highlanders yelled. The darkness thundered with the sudden tumult. The soldiers rushed for the bridge. They threw down their rifles without firing. They brandished their broadswords, but only to creep across the stringers. Duncan shoved and trampled frantically until he felt the timber under his feet.

Little points of light flashed up there in the woods. They were like fireflies. There were no lightning bugs in February, he remembered. It was a hell of a job walking this footlog. You stuck in your sword, braced your foot against it, and took another step and balanced while you pulled out your sword and stuck it in for another step.

Colonel Donald MacLeod was across, still near the bridge, but Scalpie Campbell was running up the slope, yelling like the devil. Everybody was yelling. Everybody was pushing and shoving. The bagpipes split your ears. The little specks of light came and went. It was a slow job, getting over. Damned Whig trick, greasing the stringers. He had a sudden throttling sense of alarm.

Something was wrong! It wasn't right! Something in his brain shrieked a warning. If they didn't yell so, and the bagpipes didn't scream so, and if those behind didn't push so, you could hear yourself think. But he hadn't time to think. He had to get over. Wrong or right, this was the first job.

Some of them couldn't hold their places and fell headlong into the freezing water. Duncan laughed, high, like a horse's whinny. They splashed like rafting logs. Some of them screamed when they went under. No wonder. That water was cold enough to blister you. Duncan laughed again and shut his mouth. His laugh sounded crazy.

Colonel MacLeod was walking around the head of the bridge like a dazed man, waving his arm. What was the matter up ahead? Any countryman could walk a footlog. What was Colonel Mac-Leod's trouble? He fell over, and got up and waved his sword, and damned if he didn't fall again.

"God damn it, Laughlan," Duncan shouted, half laughing, "don't jostle me like that!" Then he whooped. Laughlan Bethune tee-tered desperately and shot to the water, head down. Then Duncan was teetering, too, dancing and waving his arms, trying to stay upright, but Laughlan had knocked him off balance. Both heels slipped in the goo, and he went down standing up.

Duncan shrieked. His kilt ballooned, and the water rose under it like a knife circling his belly. His knees bent and his head went under. He stood straight and the water was under his chin. He yelled. He laughed. A pack o' loons, couldn't walk a footlog!

"Goddlemighty!" he protested, dodging. Half of them were slipping off. A clumsy fellow fell on him and knocked him under again.

He came up and the fellow stared straight in his face—dead. The churning water rolled the man over, and his arm crumpled and struck Duncan on the cheek.

Duncan stared, breathless, and another dead one fell and knocked him under. He dived out of the way and came up with a dead man across his shoulder. He fought to shed the limp thing. It was John MacArthur.

It had all happened in a moment. Duncan gripped himself. He was cold. Freezing cold. Cold inside. Colder than the water. He must hold himself. It was not true: this deluge of the dead and dying was not truth. No more than if a horrendous dragon drew across the hill breathing fire and smoke. He had gone crazy. He must get back his senses.

There was a little twinkle of lights back in the trees. He looked. There they were. Still flashing. Scalpie Campbell, tragically alone, was going toward them. Toward the upper yellow gash on the hillside. Charging toward the crackle of the winking lights. He was like a man running on air—long, slow, high-kneed strides, waving his sword, calling his men. No one followed him. And in the same slow motion he dived to the ground. He struggled up to his arms' length and then sprawled out, still.

Duncan strained to cry out. He could not. It was like a dream. His voice was a thin squeak. Nevertheless he lunged out to go to Scalpie. The icy water pushed against him. He could not rush. The mud on the bottom was deep ooze, and his feet slipped and tangled with roots. He lifted them to swim, and his overthrown arm went across a man's body. Kenneth Murchison moaned and sank under Duncan's pressure.

Duncan sprang back and caught Murchison and lifted him back to the surface. "Ken! Ken!" he cried. Murchison was bleeding at the throat. The blood spurted into the water and made it red. Duncan pushed on to the bank. He laid the clansman on the grass. He stood ready to spring, his arms out like a runner, ready to dash to Scalpie's aid or to spring back and rescue the drowning wounded. The field up the slope still was bare. Not a soul stirred upon it. Near the bridge Highlanders lay prostrate or writhed on the ground. Others struggled to get across the slippery stringers. Back of them the angry Scots pushed blindly and roared for those ahead to make way. But the two lines of men moved like snails. Some fell off. Some were shot off. Those who got across started running for the Whig breastworks and fell.

The water churned and clotted with the dead and the living. Duncan let the unhurt rescue the hurt and turned toward Scalpie. A tall soldier on the bridge teetered over him—a gangling, awkward fellow. He screamed and plunged. Malcolm, Mary's brother. He struck the water in a clear spot and went out of sight without another sound.

Duncan dived from the bank, grasped his clothing and stood up. Even so, strain on tiptoe as he would, he could not bring Malcolm's head to the surface. He plowed under blindly. He came up the opposite slope and laid him on the grass. Malcolm was dead. Undoubtedly. Duncan shook him and called him. But the bullet wound on his breast told too grim a tale. Duncan looked at his face, but his thought was not of Malcolm, but of Mary.

Up on the road the packed Highlanders crowded and raged. They did not yet understand the delay.

"Ye canna cross the bridge!" Duncan yelled to them. "Ye canna cross the bridge! Ye maun wade the creek!"

But it was like shouting in a storm. They couldn't hear him. Their own Gaelic roars smothered his voice. He barely could hear himself. He knew the way. He waved to them to follow. He struck for the water again. Nobody even saw him. Nobody came. He glanced toward Malcolm's body to mark it in his mind and plunged into the creek.

The dawn was still gray. What had seemed to him to be hours was not yet five minutes.

Duncan, waist-deep in the current, jerked and stopped. A thunderous explosion wiped out the crackle and roar of the conflict. He felt the concussion and quivered still.

Shrieks of pain came from the road. The whole cluster of Highlanders flew apart as though it, too, had exploded. It was the cannon. The Whigs had opened on the trapped men with grapeshot. The rifles had been murder, but the cannon was massacre. The fallen Scots screamed and twisted, but they were alone. The others had sprung to the roadside and lay on their bellies in the grass.

Except one man. Duncan recognized him. His name was Farearst Campbell, Farquard's cousin. He was not even in the advance guard, but had run up from behind. When the massed Scots leaped to the grass, they made way for him. He sprang upon the soapy logs, waving his sword. He ran all the way over, miraculously, like a winged man in the air. He called in a loud cry: "Scalpie!" There was a sob in his voice, a great, deep sob. "Scalpie!"

Duncan could see the bullets come through him, bursting tatters from the back of his jacket.

He ran halfway up the slope before he fell. His last sound was a strangled: "Scalpie!"

Duncan continued to stand still, for even before Far-earst had fully fallen, the Whigs charged, yelling, down the hill. He sank in the water up to his nose and watched. They came orderly enough, for Whigs, running in a good line, firing as they came and stopping to reload as the second line came in front. Alexander Lillington ran at their head, shouting like a madman. A detachment carried planks. Before the Scots had recovered from the cannon blast, the Whigs were on the bridge, relaying the floor. Some of the Highlanders, leaderless but unafraid, raced to them with swords, but fell on the way.

Duncan stood in the water, looking up the road, and moaned: "Oh!" Again and again "Oh!" As far back as he could see, the Scots were bursting from the line and running for the bushes, a mad rout. Nowhere did the line make a stand. The Whigs had broken across the creek higher up and had struck them on the flank. Nothing—nothing whatever—of MacDonald's proud Highland army was left. Not even the wagons, for all the horses, too, tore through the woods. Disgrace and shame had burst upon the clansmen.

As eager as he had been to stand beside Scalpie Campbell, the whole quick battle had ended with Duncan barely more than a spectator. He hadn't fired a shot. Few Scots had. They had marched into the trap to stand and be slaughtered helplessly.

The victorious Whigs raced across the bridge over his head, and Duncan turned and, pushing the half-floating corpses out of his way, slowly worked downstream until the bushes hid him. There was Malcolm. Even worse, there was Mary to face—to tell. He stood over the body and stared. He was numb. As numb as Malcolm. The Whigs might have seen him if they had looked. But they weren't looking for individuals. Up ahead they were taking the Highlanders by squads and companies. If they took him he wouldn't care. He wouldn't care if they did not. He had no feeling but an overwhelming numbness in his body and in his soul.

He took Malcolm in his arms, like a baby, and started home. The body seemed without weight. The morning had opened gray. And now it still was gray, gray with frost and death and defeat. His sodden clothes dripped cold water. So did Malcolm's.

He skirted the creek underbrush, moving downstream, away from the shouts and the shots to the right. Presently, moving as he was, he would be out of the area of action. The ground huckleberry bushes scraped their stiff branches against his shins, and the brier thorns raked his legs, but he did not notice.

The turmoil and the shouting raged nearer. The sound of a galloping horse drew his way. Duncan stepped into the shelter of small pines and looked. The horse, with three men astride it and one running behind, holding to its tail, burst through a slough, with the outdistanced Whigs running down the opposite hill, shooting and yelling. They gave up the chase and turned back. The horse, with its wagon harness flapping and rattling, charged on by, Colonel Cotten swinging desperately to its tail. Thus escaped what was left of Cotten's command.

Duncan turned into the pine forest, away from the little bushes which scraped and scratched him. But by now the yelling and the shooting were far to his right, and he needed the open ground. He was stumbling. The body suddenly was unbearably heavy.

Nevertheless he staggered on through the trees. He saw three empty turpentine barrels ahead, and they somehow gave him new heart. They were familiar. Something he always had recognized as helpful. They were screened from the conflict by the trees. He took his unwieldy burden to them. He laid the body on the brown carpet of pine straw and stood up to gasp and look.

In a minute a man burst through the trees and stared wildly about. He wore the tartan of the MacLeods, the same tartan that covered Malcolm.

"Alexander!" Duncan called in a loud whisper.

Colonel MacLeod, Anne MacDonald's husband, swung around, snatching at his dagger.

"Na! Na!" Duncan called. "I wi' not harm ye."

Alexander, his eyes flashing consternation, peered back through the trees. He strode over to Duncan, panting, too much out of breath to speak. He had taken a long run for a man more than fifty years old. His eyes fell on the body, and he looked at Duncan.

"Malcolm MacLeod—y'r cousin!"

"The first I knew," Alexander shouted, "the Whigs charged out of the bushes upon us, and my men——" He waved his arms. "Not a shot!"

Duncan said: "They got Scalpie Campbell!"

"What happened to Donald MacLeod? Did ye hear?"

"Dead. I saw him fa'."

"I'm headin' f'r the coast. Wi' ye go?"

Duncan's mind leaped at the idea. He could go to the coast—join Cornwallis, go to Nova Scotia, become a soldier in the British Army, march in strange places. He could escape the torment of facing Tom Brown and old Tom Hadley. He could escape the jibes and the sneers. But there was Mary. She would be alone. Flora had set her adrift, and her brother was dead.

"Na," Duncan said. "I wi' go home f'r what may betide."

Alexander MacLeod nodded. It was no time to argue. Each man for himself as he saw fit. He said: "Tell Anne and Flora that Allan and Alexander are unhurt, but captured. I dinna ken what may be done wi' 'em. Tell Anne she shall hear frae me the first opportunity."

This gave Duncan a flash of anger, for in some way not yet reasoned out he blamed Flora MacDonald for the disaster. He had taken her counsel, and this had happened.

There were new shouts beyond the sand ridge. Duncan and Alexander dashed for a pine thicket. They lay and peered out while a party of Whigs, gay and triumphant, marched rapidly by. They paused to see the strange sight of the water-soaked Malcolm on the straw, but they did not touch him.

When the Whigs had gone, they stood up. They paused, as if thinking what to say. They had no words. Not even thought. Only an overwhelming, nauseous sense of calamity.

"Weel," Alexander said, "I bid ye farewell." He turned toward the swamp. Duncan saluted in silence. He thought of Malcolm. He could not leave the body in the open. On account of the wolves. He could not bear it forty miles home. It was too heavy. The turpentine barrels would serve.

Fifteen minutes later he stood up, satisfied. The barrels, end to end, wedged between small trees, their heads, except the end two, bashed out, made a piny woods cairn that even wolves could not violate. Thus Malcolm could lie safely until he could return with the cart. Without looking back, Duncan struck out through the brush.

Home was far away, but there was nothing warming in the thought of home. The sun rose higher in the sky, but it was not a warm sun. It but gave him a sense of direction. He thought of nothing. His mind did not work. He stamped ahead, his feet pounding the soil, with nothing to tell him how far he went and nothing in him to care. He was cold and wet, but he gave that no heed.

The sun swung higher. He had the instinct to avoid the roads. Finally he came to the Black River. He knew that it was below its confluence with the South River. He swam over, and then knew that somewhere above, between the South and the Cape Fear, was his destination. There were no more rivers to cross, but there were a thousand sandhills and swamps. It did not matter. His clothes were dripping wet again, but that, too, did not matter.

That night, sometime—he did not know when, only that it was dark—he stamped upon Mary's little porch and dully said: "Mary!" She would not be asleep. She would be waiting.

Her voice tinkled inside. "Yes, Duncan."

She wore a tartan robe that covered her to her toes. She was holding to his arms, grasping him. "Ye're wet! And sae *cauld!*" Her eyes gleamed with fear. She was tugging at him, pulling him into the house. Minnie Meacham was kindling the fire. The little tongue of flame was struggling up from cold ashes. Mary was saying: "Hurry, Minnie! Oh, do hurry!"

He stared at Mary. He had to tell her. That was what he had come for.

"Sit down, Duncan!" Mary said, placing a chair behind him. "Sit down, Duncan, an' take off y'r wet shoon!"

Her hands pressed on his shoulders. He felt himself sink to the chair. The fire, feeding on fat pine splinters, grew big, and its sudden heat stung his bare legs. But his sunken eyes were on Mary, and he could not speak. He had to tell her about Malcolm. She was bustling about the room, hanging the screen of a blanket behind his chair that he might catch the full heat of the young fire.

"Malcolm," she said in a little voice, never ceasing to busy herself, "is—dead?"

A great surge of relief spread through Duncan.

"Aye!" he shouted. That was too loud. He shouldn't say it that way. "Aye," he repeated, whispering.

A sudden burst of strange sound answered him, like a dog howling. "Hush, Minnie," Mary was saying.

"I left him coopered in three barrels in the pine trees," Duncan said, staring woodenly into the fire.

Mary was silent, and he looked up at her. Minnie howled again, but Mary did not stop her. Mary's face was frozen in horror, and it dawned on him that she misunderstood.

"He is in one piece, and safe," he explained. "We maun go f'r him. I wi' go—ye needna."

"I wi' go wi' ye," Mary said.

"The Whigs"—Duncan now looked at the fire again—"riddled us."

She stood still, looking at him. She said nothing. Asked nothing. Her face was curiously pale. Her brown eyes were large and dry and dark. Minnie sat in the corner, sniffling.

"They tricked us at the Moore's Creek Bridge," Duncan said, himself thinking the thing out for the first time. "They killed off our officers and charged into us fore and flank before we knew to drop back and defend oursel's."

Mary reached out to grasp a chair. There was none. She sat on the floor, her great cloak rumpling around her. She looked into the fire and listened, as though from a great way off.

"Speak, Duncan!" she whispered.

"Moore's Creek," he said, in the same dull tone, "ran red wi' the blood o' Scots—like the pools o' Drummossie Moor."

"Are ye hurt, Duncan?"

"Na. The Whigs shot the Hielanders frae the bridge timbers, and they fell like squirrels fa' frae the trees."

"Minnie, please stay y'r snivelin'—make coffee."

"Some went tae the bottom and didna come up."

Duncan spoke to himself as much as to Mary. As the flashes of memory came, he spoke them aloud.

"I pulled Malcolm frae the water, but he ne'er spoke. Alexander MacLeod wasna captured, but Allan o' Killiegrey and his son were taken."

"Poor Flora!"

"Scalpie Campbell charged up the slope, wi' ne'er a clansman behind him. He shouted: 'King George and Broadswords!' but ne'er a broadsword split a Whig head. He stepped high and pitched to the ground."

Mary crawled over the hearth and swung the pot sling over the fire, putting the kettle into the blaze. Duncan looked down, and his legs were matted with the blood which had dripped from the brier scratches along the way.

"Weel," he said, standing up, "we maun go, Mary! Come to think o't, ye maun go, too. I dinna ken the intention o' the Whigs. They might take me on the way, but ye could drive Donald Bane back home. Tom Brown and Tom Hadley wouldna let them harm ye—surely."

But Mary only said: "Sit down, Duncan."

"But we maun be ganging, Mary. 'Tis a long way."

"Aye," said Mary, " 'tis a long, long way—but the living maun take precedence o'er the dead. Sit down, Duncan."

He did not know what she had said. It had the vague ring of common sense. She had said "sit down," and he sank back to the chair. She was washing the blood from his shins before he realized what she was doing.

"Na! Na!" he said, reaching for the rag. He took it and dabbed at the blood splotches and dropped the rag back in the basin. She recovered it and continued cleaning his cuts.

Minnie handed him coffee in a bowl, and he drank it without tasting it. It felt warm and good. Mary sat beside him in a chair and gave him a plate of food. He had no wish for it. She fed him, a mouthful at a time. He chewed and swallowed to get rid of it. It had no taste.

"Ye maun get in bed now," she said, "so we can dry y'r clothes."

"Na!" he protested, "we maun be ganging. Malcolm awaits us."
But he had no will to resist her. He undressed behind a blanket
and fell into the bed. The last he remembered she was drawing
the covers around his neck. But he neither slept nor remained
awake. He saw little flashes of fire in the darkness, and dead men
fell on him and splashed cold water. Whether it was memory or
dream he could not know, for he was numbed in his body and in
his mind and he was not asleep or awake. It was a dream when
Tom Owen and young John Hadley and Simon Hadley and
Andrew Beard gathered around him to sneer and jibe. That, yet,
had not come to pass. The soft sobbing beyond the blanket was
not dream, but Mary, drying his clothes.

CHAPTER 10

THE PALL OF CALAMITY was on Duncan still when he and Mary
drove the cart down the long, silent sand reaches toward Moore's
Creek. They had walked from Mary's cabin to his to get the horse.
Gillie Black had the wish to go with them, but Duncan thought to
say:

"Na. Ye wi' stay and keep the place. Ye wi' let no one see ye,
friend nor foe. When one comes ye wi' make secretly for the
swamp. I dinna ken what the Whigs may do, but I winna hae ye
confiscated."

They had not driven a mile before they saw a squad of soldiers
guarding the road. One of them left the group and started walking
toward them, carrying his rifle in his hand. It was old Tom Hadley.
Duncan watched him without changing expression.

"Let him come," he growled. "I wi' kill him. I wi' twist his
thrapple wi' my bare hands and pull it out by the roots. I wi'——"

"Hush, Duncan." He looked at her. She had not lifted her voice.
As though he spoke without sense. He said no more.

Tom wore his new authority carelessly, a gray old cuss, with
eyes still sharp and kindly.

"Hi, Dunk! Hi, Mary!" He greeted them as if nothing lay between them. "Mighty sorry about Malcolm, Mary."

"We go for him, now," she said.

"Yeah—well—it's the best thing to do. Lots o' them boys'll not rest in marked graves, I'm feared."

Duncan slapped the reins on Donald Bane's rump. "It's a long way," he said.

"Yeah. Well—wait up a minute, anyway. I got to talk to you about something. I got to disarm ye and give ye the oath."

"Aye. Ye did disarm me—at Moore's Creek. My sword's i' the mud at the bottom o' the stream."

"Um-huh. Well, that's that part. Now I got to swear ye in."

"I dinna ken y'r meanin'."

"We're goin' to make a Patriot out o' ye."

"Ye mean a Whig?"

"Yeah, um-huh."

"Na."

Mary leaned over and said: "Mr Hadley, please—can ye not wait until we come back? Duncan is sore distressed and I fear——"

"Now, Mary, you let this be. No tellin' who-all ye'll see before ye get back—and we better straighten this thing up right among the home folks."

"But I winna take y'r damned oath," Duncan said flatly.

"See?" Tom said to Mary. "I figgered he'd be like that. Suppose ye'd run into some o' them Kenans or Dicksons over in Duplin—they wouldn't stop to reason with 'im like me. They'd just take him, and no tellin' what would happen. Now me—I'm different. Me and Dunk used to be friends. He's just a bull-headed Scotchman, and if anybody knows the Scotch, I do. Git down offa that cart, Dunk. We got to talk this thing over. Man to man."

Duncan frowned, but Mary prodded him, and he and Tom Hadley walked out of hearing and stood in the sand and talked.

"Now—now—listen to me, Dunk. I'm your friend, understand? As fur as a man can be a friend to a Tory, understand? I know you ain't goin' to take no oath. If you did, you'd still consider your Scotch oath the biggest. Can ye keep a secret—just another secret between you and me?"

"Whatever I say, I'll do. Ye know that, Tom Hadley."

"Aye—well I do. Now, you just hold up your hand and I'll talk to you about the weather, so them boys will think you're taking the oath. That's all I ask. Then I'll give you a piece of paper that'll save you trouble wherever you go. All I ask you is to stay out of trouble, and if you feel like, sometime, you've got to fight the Patriots again—just come to me and tell me, first. Will you do that, Dunk?"

"Aye. I'll tell ye before I march again, Mr Tom. I know ye well eneugh to feel ye do me a favor. I am grateful—though I'll kill ye yet."

"Uh-huh. Well—I'd as soon it'd be you as anybody."

So Duncan held up his hand in the plain sight of the soldiers and Mary, while Thomas Hadley told him the best signs for fishing. Then he gave him a paper, certifying that he had been disarmed and had taken the oath of neutrality. Duncan did not realize then or for a long time how completely successful had been Tom Hadley's homely strategy.

They traveled all the day and all the night, stopping only long enough to eat and feed the horse and give him such rest as was necessary. They slept in the cart, first one driving and then the other. Now and then Mary gave way to fits of weeping, but mostly she was dry-eyed and silent, staring straight ahead.

It was nearly noon that Friday when they drove the cart back into Duncan's place. Duncan unhitched the horse to feed him in his own stable and rested the cart shafts on two up-ended barrels to keep the load horizontal.

Then, with a curious calm, he went to his stout house and took out two long pine planks—perfect planks, they were—and laid one of them on his workbench under a tree. Mary sat with the dead, on a box near the cart. Duncan had never made a coffin. He had seen fancy coffins, bulging out at the elbows, with little carved stanchions rising at the head and the foot. He wished he might make one for Malcolm, but he hadn't the skill—not today. Or the will to figure it out.

That evening they buried Malcolm in a grave in the sand on the second hill back of Mary's cabin. When Mary read a line from the Psalms they repeated it, Duncan and Gillie Black and Minnie Meacham. When Duncan and Gillie had rounded the yellow mound and had pushed two sticks in the ground to mark the head and the foot, Mary knelt and said a little prayer, and they all said

"Amen." They all walked back to the cabin. The war was over, so far as Malcolm, the schoolmaster, was concerned.

Far away, from somewhere beyond the woods, came the faint strain of Angus MacCooish's bagpipe. It was like a part of the mournful breeze that came out of the gloaming. He played the coronach, the old Highland dirge for departed greatness.

Duncan slept soundly that Friday night. He lay on his bed, and the dry, stifling sense of calamity continued to envelop him, but then he was asleep. He knew no more until noon Saturday. Gillie stood in the door, uncertain whether to awake him for food or to let him sleep. The Negro's smiling sympathy made him look to Duncan as a grinning black fiend, and he turned over on the other shoulder. He lay so; still; aching in his spirit; sore in his body. If he could go back to sleep—— He flung the cover back to the wall and sat on the side of the bed, his bare feet on the cold floor. He looked at them, not moving. His eyes stung and felt gritty. He felt as though his joints were dry. He knew that if he moved he would have body pains, a different one for each motion.

A jug of whisky sat on a shelf across the room from him. He looked at it with a flash of interest. And then away. Liquor couldn't change the thing that had brought on his soreness. He stepped across the room and filled a cup and drank it in one long draught.

His philibeg was on the floor, where he had dropped it last night. The sight of it gave him anger, and he kicked it to the back of the room. He reached for his homespun trousers and wool jacket. Gillie brought him coffee and eggs. He drank another cup of liquor first. He ate the food and drank the coffee and then took his jug and his liquor cup and went up to his stout house and sat on a sill. He looked on the swamp and drank liquor until dark. When he arose he was as sober as when he had sat down.

It now was Saturday and five days since the battle. The defeat and the desolation which had come to him had not ceased. Daylight and dark were the same. He threw himself upon the bed, and his body, shrieking for surcease from the torture, drew down the veil of sleep once more. He slept for hours. When he awoke it was still dark, but whether it was the same night or another he did not know. The fire was on the hearth. Gillie was sleeping in front of it, keeping it burning until his master should burn his way through the turmoil. Duncan went to his jug and drank a cupful. It burned and stung him going down, and made him gag, which was the nearest to normal he had felt since the battle.

He flung open the door and stood in it, looking out. He heard a noise, and in a little while three men came up, with bags on their backs.

"Dunk!" they called, guardedly. "Anybody here?"

"Na. Who is it, and why d'ye na come to the door?"

It was the Ross boys. They had been in Leggett's company. They lived beyond the lake to the east, where there were many Whigs.

William Ross, the eldest, came up and set his bag down. "We're headin' for Brown's Marsh. We're goin' to lie out," he said.

"Aye. And why?"

"We ain't goin' to take no damn Whig oath. Damn 'em! We'll lie out until Cornwallis comes and jine up again."

"Cornwallis?" Duncan frowned. In all these days he had not thought of Cornwallis.

"Ain't you lyin' out, Dunk?"

"Na. I'm just back. I've na had time tae think."

"Did ye git captured?"

"Na."

"Well, damn nigh half of 'em did. They even got General Mac-Donald—but I reckon you heard that."

"Na."

"Well—so long, Dunk. We got to be hittin' the grit if we get to Brown's Marsh before daylight."

They moved off into the darkness, and Duncan looked after them until they disappeared. Cornwallis, hell! Cornwallis wasn't coming. If he had been, he'd have been there when he was needed.

Tom Brown came by the next day. He had six riflemen with him. But they stayed on their horses a hundred yards away while Tom came over, alone and unarmed.

"Got a drink, Dunk? God, I'm dry!" He spoke heartily, but with a wary look.

Duncan did not answer but looked at him without speaking. He turned inside the cabin, however, because hospitality was an instinct, and even an enemy might have a drink if he asked for it. They drank together in silence, Duncan bitterly.

"Damn!" Tom was amiable. "You fellows cert'ny did a piece o' marchin' through here. I was with Moore at Rockfish, and we tried to head you off—but, hell, when we got here you were slap outa the neighborhood."

Duncan shrugged.

"I spect you're pretty sore, Dunk," Tom sympathized. "Still, hell is hell and war is war. Don't take on any more hard feelin' than you must. God help us, an' we'll be friends again someday."

"Ye wouldna," Duncan's voice strangled, and he raised his hands helplessly, "let good enough alone!"

Brown chuckled in agreement. "Maybe. We're that breed o' dogs, I reckon. Slick notion, eh, greasin' them stringers on Moore's Creek Bridge? Tom Rowan thought it up."

"I hope then," Duncan said dully, "that he chokes to death."

"But that saved a lot of lives, Dunk. Lots of 'em. If them boys had a-got to each other with bayonets and broadswords, they'd have killed hundreds—yes, sir, hundreds and hundreds. As it was, you-all didn't lose fifty dead, and we didn't lose but one."

Duncan lifted his head. There wasn't anything for him to say. Fool talk. He started to walk.

"Wait, Dunk. Let's forget the damn war. Course I've got some little duties to see to. They've made me a sort of ringleader in the district."

Ringleader? Who had said something about a ringleader? Aye—General Donald MacDonald. He had said the Whig ringleaders would go to the firing squad. "Humph!"

"Well," Tom Brown boasted, laughing defensively, "I'm as good as they've got."

"I was thinkin' o' something else," Duncan explained.

"Did Tom Hadley see you? I told him to."

"Aye, he gie me a piece o' paper."

"Good! That's all I wanted to know."

"What's comin' next, Tom?"

"I hate to think, Dunk." Tom Brown shook his head, and there was no smile in his eye. "This thing started with neighbor killin' neighbor. I pray God it don't wind up the same way—specially in Bladen."

Duncan scowled. He lifted his hands as before. "But ye wouldna——"

"Yeah, I know: let good enough alone. Let's have another drink, for auld lang syne."

Tom Brown spoke no more of the war. He spoke of horses.

"You and I," he laughed, as though there were no conflict, "got to have that horse race some o' these days."

The Whigs left soon, continuing their damnable overlording of the Loyalists. Duncan sat gloomily and watched them go. He did not stir from the place for nearly a week and then remembered that he had promised Alexander MacLeod he would report his escape to Anne.

He went neither to Killiegrey nor to Glendale, but beyond Cross Creek to Barbecue Kirk. The Reverend John MacLeod was to preach a sermon to the Highlanders in their dark hour, and all would be there.

The cold little oblong church, built by that most violent Whig, the Reverend James Campbell, who had refused even to baptize a Tory baby, was filled with Scots when Duncan arrived. He was barely able to get in. Few noticed him. They were repeating a Psalm when he pushed through and found standing room against the wall.

Preacher MacLeod was commandingly in the pulpit. He was known to dread these services at Barbecue Kirk. He had said that he'd rather preach to the most polished congregation in Edinburgh than to these critical little old Scots whose ears always were alert for false notes of doctrine.

Duncan looked until he found Flora MacDonald near the front. She was with Anne. Flora had sharp lines on her face. Bitterness and grief had cut her deep, but her head was still proud and her eyes were undaunted. He was soothed by seeing her. They couldn't put her down—neither could they him.

The Psalm ended, and the people rustled back to the bare benches. The preacher then offered the short prayer, and in it was the recurring thought: "O ye of little faith!" Duncan wondered, hearing Mr MacLeod calling on the Lord with such authority, if it wouldn't have been better had he, instead of the young Preacher Bethune, been at the Battle of Moore's Creek.

After that was the reading of the Scripture, and a hymn, and the announcements of the funeral sermons for those who had been buried. Then the people stood for the long prayer.

The preacher prayed for the courage and strength of the Almighty to enter upon the land, to stiffen the hearts of the people against rebellion and the blandishments of the ungodly and the unorthodox. He prayed for King George, he prayed for the clans of Scotland, that not one member should forget the honor of his oath to make it strong. He prayed long and loud and had reached that peak of beseeching which the initiate recognized as the point where he had started to "pray downhill" to the end—when came a new sound, and the congregation stiffened. All by that time knew it. It was the tramp of soldiers and the knock of the hubs of army wagons. A break came in the preacher's voice as he both tried to listen and to pray.

Whigs! No Highlanders, beaten as they were, could march now. The tenseness writhed through the worshipers, but the preacher held them still. His voice mounted. No one listened for what he prayed. Perhaps he did not know himself. But his great voice rose high and pitched supplication upon supplication to the Great Throne, while instinctively the people remained still, held in the attitude of prayer. Few even dared to cut their eyes out the windows. Duncan did. Soldiers were moving among the shivering horses, almost surrounding the church. They wore bucktails in their hats, if more were needed to make them known as Whigs. They leaned on their rifles and respectfully were still while the preacher prayed and prayed.

The prayer went on and on, for in it was safety. At its end, who knew what?

But even prayers must cease. That one did with three lingering "amens." Preacher MacLeod dismissed his congregation. He had preached no sermon, but it might be assumed that he could not preach the sermon he had prepared, with a company of Whig soldiers surrounding him.

The congregation began to dribble from the door. Men only. And few men. Duncan was among them. Preacher MacLeod pushed his way out soon. Colonel Richard Caswell met him with bared head and extended hand. But the preacher did not see the hand.

"Our mission is unpleasant, but necessary," Caswell said courteously. "We are under orders to prevent the carrying of arms. That is our purpose and, having seen to that, we wish you to look upon us as warmly as you will as friends and fellow countrymen. We permit ourselves none of the excesses of victory, and you may assure yourselves that no harm will be done you."

He extended his hand again, and Mr MacLeod took it and opened his mouth but for the moment could say nothing. Finally he said: "My dear sir—my dear sir."

The sincerity of the Whig conquerors was too evident for the men and women of the congregation to be long afraid. The soldiers accompanied the men to their carriages and rigs and collected a few pistols and one or two rifles, but there was nothing significant of an armed gathering.

The women gathered around Colonel Caswell. He was one of the heroes of Moore's Creek, and the news of his gallantry had preceded him. They asked him anxious questions as to the welfare of this one or that of the Tories who had not returned. More than six hundred had been captured. As far as he could he gave the names of the dead, both those who had fallen at Moore's Creek and those who later had died in Wilmington under the treatment of Dr Cobham.

"And when you captured General Donald MacDonald," a bristling little old Scot with hard, cold eyes and white hair demanded, "did ye hae trouble takin' him?"

Dick Caswell paused and spoke carefully. His mission was to make peace as well as disarm the clansmen. He knew the Scottish tradition that the chief was not to be taken until the human ring around him had gone down in slaughter. For the clansmen of old to do less for their chief was disgrace.

"Well, no," Caswell said frankly. "We found General Mac-Donald the day after the battle. He was at the farmhouse where he was taken sick. He still was sick. He was quite alone when we found him. He showed his commission to us and offered no resistance. We gave him such attention as we could."

Some of the old Scots in the circle looked actually ill.

"Not a man? Not one clansman tae defend him?" They were aghast.

"General MacDonald," Dick Caswell said, "is a very brave man. My impression," he lied gallantly, "was that he dismissed his guard, ordered them home, to escape capture."

"*Ochan! S' ma leon!*" wailed one of the ancient sires, turning away to hide his shame. Colonel Caswell had fooled no one, but he did captivate the Scots in trying to shield their disgrace.

For Flora MacDonald, Colonel Caswell had a deep bow, and she, in her turn, was no less gracious.

"May I hope, now, madam," he asked, "that we all may hence-forth work together for the happiness of our land? There is great division and great grief, and a divided leadership delays the process of restoring contentment."

It was a bold bid for Flora's support, and the Scots, including Duncan, leaned forward to see how she would take it.

"We must all pray God," she said, "for the wisdom and the courage to stay i' the right."

"Indeed, that is true!" Caswell said eagerly, seeming to sense in Flora's words a weakening. That came from the Whig accusation, weeks before the battle, that the MacDonalds were trading their influence to the Crown for princely reward. But the Scots, hearing her, knew that she merely parried words. Caswell thought, they knew, that since the MacDonald's original plan was broken they would seek the next best bid. That was quite plain now. The Scots saw clearly and settled back on their heels. Caswell would press his point and next would be back on *his* heels.

"Then, madam, let us have a conference soon—you, Chairman Harnett, Maurice Moore, others of us—and study the situation."

The Scots shifted their eyes from Dick Caswell to Flora. He had misunderstood.

Flora was quite magnificent. She was feminine, sweet of voice, calm of eye, but her manner left no doubt with Caswell or with the Scots. "Ye have been most gracious, Colonel Caswell. Please do not press us where we cannot be equally so."

Caswell's eyes opened with surprise, but he was quick to re-cover. He must raise no issue. He bowed. His acquiescence was reluctant, for the gaining of Flora MacDonald would have been a great gain, but he accepted the situation. The Patriots had defeated the broadswordmen, but they had not yet defeated Flora Mac-Donald.

Scots scattered from the cold and dreary kirk, those from distances going to the homes near by for dinner. Flora and Anne went to the house of one of the Camerons, and Duncan went with them. At all the tables that day there was an exchange of news—how Scalpie Campbell had died, how the clansmen had fallen into the creek, how, leaderless, they had scattered to the woods, how Governor Martin had failed the clansmen in his great promises, how this wife and that sweetheart and these children were desolated as the list of the dead became known.

One of the Cameron boys rode Donald Bane, and Duncan rode in the carriage with Flora and Anne. Anne had tried to get to him since church was out, but the crowds had prevented.

"Do you know anything of him? Have you heard anything?" Anne was beautiful, too, when white-faced and pleading.

"Aye, I know a'," Duncan said. "He is safe."

"Oh, thank God," she said, half weeping. "I have heard everything—that he was killed, that he was captured, that he escaped."

"I saw him at the swampside," Duncan said, "while the rout was still on. He was makin' his way to the governor's ship. He said for me to tell you. He will communicate wi' you when he can."

"Oh, thank God! Thank *God!*" She wept completely.

"I didna see Allan, neither did I see Alexander," Duncan said to Flora.

"I hae heard," she said simply. "They are in prison—up the State, in Halifax. God wi' keep them."

At the dinner that day Duncan's story was a monologue. He began at the point where he had left Flora on her white horse, while the bagpipes were still screaming in Cross Creek and the Highland march out was on. He told why he had gone to Mary, and how Mary had urged him to rejoin the clans. Flora listened with pained eyes but made no effort to stop him. He told it in no sense of revenge. It was a part of the story, and there were worse parts to come. He told of the march and General MacDonald's illness, and the quarrel among the officers, and of Malcolm MacLeod's running up to join the advance guard. He told about Scalpie Campbell's death and Donald MacLeod's, of how he saved those whom he could from drowning.

It was a long story, and everyone had finished eating and the food was cold when he ended it. They sat for a long time in silence and thought upon what he said. Then, one by one, they got up from the table and went out. Duncan went with them. The little old carls, their white hair flaring, their eyes glittering, gathered under the trees to dispute most bitterly on why the march out went awry.

Flora MacDonald later in the chill afternoon decided to spend the night there. Duncan decided to go home. Flora put a plaid shawl about her head and walked with him down the lane.

"I wanted to speak wi' ye alone," she said. "I wish ye to bear to Mary my supplications for forgiveness. I was proud then, and vauntie. God has seen fit tae bring upon me grief and humbleness. I hae been punished sorely f'r my sins o' vanity. 'Twas God's will to humble me, and I am maist gratefu' to Him. I still hae the sense o' bein' i' the right in servin' the Crown—and sae maun ye, Duncan."

"Aye, Flora. I do. More than before."

"That is good. Be sure to plead my cause wi' Mary, and make her forgie me. Tell her, if she can, tae come to Killiegrey and comfort me in this, my hour o' loneliness and peril."

"Peril, Flora? Peril?"

"Aye, Duncan. Who can say, now that they hae tasted blood, what atrocities are on the way?"

"But Richard Caswell and Cornelius Harnett and James Moore and Francis Nash, they wi' na permit——"

"Duncan, listen. This is revolution—bloody, blind, irresistible revolution. The country is rotten wi' it. No man and no set o' men can make it cease or turn its course. There is only one way, and that is for the King to quench it wi' the blood of those who spread the fire. If he can."

"But, Flora——"

"Within the twalmont ye shall see. America will attempt to split away frae the Crown and be independent. The Crown wi' na permit it, o' course, but before order is restored ye shall see human slaughter to make ye sick, Doon-kan. Wae's me, that I e'er came tae the land." Tragedy sat upon Flora MacDonald's face, and grief was in her voice. "Moreover, here in Carolina, as ye wi' see y'rsel', the tide o' wrath wi' rise higher and higher, and neighbor wi' turn upon neighbor. There wi' be houses tae burn and men tae hang and women tae mourn and hae their grief run o'er roughshod."

"But, by the Almighty, Flora, ye see through the eyes o' grief, darkly. Ye speak like the Whigs, puffed up wi' their brief glory and seein' monstrous victories ahead. This distemper will clear quickly when the King——"

Flora placed her hand on his arm. Her hand trembled.

"Doon-kan, I hae seen the 'Forty-five frae beginnin' to end. I ken how rebels feel. We now are but at the beginnin'.'"

"Be ye right, then so be it. When the time comes I wi' drag the bottom o' Moore's Creek for my broadsword."

"Aye. Ye canna help it. 'Tis the call o' the oath."

"Aye." Duncan drew his breath between his teeth and snorted. "Flora—the damned Whigs! They wouldna let well enough alone!"

Flora shrugged and smiled wanly, as in a weak effort to throw off the subject. "Perhaps," she said, "my doleful predictions wi' na come true sae soon. The Whigs seem minded to be courteous yet. In the meantime, ye see tae Mary."

"I wi', Flora. Perhaps now she wi' hate the Whigs who misguided her and killed her brither."

"Na." Flora shook her head. "Na. Mary knows her mind. I hae the soul o' a rebel at times, too. She has the consciousness o' right, and she wi' stay firm, though it tear her heart out—as it did tear her heart out when she sent ye back to the standard." She sighed tremulously. "Duncan! This coming time too much brings its horrors to me in advance! I fear for my strength tae be tested by it." Flora MacDonald permitted herself that brief bit of human fear and then lifted her chin and turned around. "But whate'er betide," she said firmly, "we maun divine the right and abide to't."

They walked on the dead grass between the rail fences back

toward the house. The chill wind flowed against their faces. Flora's eyes had thoughts beyond Duncan's ken. Her left hand held the tartan shawl at her breast, her right fondled the little round locket of gold at her throat. Duncan struggled with a thought.

"Ye shall hae no fear f'r y'r strength, Flora," he boasted, feeling boyish. "The Cape Fear Hielanders winna fail ye."

"Doon-kan!" She put her hand on his arm, but they could speak no more until they reached the house.

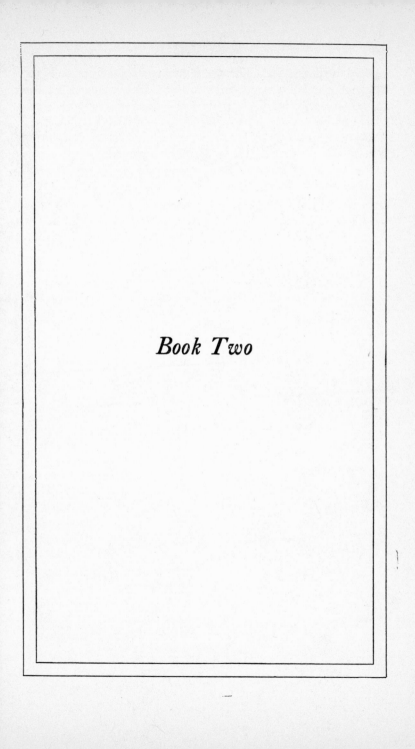

Book Two

CHAPTER 1

ALL THAT HOT SPRING MORNING the Whigs had chased him, and now it was high noon—Saturday, May 4. It was but sixty-seven days after the bitter frost of Moore's Creek, and Duncan hid and sweated in a cave of honeysuckle vines in Brown's Marsh. He was on his way to war again—for the Crown, for Flora MacDonald, for his way of life. The Whig horses stamped and splashed and rattled the brush, sometimes not more than a plow line's length away. Barely breathing, he stood in the moss with Donald Bane's head in his arm, rubbing his nose to keep him quiet.

The Whigs had been hard upon him this last half-hour. Except for Loyal liers-out and their aid, he would have been captured. The Ross boys and others hiding in the swamp sprang to the creeks, muddying trails in all directions, and confused them. Even so, the Whigs left no opening for his escape, and he held still while the horsemen beat the bushes. The littlest Ross lad lay in the vines to help him watch. Tom Brown plunged down the trail, splashing mud. There was no mistaking him. He rode harder, shouted louder, laughed longer than the rest.

"A yearling calf to the man that takes him!" Tom howled. "We haven't let a damn Tory through yet, and this is no time to start."

Duncan, as tense as he was, smiled shortly. He rubbed Donald Bane's nose the more, and the nag, as if himself knowing the need for silence, merely pricked his ears toward the shouts. A bonnie fellow, Donald Bane. Given a fair break, they'd make it yet.

They had done well, anyway. Already twenty miles from home, with, mayhap, fifty miles more of swamps and pine levels and sandhills and they would be safe. Safe with Cornwallis, at the mouth of the river. Safe with the British fleet which crowded the channel. For all his doubting and glooming, the Crown's forces had come. The days of the Whigs were numbered, thank God.

Duncan had heard of it last night at his cabin. A messenger had hailed him at the door. Duncan had stepped out and grabbed him by the collar and shaken him. "Ye lie!" he had shouted in the fellow's face. "I'll wring your neck! Ye're a Whig spy to search out the Loyal!" But the man had told him not to be a fool, but to go—Governor Martin had sent for him.

Duncan had slept out in sight of Tom Hadley's house on Carver's Creek. He had awakened old Tom before daylight to give back his parole paper, according to pledge, and then had galloped away, laughing. Old Tom had had a fit. He had yelled and sworn. He had blasted his hunting horn to give the alarm. After that Duncan had dodged Whigs all the morning—into swamps and out, across pine levels, with rifle bullets smacking into the trees to his right and left. They had always headed him off. They knew the country. Give him an open road and Donald Bane and he asked but half a chance. Tom Brown had the only horse to match him.

The Ross lad squirmed excitedly under the vines. He was as muddy as a turtle.

"They're leaving," he whispered. "Up the swamp. You can git out now."

Duncan nodded.

"We fooled 'em," the lad grinned. "They think you went yon way."

They waited. The Whig horses splashed up the creeks. Presently the sound of their going grew dim, except for an occasional shout. The two still waited, for the Whigs were tricky. It might be a trap. The Ross boy crawled out for a look around and said all was clear.

Duncan, muddy from head to foot, picked his way through the brush to the highland and waved farewell to the boy. Aye, here was freedom! In a few more hours he would be out of the Bladen Whig centers and approaching Brunswick. Donald Bane still was fresh and eager. He broke into a swift, long-reaching run over the grass. Duncan gave him the rein, and he sped through the open pines. It felt good. Duncan's shirt bloused out behind, and his hair pulled at his scalp as it straightened in the wind.

Duncan went a mile before he found a road. As he turned into it, he looked over his shoulder. Tom Brown and three militiamen bore down on him, galloping not two furlongs behind.

Duncan shrieked, and Donald Bane quivered into a knot beneath him. The nag came alive with a new urge. His nose went straighter, as if reaching for more distance than his pumping legs could attain. It was as if Donald Bane knew now that the long-delayed race had come and that his master's life was the forfeit. Duncan leaned to it. Horseflesh gave and horse heart gave, and quarter-miles flowed under the crackling hoofs as if jerked through.

The road was firm, with a bare blanket of sand to make a cushion. Donald Bane's burst of speed was so plunging that Duncan did not look back for more than a mile. When he did there was only one horseman in sight, Tom Brown. The other two had dropped out. Donald Bane had moved up beyond the range of Brown's bullets, but that was all, and Jess held his own.

Ahead was a straight green road as far as Duncan could see. The limp young oak leaves walled the King's Highway like silken patches. They made a hush, and the muffled hoofbeats rumbled down the verdant avenue like faraway guns. Duncan had loved Donald Bane, but now the horse between his legs was his own flesh and life. His urges and the horse's urges were one. The pounding on the ground was in rhythm with the thumping in his heart, and the swaying flow of Donald Bane's back was like the rushing, fighting flow of his own spirit.

Almost, Duncan forgot his own danger. The beast's magnificent spurt, his long, driving bolt which showed no sign of ceasing called to something in his soul, and for that moment he gave over to the consuming thrill of the race between the two horses.

The road was fairly good, and for three miles the race held so even, at breakneck speed, that if there was a step's gain or loss it was not discernible.

Whigs were on the road, but Duncan overtook them and passed

them before they heard Tom Brown's warning shouts. It was as though they were not on the road at all. At one of the farmhouses a man came galloping down the lane, laying the timber to his horse, but before he could join the race both Duncan and Tom Brown were beyond him.

It could not keep up. The pace was ruinous to the horses. Duncan knew now that Donald Bane could speed down the road for more miles yet. He would go on and then cough and stagger and die. Horseflesh could not stand it. Most horses would quit before they were in that danger. But Donald Bane would not, and perhaps Jess would not. Game horses plunged until something burst in their hearts, and then they were dead.

He rounded a bend in the road and, on sudden impulse, leaped to the ground and drove Donald Bane into the brush. Then Duncan climbed into the thick leaves of a hickory which hovered over the trail, daring, unarmed, to settle the matter there.

If it was foolhardy, Duncan gave it no thought. If his half-schemed plan failed to work instantly, he was helpless. There, already in sight, was Tom Brown's red-bearded face, hot and hunting. Tom, alarmed at the suddenly empty road, jerked the bridle rein, and just as Jess shot under the tree he reared high. Duncan pitched down across Jess's back, dragging Tom Brown to the ground with him.

Duncan had one priceless clock-tick of surprise in his favor. That was all. Brown was as strong as he and as ready. Even before they hit the sand they were fighting, and Jess fled with his stirrups dangling.

Tom Brown clouted Duncan's face with his fist while they were yet in the air, but that was as nothing to the shock when their heads struck earth and bent their necks and smacked them flat. Duncan had what he wanted. He had thought of nothing else. When one arm spread out to snatch Brown from the saddle, his fingers had gripped the handle of Tom's dirk. Even as he struck the ground he whirled, and when Brown shrieked and jerked to rise, Duncan's eyes glared down into his not a foot away. Tom's eyes were killing eyes.

"Ware, Tom Brown!"

Brown gasped in his face, and his body grew hard to lunge. But he held his madness, and his eyes narrowed. Duncan felt Tom's hand feeling for his knife.

"Yield, Tom Brown! I'll kill ye!"

"Kill and be damned, you bastard!" Tom Brown was wild and helpless and defiant. His knife was gone, and he felt its point pricking at his throat.

"I wouldna kill ye. Yield!"

They glared, and the fire of courage flashed like sparks from eye to eye, and death hovered there and waited.

Then Tom Brown fell back limp on his shoulders and laughed. He laughed loud, and Jess, the horse, turned in the road where he had stopped and looked around.

"I give up," Brown said.

"On y'r word?"

"On my word." Tom's face was redder than the sunset with rage and shame, but his word was good.

Duncan stood up and drew a long breath. It was well.

Tom got up, spitting sand.

"My day will come," he promised.

Duncan grinned.

"Ye've had your day, Tom. It's over."

They whistled for their horses, and the horses came. Fine horses, Jess and Donald Bane. Both of them still panted and heaved at their flanks, but they came, ready to start the race again.

Tom Brown mounted Jess and walked him back toward home. Duncan stood beside Donald Bane to let him pant. A quarter-mile away Tom Brown laughed. Duncan turned and Brown still laughed, raising his arm. Duncan waved and drew into the saddle.

He was a long way yet from Fort Johnston. There was the Loyalist in Upper Brunswick who would care for Donald Bane and return him to Bladen. And there were James Moore's ten thousand Whig troops to dodge as he footed it through the swamps. Aye, he was a long way from Fort Johnston.

It was late Friday afternoon before Duncan, mud-covered, disreputable-looking, stood in the bushes and looked through upon the British camp. His heart thumped at the glory of it. He forgot to be resentful that the British had failed him at Moore's

Creek. He wished to cry out for pure joy. There, where less than a year ago he had seen Fort Johnston as a whipping yellow mountain of fire, with jeering Whigs where he now stood, ranged row on row of tents. Redcoats by the thousand, literally thousands of British soldiers, loafed in their streets. Now! Now, Tom Brown! Now, Tom Hadley! He was free. Free to help wipe out the stain. Free to make the Whigs of Bladen pay—aye, pay!—in groans and humility.

"Come art!" said a voice behind him. He whirled, and four bayonets held on his belly. Four redcoats pointed them. Their faces were disgusted and pained, as though they marched with sand in their shoes.

"But——" Duncan spread his hands. He laughed. This was good. "I am Loyal. I came to join the——"

"March!" The wooden-faced one nodded his head.

"But, damn it! I winna be——"

"March! Ye will tell it to Colonel Tarleton," and they hustled him across the sand and into a tented street. Soldiers stared at them as they went past. They went into a tent bigger than the others. The soldiers saluted and came to attention before a smart, youthful officer sitting at a table.

" 'E was skulkin' in the lines, sir!" the soldier said.

The turbulent little colonel stood up and stamped. His black eyes barely saw Duncan, but lashed out at matters more pressing.

"Damn it! When will we get some *horses* in this hellish camp?" he shrieked. "Sand!" he shrilled at the redcoats and beat the table furiously. "Sand! Sand in your boots! Sand in your hair! Sand in your food! Sand in your teeth and in your•bed! When will we get some *horses?*"

Duncan looked at him uncomfortably, neglecting his own anger. And curiously. The petulant young man, no more than twenty, had the imperious black eyes and the fine, smooth skin of a woman. His dark face had the flashing beauty of a woman. But there his femininity stopped, for Colonel Banastre Tarleton had the short, wedgelike, spring-steel body of a horseman. He pounded his palm with his fist. His fist was heavy for his size. His fine russet turn-down boots, halfway up his thighs, squeaked under his pent-up twisting. Tarleton. The man who should live to boast that he had killed more men and raped more women than any man in America.

"Who is he?"

"We found him spying on the camp, sir."

Tarleton looked at Duncan for the first time. A hot, jarring look. "Muddy swine! Take him out and shoot him. Report that he resisted."

"Ye—yes, sir!"

The soldier touched Duncan with his bayonet. Duncan thrust it aside angrily, addressing Tarleton.

"Ye're a hasty fool, ye ramstam knurlin! Ye will report tae——"

"When you address me, yokel, say 'sir'!"

"Then ye say 'sir' when ye talk t' me." Duncan spoke quietly to hold his ire.

"You're speaking to a colonel!"

"Then act like a colonel!" Duncan bellowed. "I am a Stuart, but I do na hold mysel' too good t' speak to a fledgling sojer—e'en ye failed tae come when ye were needed."

The four soldiers already at attention snapped still more so, like horses jerked by a rough hand. Tarleton's lips quivered thin, but something in Duncan's shout bade him see to his own dignity.

"Shoot me—Duncan Stuart!" Duncan spat on the ground. "I'm here to see Lord Cornwallis!"

"You're a Whig spy, and you'll be shot like a dog!"

"I'm to see Lord Cornwallis wi'out delay, and I'm weary o' your——"

Tarleton flung his arm and turned to his chair. "Take him away!" But what might have happened did not, for Governor Martin, silk-hatted and black-coated, came in at the moment and, after a staring instant of disbelief, fell upon Duncan with joyous cries.

"You're a godsend! A godsend!" Martin shouted. "You're the first to get through the Whigs in a month!"

Tarleton sneered. "No trouble for your muddy friend, Governor! We caught him spying the camp."

Martin shook his head impatiently. "You have information?" he asked Duncan anxiously.

"I dinna ken," Duncan said doubtfully. "I hae seen Whigs. I hae o'erheard them talk. I saw their camp. They boast ten thousand ill-trained militiamen."

"What?" The impetuous Tarleton, in new mood, leaped over the table and stood before Duncan, almost quivering. "Ten thousand? Did they have *horses?* Did they——"

"I hae told ye," Duncan said quietly, "to notify Lord Cornwallis that I am come t' see him."

Duncan felt most proud and uncomfortably disreputable in his working clothes, powdery with dried mud, as they escorted him down the streets of tents. Officers greeted them, and redcoats came to salute as Governor Martin and Tarleton hurried him along as a person of consequence.

Sailors waited for them at the wharf, and they stepped into a small boat. "Flagship!" Tarleton ordered.

Duncan was fascinated. Ship spar against ship spar tangled the sky. It looked like nothing so much as a burned-over swamp with bare tree limbs bristling nakedly.

"Now! Now, by God!" Duncan whispered. "Now!"

He counted the ships, enormous, powerful hulls sitting on the water. There were so many that he gave up counting. Great battleships, the *Bristol* with fifty guns, and the *Experiment* with fifty guns, and others with forty and thirty-six and twenty-eight, looming magnificently over the others that cluttered the channel.

Overhead sailors leaned on the rails and looked negligently down upon them as the rowboat scuttled through like a minnow among whales.

An hour later Duncan was almost exhausted with the grilling. The mud on his clothes now was a badge of honor as he recounted his exploits in coming through the Whigs. He was important. His words carried weight. The anxious faces of gold-braided high officers waited on him to speak. And Duncan, too, was anxious, for it seemed to him suddenly that the whole course of the British campaign depended upon what he said. The officers were divided, just as the clan leaders had been divided in Cross Creek at the Highland march out. Desperately he fought the idea, but it was coming to him that many of the British were anxious to give up the campaign. They talked of sailing away, of not fighting —of leaving the Cape Fear to the Whigs. But, na—they couldna. It was unthinkable.

They faced him; Governor Martin, nervously. His face twitched, urging him to say the right thing. Governor William Campbell, of South Carolina, sat glowing with half-concealed satisfaction. Governor Campbell had fled Charleston as Martin had fled New Bern. He wanted the British to invade South Carolina instead of the Cape Fear. Sir Henry Clinton, commander in chief, looked on gravely. Sir Peter Parker, the admiral, barked fierce questions. Lord Cornwallis spoke quietly, but his words were those of authority. Colonel Willis Webster and a dozen staff officers grouped behind the heavily braided ones. Duncan found himself, regardless of who asked the questions, addressing his anxious responses exclusively to Cornwallis. It seemed to him that when the final decision to go or stay was spoken, the earl would speak it.

Lord Cornwallis had blue and contented eyes, a full face but one of firmness. He had the big belly of an easy liver, but he had power. He was not yet forty, and he took on none of the pompousness of his more elaborately uniformed associates. He leaned back, thinking.

"Oh, my horses!" Tarleton exploded enthusiastically. "Ten thousand clodhoppers to ride down and cut to pieces! *Ten thousand!* Give me my Legion and my orders, *sir!*"

Governor Martin beamed at the prospect.

"I wi' ride wi' ye," Duncan said grimly. The sight of Tom Brown's bearded face, glaring unbeaten into his, flashed in Duncan's mind. Turning to Cornwallis, he demanded: "We wi' herd them to Moore's Creek! We wi' wipe out the blot!"

Cornwallis rubbed his face bemusedly, keeping his own counsel.

"The sooner we attack——" Tarleton urged, and Martin broke in eagerly: "Yes, the sooner——"

Cornwallis cut them all silent with a glance. "No! The man James Moore is no fool. His strategy at Moore's Creek shows his ability. He is no fool, and remember that. Then why should he oppose us with ten thousand ill-trained, badly equipped militiamen? Now—why?"

"Hrr-r-r-r-p!" Sir Henry blasted. "I say he is inviting us to blow up his dirty rabble so the land can have peace again. The man is an aristocrat and wealthy. British victory would serve him well."

"In due deference to your wisdom, sir," Cornwallis answered, "I say no. Moore is a deliberate revolutionary, risking all. He will not play false. He has a plan, and I think I see it. Frankly I am afraid of his trap, and I'm damned if I put my army in it!"

Duncan jumped to his feet and beat the table. "Afraid?" he demanded hoarsely. "Afraid? O' the Whigs? Na! Na—I say!" His built-up hopes once more were going to dust. It was disgrace piled on disaster. "Smash 'em!" he screamed. "We, the Hielanders o' the Cape Fear, suffered and died when ye failed us last winter. Ye shan't do it!"

"*Ten thousand!*" Tarleton waved his arm. "Ready to be cut to pieces! Let's at 'em!"

"Patience! Patience!" Cornwallis smiled on the two of them. Duncan shrugged. He did not like Tarleton, and it galled him to have the fire-spitter on his side. "You'd have no battle. You'd meet a phantom army. Just enough to lead us on and on—into the wilderness. They'd drive off the cattle. They'd harry the disconsolate Highlanders. They'd break up the Indian uprising. They'd cut our communications. They'd ruin the crops. They'd starve us out, and then, bit by bit, slaughter us. The man Moore is smart, and we must not forget that, but be smarter. We must drive him to the sea instead of following him away from it. We must invade South Carolina and come down the Cape Fear from the upper reaches. There's your victory."

"Well, by heaven," Sir Henry exploded, "King George always favored blasting Charleston instead of the Cape Fear!"

"Eh?" This from the dismayed Governor Martin, who had thought the King was his staunch supporter. Duncan sat disconsolate, looking at the floor, while the officers turned from him to the new plan.

When the council broke up, General Cornwallis placed his arm over Duncan's shoulder and led him to his own table for dinner. The Highlander's dejection faded slowly as Cornwallis went to great pains to make clear that the Cape Fear was not to be deserted. The valley was to be cleared of Whigs as part of the campaign. He promised, even, that the decisive battle might be at Moore's Creek as the Whigs set about to defend Wilmington. It was not what Duncan wanted, but it would suffice. Governor Martin would be disappointed, but Duncan wished no credit from the King, but victory and vengeance and restoration of self-content. It would suffice.

Cornwallis asked many questions. He wanted to know how the people lived, when the corn would be ripe, if the cattle were fat and if they were many or few. He wanted to know how the roads lay and if the streams were difficult to cross. The general called a young officer of the Scottish regiments, one of the Queen's Guard, and ordered that Duncan be outfitted in a uniform of Stuart tartan. Cornwallis was very kind and sympathetic. More than anyone, more even than the ambitious Martin, he seemed to sense the soreness in the Cape Fear soul.

Duncan was assigned to Governor Martin as a courier, and his duties were negligible. He spent much time at first with the subalterns on the *Bristol,* but he soon wearied and sought more solid companions than the houghmagandie-bent young Englishers. They plied him with questions about the daughters in the Tidewater mansions, being more eager to find them of pliable virtue than their fathers and brothers loyal to the Crown. They had a book which was much in vogue, Dr Madan's *Thylipthora, A Defense of Polygamy,* and they read it incessantly with a consuming relish.

"See, Duncan," one bold-eyed one slapped the book, "we have written authority!"

"I dinna ken what more authority ye need," Duncan grumbled, "than the consent o' a lass, a sheltered nook i' the woods and the power that God gi'e ye."

"Consent, the devil! These Carolina plantation lovelies will not be tardy with their consents—and if they are, by the Almighty, what's the difference? The soft-bosomed sex never expects parlor tactics from conquering warriors."

"Aye—but it may not be as ye foresee."

"Never fear! They'll be damned grateful."

Duncan turned to the less boastful Highland regiments for his conversations. The Scots, also, were all too responsive to their primal urges, but each man considered it his own private sin and no subject either for perverted philosophy or oratory.

"Must one read a book," scoffed a kilted stalwart of the Black Watch, "tae ken ways of pluckin' a tap-pickle?"

Duncan saw no excitement, missing even that raid which Cornwallis led up the river. That was a disappointment. The British ravaged Bob Howe's plantation and came back with a dozen cattle and one dead soldier.

By the third week he was tired of it. He had no ambition to be a soldier or to live a soldier's way. He wanted to rout out the Whigs and return to his plantation to build it and live his life's plan. He wanted a mistress—aye—but that, too, was part of the plan and was not to be tarnished by rampant promiscuity.

Then suddenly the camp was a storm of activity. Soldiers broke camp. Tents came down. Men herded their women and loot into the transport ships or drove the harlots into the woods to live off the country. Many women railed and swore and wept and fainted when the redcoats abandoned them in the raw wilderness that day the fleet sailed.

It was on a cool Sunday morning in June, just before the sunrise, when Duncan, to thrill at the sight, looked back on a breath-taking ocean of black and gold. A massive, curving line of ships, with full-flown white sails, bent up the coast toward Frying Pan Shoals, and they drove down toward a flaming horizon walling up from sun-sheened red water. Ten majestic men-o'-war, carrying their three hundred guns, squired the great fleet southward. Charleston must be foolhardy, indeed, to offer resistance. Duncan was awed and humble and grateful. The glory of heaven—of deliverance— of Britannic might—shone in that sunrise.

The armada cast anchor off Charleston. It waited. The wait extended and nothing happened. The men became restive and officers fretful. For a week the proud fleet lay there, preening, displaying its power to the rebellious flat-lying citadel of the American patricians. And then two weeks. And three—dreary, monotonous, damnably hot weeks.

"Wait! Wait!" Sir Henry baffled his impatient officers. "They can't be entirely witless. They'll surrender without a shot."

And there was meat in Sir Henry's words. Charleston was in no position to fight the best navy and the best army in the world.

"Egad!" Sir Henry took dry amusement in watching the bare-bodied men who labored night and day in full sight of the ships, building their homely, ludicrous out-side defenses on Sullivan's Island. "Look! A fort of sand and logs! *Sand,* mind ye! And *logs!* 'Twould be an insult to His Majesty's navy to order an attack on such a thing." Sir Henry took his glass from his eye and waved it as a wand before his companions at the rail, denoting he was about to engage in levity. "The old bugger with the tobacco pipe, I take it," he offered profoundly, "is head logger—ha-a-a-a-ah—hah-hah! Ha-a-a-ah—hah!"

Governor Martin and Governor Campbell laughed loud. They had found it wise to laugh when Sir Henry attempted jokes. Sir Peter Parker did not trouble to smile.

The officers walked down the deck, but Duncan remained at the rail to watch the defenders. The big, bare-bodied, squat man in charge gripped him. With his glass he could see him distinctly— even, when the air was clear, to catch the expression in his un-worried eyes. The man was working, doing things, commanding mildly and making men work like slaves. Worried, sick to the heart with monotony and inaction and the complacency of the high command, Duncan found escape in the action of the inde-fatigable man who built a fort under the muzzles of British guns. It was futile but it was action, and Duncan watched him by the hour, almost, he felt, knowing the Whig commander's words when he gave orders. Duncan took on sympathy for him, for one broadside belch from the flagship should scatter his logs and his sand and kill every man there. But he handled logs, and Duncan knew about logs. He watched the palmettos go in place. Some-times he would contend silently with the rebel officer on how to do it. Duncan knew better ways. But in the end the rebels did the job, and Duncan found no fault in it—for a brown toy fort built on a white carpet. Duncan had a sense of proprietorship. He had helped make it. He felt he knew the chief officer, with the calm

eyes and unhurried ways, better even than he knew his own commander.

The contented old bugger with the tobacco pipe is forty-six-
year-old William Moultrie, and he has as little respect for the fancy
trappings of high rank as he has for its opinions. This sultry hot
morning in June finds him, as he has been for several weeks, busily
engaged constructing his homemade fort. The fleet looms threat-
eningly upon him. The illusion, from his flat, water-level position,
is that the British ships are up a slope of water from the beach,
and, if liberated, would float down to him. He does not waste time
on such speculations, nor does he hurry. With his sun-blackened
body bare to the waist he goes leisurely from gun emplacement
to gun emplacement, inspecting. He does this frequently, and then
as leisurely goes back to the end of the wall where men are working and supervises the operation. As often as not he is the one who
grapples the end of a palmetto to fling it into position.

A curious contrivance of defense, this awkward fort of soft,
fibrous logs which sets its scaly face against the pride of British
might. Negro slaves float the logs to the island on flats. Soldiers
cut them to length and bolt and chain them together and toil them
into the wall. Negroes and white soldiers fill between the log walls
with sand. When William Moultrie walks on top and surveys his
curious handiwork, he walks on a sand bulwark sixteen feet wide.
Before him are the channel and the open sea. It is up this channel
that Clinton plans to sail.

Behind him, across an inlet, is Long Island, with its sand and
clumps of myrtle. Moultrie gives thoughtful looks to Long Island,
for the enemy easily could land a force there, and his fort has no
protection from that quarter. It will be weeks yet before he can
complete the rear wall, and the British will not wait.

Now comes a boatload of dignitaries over from Charleston. William Moultrie gives them slight attention. They come with advice
and argument, and William Moultrie has had all the advice and
argument of which he has need. Over in the city, flat against the
low-lying green trees, they have the liberty, so far as he is concerned, of making endless disputation. They have the soldiers and

the breastworks upon the Battery, and the powder and the high-ranking officers, and the time for councils of strategy. There they have the opportunity of bowing and tripping and exercising their chivalric arts before the fine ladies of Charleston. And there, unless he can finish his fort quickly, the British fleet will sail in ponderous triumph and blow the town to pieces. Yet they take time to argue with him.

General Charles Lee it is, this time. William Moultrie swings a palmetto log viciously around and composes his temper to greet the gentlemen. There is his friend, Whig President Rutledge, South Carolina's Cornelius Harnett; and lesser officers from the troops. General Lee, the eccentric, the favorite of Congress, he of the profound military wisdom which so brashly challenges the test, leads the group. The party, except for Rutledge, is more interested in the fleet than in the fort.

They come along the top of the wall as Moultrie wipes the sand from his hands on his breeches and walks to meet them. They keep their eyes on the ships and estimate their gun strength. That being so, Moultrie stops walking and waits easily, smoking his pipe, until they come to him.

"I still say, sir," General Lee declares, twisting his head and chopping down with his face for force, "that you but waste your time. I admire your bravery, but my advice is that you suspend operations and join the force in the town."

Young officers bow decisively in agreement, but they have the good grace to say nothing.

"I am grateful for your counsel," Moultrie says. He is calm, and as he speaks keeps an eye on the men placing palmetto logs.

"You can see," Lee says, waving his arm around the beach. "The Britishers will send their men-o'-war somewhat at this angle. In order to make short work of it, Sir Peter will unleash all ten on you. After you have taken a hundred shells, these soft logs will be hash and your sand will be level. Your guns will be silenced and you will be lucky to save one man in ten. Thirty-one small guns, Colonel Moultrie, just can't demolish ten of the best warships in the world."

Moultrie takes out his pipe and blows smoke calmly. "I ought to have more ammunition," he says, agreeing that far. "I've twenty-eight rounds of shot, and not quite enough powder for that."

"We need all the stores for the defense of the city," Lee rebukes him.

"I'm defending the city," Moultrie answers quietly.

The weather is very hot, and the wind is from the landward. Mosquitoes and sandflies swarm upon the low island, from the marshes beyond. It is enough to make a perspiring general, helpless for lack of formal authority among these rabblish troops, very angry. He becomes purplish, and Rutledge diplomatically leads him on.

Rutledge comes back and whispers to Moultrie: "I will send you five hundred pounds of gunpowder."

"It will be needed."

Sir Henry finally knew a great wrath. He told Governor Campbell that threats and promises were useless, that the South Carolinians must smell gunpowder and feel steel.

" 'Twill do the damned rebels good!" he now thought righteously.

Therefore on Tuesday, the twenty-fifth, there was vast commotion on the water, and General Clinton beached more than two thousand soldiers on the gleaming whiteness of Long Island. From this blistering hot camp he purposed to wade the inlet and attack the fort from behind when the fleet had reduced it. The plan of battle had been worked out with Governor Campbell, who knew the territory, and from now on the reduction of Charleston was to proceed like clockwork. By the end of the week they would be marching into the country, knocking the South Carolina Whig planters right and left, while the Indians raged down from the mountains.

It would be spectacular, and Duncan held his country gawking in check to ape the suddenly brisk officers. Aye—now! It had come. He was with Governor Martin on the *Bristol* and would be in the thick of it. They would drop a ton of bombs on the curious log fort and smash it. Then the men-o'-war would sail up the channel to the city. There would be smoke and explosions and bursting buildings. And then, silence. And fleeing Whigs. He was impatient. Impatient for it to have an end. It was nearly two months since he had left home. He had thought then that the war would have been won by now. It hadn't begun.

The bombardment commenced at ten o'clock on Friday morning. The warships dropped down from Five Fathom Hole, where they had more lately been stationed, and with anguishing deliberation made their ominous line before the fort. The ponderous *Bristol* and *Experiment*, with their fifty guns each, took the direct positions not a half-mile from shore, and the eight others flanked them. Far back of the line the transports readied to sail up the channel, and the soldiers on board prepared to land.

Duncan leaned on the quarter-deck rail, straining his eyes from ship to ship and at the unhurried man Moultrie in the fort. The tremendous thing was about to begin. Sir Peter jerked back and forth on the deck, with short, nervous strides. He looked at the ships through his glass and shouted orders, though his aides were at his elbow. Important, gold-braided officers and the special guests from the army stood by. Governor Martin was there, glumly silent. It was a bitter day. Neither had his army commission been restored nor his province been chosen for the distinction of the opening subjugation. Governor Campbell was there, eager, pale, tensing for *his* deliverance—just as Duncan would feel when he marched through Bladen with the conquering British Army at his back. It was a great, trembling, silent moment.

The little men at the fort kept working as though nothing threatened them. Duncan looked on in dismay. Didn't they *know* that red hell would spew on them this hour?

He stiffened, breathless. It was the signal. The *Thunder* bomb ship at the end of the line let go. Duncan frowned and rubbed his face. He was surprised and let down. Just a mushroom of smoke, a dull roar down the water and a splash of sand on the beach. The men on the wall ran and jumped behind, as if it were play. And then silence, and the blue water and the white sand and the logs were as before.

Now there was a blasting broadside from the *Bristol,* and the ship quivered. Duncan hugged the rail for support. He was smothered in a vast swirling thundergush of black cloud and unleashed power. Storms of smoke shot out under him to rise up and blot out the ship.

The wind blew the smoke across the deck, and the officers stared, speechless. Finally Captain Morris wondered, disbelieving: "Well, damn my gunners! Can't they hit it?"

The brown fort hovered on the beach quite as before. If a shell struck, it hurtled into the soft logs and was smothered in the sand. The defenders were serenely there. If they were being attacked, they did not seem to realize it.

Now there was a bit of smoke behind the wall. An explosion. A shriek through the air. A crossarm high on the mainmast of the *Experiment* dropped down wearily and hung in the ropes.

The officers swore. It was not important, but the damned clodhoppers had drawn first blood. Captain Morris stalked from the deck to bawl his fury among the gunners.

Thunder ripped. Fire belched. Wood splintered. Decks trembled. Duncan could not follow all that happened. Officers stamped back and forth and orderlies raced through the fog. Men shouted and swore. Now and then one screamed. One man was blown clean from the ship to disappear in the water.

He had that curious, helpless feeling that he had had standing in the water at Moore's Creek. Something had gone wrong. Somebody had miscalculated. True, the ships slung their tons of death at the fort, but the fort merely stood there and absorbed it, when long ago it should have been leveled. It was not admissible that the mightiest seagoing fortresses of the Crown should long be impeded by a homely thing of logs manned by countrymen. But there it was, still brown and unmoved on its incredibly clean white sand.

And not only that. Calm, slow little clouds of smoke rose at intervals behind the wall. As though the British ships were not hurling more explosive to the hour than they were to the day, the men beyond the logs worked leisurely. Their twenty-six-pound shot and their little nine-pound shot burst through the air with equal precision. A rudder post blew out or a bowsprit dropped or a topmast fell over and sagged in its rigging. In the swirl of smoke and boom of cannon there now and then came the lightning smash

of crushing wood, and a shell burst through into the lower decks
of the *Bristol.*

Duncan could imagine the man Moultrie, still bare to the waist,
still smoking his pipe, going from gun to gun, being as careful
not to fire as to fire.

It was as if the commander of the fort should say to a gunner:
"Drill me a six-inch hole through that pustle-gutted army captain
on the after deck," and pass on, knowing that it would be done.

Two hours went by, and the rumble and the thunder and the
shrieks in the air became monotonous. The wind kept pushing the
smoke away. Now and then it lifted for a clear picture. Sir Henry
and his men on Long Island had not moved. On Sullivan's Island
the reason was seen. Bare-bodied Whigs hid behind the dunes,
hugging the sand, waiting for the British to come in range. It was
but a little force. Clinton had ten to their one, but each man of the
rebels could pick off ten before the redcoats could cross the water
and get in position to fire. Clinton discreetly held his distance and
fought mosquitoes instead.

But, here, around the point, three ships moved up for an enfilad-
ing fire on Moultrie. That should end it. Officers wiped sweat and
sighed relief. Duncan waited for the end. But, no. The ships knew
nothing of the sandbar there, and now they were grounded and
helpless and the smoke shut them out.

The *Bristol* shook with a direct hit, and the screams below lifted
out of the reek. Duncan ran down the companionway, down into
the dungeon of stench and shrieks and scattered human entrails.

A naked man, except for the strip of cloth around his middle,
lay on the floor. He had no face, only a red, mangled, scooped-out
cavity in its place. Another lay against the wall, with his leg lying
insanely across his chest. Behind the gun a half-crazed man,
amazed and jittery, picked with his finger at a steel bolt that pro-
truded from his stomach. Men with stretchers came running and
took them away. Duncan shouted. He didn't know why. He ran
back to the quarter-deck and gripped his rail.

No one was on deck but Captain Morris, and Duncan saw him
stagger and rushed to him before he fell. Stretcher-bearers came,
and Duncan helped take him to the surgeons. The captain's neck
was bleeding, and his arm was smashed at the elbow. Surgeons'

helpers gripped him and bound him to the table while the surgeon prepared to saw off the arm. A red-hot shell hurtled through the wall, and the two helpers became stinking, frying smears in a pile of splintered wood. Other helpers appeared, and the surgeon took off the captain's arm and threw it on a shelf.

Captain Morris, his arm now a white-bandaged stub, got down from the table and started back to the quarter-deck. The surgeon shouted to him. So did Duncan.

"Na!" Duncan screamed. "Ye canna go back!"

The captain turned slowly and leaned over to hear. One had to shout in the noise.

"Ye're too weak! Ye canna!"

The captain shrugged and went on. Duncan turned to the surgeon and shook his head. He followed after the captain, out to the quarter-deck, into the splitting shriek of missiles. The captain buckled in the middle and pitched to the deck like a wet rag. Another shell struck him, and he was dying.

Later in the afternoon the smoke lifted just as the fort flag went down. Sweating, blackened sailors cheered. The ships were a line of shambles. Proud sails hung crazily on broken masts. More than a hundred men were dead. Almost as many more were wounded. The curious fort had held out extraordinarily. But now it had fallen. The sailors cheered.

They cut the cheering short. An American soldier was out on the wall tying the fallen flag to a swabbing staff, and the flag flew again. The ships rained their shells at him, but he walked away and dropped behind the wall unhurt.

The night came, but there was no darkness. Shells bursting over the ships and over the fort made a hellish glare that rumbled and grumbled and was split through with shrill sounds.

At nine o'clock the wind and the tide changed and bugles rang from ship to ship. A great quiet came. There was no glare except from the fast-grounded *Acteon* ship. The crew burned it and escaped to the *Syren* and the *Sphynx,* which had floated themselves from the sandbar.

Moultrie, no doubt, still smoked his pipe and waited for another belch of flame to guide another well-placed shot into the tattered ships. But the men-o'-war prepared to fall back. Moultrie had no marks to shoot at, and silence was terrifying. Duncan stood at the rail and shivered. The silence cut through him like something cold.

The *Bristol* swung her prow slowly around to the sea. Two young officers, taking advantage of sudden leisure, gulped liquor in the cabin and lit their tobacco pipes with a torch. Flame spat from one of the fort guns. A shell over the taffrail smashed through the cabin and wiped them out. It killed three men on the main deck and, having raked the ship from stern to stem, drilled through the forecastle and into the water. Duncan did not move— it was but one more—but stood there, overwhelmed.

Governor Martin found him so. The governor was cold, too, and his face was white. He spoke through clenched teeth.

"An important and dangerous assignment for you, Duncan," he said. "Can you undertake it?"

"Aye." It did not seem important. Nothing was dangerous, now.

"The Indians. We must stop them!"

"Indians?"

"Yes. They were to start out of the mountains as soon as their scouts heard our guns at Charleston. We were to have met them in the foothills. But now——" Martin flung his hand back in despair. "Duncan," he said, as though ashamed to say it, "the fleet is sailing! They are abandoning the South. The ships are going to New York."

The two men looked unbelievingly into each other's eyes. They had driven for this day. Since Moore's Creek they had had no thought except for the coming of the British and the breaking of the Carolina revolt. And, after that, peace and the rule of the Crown.

"Na!" Duncan whispered.

Martin said nothing.

Duncan grasped his shoulder, shouting: "Na, I say!"

Martin looked to the sea.

Duncan groaned. He swung to the ship's rail as if to shake it. "Tom Brown t' gloat! Flora MacDonald t' suffer! Whigs over-lordin' the Hielanders! Na! They canna! The King winna permit it!"

Martin took control of himself and of Duncan. He spoke

crisply: "The Indians—they must be stopped. The time is not right. They must hold until the British come again. Their scalping and clubbing and burning is needless now. You must hurry."

In half an hour Duncan dropped overside into a boat which sailors held. Next he was in the woods north of the city. Below him he could hear the drums and explosions of celebration. Behind him were the dim lights of the ships moving farther out to sea.

CHAPTER 2

IT WAS DARK, and Duncan struggled to come from under. He smothered. Something was around his neck. He tried to scream aloud but could not. He was stifling. Indians with bent and gleaming brown backs leaped over things, and other Indians followed swift on their heels. One reached down and jerked the frock off the dead girl, and her form flopped limply on the clay. The Indians ran, and their yellow and green spots swam before his eyes. But he could say nothing. He was stifling, and he had to come from under.

There were sounds, murmuring sounds. Women's voices. A woman screamed in terror and pain. Murmuring words. A shriek. Duncan heaved. He had to come from under, by God. He'd get out. Tremendous pressure built up in him to tear his way through, to where he could see. He opened his eyes. He was perfectly still.

It was peaceful. Quiet. He was in a log house, and the trees were green through the window. It was cool. A sweet breeze blew through the door and waved the curtains. He was lying on his side, his eyes open, bewildered by the peace which so suddenly came.

A woman screamed: "I'm dying! I'm dying!"

Another woman's voice, deeper, musical, assured, answered her: "Easy! Easy, wench! Would you kill the innocent babe with your flingin' about?"

"I'm dying!"

Duncan started to look over his shoulder. A thousand hot needles stuck him—in his arms, along his back. He hadn't moved an inch. He eased to, lay there and panted.

The woman, amazingly comforting in tone despite her hard words, said: "You'll not die. Now strain! Strain, you duck-legged ninny!"

There was scurrying. Murmurs. A Negro woman brought steaming water. Murmurs. A sob. A piping wail. A laugh.

When Duncan awoke again, it was twilight, a soft, cool twilight, with the red of sunset across a hill.

"Ma-a-mmy! That man's got his eyes open!" The soft thump of a child's feet raced down the porch.

In a moment a woman came in the door. She looked at his eyes questioningly. He looked back at her. It was strange. There was something about a baby. And Indians. But the woman was Martha McGee.

She was as large and firm-fleshed, her skin was as smooth, her eyes were as blue, as deep blue, as they were that night in Bladen. She wore a white apron, tied about her good round hips, and a white starched neckpiece that met over her throat.

"Ye're a good-lookin' woman," Duncan mumbled.

Her chuckle was solid and rich, from down in her lungs. "You men! Show you a woman and you kick right out of your coffins."

"I didna mean it."

"No?" she bridled.

"I didna mean to say it, I meant. I intended to ask ye where I am and what I'm doin' here, Martha McGee."

She laughed and dropped down in a low splint-bottom chair at his head. He saw her with greater ease now. He liked to look at her. She drew the sheet on his shoulder and smoothed his pillow. Her eyes moved over him easily. Her gaze salved him. She comforted him.

"You are at the Widow McGee's," she said lightly, "on Deep River. What you're doing here, I don't know. I've sat here in this chair off and on for six days and nights, wonderin', Duncan Stuart."

"Deep River?"

"Yes. The Quakers brought you up the lane last Thursday. You cried over and over: 'I' the name o' the King—stop! I bear a message frae the King!' Crazy as a loon."

"Aye?"

"Yes."

"I must ha' come a hunner miles."

"I don't know. We quieted you, me and the niggers. The back parts o' your clothes were all parched and dropping off. Your whole back was as raw as sausage meat, and your hands were blistered. You had a bullet hole through your right shoulder and blood down to your foot. You were a right smart mess, if you ask me. Did the King's Indians roast you, or what?"

"Aye."

"Then, f'r God's sake, why were you goin' around yelling for the damned king?"

"I dinna ken," Duncan mumbled.

Martha leaned closer, the better to hear his disjointed recollections. "Tell me. Can you?"

His straining thought was of clouds of cannon smoke and thunder, of splitting timber and wounded men, and of tattered ships moving out into the dark. There was a sorry satisfaction in it. The British could not now be disdainful of the Scots at Moore's Creek.

"Aye. Some part. I was dispatched by Governor Martin to halt the Indians. But I was late."

"They killed thirty-seven."

"Aye? I didna ken. I was at a cabin. Two bairns played in the yard. The redskins fell on them before I could prevent it."

"But they burned you, too."

"Aye." But his mind still gripped the picture of the bairns and would not let go. "Aye." His ponderings swirled with whoops and flame and ungodly hurts. He could not think what to tell Martha. "I shouted: 'Stop! I bear a message frae the King!' but they didna comprehend, and laughed, because they thought I begged for mercy."

She bent and kissed him lightly on the cheek as she would a baby.

"An interpreter came in from the woods and heard me. He cut me loose from the stake, and we all ran, for the Whig riflemen came. One took me in the shoulder. I fell i' the weeds. I canna recall more."

"Don't try."

"By what means I came to be this burden on ye is na in my mind."

"What difference? The Lord puts it on me to worry with the sick, all alike, Whig or Tory. Your burns are healing good, but your shoulder ain't doin' well. You'll drink some chicken broth now—then, back to sleep, sick man."

"Ye're a good woman, Martha McGee. I'm sorry to make trouble."

She whispered: "I'm glad."

Martha sat and talked often with Duncan those seven days yet that he stayed at McGee's Mill. Thinking about it at night, when all was quiet, he could not see how she did all that was upon her and yet seemed to have abundant leisure to sit with him. Most women in the neighborhood demanded that she be the midwife at their times of lying-in. She operated the store and bought furs and wax and the dried leaf of the deertongue for tobacco makers. She sold salt, sugar, coffee, ribbon, beads, buttons, anvils, strap iron. She ran the gristmill. She did not attend church, though she scoffed none at religion. She was a busy woman and a successful woman, and she was loved, even though she bossed everybody overmuch.

One of these neighbors came on a horse. Duncan, who still could not sit down, was out of bed, standing in the door. The man had a keen, penetrating glance, as though he were never satisfied until his adversary shifted his eye. Duncan knew him, Dr John Pyle, colonel in the Regulator brigade when the Loyalists marched to Moore's Creek. Pyle looked at Duncan as though he had never seen him before. Martha McGee sat on the porch, and Pyle made no move to leave his horse, merely sat there and talked.

"Well——" he spoke abruptly and paused. "Well, Martha," he said, "I've taken the Whig oath."

"Phut!" Martha scoffed. "You're no more a Patriot that I'm a ring-tailed coon. Your oath's not worth a mou'ful of mush."

"But I say, Martha—I really have. I swore fealty to the new regime down at Cross Creek. I thought you'd want to know."

"John Pyle, I've known you for years. You're honest, in your lights, but you are mule-headed. You swore your oath to save your property, that's all. If the British ever come through here, you'll be high-tailin' all over the woods, waving flags, trying to make the King think you won his war."

"But, Martha——"

"Go on, John! Don't try to pull the wool over my eyes. If you'd been such a high-rearin' Whig you'd ha' gone with John Clark and Ben Cleveland to whip back the Indians. Did you? No!"

John Pyle flushed and had little more to say. He rode off, with Martha McGee chuckling after him derisively.

"He thinks he's so damn smart! But I'll say this for John," she added reflectively, "he's one of the few men, since Mr McGee died, that hasn't come around me wingin' his spurs."

Whether she spoke in pride of her attractions or in disapproval of her yearning admirers, Duncan did not trouble to decide. In his condition his interest in her person—or any woman's—was as pure as the driven snow.

"Weel—ye canna blame 'em o'ermuch," Duncan considered.

"And there goes you!" she chaffed.

"No fear o' me ravishin' ye now, though I had the heart," he declared ruefully, raising his shoulder and twisting his back gingerly.

"That's the fact—no fear o' you." She laughed easily. "How do you like this Deep River country?" she asked him. She made no reference to their former discussion of that subject, but Duncan felt embarrassed.

"It's bonnie. Y'r goodness to me made it so."

"Duncan," she asked abruptly, "why don't you get some sense and join the Whigs?"

"Na."

"You're standin' in your own light."

"Na."

She was quiet for a time, pinching her fingers in her lap and looking down at the mill. She sighed. She shook her head. Then she laughed. "Steve Lewis," she said, "still hangs around, but I'm as honest as ever."

After that she was none the less kind, but Duncan felt a change in her. That night she was washing his back and shoulder with hot salt water.

"I ought to be saving this salt for some good Whig," she said, shortly good-humored. "The supply is low, and the price is going high. Wouldn't surprise me, unless we run the British out of the country, salt will sell by the grain."

"So bad? I hadna heard."

"I've done a good piece o' doctorin' on you, if I do say it myself. You're healing fine."

"I'll be gettin' home, then, thanks to you."

They parted in calm. There was continuing friendship. That was all.

Duncan made his way to Cross Creek slowly and painfully. He spent two days at the home of a Scottish family near Flora Mac-Donald's old home at Cameron Hill, and they treated him kindly. He found more Scots now, and his way was easier. One of them took him in a cart from that settlement to the next, and another in turn sent him on. He lay on his belly on the floor of the cart. The going was rough, but it was better than the pain with every step when he walked.

When he reached Cross Creek the town house in the square was alive with people. Whig soldiers lounged about. Duncan had heard they would be in charge, but he did not mind Whig soldiers under the command of officers. There was no spite in them, such as individual Whigs were beginning to show.

A Whig soldier slapped him on the back. Duncan cringed.

"Oh! Sorry!" the fellow said. "I didn't know you were hurt. All right now?" Duncan nodded. "Line up over there under the balcony with the rest. Colonel Folsome's to read a paper."

"What paper?"

"Colonel Folsome," rolling the phrases with relish, "is to proclaim the Declaration of Independence of these United States of America."

"Ye mean," Duncan gasped, "that the country has seceded?"

"Exactly!" the soldier said proudly.

"Then I wi' na listen to such sedition!"

The soldier's eyes narrowed, and his jovial smile went hard. "Say, you, get in line with the rest o' the damn Tories before I hand you in, spitted on a bayonet!"

"But I dinna wish tae hear," Duncan protested. "The King——"

"Scottie, listen," the soldier said, patiently angry. "There ain't no damn king, so far as this country is concerned."

"Ye ha' na the right to say the King——"

"Hey, George!" the soldier turned to another. "Put him in the front line. Remember your orders, treat him kindly. If you stick him, make sure it is an accident."

Duncan found himself in the front-rank group of discomfited Scots. He and they stood mute, with drawn lips, pale faces. Duncan felt as though he witnessed a cataclysm—a tearing asunder of all sound things.

The Whig officer stood on the balcony, pale himself, and fingered the paper which he was to read. It was as if he, too, realized that the thin instrument would, like a sword, sink incisively into the civic tissues which had held the people as one and make them two. He unrolled it, explained his authority, and paused for another explanation:

"Through the misfortune of great disaffection in this county," he said, "the Committee of Safety deemed it an undertaking too hazardous to bring this document to you in peace. In other counties the Declaration of Independence has been received with fervid enthusiasm. It is my sad duty to bring it to you on the point of a sword. I, therefore, am prepared to enforce your respectful attention. Even so, to you, whom I would prefer to address as fellow citizens, I do not raise the sword. I invite, with utmost hospitality, your consideration. I read:

"'When in the course of human events, it becomes necessary for one people to dissolve the political bands which have connected them with another . . .'"

Duncan's brain swirled. It had never seemed possible that the Whigs, under show of guns and swords, should boldly stand here in Cross Creek, the citadel of the Highlanders, and proclaim their arrogant independence without broadswords cracking their skulls.

He did not, he could not, follow the stately words. Only now and then a phrase penetrated his understanding. "'We hold these truths to be self-evident, that all men are created equal . . . long train of abuses and usurpations . . . The history of the present King of Great Britain is a history . . . He has refused . . . He has forbidden . . . He has endeavored . . . For cutting off our trade . . . He has plundered our seas . . . He has excited domestic insurrections among us . . . the merciless Indian savages . . . We,

therefore, the representatives of the United States of America . . .
are and of right ought to be free and independent . . . we mutu-
ally pledge to each other our lives, our fortunes and our sacred
honor.'"

"The King did nought," Duncan whispered to himself, "save
punish lawless rabble."

At the close of the reading the soldiers cheered. Some sections
of the crowd cheered, but the greater number stood in silence,
seemingly stunned by what they had heard.

Colonel Folsome said kindly: "All you who will are invited into
the building to take the oath which makes you a free citizen of the
new nation. I warn you that never again shall this land bow the
knee to the King of Great Britain, and never more shall we subscribe an oath in his name. When you take this oath, you repudiate
all oaths of the past which conflict with it."

He now raised his voice: "Now I speak as a soldier. It is my duty
to warn all who might interfere with anyone who becomes a
Patriot that the full strength and punishment of the military arm
will fall on you."

Duncan turned away bitterly. Many of those in the crowd went
into the building. He did not look to see which ones. His anger
smoldered, and his helplessness made him shrivel. He stumbled
down the road to Campbelltown on the riverbank. He felt like an
old, weak man, hobbling along with his stick.

Many passed and repassed him, but he did not speak. Nor did
they. Some were Whigs and did not care to speak. Others were
Loyalists and deemed it wise not to. But before he had gone half
the way, Archibald Black walked to him from toward the river.
Archibald was old Kenneth Black's son and a good friend of the
Crown. He walked among the Whigs as though they did not
threaten him. When he saw Duncan he came with surprise and
concern, looking his distress at his faltering step. He wasted no
words of politeness.

"Now, Duncan—tell me."

Archibald held out both hands as though he wanted to throw his
arm around Duncan's shoulder and yet was afraid to touch him.

"I am sorry," Duncan said, "I canna gi'e ye my hand," turning it
over to show the healing wounds. His lips twitched. He wanted

to laugh joyously at this new warm feeling of friendship, and was afraid to, for fear of weeping.

"No matter," said Archibald. "Tell me—better yet, draw aside from the road under the tree here and we can speak freely."

"I dinna like it," Duncan protested, nevertheless going. "I am an honest servant o' the King, and it gi'es me no shame—yet we have to skulk among the traitors as though it were us who performed the crimes o' tyranny and sedition."

"The truth," Archibald agreed. "But, now, tell me. I last heard o' ye in May. Ye escaped frae a Whig band and went to join Cornwallis. Now it is August, and ye are in Cross Creek, sore wounded and creepin' like an auld man."

"Aye," said Duncan. "Frae May to August was a long time this year, though it seems to me on'y a fortnight."

Duncan told him—about the brave sailing of Sir Henry's fleet to Charleston and its disaster, about his trip to delay the Indian uprising and his own involvement in the massacre. About his painful way back to Bladen.

"But, no," Archibald protested. "Ye canna. Bladen has become a hellhole since ye left. Ye're in no shape to fend for y'rsel'. Come wi' me to Drowning Creek and we wi' mend y'r ailments, then ye can take y'r place at home as a brave man should."

"Na. I wi' go on home."

"Na. Ye winna," Archibald said with equal firmness. "Flora MacDonald would tongue-lash me unmerciful were I to permit ye to go in y'r shape among the Whigs and the Loyalists o' Bladen wi' their nightly raids and clashes."

"But I *maun*. I maun go." Duncan was suddenly eager to be on his way. "There is Mary MacLeod, Malcolm's sister," he explained elaborately, "who needs my protection among such violence."

"That Whig filly! Bah! Ye would but hamper her. The *Whigs* give her *abundant* protection—an' don't f'rget it."

"I dinna ken what ye mean, Archibald Black!"

"I mean her house is a gatherin' place f'r Whigs. She's all for 'em, hand in glove. They hang around her like swine under an apple tree. Na, Duncan. Forget Mary and come wi' me. Ye shall see Flora MacDonald, and she wi' esteem it good fortune that she can help to heal y'r wounds. Y'r Mary is na yours now."

The three months of Duncan's absence had wrought tragic changes among his friends. From February's Moore's Creek to May's Cornwallis had been a period of quivering uncertainty, but the lines had held. The Whigs had made no vicious effort to over-run the Loyalists. But after Duncan had sailed with the fleet, the Whigs had moved swiftly. No Highlander who threatened to lead was permitted to be free. The deadening pressure of the rebels was upon the whole valley, and suspected Loyal leaders were herded to prison by the scores.

Flora had taken him to Killiegrey. Maggie Black spent most of her time there. Anne, with her babies, was there much of the time. Children and wives of the menservants who had gone to war with Allan MacDonald were with her and worked the patches and fed the pigs and carried on for such necessities and comforts as were to be had, but, even now, poverty hovered over the place.

Duncan was at first too ill to give much thought to his future. The fire wounds had been deeper than he thought, the bullet wound now was better healed than they. Weakened and dis-traught, he found it better to cease his fretting and give himself over to Flora's ministrations. She was most solicitous.

She sat beside his bed, and he thought how similarly to Martha McGee she affected him. Both looked on him with understand-ing eyes and knew how to make decisions of wisdom.

Now Flora's blue eyes were deepened in their blueness and darkness, as though rankling pains tore in her soul. But her words were cheery and brave.

"How can ye be so bonnie and gawsie, Fionnaghal?" he won-dered. She merely looked down in his eyes and smiled.

"Allan is gone," he said, recounting. "And y'r son, Alexander. And Alexander MacLeod is gone frae Anne's arms."

"Aye," she said quietly.

"And the strong men—Hector MacNeill, and Duncan Ray, and Archibald MacDougall. Gone."

"Aye."

"Donald MacDonald is gone and Donald MacLeod is dead."

"Aye."

"And those who might be stalwart f'r the King are mute—Far-quard Campbell and Thomas Rutherford and Gilbert Johnston."

"Aye. But old Gilbert is dead, too, now."

That was a new stab. Old Gilbert was a friend. But stabs came
freely these days. Duncan did not change the subject.

"And ye, Flora, who hae known the friendship o' destiny, live in
a strange land, in poverty, like an indented woman. I dinna ken
how ye bear it. It makes my spirit droop."

Her hand cuddled into his sound palm impulsively. "You dear
laddie!" she murmured. For a while she said no more, holding
the moment, enjoying his simple adoration. Then she explained:
"Think ye," she asked, "that the King i' his majesty wi' permit
things to be long like this?"

"I dinna ken," Duncan said hopelessly. "Moore's Creek, Cape
Fear, Charleston—Whigs soldierin' o'er the land. The King flouted
and despised an' made a laughin'stock on the highways, wi' his
men-at-arms makin' stage-play battles an' runnin' away."

Her indulgent chuckle made him wonder the more. He was not
quite so despondent as his words indicated, but he needed to
know, for his own stability, the source of such cheerful bravery as
she had.

"I hae said," she repeated, "that His Majesty will not long permit such things. And now I say more yet. Doon-kan, keep this e'er
in y'r heart and ye wi' hae no doubts—we keep our oath—we are i'
the *right*. And the good God keeps the right. The doited victories
o' the misguided canna long prevail. Your duty is to keep a stout
heart and be ready."

"Aye," he said, not fully satisfied. "Even so, but the Almighty put
a great burden on ye and auld Kenneth, leavin' it to ye to keep the
Highlanders stout-hearted."

" 'Tis na sae hard," she smiled again, liking the thought that she
was the moral commander of the disorganized clans.

Old Kenneth came in just after that. Old before, he was older
yet now and, somehow, stronger. Where his fat had shriveled, his
sinews seemed bigger and more tenuous. His face was the face of
a pale old man, but his eyes were solid blue and thoughtful. His
countenance was that of one who was stern and kindly.

"Ye wi' heal y'r sores as quickly as may be, Duncan," he said,
and Duncan himself caught the impatience to be sound. "The
Lord in the past has seen fit to confound His enemies at times wi'

the auld and the inept, but it is better to have stout ones, such as ye. We Scots left i' the sandhills hae our work tae do."

"Aye," said Duncan. But it was a week later before Duncan was informed of the inner meaning of Kenneth's words.

"Think ye," demanded Kenneth hotly as he and Duncan strolled, "that we wi' bear the additional disgrace o' permittin' Flora Mac-Donald tae be hounded by the irresponsible Whigs? I wi' lose my life, Duncan, before I permit it—and sae wi' ye."

"Aye," said Duncan. "E'en so," he added, "I hae that faith in the Whig leader, Cornelius Harnett, that he wi' na permit disgracefu' indignities upon her person and property."

"Pish!" Kenneth Black scoffed his distrust of all Whigs.

Kenneth seemed to prevail in that exchange, for when they rounded the bend of the road and looked up the lane a company of soldiers stood in line before the house while a young officer talked with Flora at the door. They hastened their steps, but neither could run.

"Here! Here!" Kenneth demanded, striding up to the door. "What is this?"

The long-faced, pleasant young officer turned on him curiously. "How is it your concern?"

"Don't! Don't, Kenneth!" Flora begged.

Kenneth blazed: "I wi' na hae ye interrogated by this rabble!"

But the young officer was not disturbed. "Please be quiet," he said. "I take no pleasure in this, but it is my duty. I have instructions from the Council of Safety—signed by the chairman, Mr Cornelius Harnett, if you are interested—to take inventory of this property."

He smiled. Duncan knew those Whig smiles. Flora smiled, too, somewhat guardedly.

But old Kenneth blustered yet. "I forbid it! Ye shall na!"

Captain Ingram did not answer, merely nodded over his shoulder, and a sergeant and a squad of soldiers surrounded old Kenneth.

"Co-o-o-ome on, Grampa!" the sergeant soothed him. "An' don't you hurt none o' the boys. They ain't old war horses like you."

Despite his healing wounds, Duncan had a mad impulse to spring upon them, but he caught sight of Flora. She hid her face behind the door jamb to smile, and now Duncan felt like smiling, too—if she did. The soldiers led old Kenneth out to the gate, where he stood in outraged silence.

"He will not be hurt," Ingram assured Flora. "And I will cause as little inconvenience as I can."

"Ye are most circumspect," Flora answered him, not approvingly. "It would serve me better were ye less considerate. At least, I seek no quarter."

"I'd be disappointed," Ingram said, "if you did. It would ill suit the one who so gallantly rescued the Bonnie Prince."

Flora laughed heartily. "Now you've destroyed my resentment entirely," she half pouted. "I only hope that the Whigs may continue chivalrous to the end."

"Have no fear of our soldiers," Ingram replied. "I cannot speak for these neighborhood bands that spring up and prowl."

"Aye," Flora said, troubled. "But what can I do for you, Captain Ingram?"

"I think it will be sufficient for you merely to tell me what you have. That will save our going through your house and barns."

Flora's eyes widened. It was as though a housewifely fear disturbed her. "No," she said. "No. Ye will look and see and make y'r own list, Captain Ingram."

He shrugged. "That means you have hidden well the fine silver given you in London." He didn't seem disappointed.

Duncan, resentful, still had a surface liking for the young officer. He made things no more difficult than his orders required. Flora MacDonald thought so, too, for she said:

"When the day of reckoning comes, Captain Ingram, ye hae my permission to call me as a witness for y'r mercy."

He gave her a look of mock terror. "Does Great Britain still hang and quarter 'em as they did Wallace, and swing their hams on the city gates?" he asked.

The sandhills were brilliant, red flame again when Duncan, not strong but with a whole skin, finally went through the November scrub oaks on his way home. The oaks made him think of Mary. He never saw their autumnal crimson except to remember the morning they had stood on the river bluff and looked across at the place where her cabin was to stand. She had been afraid that morning—aye—but she had got over that. Her desertion of the Loyal cause came more and more bitterly upon him as he neared the neighborhood. His other wounds had healed better than that in his heart.

It was night when he reached her cabin. He had said, many times, that he would not go there, and had meant it. He passed Owen Hill and did not stop, and Brompton Hall and did not stop, although he was more than half minded to pause and tell young Gilbert his grief for old Gilbert. But na. They were Whigs. He did not change his mind about going to Mary's cabin. He merely went. Something drew him. It wasn't a matter of decision. His steps became faster, and he was there.

There was laughter inside. Women's—Mary's, Tom Hadley's daughter's, the cackle of Minnie Meacham. Men's—Billy Brown's, Hector Owen's—Sonny Johnston's—two others that Duncan did not know, and a third who was a Gillespie. Duncan looked through the open window from the darkness and saw Mary among them. His eyes were like those of a hungry man looking on food.

He felt strong, and warm in his breast. The Whig striplings— he would brush them aside. He saw Mary's eyes, and they were as before, calm and brown and true. Aye! They had told him wrong. There was nought the matter with Mary, save her misguided Whig notions. It was worth the trip just to look at her.

He paid attention to the others before going in. The Gillespie youth was teasing them—at least they were teasing him. He bore decrees from the Provincial Congress. They plagued him to read the proclamation, but he liked their teasing too well.

"It will end the war!" he declared mysteriously.

"Go on, Gil! Read it!"

"Oh, it isn't for you! It's for the damned Tories."

"Please, Gil." Mary's voice pleaded, but her head did not. It was upright, like that of a princess. "What about the Tories?"

"It gives them free pardon—if they take the oath."

"Oh. If."

"Except those that aid the British."

"What for them?"

"They are to be shot."

The Whig bombast about shooting him did not make near the impression on Duncan as his belief that Mary turned pale.

"Let me see that paper, Gil!" she demanded.

"No."

"I mean it. I want the paper!"

He smiled provokingly. "For a kiss, I might."

Duncan smiled in grim satisfaction. The lad was a fool. Mary wouldn't. His breast wrenched. "It's a poor trade, at that," Mary said lightly, going unabashed to the Gillespie.

As though a great hand snatched him, he stood at the door. The young ones were laughing uproariously. But Mary did not laugh. She had the paper in her hand, staring over her shoulder at him in the door, with the Gillespie boy's arms still around her. Her eyes were big and brown and staring and afraid.

If Duncan's face was haggard, it was no more than a reflection of the bitterness in his soul. He could forgive her disloyalty to the Crown as a frailty of mind, but disloyalty to him was perfidy.

The others whirled around to face him. Minnie Meacham gasped her terror, "Lawd ha' massy!" for Duncan strode into the cabin, looming over all.

He snatched the paper from Mary, snarling at her. He tore it into shreds and pitched it in the Gillespie boy's face.

"I winna take y'r damned oath!" he shouted. "And I wi' serve my king! T' hell wi' y'r piddlin' decrees. The first Whig whoreson t' put foot on my land, I shoot!"

He so stunned them that he had turned out the door and was gone before anyone moved. He ran through the darkness, faster yet, because behind him there was a wail—a lingering, desperate wail, calling him back. Mary.

CHAPTER 3

Duncan had spoken from a white-hot soul when he defied the young Whigs to come upon his place. He would shoot to kill, as certainly as God gave him sight. He went home, seething. He had been buffeted as far as he would go. If the Almighty intended for him to have anything on earth on which to be master, it was his land in Bladen. Everything else had been snatched from him— Mary, the Crown's protection, Flora MacDonald's well-being— everything but his naked land. On it he would take his stand.

Duncan panted on home, for he had run away from Mary's cabin, and now he was too weak to run. Nor had he paused to take his breath, but had pushed on with all the strength he had. He was in his own field now, in sight of home but for the dark.

Someone laughed. It was a mocking laugh not ten feet away in the bushes. Duncan demanded:

"Who is it?"

A muffled voice answered: "Who you reckon?" and laughed again, and at that instant something soft, like a padded club, struck him on the back of the head. Duncan pitched forward and fell. He was addled, not hurt. He scrambled up, spitting sand, swearing, but all he heard in answer was the sound of running feet and derisive laughter. He staggered on home, drunk with his own rage.

He went to bed as though it were last night instead of seven months ago when he had last slept there. He glared at Gillie Black without speaking. He cared nothing, but lay on his bed and cursed, thinking of Mary MacLeod standing so readily in the Gillespie boy's arms. He must kill the Gillespie boy.

The next morning Duncan found his old rifle where he had hidden it in the swamp. He spent the day molding bullets. He could buy none, for the Whigs were sweeping the country for them. He found an old crosscut saw from which, when he had time, he would cut and fashion a sword. He made a gun rack of hickory forks just inside his cabin door, where he could get his rifle with least trouble.

He had not rested a moment through the day. But now night came on, and he wandered about the place. He rubbed Donald Bane down with a corncob and grumbled that the horse was too fat. No work.

"Did ye na have trouble wi' the Whigs in my absence?" he asked Gillie.

The black boy grinned and shook his head, overjoyed that Duncan at last had spoken.

"Dey comed," Gillie said, "but dey said dey wouldn' take nothin' till you comed."

"Who?"

"Whigs. I dunno who. Dem here goes other places and steals, and dem other places comes here and steals."

"Oh, they're coming back."

"Dat's what dey said."

"Then, Gillie, we'll kill 'em."

Gillie's lips quivered, and his eyes went white in the dusk. But he said: "Yassuh."

Duncan thought of his gun and started for the house. After this he must carry the gun everywhere he went. He had just passed the pine clump at the top of the rise when he saw a tall figure in his path ahead.

"Hold up, mister," the man said, drawling in good nature.

Duncan held still long enough to draw a breath. "Ye're a damned Whig," he shouted, "and I'll cut your heart out!"

"Uh-huh. No suh."

This voice came from behind, and Duncan whirled. Three men stood there with rifles.

"We don't want no trouble with you, mister," the man in front said. His voice was still slow and amiable. Duncan was not deceived. The Whigs would be amiable, even slitting a throat. "But our army up Nawth, it needs rations. We want about fo' bushels o' cawn offa you—that'll be aplenty for now, I reckon."

"But I'm a King's man!"

"Oh, that's all right," as if accepting an apology. "I like for a man to talk straight. I might be a King's man myself—if I didn't think he was such a goddam, piss-anty butt-faced son of a bastard whelp of a skonk. But yo' cawn'll suit us all right, mister. It's as good as any."

They trussed up Duncan with one of his own plow lines. They raided the place leisurely. They broke his gun. They took the corn they wanted and, one of them taking a fancy to Donald Bane, took him, too. Also they took Gillie Black. When they were safely out of range, they said, Gillie could come back and untie him. Duncan protested bitterly, but they took Donald Bane just the same.

Duncan wallowed in the sand and strained the rope, shouting insane oaths at the raiders as long as he thought they could hear. Then he wept, racking his lungs and tearing his soul at his sheer helplessness.

He must have gone crazy. The only thing he remembered through the night was Gillie gasping over him, moaning like an overzealous dog, cutting his bonds. When he recovered his senses he was trying to repair the broken stock of his gun with his hand-axe. Then he knew he had been crazy.

"Where did they go with my horse?" he asked, and Gillie answered for the hundredth time:

"I dunno whey dey went. Dey runned me back an' kep' gwine."

"I'll find Donald Bane and I'll split their skulls wi' my broadsword."

He realized that he had no broadsword. The words had a vaguely familiar ring in his mind. He had said them over and over through the night. He had the feeling that they had come out of darkness, but now it was morning and the sun was shining.

A horseman trotted through the trees toward him from beyond the frame of his stout house. Two horses. One man. Duncan started swearing hard, bitter, monotonous oaths which neither rose nor fell in inflection.

It was Tom Brown. He came smiling, but with his arm handy to his gun. Duncan's flow of recrimination did not halt or change its tone. Brown had brought Donald Bane back. He threw the leading rein to Gillie and turned back on his trail without explaining.

After that, when Whigs came to take his hog meat or his corn, Duncan offered no resistance. They always had a gun at his back before he knew of their presence, anyway. He merely sat and glowered. When they made the empty promise that the Continental Congress would pay, he said nothing. What could he say? The army was stripping the country. Whig or Tory, what did the army care? If he objected, the raiding squads would arrest him and hold him in prison. Many of the best Scots were in Halifax jail. Everywhere Duncan turned was some sharp prick of Whiggery to drive him back to sullen frustration.

It was a new, vicious, bloodless phase of revolution. In the cold winter evenings he sat before the fire and molded bullets, and each one he cherished like a gem. Some he placed in a leather pouch and some in a cloth pouch. Those in his leather pouch were for hunting, for the Whigs had taken all his meat, and he ate wild turkeys and fish and quail. Those in the cloth pouch he hid like a miser, for some time, some day of God's choosing, he would bury each one in the chest of a Whig.

The Whigs had changed color since they had started. The old, aristocratic ones were clearing out. New nobodies were coming in to take their places. James Moore came home and died of gout in the stomach. Maurice Moore died in the same house on the same day. Robert Howe, who, detestable as he was, still was better than the nobody Whigs, was away at the war. Cornelius Harnett was elected to the Continental Congress. The wise and moderate Samuel Johnston had been shelved, and the sharp and envious ragtag-and-bobtails were in power.

It took a little thing like salt to arouse him. He came home one evening from his cave. For protection he had dug into the sandstone bank of the Cape Fear. From a secret door he could crawl to it and, if need be, live in the cavern indefinitely. Under a curtain of overhung tree roots he could see the river, and, if he wished, make his cave a fortress. It gave him comfort to have such a place. When he reached home Alexander MacHolm was there, passing through from a trip to see a cousin on South River.

"I feared I might na see Andrew again," Sandy said, explaining his trip.

"And why?"

"I and mine, we're t' gae next fortnight."

"Na, Sandy! Where to?"

"Nova Scotia, on farms from which the Acadians were driven."

"Na, Sandy! Ye shan't! If ye leave, then ithers may leave. The Cape Fear may be stripped o' Scots! There's been talk o' it."

"Aye." Sandy was grim. "An' so be it. I came frae starvation in the Western Isles to starvation here, and a thin belly is painfu' anywhere. In Nova Scotia, I'm told, one at least may hae salt t' cure his meat and sprinkle his greens. Gin ye like the Cape Fear, then take my part."

Sandy walked on, and Duncan looked after him. A shaken feeling crept into his mind. All the while, in the tumult of his spirit and through the pain of his body, he had relied unconsciously upon the stability of the legion of clansmen clustered along the Cape Fear and through its valley. The thought of them was like a pillow on which to lay a weary head. As long as the Scots were there, with Flora MacDonald to lead them, he had the courage to hope and bide his time. But if they broke away and left an empty valley? He shuddered.

Gillie served his supper, and for the first time the absence of salt was unbearable.

"Salt!" he demanded. "Everything is so goddam fresh!" In his mind had come the conviction that what was about to drive the Scots away was the lack of it. If they had salt, they would stay.

He rode up the valley that night, stopping at Highland huts along the road. In Cross Creek was salt, he told them. The Whigs had it. The Loyal must have their share. Men joined him. Women sped them on. It became a crusade of hope—for sick children, for old people, for distempered women. Snatches of talk rang in his head as his company grew and grew.

A woman said: ". . . and Grampa, with his yaller janders, jest give up. The last words he said were 'no salt, no salt.'"

Another woman said: ". . . and all my bairns are sick. With their rich blood and all and no salt to thin it—they'll die!"

To Duncan, as he rode along in the dark, salt, suddenly, was the most precious thing in the world. They'd take the Whig salt if they had to break down the warehouse.

They were not alone in their desire. When they reached Cross Creek, hundreds of people mobbed before the salt house. Women screamed vengefully. Men shouted. Some threw rocks. These whizzed through the air and pounded against the walls.

"What kind of a government is this?" a woman shrilled. "No salt!"

A man on the other side of the crowd shouted: "Open up! Open up, there! For the love o' God, would you starve us?"

Rocks rattled against the walls and bounced off to roll on the ground. When Duncan and his down-the-river men rode in, the mob cheered.

"Go away! Go away!" a frightened voice shouted from an open window.

The people stood aside when Duncan strode through at the head of his group.

"Open the place!" Duncan shouted angrily. "We're here for salt!"

"Go away!"

"We'll break the door! Open up!"

Just how far Duncan's stubborn anger might have led him never had a chance to show. Terror-stricken women screamed and ran, and many of the men fell back.

Not a hundred yards away a company of Whig soldiers pounded up the hill, their bayonets set. They filed before the warehouse and turned their guns to the mob. A flushed, square-faced officer glowered at the crowd and picked Duncan as its leader. "Now what?" he demanded.

Timid heads came from windows all along the street. Anxious men and boys crawled on the ground to safety behind trees and peered out to see the battle. The Highlanders, one told another, had come to take the town.

Something solid and satisfying warmed Duncan. Here, for once, he could come to grips with an issue. "We want salt!" he shouted.

The square-faced officer frowned, and shrugged, as if disappointed. "Is *that* all?"

He turned to the storehouse: "In there! Open the door!" Then, back to the crowd: "Go in, one at a time. Have your money ready, a pound a bushel."

The people who a minute before had been murmuring and shouting now cheered. The money was nothing. A North Carolina pound wasn't much. The state treasurer hauled it around by the cartloads without guards.

Duncan went in. It was government salt, and he had to take the oath of allegiance before he could have it.

"Take the oath," said the commissary man. "Swear before God on the Holy——"

"By God, no!"

"Huh-h-h? Sorry."

"Well, damn y'r sorrow—and y'r salt—and y'r oath!"

Duncan stalked out without salt, but he had no complaint against the Scots who took the oath with tongue in cheek and returned home with salvation for their sick.

"Now, preach everywhere ye go," Duncan admonished his companions, "not to join the break-away. Stay here. 'Tis *our* land. We'll na let the damned Whigs take it from us."

Suddenly the possession of salt became the ruling impulse of his soul. It was as though the Whigs had forbidden it and he was determined to prevail over them. He stopped at home long enough to fashion a sheet of tin into a salt pan and set out for the coast, where the salt pans steamed.

It was two days later when suddenly the June breezes became cool and refreshing. On turning a bend in the sandy road down near the South Carolina line, a panorama of blue sky and white sand and foam-flecked green sea spread before him. Far down the beach were dark specks of people, scores of them. He rode toward them—like some rustic, bright-haired Bellerophon on a Pegasus which had yellow wings of corn fodder.

He drew attention. A crowd gathered around him when he stopped, some of the women eagerly.

"I came to make salt," he said uncomfortably. He had not expected such a crowd, although he knew that both Whigs and Loyalists, especially the women and the sickly men, came here for the summer.

"Oh—*salt!*" murmured a girl, for no more reason than to smile agreeably. "Yes, indeed!"

Others murmured. The elderly women looked at him with sharp, wise old eyes, to appraise him, and not without approval.

An old man quacked: "Plenty of it here, young man. Plenty."

"I don't see the salt pans." Duncan looked around.

"Oh, no wonder you are confused," a pale, slim young woman in black smiled at him. She was pretty. She had blue, dark eyes and eager red lips. "Over this way," she pointed. "On the sound side. Where we camp—and where the wind doesn't blow sand in the salt." She walked over beside him, as if laying claim. The older women looked at each other significantly. "I'll show you the way," she said.

She was light and she was dainty, and her black gown swirled coquettishly in the breeze. They walked along together. She was, she said, not well. She took his arm and leaned on him. He liked that. It was as if a cool sweet wind blew through the turmoil of his spirit and left peace and beauty and good cheer.

Halfway over the causeway to the mainland she said she felt faint. She wondered if she might not sit in the saddle. Duncan saw no change for the worse in her, but he risked no questions. "Just lift me," she said. So she was in his arms for the slow tingling moment. She seemed quite happy. He walked beside her, as, on a long-gone day, he had walked beside Mary MacLeod going up the river. The woman became most cordial. "You must stay a long while," she said. "My husband returns home tomorrow."

They stopped at the salt pans. Negroes poured water from the sound into them. Some were steaming. Others were not yet evaporating. Some had the thin skim of dry salt on their bottoms.

The woman in black pressed his arm. "Remember to stay." She lingered briefly and went on to the cabins. In a little while he saw her strolling with her husband.

Duncan tethered Donald Bane with other horses in a grove of myrtle. That night he slept on the beach.

It was like another world. The clean, cool breezes swept away every worry. But he was hungry, hungry for peace, hungry for stability, hungry for the Mary MacLeod he once knew. He slept long, and when he sat up and looked at the sunrise he was unutterably lonely.

Then he sighed, shook the sand from his hair and stood up. He would buy salt and leave at once. He was in fairyland; it was not real.

If it could be expressed in terms of sound, the Cape Fear Highland break-away might be likened to the long, rumbling roll of an earthquake, with a sudden ominous rent on the face of the earth.

The first Duncan knew of it was when, coming back with his bushel of salt, he heard the faraway wail of Angus MacCooish's bagpipe. Something was wrong. Duncan did not know what, but it was rich in Angus' lamentation.

When Duncan turned into the King's Highway at Carver's

Creek he saw what he most dreaded to see. The road was lined with carts. The carts were piled high with household goods. Scots were streaming down the road. Hundreds of them. Duncan groaned. Accustomed to defeat this last year and a half, as he was, this was the most scorching of all. If the Scots went, then there could be no little Scottish empire in the Cape Fear. Flora MacDonald might call, but none could answer.

He jumped to the ground and stood in the path of a big dark Scot. He did not know the man, but that made no difference.

"Don't go!" Duncan caught his arm. "Stay. The King's peace will yet come!"

The man only flung his arm aside and kept walking.

They were angry, these Scots in the break-away. They had been promised much, and the promises had failed.

It had started in February. Just a year after Moore's Creek the Scot stream had started trickling for the same sea that Scot blood had flowed into. Then the flow had ceased and now, in June, it had started again and become a torrent.

The Whigs were aghast. They made efforts to persuade the Scots to stay, but they were powerless to stop the emigration.

The Whigs did stop their coercions. Their Congress abolished the allegiance-or-death decree. Tom Brown and other Whig leaders and Duncan Stuart for the moment forgot to be enemies and worked together to stem the common disaster. The Cape Fear was about to be depopulated, and they resisted it night and day.

No one ever knew how many Highlanders left the valley. No one ever knew how many had been there in the first place. Some said that sixty thousand lived along the stream and that of these forty thousand departed. They went back to Scotland, to the West Indies, to Nova Scotia, to the fastnesses of Canada. Ships filled with them at Wilmington and Brunswick and Charleston and New Bern. They jammed the highway leading down the river, and sometimes on the river their boats were so clustered that one could walk from bank to bank without wetting a foot.

The oppressions of the Whigs had ringed them around and stifled them. When they left it was a stampede, and heartstrings tore and bled in the ruthlessness of the break.

Mothers left gifts wet with tears with daughters who had mar-

ried young Whig husbands. Brothers embraced sisters as they
parted, perhaps forever. Strong men stood in their clearings, now
fertile and promising, and swore bitter oaths at the waste of a lifetime. Bairns, born in the new land, screamed their terror at being
led away to strange new abodes.

Mary MacLeod was as distressed as was Duncan, and he more
than once met her as they went among the cabins to plead against
the departure. But he passed her silently and gave her no chance
to speak.

Once she faced him. "Doon-kan!" she said. "Wait, please," and
walked toward him.

"Aye," he said and stopped, but he bethought himself before she
reached him and walked on.

After these encounters his brooding spells were worse than before. He stood on the riverbank at Elizabethtown and saw the
Scots flowing downstream. It was a tide. It was the outflow of the
tide that had come in when Flora MacDonald came to Carolina—
back when Scottish lassies blithely sang: "I gae to Carolina for to
mak my fortun'!" It was flowing out, and it had to flow out before
another tide could come in—a raucous tide, of swelling waters and
clashing waves.

A dark-visaged man stopped beside him and talked. It was
Willie MacCallum, and Willie had deep blue eyes that knew to
suffer and not hate.

"We'll be back—we men," he said—and he spoke of the thousands that did come back, with Cornwallis and the hellish Tarleton. "Come wi' us, Duncan," he said abruptly.

"Na." Duncan wished for him to be silent, but Willie persisted
as one who had a point to make.

"Ye'll na turn Whig?"

"Na."

"Then, Duncan, now, come wi' us and take y'rsel' frae the mud-
dle o' the Hielanders here. Ye can come back and fight the better.
It is a point o' common sense."

"Na."

"Then why, Duncan?"

Duncan answered slowly, for in every thought he had of leaving

Bladen the vision of Mary MacLeod moved through his mind, and he could not think clearly. It was maddening.

"Weel—Willie MacCallum, I am here. I wi' na be chased from Bladen by the rabble. If the King will make my land safe for me, I will help him. If he will na, then I will make it safe for mysel'. I'll na move an inch."

"Ah, weel, Duncan. Ye choose the hard way. I pity ye and admire ye. My mind is that the contention will na be settled until neighbors settle it, o'er rifle sights. I hae no relish for that kind of war, and I'm leaving."

"Ye speak the truth, Willie. It will na end until Tom Hadley shoots at me and I clout his boy wi' my broadsword, and his cousin wi' kill my friend and my friend's brither wi' burn his house and rape his wife. Ye're lucky, Willie, that y'r conscience permits ye to go."

"Aye—but when my wife and bairns are safe, I wi' come back."

"Aye."

"Duncan."

"Aye, Willie?"

"Ye'll hae na hard feeling if I counsel ye?"

"Na."

"Word o' the Stuarts?"

"Aye."

"Then, Duncan, ye should wed the MacLeod lass and come wi' us."

"Na!"

Willie MacCallum's well-meant advice was like a knife in his back, an unlooked-for pain not to admit, even to himself.

"Ye love her. 'Tis too plain," Willie blundered on. "And she is nigh doited wi' love o' ye."

"Stop, Willie!" Duncan stepped away, to hear no more. He stood tense. He would not speak to Willie of that matter. Someone stepped in the leaves behind him, and Duncan saw Willie going down the riverbank. That was good.

"Doon-kan!" Mary MacLeod was at his elbow and whispered to him. He jumped as though she had jabbed him with a pegging awl. He glared down on her, but she gave his frown no heed. Her brown eyes were soft with tears about to fall, and her voice was tender. "Doon-kan, I told Willie to say that. I hae no pride, Doon-kan. I am weary and lonely, and I love ye. Wi' ye na let us, Duncan, forget the cause o' patriotism and go wi' the Scots to some far place where we can forget?"

"Na." It was a bare whisper, hardly more than a gasp, but it shook Duncan in his chest.

"Please, Duncan!"

His lip curled. "Leave my stout house?" he demanded. "Leave my plantation? Leave it a' to traipse wi' a Whig filly? Na!" he cried loudly, to cover the senselessness of what he had said.

"Doon-kan, I am abasin' mysel' before ye. Let us forget——"

But Duncan was running up the bank in terror. He looked back, and Mary had her hands out to him, still pleading.

Before he reached home he had thought out a good reason for his refusal to go with the Scots. He would never leave Bladen, he told himself, as long as Flora MacDonald stayed on the Cape Fear. That was a better answer. Only, he grumbled, he had been too long thinking of it. Even then, in his thought, visions of Flora jumbled with those of Mary MacLeod.

CHAPTER 4

Flora MacDonald was under arrest, charged with sedition. The Whigs, taking advantage of that period of inertia among the Scots after the break-away, sought by drastic action to wipe out all resistance on the Cape Fear. But the clansmen heard the news with aroused dismay and moved up the river stealthily.

None of this new consternation appeared on the surface that winter day at the trial in Cross Creek. The scene, tense as it was beneath, outwardly was most casual as Duncan wandered from one little group to another of the Highlanders. To the crowds of Whigs they showed nothing of a desperate plan.

Jamie Cameron, in true horse-trading indignation, lifted his voice to John Anderson: "I winna gie ye twa thousand dollars atwixt y'r nag and mine."

"Weel," John deliberated loud enough to be heard by any passing Whig, but eyeing Duncan who had just walked up, "I wadna tak the money, anyway. I've got a tubful of it at home, and it is good for nought. I'll gie ye my nag f'r y'r nag and a grubbin' hoe."

Duncan said in a low tone: "I go t' the courthouse now. If ye hear me shout, come. If it's peace, I wi' walk out beside Flora wi' my hand raised. But if I cry: 'Flora's locket!' then strike!"

Then men nodded and turned back to their horse-trading and references to ludicrous sums in worthless North Carolina currency.

Flora was on the witness stand. She saw Duncan. She knew nothing of his plan to rescue her if the Whigs sentenced her to prison. She looked relieved at seeing him, but gave him no sign of recognition. She was waiting, covering her anxiety with calmness. She might have been sitting in church. He spied six other stalwart Scots stationed in the hall, each in his appointed place. Whig soldiers leaned on their guns in the corner. Men and women crowded the little courtroom and gaped at the famous prisoner. Speaking among themselves, they had called her a she-devil and a troublemaker. They had proclaimed that she ought to be shot for a murdering Tory. But, face to face with her stately dignity, they merely stared and showed more curiosity than spleen. Duncan, steeled to the crisis, felt neither anger nor fear, not even sympathy for the woman whose harassed blue eyes looked back on the people. When certain things happened, he would do certain things, and he had no time to have feelings.

The thin, gray old magistrate looked at her acidly. His course was laid, and the hearing was empty form, but he was more agitated than she. Malignant as he was, he had no desire to arouse a Highland hornets' nest. He licked his lips into his sunken mouth, first the upper and then the lower, and continued to stare in sour deliberation. Then, apparently satisfied that he had impressed her with the majesty of the law, he barked:

"Missus MacDonald, you stand cha'ghed befo' this co't with spreading sedition. Speak fo' yo'sef, befo' the co't sentences you."

Flora's blue eyes gleamed suddenly. She drew her head sidewise in amazement, but her eyes on him. She chuckled.

"What's to laugh at?"

She gasped: "You—you—you said you would permit me to speak before you *sentenced* me. Am I condemned, then, in advance?"

The old fellow shook his head, angry at being caught in his own words: "A slip o' the tongue, madam. A slip o' the tongue. Proceed!"

Flora, alarmed, but still smiling, turned from the frost-bitten justice to the young army officer. The young man looked away uncomfortably. Duncan thought he was one of the Emmetts—a good family, but Whigs. At any rate he had the decency to be embarrassed at the court's openly displayed hostility.

She looked back at the magistrate. "Excuse me," she sobered. "I meant no indignity to your court."

"No offense intended and none taken. Proceed, madam."

"Then please tell me in what *way* I am supposed to have spread sedition?"

"You are cha'ghed with persuadin' men not to jine the American army and stirrin' up trouble agin the government of this free and independent state of No'th Carolina."

"Very well. Produce your evidence. I will answer it."

"That ain't the p'int. I want to know did you or didn't you."

"I will face the one who said that I did."

"Answer my question!"

"Are you telling me to convict *myself?* I ask a fair trial or none!"

"Hur-r-r-r-up!" The old magistrate jumped up angrily, clearing his throat. Duncan was uncomfortable. Flora was forgetting her main danger for the momentary clash.

The old magistrate snapped: "Listen, madam! What I want you to say is whether you was seditious or wasn't you?"

She shook her head helplessly. She pointed to the crowd. "Please," she begged. "There isn't a person in this room who wouldn't demand a fair trial. I ask no more."

Duncan caught the young army officer looking concernedly at him and at the other Scots. Also he was watching the increasing number in the audience discreetly nodding their heads, taking sides with Flora. Her spirited protests had gained their sympathy.

"Then, d'ye deny," the magistrate stormed, "that ye lent aid to fugitive Tories, that ye counseled the Scotch to resist the Patriots, that ye spread sedition up and down the Valley, that ye held up the tyrant George to make the people subject to him?"

"I deny nothing. I affirm nothing. I am ready to speak the truth when ye have faced me with the evidence which, even under Whig law, ye are bound to do."

"Bah!" The old magistrate rapidly was losing control of both himself and the situation.

"I came to this country," Flora continued, "to find peace and plenty, and to abide by the oath and obligations which of old time were upon me. I seek no controversy. Even so I am shorn of my husband and my sons and reduced deeper in poverty than I have ever known. Now you threaten me with prison because, forsooth, I only seek in my humble way to remain honorable though I lose all else."

"Honor!" the magistrate scoffed. "What do you call honor?"

"In this case," Flora replied quietly, "I have refused to turn traitor to my oath and my king."

"Aha!" The magistrate, triumphant, turned his toothless grin on the audience. "Ain't that sedition? Ain't it?"

The people looked back silently. If the magistrate looked for applause, he was disappointed. Duncan had an insane impulse to vault the crowd and grab Flora's tormentor by the neck.

The young militia officer, who had gone outside a few minutes before, came back gravely. Perhaps he had seen those horse-trading Highlanders in a new light.

Flora, having said that much, now held her head proudly, as if defying the court to torture her more. Duncan was tense and white.

The magistrate said: "By your own words, madam, I hereby pronounce you guilty!"

Flora dropped her eyes, loosed her hands into her lap. Her shoulders slumped imperceptibly. She said nothing. She had gone to the Tower of London gallantly, but a Whig prison held no glory.

"The co't sentences you——" The old fellow paused as if to enjoy the sweetness of his morsel.

But now the officer of the militia leaned over his shoulder, whispering urgently. The old man frowned in protest. The young man insisted. They whispered sharp words at each other. They left the bench and went to the corner of the room to whisper there. The old man then shook his head resignedly and returned to his seat.

"The co't sentences you," he continued rapidly, "to remain in its jurisdiction subject to its decrees, and to violate no jot nor tittle against the peace and dignity of the free and independent state of North Carolina, so help you God." The magistrate whacked the desk with his gavel and glared ferociously.

Somehow the sentence sounded terrible. Incoherent, it had the ring of great punishment.

Flora looked at the magistrate helplessly and shot an appealing glance to Duncan. The audience was as confused as she. Duncan made ready to spring the instant the officer should move to take her.

The magistrate gathered up his law book. "Now," he said angrily over his spectacles, "you go home and behave yo'self!" He stalked out, far from triumphant.

Flora's face cleared, but she dared not laugh. She had offended enough. She bowed her head in submission. Duncan came to meet her. She took his arm, and they walked to the door. No one spoke to her, but the crowd looked after her, curiously abashed. Duncan passed through the door with his hand raised in peace, and the Highlanders went about saddling their horses and making ready to ride.

The Scots were grimly silent. They found Flora's rig, and Duncan sat beside her to drive. A Scottish lad rode Donald Bane with the others. With the horses walking, they headed into the winter winds up Haymount Hill toward Killiegrey. Behind them by twos and threes came the bodyguard of Highlanders, men of gaunt faces and gaunt horses, their kilts faded and patched and none the less proud for all that.

When they were out of the village, Flora MacDonald spoke her first word. "Doon-kan!" and wept.

It was a long dreary ride to Killiegrey. The silvered bare oaks whistled shrill in the cold wind. The horses' hoofs clopped hollowly in the sand. There was so little, so eternally little, to say.

Duncan thought of Flora and her impoverished cavalcade with

a silent groan. He remembered the time when she was the Scottish fine lady who so dashingly had pranced upon her white horse, inspiring the kilted clansmen to march for king and country.

But now her dress—the same black silk dress—was turned and patched and took its only pride from the queenly figure who wore it. The harness on her horses was held together by cotton strings. The leather sheathing was torn from the rig, and the rough boards showed through. The whip socket held only a broken hickory switch. Flora MacDonald had reason for her disconsolate silence.

They were a part of that strange quiet which had reigned over the Cape Fear these months past. It was as though, now that the first crashing blasts of the break-away were spent, Nature brooded upon the wreckage of her own storms.

Empty cabins of departed neighbors, with doors and windows to creak in the wind, looked back at them over grass-grown corn rows, forlorn monuments to vanished hope. Here and there might be seen someone passing through, inspecting, hoping to pick up stray corn or a broken pot. In one a squad of men camped, but who knew who or what they were? Deserting Continentals from Valley Forge, perhaps—perhaps a gang of marauding Loyalists. The woods were full of them, and they changed their colors as occasion required.

The requisitioning of war was rapidly becoming mere pillage, and no one could tell now whether robbery was sponsored by law or by greed. And it made no great difference. America was in gloom. The brash new United States of America was heartily weary of war, even now, before a decisive battle had been fought. The only bright ray in the murk was that Britain was as gloomy and weary of it as were the rebels. The people of the mother country increasingly rebelled against the slaughter of their American friends and kin. It was a time of great weakness of government in America, and there was danger of anarchy.

Only once after that first burst of tears near Cross Creek did Flora weep again that day. That was when they came against the deserted cabin of Archie and Jean MacCulloh. Flora had loved Jean—and now they were gone—where? Flora wept softly on Duncan's arm.

"What hae I done?" she asked herself. "What hae I done?"

"Be brave, Flora MacDonald," Duncan said. "The King wi' not long permit such oppressions upon his subjects. Ye said that once t' me. I say it now to you."

"I don't know, Doon-kan. I don't know," she said dejectedly.

"But ye must keep it in y'r heart, Flora. Ye *must*."

"But I am such a weak woman, Duncan. So alone. So helpless. So deep in the wilderness of a strange country, wi' my Allan gone away, wi' enemies round about me."

"Na! Na, Flora!"

"Aye, Duncan," she sighed. "My health is tender, my bairns in danger—one never knows what a night may bring forth—I no longer am the brave woman ye call me. I pray the good Lord that He may see my weakness and have compassion, to put me again on the sweet soil that gied me birth, and let me live and die there in peace."

"Na, Flora!" Duncan's cry was so much a moan that she forgot her own pains to grasp his arm and search his face. "Ye canna, Flora! Ye canna! Many Scots are gone—thousands o' them, but thousands still remain. I am here, and ithers like me. We depend on ye, Flora. Ye hold us thegither. But if there be none t' lead us, then we may as well stick out our necks and let the Whigs chop their will."

"Ye do! Ye really do, depend on me—don't ye, Duncan?" Flora suddenly was eager. Her physical weaknesses, her personal troubles, were swept away. Her eyes shone again with the light of leadership. She extended her hand impulsively. "My hand on it, Duncan! I wi' not desert ye, as long as ye bid me stay. I wi' be strong. Ye speak the truth. This nightmare o' threat and oppression shall pass. We wi' be happy yet, Duncan. Eh, Duncan?"

"Aye, Flora!"

"We shall know peace yet, eh, Duncan?"

"Aye, Flora. But war first, and courage."

"Aye, Duncan. War first, but then—peace and rest."

"Aye."

"I think I could stand it better, Duncan, were there immediate gallant things to do—instead of fears by night and dread by day."

They spent the night at Kenneth Black's. Most of the clansmen left at once for their homes. Half a dozen remained to accompany her to Killiegrey the next morning.

Flora's scream was Duncan's first alarm. The three of them, he, Flora and old Kenneth Black, were turning into the lane up to Killiegrey. The six clansmen had turned back when they had come in sight of the chimneys, but now Kenneth dashed back to overtake them. Duncan whipped the horses to a gallop, and they raced up to the house.

Women were screaming inside. The house was full of marauders. They tumbled house furnishings out the door and scattered clothing on the floor.

Flora jumped from the rig and ran toward the men on the porch. "Stop!" she cried. "What are you doing in my chests? Stop instantly, sir!"

Duncan ran with her and tried to hold her back, but she would not be detained.

A long-faced man, wearing a ragged greatcoat with a rusted sword at his side, frowned up from pawing in a chest of clothing. He said nothing, but lifted his upper lip and snarled. He glanced over his shoulder and waggled his thumb. "Take 'em!" he said and went back to his search.

Eight men circled them with swords and bayonets. Duncan laughed. He couldn't fight that many. He couldn't even attempt to escape and leave the women.

"Keep y'r dirty steel at a distance," he growled. "We wi' not resist."

"Put them with the others," the sword-swinging commander ordered. "If the old hen starts cacklin', slap her down. We got to levy on this house and be gone."

"Levy—how?" Duncan demanded.

"In the name o' the Continental Congress and the high command o' the army!"

"Bosh! Ye're a bunch o' desertin' scalawags!"

The fellow grinned. "Well," he said, "this is one way to collect overdue pay."

Back in the hall, before the fireplace, were lined the women and old men. Duncan and Flora were hustled among them. There was

Anne, pale, pretty, attempting to be brave; one of the servant girls, a comely lass of seventeen, and four or five others. Two old men were tied to chairs near the door. One's face was bleeding. The fire helped, but the day was cold, and the wind blew through the windows which the marauders had burst open.

The invaders found wine. The six men who guarded the prisoners kept the jugs in motion, up the line and back again, with a swaggering cockeyed soldier taking the lead.

When.they had enough to drink, they began to eye the women.

"Carefu' tae you!" Duncan muttered.

"Shet up!" Cockeye warned him. He walked over and waggled Anne's chin between his thumb and finger. She jerked her head. Duncan lunged for him. The fellow must have expected it. He plunged his rifle butt into Duncan's stomach and reared back to laugh. "Tap him," he ordered.

One of the guards hit Duncan over the head with his rifle butt. Duncan didn't seem to feel the blow. He still had his mind on grasping the bugger's throat, knocking his head against the floor and throttling him. But he couldn't reach him. He was taking long, gangling steps backward until he bumped into the wall. Then he slid down, and things grew dark. And darker yet. And still darker. He seemed to be sinking into an abyss.

The next he knew he was seeing double, as if he were drunk, with an overpowering gripe twisting his belly. He couldn't raise his hand. He couldn't draw up his feet to rise from the floor. He strained until his temples throbbed, but he couldn't move.

The limber-jawed one with the cocked eyes slapped Flora Mac-Donald on the cheek.

"Shet up, ol' woman! Any more sass and I'll fry your fat. Stand where I tol' you."

He was not angry. Worse, he was arrogant and derisive. He laughed much. He went back to the terror-stricken Anne. The other soldiers looked on, enjoying the show.

"Watch 'er, now—watch 'er!"

His glance was as filthy as his teeth. His long saber flashed when he unsheathed it. Anne shrank back, but he caught her by the collar of her dress and held her.

"Now when I do this," he said over his shoulder to his companions, "watch 'er—wha, ha, ha, ha, ha! When the cold steel hits her skin, watch 'er spraddle back an' twist. Wah, ha, ha, ha! They'll do it every time!"

He slipped the point of his blade down by her chin into the bosom of her dress. Her eyes and her unuttered shriek told of her horror. As the flat steel went down to the hilt, her breast shot forward and she jumped back and stood awkwardly rigid.

"Wha, ha, ha, ha! Didn' I tell you?"

He gave his blade a twist and a jerk, and all her garments lay open from her throat to the floor.

The rowdy whooped and danced a jig, sliding to an obscene stop before her.

"Want 'er?" he demanded over his shoulder. "I'll take this'n," and collared Nellie, the servant lass.

Duncan slumped vaguely forward and balanced himself uncertainly, weaving on his knees. Only the lines of strain on his face, as though he pulled against the weight of the world, told of strength. His arms hung down limply.

"Tap him again, he's comin' to," Cockeye ordered. He gave attention to Nellie, again sheathing his flat, cold blade in the bosom of her frock. She screamed. Her breast arched. She jumped back and stood like marble.

"See? See?" Cockeye yelled. "They'll do it every time!"

His blade turned and slashed, and Nellie, too, was brought to the shame of her mistress.

"Stop it! Stop it!" implored Flora. "Hae ye no respect for womanhood? Hae ye no love f'r your mithers?"

"Whur's that silver?" one of the men answered her.

An old woman down the line croaked: "Shame on ye murderin' monsters! One wi' the feelin' o' manhood wouldna stoop tae such beastiness!"

"Shet up, Gramma—you ain't seen nothin' yet!"

What might have come next was not revealed. The sound of frightened shouts and scampering came from outside.

"The cavalry! Cavalry!"

"It was a goddam lie! She didn't have no silver nohow!"

The marauders broke from the room pell-mell, not even stopping for the wine. They threw themselves on their horses and dashed over the torn-down fences headlong for the brush, shedding stolen pewter as they went. They entered the woods just as old Kenneth Black and the clansmen galloped into view down the road.

Kenneth was almost apoplectic, and the five others were but little less. He stood purple-jowled and cursed in harsh Gaelic oaths that made no sense except in ferocity. But there were only two guns in the whole company, and their men were outnumbered four to one. Flora MacDonald's good judgment held them there.

While the danger lasted, Flora had an iron nerve. When it was over, she succumbed to depression and sat dry-eyed in the midst of her torn belongings.

"Wae's me," she wailed. "Why did the Heavenly Father permit me to come to this accursed land?"

Old Kenneth took charge. "Get out the wagons and the carts!" he commanded. "Sandy, ye ride the mare home and send all the wagons and carts o' the place. I wi' tak Flora MacDonald home wi' me. She sha' na spend anither day wi'out protection."

Flora, the queen of the Carolina Highlands, looked up darkly. She said nothing. The servants leaped to the task of moving.

That afternoon, when the sun hung coldly above the horizon, Flora MacDonald stopped the baggage-laden cart on which she rode. She looked back at the bleak thing which was Killiegrey. Once of rosy dreams and fair promise, now its bare windows were empty and dead. Its halls, so recently ringing with the laughter of good living, now were but hollow caverns.

"Allan, my darlin'!" Flora whispered.

CHAPTER 5

FLORA MACDONALD's miserable comfort in Kenneth Black's cabin was no more comfortable or miserable than the bleakness which spread upon the whole land after the break-away. She no more knew what was to become of her than did any other Tory—or Whig. All were in want. Happy was that one who lived off the beaten trail, whose little hoard of food met no envious eye. In the North that spring and summer of 1778 the armies maneuvered cautiously. In the South the pestilence of gloom settled upon all alike, and avarice and greed sucked deep of the blood of patriotism.

Duncan morosely watched the stagnation set in for rot, and turned his hand neither for good nor ill. He, too, had stagnated. His life's course had been dammed. His friends had been routed and browbeaten and humiliated and imprisoned and killed, his own king was helpless to enforce peace in the Carolinas—and all to what end? Only for a barren land of sapped farms and hungry people, who already had forgotten their high principles for preying and pillage.

He sat at his cabin door in the shade of a tree, slapping flies, drinking white liquor and reading, and laughing sardonically at a copy of a letter written to the people by Judge Sam Ashe. The impoverished rice planter wrote despairingly:

"For God's sake let's arouse from our supineness. Let the love of country rise . . . superior to base passion for gain!"

"Gain!" Duncan chortled to himself. "Gain what? There's na enough in the whole damn country to fill a peddle pack."

Duncan was half drunk and hadn't noticed John Slingsby approaching over the soft sand.

" 'Tis true," the newcomer sighed, looking down on Duncan.

Duncan threw the letter aside and looked up, frowning. He'd had no truck with Slingsby since the latter had taken the Whig oath in Wilmington.

John Slingsby was tall and spare-built, with an earnest eye. Everyone had always said he was honest, and Duncan had not doubted it until John had turned coat.

"Why did ye come to me?" Duncan asked bluntly.

"I have recanted my oath to the Whigs," John said quietly, taking a chair and leaning back. "I thought you would like that."

"Aye."

Duncan answered listlessly and looked over the swamp. It made no difference now. It did not even remove his resentment at John's having taken the oath. He spoke no more of it, and

Slingsby did not mention it again. They wondered how things would end. They did not trouble to guess.

Slingsby had deeper lines in his face. His hair was silvered and not so jimply kept as once.

John must have been appraising Duncan also, for he said: "You look more the man, Duncan—less the lad."

"Na, John," Duncan judged. "I know mysel' too well. I once had vauntie notions. I entertained some thought o' glory and honor, but now all I can think is that my king is weak and needs me, and I, too, am weak."

"Aye," Slingsby nodded. "I said ye were waxing strong."

Slingsby looked at him earnestly, as though he, also, wished to make a confession. But old Tom Hadley rode up and looked down on them from the saddle. He chuckled. He was grayer than before, and his clothes were faded colorless.

"First time I've seen you to talk to, Dunk, since you gimme the slip that time. Jest ridin' the country, me and Tom Brown—thought I'd drap by and gab awhile. How's things in Wi'm'ton, John?"

"Light, Mr Tom, and sit," Duncan said, beginning to smile. This was like old times.

"Yessir," old Tom chuckled, and Duncan found another chair, "that was the damnedest thing to happen to me in this war. The boys ain't stopped laughing at me yet."

"Weel," Duncan said, "it did me little good and ye little harm. Tom Brown caught the brunt o't."

"Ye-e-ah!" Tom Hadley tipped back his chair and settled its legs in the sand. "Jest how did you and Tom make out?"

Duncan paused. He thought of Tom Brown on his back and himself with a dagger at Tom's throat. The memory suddenly was revolting. He looked at Hadley and knew the old fellow was trying to worm the story from him.

"What did Tom say?"

Old Tom shook his head and laughed. "I've an idea you outsmarted him worse'n you did me. He wouldn't tell."

They smiled mildly, and then their faces sobered and they gave thought to the things that leaped in their minds. Old Tom rose as if to go and sat down again. Perhaps it was to see who the horseman was that came over the creek. Duncan knew without turning. The horse was Tom Brown's Jess. He could tell by hoofbeats.

"Ay-y-ye!" Tom Brown shouted from behind the trees. "Anybody home?"

Then he came around the path and saw them.

"Let's all get drunk," he demanded, and he did not smile. His eyes were dead with worry and dread and disappointment. "Swear to God I'll go crazy if I don't get drunk."

"Ye needna be so low, Tom," Duncan offered, setting out another chair. "Think o' me. And my kind."

"Aye, Duncan." Tom dropped from the saddle, his voice softening. "I can think o' ye, or anybody I know—Whig or Tory—and weep at the damned plague on the land. Thieves! Robbers! Night riders! Skunks! It's enough to make an honest man puke. Where's that liquor?"

The day was hot, but Tom Brown conceded nothing to temperance on account of that. He swung the jug to the crook of his elbow, hoisted its bottom and drank deep. The fire of it brought tears to his eyes and a gasp from his lungs. Old Tom Hadley raised the jug with both hands. John Slingsby, used to the finer liquors in Wilmington, gagged but held to it. Duncan, already rosy and sweating, put down another without effort. The first one was the hardest.

Their conversation was dry. There were thoughts to think but little to say. Yet, in their common gloom, they discarded the enmities of the tragic two years of war and held together on the remnants of the friendships which had existed before.

Hadley reached for the jug. "If they'd jest stop talkin' and start fightin' we might get somewhere."

"Weel," demanded Duncan, "how'd ye like to be like me—no army t' fight in, no fight if ye were in the army, wi' y'r king impotent t' subdue rebellion and this rebel Governor Caswell just waitin' for ye to grow anither ear o' corn so he can grab it?"

"Tough," old Tom sympathized. "It *is* tough."

"No salt," Duncan moaned, handing the jug to Slingsby.

" 'S a fact—no salt—no shoes," Tom Brown lamented, "and this cussed paper money litterin' up the house—the women all out o' heart. Swear to God—— Yeah, John, don't care if I do."

"I got two shoats in the swamp," Duncan said, "and I don't have a notion there'll be corn to fatten them. If there is enough, some Whig polecat will requisition the meat for the army."

"If you think you're the only one to suffer," Tom Brown said, "take a look at my smokehouse."

They all took another drink. They had to drink fast, the way they sweated, to acquire intoxication. But, being determined, they held to it. Good cheer never came, only greater gloom. They attempted to sing "Auld Lang Syne" but there was no spirit in it. Finally, as the sun went down, they were quite drunk, lying on the ground, hard asleep, taking their hard-won respite.

It was early fall when Duncan was summoned to Brompton. The first autumn chill struck moistly through him as he crossed the river. Duncan went dismally. Young Gilbert, since old Gilbert had died, had steadily forsaken the King's cause. While he pretended to be neutral, Duncan suspected that he kept a harboring place for Whig spies. At any rate he had no comfort at Brompton and had remained aloof. The Johnstons had not been at pains to conceal their own coolness, and, therefore, when Gilbert sent a Negro asking as a special favor for him to come that afternoon, Duncan knew it was important enough to heed.

Gilbert met him at the front-yard gate. His friend of olden days was polite and formal. They shook hands, a hard, vibrant shake in which the bones pressed upon each other. Gilbert's eye met his in a brief glance and shifted over his shoulder. He was not the proud, hospitable old Gilbert Johnston who had so warmly welcomed all Scots to Brompton Hall the night, four years ago, when Flora MacDonald had entered the valley with such fair promise.

This was a truce, and Gilbert and Duncan both put their own thoughts back in their minds.

"We hae Flora MacDonald wi' us," Gilbert explained. "She wants to see ye. Ye'll find her i' the parlor."

"Flora—is she well?" apprehensively.

"Aye, well." Gilbert's dry voice somehow was not reassuring.

Duncan left Gilbert at the front door. From far down the dark hall, he had the impression, some of the Johnston women looked at him but did not come forward to speak. He pressed on to the parlor door and turned the knob.

It was a shadowy room. The curtains were drawn as usual. The bit of fire on the hearth emphasized more than lightened the darkness of the spinet against the wall, the heavy bookcase in the corner, the black-walnut chairs with their deep-cushioned seats. It was the curtains with their faint mustiness which gave Duncan the feel of suffocation.

Flora MacDonald sat alone, dressed in black. The little flame gave ruddiness to her face and made it warm. Warm and wan. And defeated. Aye—defeated. The damned Whigs had murdered her. That was in her eyes.

She smiled and rose and held out her hands. "Doon-kan!" Her eyes were happy that one moment.

He took her hands in his as though they were a hummingbird. "Flora—are ye well?"

"Aye—Duncan. Well. And yet—not well."

"And how *could* ye be?"

"I'm glad ye came. I knew ye'd come."

"O' course—if ye wanted me. Ye kenned that."

She sighed. "Aye, Duncan. I kenned. I hae that i' my heart— forever."

"Fionnaghal—ye speak cryptically."

"Duncan, I am going home."

"Home? Killiegrey?"

Flora shook her head. Her voice was a little murmur. "Na, Duncan. South Uist. And Skye. Where I can drink the whey o' the goats o' the Western Isles. I'll ne'er be a well woman wi'out it." She looked into the fire and seemed to speak to herself more than to him. "And feel the mists o' the Isles and hear the music o' the Minch upon the rocks o' Benbecula, and hae the feel o' the solid ledges o' Kingsburgh and Ormiclade and Flodigarry beneath my shoon. They canna take these away frae me—no matter how they try."

Duncan opened his hands and stood thus. She drew away and sat down again, wiping her eyes, still talking—her voice a tinkle, her eyes looking into the coals and seeing Scottish hills.

"Na," she said to the fire. "They canna tak awa' the heather, nor the burns and the braes nor the wimpling paths where the kye walk. They can take the castles and the high estates and the siller and the gowd, and the fine gowns and the supercilious talk o' the fine folk, but they canna take one whit frae the sweet smell o' the breeze frae the sea which so aften rested me in Flodigarry."

"Flora!" Duncan protested. But she did not seem to hear.

"My foot there," she patted her knee sharply, as though she felt the soil of Scotland, "wi' fa' on the ground and be firm. It wi' find no uncertain sand for to shift and sink. There wi' be no mournfu' gray moss to hang frae the trees as though to shroud a body before her doom. There wi' be no long distances o' loneliness and sorrow. No slinkin' enemies to creep upon a body i' the dark. There wi' be no strange king to promise and disappoint— because I wi' na again put my trust in any king or prince or man o' power. I want nought but my Allan and a wee bit croft i' the Hielands. Though we be poor as kirk mice, my Allan and me, God grant we hae our gloamin' years together in peace."

Duncan had waited too long with his protest. He had expected to remind Flora that she had promised not to forsake the Cape Fear until victory should come. But now, having heard her crooning, he knew he was overruled by a higher claim. Who was he to say nay to one who asked for nought but the feel of the auld heath?

"They hae taken a'!" Her tortured eyes raised to his. "We offered a' and they hae taken it. My Allan and my sons and a' we did hae. The House o' Stuart—now the Hanover—I hae served both wi' equal desolation."

First aghast at feeling this tower of strength shattering before him, then cool and reasoning, Duncan was conscious of a certain new power. He knew now that no longer was there one in life for him to depend upon either for wisdom or for leadership. His king had failed him. And Flora had failed him. But, by God, he could stand alone. And alone, by God, he *would* stand.

Flora MacDonald no longer was the grand lady to him. She was only a woman. Less admirable, perhaps, but illimitably more lovable.

"Fionnaghal!" he whispered and dropped on his knee before her chair. She reached out to him in a quick impulsiveness and drew him closer. He felt her fingers in his hair, and it was in his mind that it was not his yellow locks she felt but those of the long-gone Young Chevalier. Silent, still, he waited while she stroked him and looked into the fire, taking this last wee bit of illusion from a life so quickly settling into a field of ashes.

"Doon-kan," she whispered, "let us a' go back to Scotland—ye wi' y'r Mary, me wi' my Allan, Sandy MacLeod wi' his Anne and bairns—what though we wear but hodden-gray and hae only the plain vittles and simple ways o' the poor—the burns and the moors and the sweet smell o' Scotland wi' be there for aye—and aye—and aye!"

Duncan laughed and straightened up, shaking his head. "And who would burn my tar and till my soil and fight my fight?"

She laughed too, buoyed by his cheer. "I ken, Doon-kan. I ken. I hae been a silly, weak auld carlin, soughin' my sore distress upon ye. But did ye ken how neefu' it were for me to do it, ye'd na hold it against me."

Duncan drew her standing. She was not to his shoulder. He hadn't noticed that before. He had thought she was taller. He spoke with more assurance now, more than ever before to Flora MacDonald.

"Flora, ye hae chosen the better part," he said. "This land is too raw f'r ye. We wi' the youth and strength wi' stay, and when we hae it smoothed an' sweetened to y'r taste, then ye shall come back and be our princess."

She smiled and shook her head gently. "Na, Doon-kan. Once my foot is on Scottish soil it ne'er again shall press anither sod. A' I ask o' the King is to gi'e me back my Allan and frae time to time let me look upon my bairns."

They stood before the fire, Duncan with his arm around her shoulders, she leaning against him.

"Doon-kan," she said, "wi' ye na marry Mary and come back to Scotland?"

"Na."

"Why? Once, i' this very room, ye longed f'r her—sairely."

"I wi' na marry Mary now—e'en she had me. She has ta'en up wi' the Whigs."

"Allan married me after I had aided the Prince."

"Mary has made her bed—she must lie in it."

Duncan's voice was cold dispassion. It bore no hint of the torture of his soul those weeks after he had seen her so contented in the Gillespie boy's arms, and of the throttling imaginings of what he had not seen.

"Duncan," Flora said to him quietly, "do not disparage Mary too harshly. When she came to America she had Malcolm—she a'ready has gi'en to the King more than ye hae."

Duncan's reply was about to come bitterly, when the door opened and he turned to see who entered. It was Mary. She bore a knitted jacket on her arm. She saw him without surprise, even with casual glance.

"How are you, Duncan?" she asked. "I haven't seen you for the *longest* time!"

While he answered uncomfortably she passed on to Flora.

"See? Flora? I've mended the jacket for you. No proud army wife shall boast that she has finer. Do you remember it? It was one you gave me to keep me warm on the ship."

Duncan was agitated beyond control. His stomach trembled and his breast swelled, and one pulled against the other. 'Twas a fair circumstance for him, as torn as he was, that the women bent over the patched jacket and paid him no heed.

When they had finished, Duncan was leaning on the mantel board with one arm, and his other thumb hung in his kilt belt. His countenance he held still by force. Flora's blue eyes were sick with the sadness in them, Mary's bright, brown ones were alive with sympathy and hope and courage. It was she, now, who led, and her sweetness poured out like a song. She was planning for Flora's trip to Nova Scotia, there to see Allan (now exchanged and back in the British Army), thence to Scotland. There was the matter of the jacket, and then it was a question of gloves—one of one pair and one of another, and both had to be patched and dyed.

"And when ye see Tam of Glengarry, gin ye see him," Mary laughed, "ye must not say to him that the Mary he wanted tramps the bogs in heavy shoes and works like one o' his ain gillies!"

"Na! Na!" Flora's eyes brightened. "I shall say that Mary has the lo'e o' many Carolina planters o' wide acres, but that she awaits her Cape Fear true lo'e, who is the envy o' them a'."

"Na," Mary said soberly. "Let him be tell'd the truth or nought."

"But it is na the truth, my dear?"

"Ye speak o' Duncan and me, doubtless. Duncan has his work to do, I hae mine."

Her words were calm and cool and carried no hint of heartbreak. Duncan was about to blurt out that his life's course was not at the disposal of Mary's whims, but that seemed no fair retort. Instead he bolted for the door, saying:

"I'll be back. My horse rubs the bridle at feed time."

He had no intention of coming back to Flora and Mary alone. He could not know that when he closed the door Mary fell on Flora's lap and sobbed bitterly.

From then until three days later when Flora's barkentine loosed its mooring at the Wilmington wharves and dropped down the river with the tide, there remained for Duncan three pictures for memory—three gray pictures.

One of these was that night at supper at Brompton Hall. Mrs Johnston's pear preserves were as good and as aromatic and as sweetly cold as of yore, yet they lacked savor. The fried chicken was golden brown, but the taste was gone. The table linen was glistening white, yet was not awe-inspiring.

Gilbert presided, and each one spoke his part for the conversation. But Duncan, in grace, could not speak his heart, for he hated Whigs, and Gilbert had made peace with them. Gilbert could not lament the unwisdom of the Tory leaders, for there was Flora—Flora, conquered and defeated. Only by the power of long habit did she sit cool and deliberate and wield the Johnston pewter as though no such thing had happened. They tested for an agreeable subject and finished the meal with stories of ancient Scottish valor.

The next picture was the day in Wilmington when the Whigs and Tories who still had money gathered around and made their offers on Flora MacDonald's silverware—the precious silver she had kept since the lords and ladies of London had lionized her. But now such things meant little to Flora. The locket on her breast, with the Bonnie Prince's yellow curl inside, the carefully wrapped sheet on which he had slept and so dedicated her shroud, these she would not part with for love or money. But the silver—

well—either that or no passage. The Whig officers had been kind. The courteous Captain Ingram had secured her the pass which made the transportation of the plate safe. Now it was on sale to the highest bidder. Duncan walked away from the sale place, because the eagerly gathering inhabitants made it obscene.

It was at gloamin'-shot when he walked down the gangplank. The ship's cook was frying fish. Flora's baggage he had stowed in her cabin. With it he had left a shapely water dipper he had made from a cypress knee. Others had presented gifts—Mrs Slingsby, Mrs Shaw. Dr Cobham had made her a concoction designed to relieve seasickness. The wharf was filled with people, some sincerely wishing her well, some merely curious. Mary Harnett was there. Cornelius was in Philadelphia at the Congress. Mary's pale brisk face was not that of the avid looker-on.

"Once I told you," she said to Duncan as he paused at her side, "to watch Flora MacDonald. I'm sorry I went out of my way to say anything against her. She's had enough bitterness. Had I the same, I pray for her strength to bear it."

Duncan pressed his lips and did not reply, but nodded. He could not trust himself to speak of that.

"How is Cornelius?" he changed the subject.

"Working himself to death."

Duncan forsook the crowd and went up the wharf where he could be alone for his last view of Flora when she came back to the deck. He stood under the stern and waited, looking up. The wharf timbers gave up their cables, and the barkentine inched into the current. The last segment of sun sank behind Eagle's Island, and the western sky blazed flame for Flora's farewell.

She stood at the taffrail, looking down. Others were there, too, but somewhat apart. When he saw her she was waving to those on the wharf. When he waved she saw him and fluttered her handkerchief. She turned quickly and looked across the river toward the sun, and he knew she turned to wipe her eyes.

"Good-by, Doon-kan!" He didn't hear it in the noise. He saw it on her lips and felt it in his heart.

The ship was in the middle of the river, swiftly on its way in the tide. The people at the wharf drifted away a few at a time. Duncan stood on the timbers, watching the ship, the black-draped little figure that stood at the rail and looked back up the Cape Fear. The purple shadows reached out, and the ship began to merge with them. He could barely distinguish her. A sudden gripping choke in his throat made him lunge out with a wide sweep of his hand as though to call her back. Perhaps she saw it. Perhaps not. Duncan thought he saw her raise her hand and wave. And if she did, then the darkness also brought him a message: "Good-by, Doon-kan!"

The flatboat, with Gilbert Johnston's Negroes on it, ready to pole back up the Cape Fear, rode high on the turning tide. The night was chilly. They had piled dirt on the floor. They had a fire and light. Duncan stepped over their long poles. He paused. There was an extra man, a white man. Duncan frowned, for the fellow had a white hickory club prowling about searchingly, whacking at things. Duncan remembered the whack; the man had asked him about ships the night Flora MacDonald had come four years ago. The same man who had tried to kick the Tory boy in Cross Creek.

The back-countryman came to him with the brisk walk of the short, strong man. Duncan stood at the fire and waited, his mind clouding.

The fellow's hard blue eyes never left Duncan. "Oh, you're the Scotchman who kicked me through the crowd at Cross Creek," he said bluntly.

"Aye," Duncan answered dryly. "Want more?"

"No. No, that was enough."

"Weel," thumbing, "get off the boat."

"Don't be so damn short. I am the one that got beat, not you."

"I hae no truck wi' Whigs."

"Who said I was a Whig?"

" 'Tis well known. Y'r name's Hanning—or Ganning—or——"

"My name's Fanning. David Fanning. I'm no damn Whig, and who says so is a liar."

"Why, then, did ye try to beat up a Loyalist boy?"

"I was a Whig then. I might have been now, but the cutthroats robbed me."

"Oh."

"I've sold my horse. I want to go up the river with you."

"Humph." Duncan gave thought. The view had shifted too quickly for a quick answer. "Ye're no Whig—so, why not? I warn ye, however, that if y'r natural contentiousness leads ye to combat wi' me, I'll throw ye in the river and na fish ye out."

"If you are man enough." David Fanning accepted the terms cheerfully and began to open his saddlebags for pans and coffee-pot.

"Shove off," Duncan said. "We'll be above tidewater when the tide tur-r-rns back."

The tide. Duncan never thought of it without remembering Cornelius Harnett's words: that more water runs out than runs in.

CHAPTER 6

KING GEORGE WAS A LONG TIME demonstrating his might in the South, but once in action the reverberations were as thunder and his strokes as lightning. Savannah—where the forces of Robert Howe, of the Cape Fear Tidewater, were riddled. Brier Creek—where the army of John Ashe, his neighbor, was routed. Kettle Creek—Stono Ferry—Charleston—all steps in the British northward march of victory, and Duncan Stuart remained in Bladen to stamp his feet and shake his yellow hair and unnaturally bellow his derision at the disconcerted Whigs. His pent-up and packed-in oppressions came out in a new, flaming sense of deliverance.

"Waste no time on me!" he derided Tom Brown at the Elizabethtown ferry. The Whigs were marching and counter-marching in frenzy, and Brown was watching the Bladen Scots like a hawk. "When His Majesty takes Charleston I go, and ye can't stop me. Till then, ye can best spend y'r time pickin' out places i' the swamps to hide in."

"I'll make plenty o' Tory skulls pop"—Brown smoothed his harsh words with a grin—"before I skulk in the swamps." Then, soberly: "And don't forget that the first move you make toward the British may be your last. This is no play war now."

"And don't ye forget," Duncan said amiably, "that f'r five years ye hae trampled the Scots on the Cape Fear, and when it comes our turn t' be on top—ware, Tom Brown!"

Brown laughed and slapped Duncan jovially on the shoulder.

For some reason, strange even to himself, Duncan filled with sudden, choking rage. "Keep y'r dirty back-stabbin' hands off o' me," he shrugged. "I'll ne'er look mysel' i' the face wi'out shame until I run ye out o' the country."

They glared at each other for a long moment, and it came upon each one that a quarrel was useless. They walked away in different directions.

When, a week later, Duncan heard of the fall of Charleston—of the ludicrous ease with which the British took Fort Moultrie—his cry was like that of a hurt animal.

"They could hae done it four years ago, if they'd had the sense o' goats!"

Four years! A senseless delay which had cost him shamefully— tens of thousands of Highlanders gone, Flora MacDonald gone, friends transformed into corpses, prisoners and enemies—and had opened the gates for poverty to stalk the land.

Young Duncan Ray was in Bladen and told him about Charleston. Ray also said that old Hector MacNeill and Archibald Mac-Dougall had returned with him from New York. They had sent him slipping through the valley for the Second Highland Uprising. The Scots were to be readied for the coming of Cornwallis when the corn should be ripe.

"But Flora MacDonald is gone!" Duncan told Ray in anguish.

"Aye, but we'll get her back."

"Aye!"

Duncan Stuart would not heed Ray's caution to stand ready and wait.

"I hae said if the British take Charleston I wi' go to them and take up the march where I left off four years ago, and so I wi'."

The fall of Charleston was on May 12, 1780. Sir Henry Clinton, still rankling from the disgrace which the slow-moving country warrior, Moultrie, had put on him in 1776, moved by land and sea and squeezed that proud city until finally the citizens petitioned their own half-starved soldiers to surrender. Duncan made a quick calculation. Camden might be next. Duncan Ray had said that Cornwallis and Tarleton would move inland between the Pee Dee and the Wateree. Governor Martin would be with them. He would leave at once—tonight.

To Gillie Black he said: "Ye again will take note that ye are in charge to do what is to be done. If, when I am gone, ye are stolen by the Whigs, ye wi' make y'r way back to me the best ye can. Ye wi' remember a'ways that ye are my property, bought wi' my money, and ye are to consider no ither man y'r master except by my authority."

"Yas'h."

"I wi' leave Donald Bane wi' ye, and all things else, and ye are t' conserve them as God gies ye strength and wit."

"Yas'h."

"Should it be that the Whigs steal Donald Bane, ye wi' follow after them and steal him back. If that should not be possible, then ye shall kill the nag t' save him the pains o' starvation and mistreatment."

"Yas'h."

Duncan left by night, wearing only homespun breeches and shirt, with neither the oat straw of the Loyalists nor the bucktail of the Whigs. He carried no weapons. He planned to say neither yea nor nay to any he should meet on the road, and to make his way circumspectly south and west until he made contact with Governor Martin.

He spent one night in the abandoned house at Killiegrey, as forlorn and as dismal a place as he had ever known. He had stopped at Kenneth Black's on the way for something to eat. Old Kenneth's eyes had shone as though heaven again was showering gifts upon the King's men. "I wad tae God," he cried, "I could gae wi' ye!"

Duncan crossed the Yadkin and bore southwest, coming now into the country of clay hills and shale. He was more and more disturbed for his own safety, for now he began to pass through the thrifty Mecklenburg country of the Dutch and the Ulster Scots, who were vindictive Whigs. Moreover, the undergrowth was less thick, and there were no enveloping swamps to dive into for havens. If pressed, he decided, he would climb into the trees for hiding.

When he reached the Waxhaws, he had reason to feel glad he had made this plan, for, approaching suddenly before him, a line of Whig soldiers, about three hundred strong, topped the hill beyond and he had no way to escape except up a tree. He went up as nimbly as God gave him strength. The leaves shielded him, but the soldiers were not keen-eyed. They were looking back in apprehension.

An officer gave them orders, and they halted and lay on the grass. They were not far from Duncan, and he could see them well and hear them talk. One of them, a big brown-eyed, yellow-bearded fellow, grumbled good-naturedly:

"Well, if we're going to surrender to this Tarleton, Preacher, it's time for you to tell Saint Peter to open that gate—*wide* and *fast!*"

They were tired. The day was hot. Nobody said much. They were dejected. Tarleton was pursuing them with race horses taken from the Charleston stables. They spoke of Colonel Buford, and Duncan had heard of the Virginian. Colonel Buford was back over the hill arranging terms of surrender under the white flag with Tarleton's agents.

The first sign of action that Duncan saw was the American officers racing over the hill, waving their swords, shouting wildly: "To arms! To arms!"

The soldiers leaped up, but they were burdened with their equipment. Their guns were not loaded. They knew nothing of battle lines.

And then came the British horsemen, charging over the crest of the hill with thundering hoofs and ungodly shrieks. Colonel Tarleton was in his stirrups, riding a bay horse, shouting like a demon, and swift upon him were the cavalrymen. The Whigs were in a woeful state of confusion. Some fired their guns, perhaps fifty of them, and some of the cavalrymen pitched from their horses into the valley.

Then Duncan saw the sight which was to remain with him for all his days. The Whig soldiers threw down their guns and held up their hands in surrender. The British were so close upon them that they could have seen their hands trembling.

What made Duncan forget the rest of it was the big brown-eyed yellow-bearded Whig soldier under his tree. He was the one who had laughed so much while the men sat on the grass and waited the order to surrender. Duncan heard the other noises, the trample of the horses, the shrieks for mercy, the splattering sword strokes, the soft, gritty, sickening swipes when the blades sank into flesh and bone. Those noises battered at his ears and were refused entrance because they were crazy and unbelivable, but under him on the ground was something he could both see and hear, and he gave heed to the point of nausea.

He saw this the more because he watched Colonel Tarleton's maniacal approach from the other hilltop. Small and compact, he sat his saddle or stood in his stirrups as though the horse and the saddle were a part of him. He leaned forward, and his shouts were high and predatory. Hundreds of horses' hoofs rumbled behind him, and the swaying bodies of the men were like tumbling waves.

The Whigs halfway down the hill no longer stood in the face of howling death but threw down everything and ran. Tarleton whacked at the neck of the first man he reached but did not cut him down. The next horse behind him did, and the other horses trampled him.

The thunder of the horses' feet swept on, but at a slower tempo as the horsemen began to overtake the fleeing Whigs. Duncan was impelled to look at Tarleton's eyes, hot, black, hungry, as he closed in, as though here now he would take his fill. It was directly under Duncan's oak that Tarleton overtook the big brown-eyed soldier.

When the man saw that he no longer had a chance to escape, he turned, his hands high, calling for mercy. He caught Tarleton's reins in both hands and stopped the horse, lifting his face to the officer and shouting above the turmoil: "Quarter! Quarter! Quarter!" But louder than his great mellow voice were his eyes, like the liquid, pleading eyes of a dog.

Tarleton looked down on him for the fraction of a second, his neck bent, his sword still high. Then, faster than Duncan's eye could follow, the sword whipped down, and the man's handless arms jumped up, both stumps being little spurting red fountains. The Whig looked at them dumbly, his eyes growing bigger and bigger, looking first at one and then the other. Then he shrieked.

Tarleton laughed and rode on. The man ran, his stumps of arms spraying blood before him. Duncan saw him race to the brow of the hill and sprawl. All up the hillside the bodies of men, dozens of them, lay on the ground, and a hot, sickening scent rose into the branches of the oak.

Duncan dared not come down. Tarleton's men would kill him before he could explain. The horsemen would be coming back this way as soon as the diminishing number of shrieks over the hill should cease. He had to remain hidden. He clung to the trunk of the tree so fiercely that the sharp bark bit into his arms. And stared dumbly, refusing to believe that what he saw was true.

The British came back over the hill, shouting victory, driving twoscore prisoners over the scene of slaughter. They made no effort to alleviate the suffering of the wounded or to bury the dead, and there was no visible soul in that wilderness to perform the office. Except Duncan.

"Water! Water!" groaned a voice from the ground, even before the King's soldiers were out of sight. Other dulled ears caught the sound. "Water!" they croaked. The field of the maimed and the dead lifted a single voice, "Water!"

Duncan scrambled down the tree, and, standing on soil, stumbled to the ground, for his knees trembled and were weak. Not ten steps away the clear blue eyes of a thin-faced man with a crimson chest whispered: "Water!" Duncan gathered up a canteen and ran down the hill to what seemed to be a creek. When he came back he had forgotten which man had called him. The hillside was strewn with men, some dead, some unconscious, some groaning and coughing and calling for water. A sense of justice bade him get his bearings from the tree and find the man who had first called. He found him, but the man now was dead and needed nothing.

After that for an hour, or two hours, he bore water to the wounded, racing, perspiring, forgetting the horror of it in the pressing immediate necessity. He forgot Tarleton. He forgot the charging horses except as something unbelievable. He carried water in little metal canteens, and as soon as he had relieved one, ten more called.

By what means the news went through the wilderness, Duncan

never knew. Somewhere in that timeless agony after the British left, people began arriving. First there were some men and then some more men with some women and then some women and some boys. No one spoke or explained. There was no time to talk.

The human instinct to organize took effect. Woodsmen fashioned rough stretchers from saplings and went among the dead and picked out the wounded and brought them together in the shade of trees.

All this, somehow, seemed to ease the tension. The work proceeded in an orderly manner, and now and then one spoke to another.

Water stood in buckets, and women tore their own petticoats and the shirts of men into bandages. One red-haired woman, Duncan noticed, was more efficient than the others. She was more deft with her hands, quicker to see with her quick blue eyes. She was thirty-five years old perhaps. She had a lively, courageous voice made more for laughing than for sighing upon the wounds of a hundred bleeding soldiers. The men called her Mrs Jackson. Her two sons, one about fifteen, the other no more than twelve or thirteen, attended her. Pale and big-eyed, the thin-faced, lanky boys were quick to obey her—whether to roll a bandage or to push in the eye of a whacked-up soldier while she held open the socket.

"More water, Andy," she called, and the lesser of the fierce-faced youngsters ran, barefooted, beyond the trench where the men were opening a grave and dipped water from the creek. "Damn British!" he half sobbed to Duncan. "*I'll* kill 'em!"

They built fires that night. No attempt would be made to move the wounded into the Waxhaw meeting house until tomorrow. The helpers sat far enough from the fire to escape its warmth and bitterly assailed the merciless Tarleton. Duncan strolled into the darkness, took his direction from a star and made his way on toward Camden.

So much alone, Duncan had grown the habit of speaking to himself as he walked. First he had whispered, but now he spoke aloud. He argued matters to himself and disputed right soundly. It helped muffle the cries of the mercy seekers, and it cut the distance to that illimitable sandy flatness which thinned under the horizon. He had walked all night, and the sun was rising pinkly.

"The looks o' the woman's eyes," he said. "They were like blue needles. They had death in 'em, like the death on the hillside. They had *a'* that death in 'em, and pity. And hate. Aye—they had hate. I wouldna be Tarleton, with any soul bearin' me that hate. But she had pity, that Widow Jackson—great pity—enough to take a man's broken jaw i' her hands like it was a hog jowl and put it back i' place. Aye—she had grit. It takes a wonderfu' woman to do that in the name o' pity. The lad's name was Andrew—a good Scot name. He was like his mither. But she said she came frae Castlereagh, so she was Irish. Ah, weel, there's bound to be *some* good in the Irish. But they are Whigs, o' course."

The thought that such spirit existed in the Whigs gave him pause for consideration.

"Aye," he said, "the war wi' not end till the Whigs are overwhelmed. Tarleton, as brutal as he be, no doubt is right. Ye hae to kill 'em to conquer 'em."

He tightened his lips and walked on grimly for more than a mile before he spoke again.

"I hae na yet killed a man. May God preserve me frae that distress o' soul."

Duncan did not go all the way to Camden, for on the road he met some Loyalists foraging for beef. They told him that the British, more rapidly than he had anticipated, were throwing up a line of forts across the province of South Carolina. The easternmost of these was at Cheraw, sixty miles away, almost on a line toward Elizabethtown. It was the nearest post to the Highland country, and Governor Martin had gone there. General Wemyss was in command of the district, and Major Archibald MacArthur held the town with two battalions of the Scottish Seventy-first Regiment. That was like going home. Duncan made his way there directly, for he had no wish now to see Camden and the bloody Tarleton.

Though the sand pulled at his feet, Duncan's spirit leaped. Not since Moore's Creek had the sense of victory been so strong upon him. He strode over the sandhills without conscious effort, driving on. Even the long march was a relief. Every step he took now, every slope he topped, every creek he crossed—all these were that much more action toward triumph and peace and restored stability.

He walked on, never tiring. Whether it was night or day made no difference. The sand was as soft for sleeping in the day as it was at night, and the stars guided him by night as well as the sun by day. He walked until he wearied, went to sleep in the vast privacy of the plain, awoke and walked once more.

Governor Martin was as sickly and as determined as ever. The day was hot. He wore no coat, but preserved his dignity with his black beaver hat.

They sat in the shade of a mighty oak and talked. At least, Martin talked. He asked questions and kept on talking, leaving Duncan no opportunity to answer. He had gone to New York after the failure at Moultrie in 1776. He had been sick. His wife had died. He had been sick again. The King had failed to restore his lieutenant colonel's commission. The Whigs had confiscated all his property in North Carolina. He had been sick.. When God gave the British the victory (which had been delayed by their own dilatory measures) he would make the Tar Heels pay and pay. Cornelius Harnett, Martin said, would pay in sweat .and groans.

"You'd heard about Robert Howe and John Ashe?" Martin asked in pale satisfaction.

Duncan managed to say: "Na."

"Robert Howe was routed so utterly in the defense of Savannah," the governor continued, barely pausing, "that Christopher Gadsden castigated him, and Howe issued a challenge. Howe shot his ear off. John Ashe did no better in Georgia when the might of the British bowled him over, and he demanded a court-martial to clear *his* name. They are not so arrogant now as they were marching on the Cape Fear."

Duncan hoped that Mary MacLeod would hear about womankiller Howe. "What can I do?" he demanded, breaking into Martin's monologue. "I am ready."

"Patience! Patience, my friend. Our impetuosity always has done us more damage than our loyalty. Let us be patient and attend the mills of the gods, which I have found, to my sorrow, grind slow."

"Aye. But now's the time f'r action."

"Yes, well-directed action, and when victory comes it will be sweeter. I shall want you for my courier, of course. Your first duty shall be to return home."

"Na!"

"Patience, I said. The assignment is not as drab as it seems. Are you not interested in seeing the British capture Wilmington?"

"Wilmington? Aye! When?" Duncan was aroused now, standing up, flinging his hair, ready to go.

"Patience. Patience. In the high command's own good time it will send a naval detachment by sea from Charleston. Wilmington will be taken. Never fear. All the Whig strength is being pulled inland and will be driven back to the sea. It is Lord Cornwallis' original plan, you remember."

"Aye."

"So you will return to the Cape Fear, and when Wilmington is taken you will report to the commanding officer and bring dispatches from him to me. I shall be with Cornwallis."

"When? When will the fleet come?"

"It is not for us to decide. You will wait. And as you wait you will aid Hector MacNeill in firming the Scots for the second uprising. They will join Cornwallis when the British sweep through North Carolina."

"Aye! Aye, aye, sir."

"But you will form no company of your own, but hold yourself ready for my service."

"Aye."

Duncan marched on home.

"This is the fifth year," he grumbled to himself as he bore east of the Pee Dee to find more level ground. "Five years o' strivin' to get i' the war and reclaim my country, and I'm na in it yet."

But if his duty was in the quiet precincts, Duncan soon began to hear rousing news. There was Ramsaur's Mill in June. The Tories were defeated, but the Whigs soon scattered, too. In August at Hanging Rock, above Camden, Tarleton smote the Whig Colonel Sumter a terrible blow. And then, ten days later at Camden, Lord Cornwallis marshaled his mighty army, and the great Whig army under General Gates was blasted to the winds. And the next day, at Rocky Mount, across the Catawba, Tarleton picked his former enemy Sumter for another disastrous blow. In September Cornwallis marched triumphantly across the line into North Carolina, just as Martin had said he would, and made headquarters in Charlotte, driving the Whig Davie's men into the woods.

Duncan had no need to firm the Scots in his neighborhood. They were ready. They were eager. He had to persuade them to hold until they were called. It was Cornwallis' purpose to roll up his army as he went along.

The great string of triumphs—Savannah, Augusta, Brier Creek, Ninety-Six, Charleston, Camden, Charlotte—it was good to have them to remember. For in ten days after Cornwallis entered Charlotte a terrible thing happened.

Major Ferguson was surrounded by ragged companies of hastily gathered backwoodsmen on the ridge of King's Mountain west of Charlotte and slaughtered. Even when the thousand regulars and Loyalists called for mercy, with Ferguson dying before them, the backwoodsmen shouted back: "Sure! Buford's quarter!" Duncan, who under his tree had seen the mercy which Tarleton had given Buford's Virginians, shuddered at what he knew happened on King's Mountain. But that was only a side issue to Cornwallis' great army, and Cornwallis was still triumphant.

Duncan heard no more as the winter advanced. Then, early in February, he heard bad news and good news. Tarleton had been routed by the Whig colonel Daniel Morgan at Cowpens in South Carolina. That was not so bad, for Tarleton could be defeated today and win again tomorrow. That was the way of the side armies. Cornwallis had not been defeated, and as long as he remained intact, triumph reigned in his rear—just as, soon, the King's rule would come again to Bladen. The other news was that Major James Craig had sailed up from Charleston and had taken Wilmington with barely a struggle. That was sound good news, for now there was a base on the Cape Fear. Duncan went immediately to Wilmington as he had been instructed.

Wilmington was hardly more than a military camp when he crossed the tidewater at Mount Misery on the Welshman Thomas Bloodworth's ferry. Long since the Whigs had driven out the Loyalists, and now the British had driven out the Whigs. Redcoats were all over the streets and quartered in almost any of the two hundred houses they liked.

Captain Sam Campbell was in charge of the camp when Duncan arrived. Major Craig had chosen him as second in command for his knowledge of the territory. Craig had begun at once harrying the country. He was out on the New Bern road on an expedition, Campbell said. They were standing on the Market Street dock watching a new shipload of soldiers disembark.

A squad of redcoats came in from uptown and reported.

"We have raided Rouse's, eight miles out, sir," a sergeant said.

"Any prisoners?"

"No, sir. No prisoners."

Sam Campbell's lips drew thin. "How many?" he asked.

"I don't know, sir. It was last night. It was dark. Their horses were tied under the trees. There must have been ten horses. We went in the tavern on them. Eight or nine fell in an upper room. One of them, Captain James Love, fought like a lion. He used his saddle for a shield. He fought us out of the house and on to a mulberry tree. He stabbed four of our men. Killed them. He fell among them at the roots of the tree."

Captain Campbell said nothing. He turned to an officer: "Take a company of soldiers and bury the dead."

Later that day Major Craig returned to the town. He saluted Campbell and went on to his room. The column of horsemen continued on toward the roofless stockade where the prisoners were kept. Duncan watched them. They had a dozen or more captives, hands tied, marching in the line. Some had blood on their faces. The day was cold, but some of them had no coats.

Then Duncan saw a redcoat ride along proudly on his horse. Behind him, like a sack of meal, an unconscious man with grayish-brown hair lay limp across the horse's back.

The man's long hair hung down over his head like a bedraggled curtain. His coat tails hung over backward. Under the horse's belly Duncan could see his feet dangling. One foot was greatly swollen and wrapped in a dirty white bandage.

"We got 'im!" the soldier called to a fellow on the sidewalk.

"Who?" Duncan asked Campbell.

"That? Oh, Cornelius Harnett."

Duncan had a sudden creeping feeling. He tried to shout robustly and angrily. But he only whispered "What?"

"Yes. The old fellow tried to escape, but they trailed him up the New Bern road——"

But Duncan did not hear the last of what Campbell said. He dashed into the street and grasped the reins.

"Stop!" he cried, his voice choking. "Stop! In God's name—would ye kill him?"

"Why not? And who *are* ye?" the Irish redcoat demanded, hacking Duncan back with his blade.

Sam Campbell was walking up rapidly and forbade the soldier to strike Duncan. Duncan grasped his wrist and pulled him out of the saddle. Not looking to see whether he would be attacked, he lifted Cornelius Harnett as gently as he could from the horse.

But gently or roughly made no difference to the white-faced old revolutionary. Whig women and other noncombatants from somewhere suddenly arrived. Their expressions were those of disgust and horror. Even Tories there stormed out when they found who the unconscious man was.

"Where to put him? Where to put him?" Duncan demanded, looking around, holding his fallen friend in his arms.

"Ochan! Ochan! Cornelius Harnett!" He groaned at the limp form. This ought to satisfy even the bloodless Governor Martin.

Soldiers came with stretchers and took him into a house. Major Craig peremptorily took charge. No one was permitted to see Harnett. Bystanders were driven away.

Finally, after an army doctor had come out of the room, Sam Campbell arranged for Duncan to go in. Cornelius Harnett lay on a cot. Duncan said nothing, merely went in and knelt beside him.

There was nothing weak about Harnett's face, even in his extremity. There was, indeed, a sort of fulgent white beauty about it. He was in the borderland of consciousness. He groaned with the gouty pains in his foot and the soreness of his body. He turned his eyes on Duncan in ponderous curiosity, and then he smiled.

"Friends," he said, relieved. "Duncan, my friend. They didn't get the money! They didn't get the state's money! I hid it where my friends know. Where you—— No. No, Duncan."

Cornelius came more awake and his eyes became cautious. "No. You're not a friend—and, yet, you are a friend. My honorable friend, Duncan."

Duncan placed his hand on Cornelius', and Cornelius grasped it. His face writhed in the pain, but he smiled.

"Remember, Duncan—what you once said about splitting my skull if it became your duty?"

"Na, Cornelius!" Duncan said in anguish.

"Well—my boy—don't worry. You'll not need to, now."

"Stop! Cornelius! You're na goin' tae die!"

"Die? Of course not! I'm too tough for that. I'll come out of this. But the damned British—they'll hold me until it's too late for you to split me."

Cornelius laughed, and Duncan laughed too, almost hysterically.

"It is over now," the old man said. "Almost over. Nothing can prevent it. Men shall be free—as free as the wind in the trees, as free as the gold in the sunset. A land of free men!"

Cornelius Harnett was crazy. With the British crushing him, he raved of victory.

"You don't agree, eh, Duncan? You never did, my friend."

Duncan saw Cornelius go into the stockade the next morning. He walked in—with a bad limp, but proudly. Duncan waved, and Cornelius waved back, as though in triumph.

Duncan turned away, and Major Craig was standing beside him, cynical.

"Egad!" the officer protested. "I feel I should apologize to the King's friends for arresting the old reprobate."

Duncan found nothing to say to that, but stood troubled. Victory was not always sweet.

Craig called him into his office and gave him a packet of papers. "You will join Cornwallis and deliver these to Governor Martin. You will go up the Cape Fear Valley and into the region beyond Guilford Courthouse, and so avoid the Whig Lillington, who is moving against us here. On your way you will take charge of a squad of Highlanders waiting to join Colonel John Pyle near Deep River, who is to join the British Army. Your impatience may have rein now. Go, and God speed you!"

"Aye!" Duncan laughed and leaped away. But what amused him was that Martha McGee was right. John Pyle had turned coat again.

Duncan had need to rush on with his twelve Tories to join Pyle. But at Martha McGee's mill he nevertheless paused for the moment necessary to pass a word with her. Men were at the mill, and the miller was grinding corn, running his mill rock hot for the haste. Whigs or Tories, it made no difference to him. Everybody wanted meal against the impending confusion of two great armies in the field. All were careful not to mention the war or to say how they stood. At the mill all were neutral. Duncan's clattering company of Tories made no stir. In another hour another company might be Whig. That, too, would make no difference. Those at the mill wanted meal to take home, and then they would be Whigs or Tories. Duncan went on up to the house.

Martha came out and stood on the stone which flagged her stoop. She looked at Duncan quizzically but not harshly, Whig though she was. Nor yet in apprehension.

Duncan said: "I was passing. I stopped only to say I continue grateful f'r y'r goodness to me. It pleasures me to see ye lookin' so hearty—and pretty."

"Gwan, Tory!" she laughed. "You needn't think you'll subdue this country with blarney. Ye dinna ken hoo!" she mocked him.

He smiled with her, but made no attempt to follow her humor. "I see y'r old enemy, Steve Lewis, has na subdued ye yet."

She laughed. "No. He still bides his time. He tried to ravish me a fortnight ago in the woods, but I took him with my gun and turned him over to the Whigs."

"I dinna ken what wi' betide," Duncan said soberly. "Lord Cornwallis sweeps all before him, and the Crown, i' God's own time, wi' hae piece i' the land. A battle wi' ensue, and the people around about wi' suffer. If such comes to you, I pray I may hae opportunity to bring ye aid."

"Duncan Stuart!" she blazed, her anger but barely tinged with good humor. "If you weren't so dumb and so good at heart, I'd bend this axe handle on your pate! Cornwallis rides to his doom, and the Whigs will be picking up the pieces in a week."

"Na," he said quietly. "Cornwallis wi' prevail. Peace wi' come, and I wi' saw the logs for my stout house again."

She shook her head, and her eyes suddenly were glum. "Cornwallis don't amount to so much. There'll be no king's peace in this country until he beats Greene and then beats Washington, and then kills out all the Whigs—and that means me as well."

"But all ye hae to do——" he protested.

But Martha said: "Wait a minute, I've got a piece of dried-apple pie for you."

Dr John Pyle was waiting at the rendezvous when Duncan and his squad marched in that cold February night. They were on an abandoned farm, roasting a hog which they had taken along the way. Dr Pyle was most happy. They would march before day and be present when Governor Josiah Martin raised the King's standard at Hillsboro. They would be acclaimed as friends of the Crown.

"Aye," Duncan said. "I wi' go wi' ye, to rejoin Governor Martin, whose courier I am."

"Glad to have you. Glad to have any tried and true Loyalist."

"Aye," said Duncan dryly.

They slept in the barn that night. Because the barn belonged to a Whig, they set fire to it as they left in the morning. Duncan winced at the waste, but it was not his company. Long since he had found a better peace by keeping quiet than in protesting against the wantonness of the violent. They stood by to see it burn, moving back a step at a time as the fire became hotter. Then the roof fell in, and a bitter hot wind shrieked through where it had stood. The soldiers turned and marched.

It was Sunday morning, but nobody moved toward the churches. People stood back from the roads to let them pass—Whigs and Tories both, for no one now could say whether a Whig wore a bucktail on his hat or an oat straw, and no one knew what stratagems of disguise Tories might attempt. Nor, indeed, was one too safe even among friends.

Duncan marched with Dr Pyle. They passed from Chatham into the Orange territory.

"We should keep a sharp lookout," Duncan cautioned him.

"The Whig Lee—'Light-Horse Harry,' they ca' him—ranges in all directions around the camp."

"Never fear! Never fear!" Pyle answered jauntily. "I have the news that Lord Cornwallis has sent Colonel Tarleton to meet us here in Orange."

"Aye—weel—still I wi' feel better when the troop is in Hillsboro."

"Allay your fears, my friend." The Tory leader threw out his hands carelessly. "My troop would not shrink from the devil and a regiment from hell."

"Aye—wi' one more drink around I suspect they'd storm the gates, hot as they may be."

Pyle laughed. "Drunk? No, they're not drunk. Only filled with the exaltation of victory and power. It is a glorious feeling, my friend. Glorious!"

Duncan shook his head and plowed on. The men were not bitch-foudrunk, but, anyway, tozie, and not the soldiers who should tread lightly and alertly through country whose every road bend might conceal hostile troops.

As they marched into Orange, Duncan dropped back to speak with the Scots who had come up from Bladen with him. The air was chill and the ground frozen. Now and then an arm went up as the column swayed and curved its way onward, and another drink went down. Fortunately, the weather was too cold for a man to get very drunk if he kept marching.

At the head of the column there was talk with men who waited, and two young men of the column dashed away. Duncan surmised that Tarleton was not far distant.

"Where's Tarleton?" he asked the man at the roadside as he went by.

The man pointed with his thumb. "Over the creek," he said. The young men hadn't gone that way, but Duncan supposed they knew the right path. The column continued to swing along, and the word went down it that soon they would be conducted straight to General Cornwallis.

And, sure enough, soon the head of a column of cavalry came around a curve in the road, and Colonel Pyle gave the order to halt. His company lined up on the side of the road as soldierly as they could.

" 'Tenshon!" Colonel Pyle shouted, and the whole column, with some degree of order, snapped to, rigidly.

The cavalry moved down the line within touching distance of the foot soldiers, making a gallant showing, and Pyle's men, overcome by the honor of being met by Tarleton's own Legion (although their black-eyed little commander himself was not in evidence), burst into shouts.

"God save the King!" they roared.

And: "God save the King!" they continued to shout.

Some of the horsemen shouted back in the hubbub, and to Duncan it sounded as if the disrespectful regulars were shouting: "God damn the King!"

Colonel Pyle was enjoying the proudest moment of his life. Duncan was sure the colonel would burst his breast buttons, he so strutted as the cavalry filed by him.

Duncan started and frowned. A new company was coming by. He had seen its commander before, a blue-eyed, pink-faced young man with the corners of his mouth thinly carved. He had seen him at——

Someone behind him was shouting frantically. Duncan took his eyes off the moving line of horsemen to look. The yelling man was David Fanning. He was standing in the bushes behind Colonel Pyle. He was shouting to Pyle, desperately. Pyle did not turn, but stood proudly facing the commanding officer of the horse troops who had paused opposite. Fanning threw up his hands helplessly and fled into the trees and over a ridge. Duncan stared after him anxiously.

"God save the King!" the Tories shouted, giving their enthusiasm full measure.

"Graham!" Duncan shrieked. He remembered the man. Joseph Graham of Charlotte—the mosquito-like Whig cavalryman, who buzzed and bit and flew on.

"Whigs!" Duncan shrieked. He struck the man next to him and yelled: "Whigs!" He struck the man on the other side and yelled: "Whigs!"

But they continued to shout: "God save the King!" and the passing cavalry looked down on them not a sword's reach away.

Duncan stood and trembled. He wasn't afraid. It was too late to be afraid. The whole king's company had bared its heads to the swords of the enemy, and in a moment the pates would be popping. His brain played tricks. He remembered what Peter Robinson had said, that a "Scotchman's hard head splits like a green gourd."

There was a confusion up the line. One of Pyle's men fired his rifle. Others did likewise. But not ten in the whole company were ready to fire.

The Whigs, shouting like demons, wheeled their horses and fell to with whipping blades. The screams of the Tories were the screams of the doomed. Two hundred men were helpless in the slaughter.

Nobody but daredevils like Light-Horse Harry Lee and Joe Graham would have put their men perilously at the rifle mouth like that. Nobody but Tarleton would have set the example to drown out the cries for mercy with the ghastly smash of steel on bone. Here was more of "Buford's quarter."

Duncan would have dashed away. He was not immediately attacked. A horseman took the man on his left and another the man standing at his right. They had refused to believe him when he had cried: "Whigs!" They still yelled "God save the King!" as if in that desperate cry were safety.

And now, on his left, the horseman was running down the Scot who yelled, and his sword was raised to slash him. Duncan had no plan. A rifle butt plunged into the horseman's side, and he went out of the saddle with his near leg in the air. Duncan was surprised. He had done that.

He still had no plan. Horses swirled around him. The man on his right had his sword fouled in the body of the fellow who had just yelled "God save the King!"

The riderless horse trampled against Duncan, and Duncan caught the reins to hold him as a shield. Then Duncan was in the saddle galloping away. Suddenly the woods were full of horses and running men. Whigs paid no attention to the men on horseback. Those on horses raced through the bushes after men on foot to hack them down. The ground was full of bodies. Some of them writhed slowly and screamed.

Duncan recognized one of the men who ran. Colonel Pyle. His arm was bloody. He ran up to a muddy pond, and though the pond had been frozen early that morning he deliberately dived in. Duncan saw his face come up in some grass. Duncan skirted the pond and raced on.

Duncan galloped wildly, not heeding where he went. He crossed a creek. He climbed a hill. It dawned on him that his horse was a good horse, fleet and lithe. At the top of the hill he looked back. Half a mile away the Whigs were re-forming and shouting their victory. If they had lost a man, Duncan hadn't seen him fall. He was too stunned to have any feeling about it. As after Moore's Creek, and as after Waxhaw, and as on the ships at Charleston, he felt as though he had just come through an unbelievable dream, and its cold ghastliness lingered, with the insipid, empty smell of the freshly dead in his nostrils.

The horse snorted and pushed on. It went in the opposite direction from the battle, and Duncan let him go. He hadn't gone half a mile from the hill, not a mile from the battle, when:

"Halt!"

The horse knew the command, pricked his ears and stopped. Duncan came groggily from his stunned silence and held up his hands. The man was a British soldier, standing with cocked rifle.

"Weel?" Duncan asked dazedly.

"Countersign?"

"Oh. No. I dinna hae it. I am frae Colonel Pyle's company."

"Yes, sir," the man answered readily. "Colonel Tarleton is expecting you. We are in camp, waiting for Colonel Pyle."

The sentry called to another, and Duncan was led into camp.

"In there," the new man said, holding Duncan's horse. He pointed to a marquee, an elaborate thing out here in the woods, and Duncan walked into the tent, still pale and dazed.

There were partitions. In the front a man, a fattish, middle-aged man, with pleasant face sat behind a table.

"Tarleton," Duncan said, looking at him.

"*Colonel* Tarleton you mean, no doubt," the man reproved him.

"Aye, Tarleton."

"What is your business, please?"

"I came frae Colonel Pyle's company."

"Oh yes, yes. Well, you'll have to wait. A short time."

Duncan sat down. There were voices. Sharp, angry, hushed—low, plaintive, protesting. A man's. A woman's. They registered with Duncan as something vague and distant.

The man behind the desk may have misunderstood Duncan's pale face. He came out and sat with Duncan, perhaps to make a screen of noise. Anyway, to talk.

He shook his head. "I have been with the Tarleton family all my life," he said. "It is trying, at times, to bear with the young man. His father——" The man shook his head hopelessly. "I will be most happy when we can return to England. But," he said, "after all, he is a most gallant horseman."

Duncan did not hear what he said. The man stopped, and Duncan felt that he had been asked a question.

"Aye," he answered.

"It makes him very angry," the man kept on, "for one to mention his—ah—amorous affairs. It is best to confine your conversation to your definite business."

Duncan sat on the canvas chair, motionless. He did not know how long. A woman came through and went out, her head down. He did not see her face. It was veiled in her shawl to hide her shame.

"Well?"

Tarleton stood before Duncan and spoke abruptly.

"I come frae Colonel Pyle's company," Duncan repeated.

"Well, where is the clodhopping fool? Why doesn't he come on in?"

Duncan was silent.

"You're Stuart, aren't you? Duncan Stuart. I know you."

"Eh?"

"Aren't you, Stu—— Say, man, are you sick? Get him a drink! Big drink!"

Duncan's fingers closed around the goblet clumsily, and the glass found his lips. It did not leave them until it was empty.

"Where is Pyle's company?"

"Cut to pieces. Wiped out."

"What?"

"Whigs split skulls—like green gourds."

Tarleton was shaking his shoulder. Duncan's head was slumping.
He couldn't seem to hold up. His glass was full again, and he
drank.

"Where? Oh——" He stopped to think. "Across yon hill."

There were sharp commands and rushing men and the trample
of horses. Duncan was standing at the table holding out his empty
goblet for more liquor.

Duncan awoke the next morning with a brassy mouth, a rich
headache and a sense of hovering doom. An orderly heard him
move on the cot and looked in the tent. He smiled and came
inside.

"Good morning, sir. The colonel's compliments, sir. He said
for me to provide you with this, sir, as soon as you were awake."

The man poured a full goblet of whisky, and Duncan reached
for it with shaking hands. He was glad of it, for as the racing
warmth of the liquor flowed a glowing course down his throat
the ghastly pictures of yesterday began to tower in his mind.
The morning was well gone when he walked out of the tent.
He walked steadily. The liquor and his memory fought for the
mastery. "Ah, weel," he thought, "war is war." The thought
seemed of vast comfort. A soldier walked by him.

"War is war," Duncan said to him, but the soldier looked at him
curiously from a somehow vaguely cross-barred red coat that
merged into another red coat. "Aye," Duncan said, nodding
firmly, and walked on.

Before he reached Colonel Tarleton's marquee he stopped to
examine a beautiful high-headed black stallion across the area.
The beast was saddled, with a heavy bridle and curb bit. Two
grooms held the horse, and it stamped and trembled. The sun
made bright streaks on its velvet-black hair. Its nimble feet, always
on the ground, seemed eagerly always on the point of leaving it,
as if the horse had no weight.

The sight of the nag pulled Duncan out of the state bordering
on drunkenness. He took ease by holding to the low limb of a
tree, but his eyes were clear, and he could observe and think.
The horse, bridled and saddled and held, somehow was like him-

self. He wanted to go to the beast and run his hand along its neck and under its mane and make friends. It did not occur to him that the horse would not. He had a way with horses. He had broken many a horse, but the horse always was his friend first.

He did not go to this black horse, however, for that was a pleasure held in reserve for Colonel Banastre Tarleton. The young officer came at that moment out of his tent and, walking by Duncan, went across the field.

He was a dandy. He wore a short white linen jacket, which fitted his shoulders perfectly, and white linen breeches which, halfway down his thighs, disappeared into shining soft russet turn-down boots. His hat was wide-brimmed, a curiously fashioned, low-crowned creation of snow-white feathers of the swan. On his heels large silver spurs, with long, sharp rowels, jingled softly as he walked. In his hand he carried a heavy leather scourge with shot twisted into its lash.

"Watch 'im," a soldier whispered. "That's a stallion he ordered up from Cumberland. No man has ever stayed on its back."

Duncan did watch. And the noble horse watched Tarleton, turning arrogant eyes on the white-hatted, white-jacketed strong little man who strode across the field. Tarleton turned malignant black eyes on the quivering horse.

There was no preliminary. The horse deigned no retreat when Tarleton marched up and took the reins, the men falling back. Then, with a truly marvelous leap, without benefit of stirrup, Tarleton sprang and was masterfully in the saddle before the beast even quivered. For a full angry second the black stallion was a trembling picture of outraged equine nobility.

Suddenly came a trampling crouch and a plunging leap and a clear scream from its high-reaching head. The entire horse was off the ground, thrusting into the air.

"Poor beast," Duncan murmured, for there is nothing sweet in seeing even a beast that loves freedom thrashed into submission.

The horse came down, humpbacked, stiff-legged for a terrific jolt, but Tarleton was a real horseman. That blow he took in his toes in the stirrups, and when the horse, swift as flame, darted out for speed and an unhorsing swerve, Tarleton coolly was set for it, sinking the long rowels into the stallion's flanks, slashing at his side with the shot-slugged whip. The stinging pain must have disconcerted the nag, for he attempted no throwing tactics but leveled out for a beautiful charging bolt around the area, with Tarleton stabbing him with the spurs and burning him with the whip as they plunged around the field.

But Tarleton's victory was not to be won so easily. The stallion came to know that he was but spending his strength in those long, flashing strides with his rider none the worse, and he began to leap and swerve and dart. Now he took his pain and gave it no heed. Up-ending, almost perpendicularly on his heels, he swapped ends, almost standing on his head. He attempted no rolling process, but his zigzag, whipping course, like a darting black snake, took him far down the field, around and back. He kept Tarleton first to one side and then to the other, with perilous moments when he all but plunged to the ground. That he did not went to the point of magnificent horsemanship, but Duncan gave him admiration only grudgingly.

The stallion's mouth was bloody foam where the sharp curb bit cut its tongue. Its sides were lathered with the sweat, and the white was streaked with red where the slugged whip had taken its toll. The rowels had cut deeply, and blood trickled down to the bottom of its belly and dripped to the ground.

And now the horse, goaded beyond stratagems, pitched down the field in a fiery straightaway, its muddled mind knowing but to run, run, run, and so escape the tenacious, maddening thing which bestrode him and tortured him and battled at his spirit.

Duncan grunted, disappointed, for that was the signal that Tarleton had won. The horse would course himself to utter weariness, and never again would he be the wild, free-charging creature of nature that knew no master. And so, around the field, and around again, and around once more in a masterful show of endurance but with no hope of success, the beautiful stallion ran himself to exhaustion and stopped, bloody, heaving, head hung, his dull eyes looking at the ground. Tarleton, his master, sat there in token of his triumph.

Then Tarleton whirled out of the saddle and threw the reins to a soldier.

Pale, black eyes still flashing the anger that had blazed at the black beast for daring to oppose him, Tarleton spoke to no one and strode into his tent. He had broken the horse that none could ride, but none called "Bravo!" There was precious little show of admiration for him. The eyes of the soldiers followed the low-hung head of the black stallion that meekly followed a man to a stable.

CHAPTER 7

MARCH FIFTEENTH was clear and mild, a capricious winter day smiling too coyly upon the close-packed columns which crawled uphill and downhill toward Guilford Courthouse. The gods of weather beamed with barbed kindness upon those men who wore the King's garb—aye, and also upon those across yon valley, who crouched behind a rail fence, looking anxiously ahead, and taking comfort in the knowledge that for miles back their Whig fellows lay in wait, ready to take their turn. In the Patriot midst was the unconquerable fighting Quaker, the man Greene who fought, lost and fought again, whose campaigns were as crowned with victory as were his battles with defeat. His serene pink face, his calm clear eye, were as regiments. No fancy uniforms crouched behind these fences and these trees—woodsmen, mostly, fresh militia. Holding the road, there, behind the first fence, was Captain Arthur Forbis, of the neighborhood, who had never seen a battle. He was to take the brunt of the first clash with the King's fine troops. He had never seen a battle, but he told General Greene that he reckoned he and the boys could do around a right smart with their rifles while things got started. About him were settlers he hadn't seen until this morning, woodsmen with squirrel rifles who said they had just dropped over to take part in the shooting match. Captain Forbis told them to pick their own trees.

Duncan Stuart that morning reported to Governor Josiah Martin as a matter of routine. But now he wore a kilt from the Fraser Highlanders, and he felt the tug of his broadsword on his belt.

"You will stay with me in the rear through the battle," Martin said to him, "so that, if necessary, I can send messages."

The corners of Duncan's lips fell low, and his mouth opened wide.

"Na," he said bluntly. He picked up a rifle and hurried forward. Fraser's Highlanders were to the right of the road, and Boze's Hessians were more yet to the right. Colonel Webster, balancing the green and red of Fraser's tartans, held the left of the road with the red-coated Twenty-second and Twenty-third regiments, with Tarleton and other outfits in the rear in reserve. Duncan passed through all these as he pushed on faster than the slow-moving columns to stand among Scots when the fighting started.

Faster yet and faster Duncan tramped. The whole army seemed to have quickened its pace. The sun slashed down through the bare leaden branches of the oaks and was lost on the brown of the earth. Through the trees, kaleidoscope-like, as far as he could see to the right and to the left were swinging lines of the red coats and of the Scottish plaids. The trunks of the trees passed between and seemed to bite little notches in the lines.

Beyond other trees and other hills were the rebels, and all the Britishers seemed to sense that soon now the armies must meet. Along the road the gun wagons rumbled. Against the low branches of the trees the brightly gleaming bayonets of the soldiers clashed and slithered. The steady tramp of their boots was like the muffled beat of drums. There was no talking in the lines, for this battle forecast its own shadow of destiny, and the soldiers grasped their guns and pressed on with set faces. As though it were in their hearts to crash into the thought of the gods and find what things foreboded, they marched faster and faster.

There on yon slope was a fence, an ordinary zigzag rail fence, set there to keep the ranging cattle and the hogs of the woods from the productive field of kindlier days. The soldiers frowned, for the fence was an obstruction to be climbed, and fences are not easy to climb in the process of marching. But faster yet they marched, because if the fence was to be climbed they had best be about it. Duncan was not in the front line. He fell into one of the rear lines, where he found a place.

He had never known blood lust. He had never killed a man. He did not know how it felt to be as Tarleton was that day in the Waxhaws when he had slashed off the hands of the pleading

Virginian. But now he was in the business. It was a service to the Crown to clear out those phantom men that lurked in the trees behind the hills he could not yet see. He would do as the Scots did. As they killed, so would he. It was a thing to be done before he could know peace and stability.

There was thunder on the road. The columns halted. More thunder and black smoke rose above the cannon and drifted with the wind. There were explosions beyond the rail fence, and before it. Shells shrieked and exploded and made fog to fill the land.

Then the bagpipes howled, and the bugles blasted, and somewhere the drums beat their staccato demand for speed and death. Officers shouted, and the stiff red soldiers and the rigid tartan-clad Highlanders poured from their lines and raced away through the smoke. Now they could see, Duncan saw well now that he knew where to look, the homespun-garbed Whig soldiers standing and lying behind the rail fence.

Before him, each line in its place but its precision broken, the Scots were rushing forward, spreading through the rolling roars of bugles and cannon and battle screams.

Over to the left the redcoats were rushing forward, but their lines were straighter, more precise than the kilted soldiers'. They, too, were getting set to take the fence. There were thousands of them, an avalanche of red, moving resolutely on nothing but an old rail fence, and nothing was happening. Duncan had never seen a great battle. This was a great battle. It wasn't as he had imagined.

Back to the rear the cannon thundered on, and now there were little popping noises. The Highlanders went forward like a wave— a wave on a smooth beach, where, first, the water tumbled and then smoothed down to a thin-edged flow and stopped.

For the Highlanders *were* stopping. In the thunder and roar and tumult and high shrill shouts coming through the rumble, the Highlanders were stopping before they reached the fence. The foremost line grew thin suddenly at a place, and great gaps opened as Scots suddenly faded. The next line fell in and filled the gaps, and it, too, suddenly went ragged as the Highlanders pitched and sprawled. Duncan's back line was drawing near, and nobody yet had crossed the fence. Scots had rushed to it and climbed high on it, and then they had crumpled backward.

Duncan could see them more plainly now. The place was smoky, and he saw through a veil, but he could see. He saw their naked legs more distinctly than anything. They were in heaps, piled like gnarled peeled-bark logs for a new-ground burning. They were dead, and wounded, and shrieking their agony. The wounded were interwoven with the dead, and the whole pile heaved.

It suddenly came to Duncan that this had to be stopped. He was coolly surprised that he hadn't thought of that before. The God-damned Whigs were killing Scots. Killing them! They had to be stopped. If anyone had given orders, he hadn't heard. He took it upon himself in his own way to stop the slaughter. It was suicide to rush the fence. The Whigs had to be picked off one at a time. He left his line and zigzagged through the lines ahead and plunged behind a tree. He knew how to fight the Whig way. It was all very well to be brave and stout-hearted, but to stop Whig slaughter one must shoot as the Whigs shot. From that tree he dashed to another, and to another yet, and then he was within fifty paces, and at fifty paces he could put a ball in a squirrel's eye. The Scots marched by him. They were dumb, standing up that way to stop bullets. He gloried in them. That was the way men ought to fight, standing up. But it was silly, out here in the woods.

There was a fellow behind the fence. He was on the ground, on his belly. You could see his eyes, black eyes, between the rails. He was drawing a bead on a Highlander. Duncan pulled the trigger. The eyes jerked and disappeared. So much for that. There was another. This one stood in a fence corner, taking sidling shots at the clansmen down the line. Duncan took a bead on his eye. The fellow, somehow, was white-eyed. Perhaps pale blue. He pulled the trigger. The fellow stooped as though he were picking something from the ground and sprawled.

The Scots were climbing the fence. Rebels were running. They were streaking across the old field away from the fence, just as five minutes before the Highlanders had been running to it. One enormous Glengarry man, with the fury of revenge, pitched his bayonet into a fleeing Whig, threw him back over his head and kept striding.

The fight was over for this moment at this place. To the right the Hessians were not across the fence. They rushed it in waves, and the Whigs clubbed them back. The Hessians recoiled. Their officers flogged them with bull whips, and they rushed again, and the Whigs clubbed them back, and they fell among the Hessians that had fallen before. Then the Hessians fell back, fired and rushed again. This time they went over the fence, and the Whigs fled to the shelter of the young pines. Before him, where the Scots had chased the Whigs, the path was strewn with Whig dead. But before the Hessians there were few. They did not know how to kill. British cavalry now was flanking the retreating Whigs, and Duncan looked and frowned at this strange sight in the tall grass. A cavalryman raised his sword above the head of a racing rebel, and the Whig disappeared as though wiped out.

The redcoats were over the fence now, too, but behind it they left a rich red line on the ground. Duncan ran after the Scots. As he came over the brow of a little hill, he saw a pitched battle of bayonets down by the creek, and he raced for it, his bayoneted gun held like a pitchfork.

Just as he got there he saw two officers fighting. Other soldiers on both sides, some of them anyway, had stopped fighting to witness it. It was a feud fight, somebody shouted. All around the battle raged. Guns thundered and men shouted and gutted their enemies with bayonets. But here was a little whirlpool. Two sworn enemies had stopped to settle their controversy. The Maryland Whig, a captain, parried the sword of the Scot, a colonel of the Guards, and then like lightning whipped down. The Scot's head curiously halved and lay open upon his shoulders. He fell, and the Whig captain fell on him, and the Guard who had shot the captain fell on top of both, and a Whig soldier pulled his bayonet out. Cavalry galloped down the hill, and the Whigs fled. The Whig captain was not dead. Duncan saw him attempt to rise.

Duncan was in a little ravine, picking off Whig calvarymen, those of the same Colonel Lee who had cut up Pyle's men, when he saw General Greene ride by with a Whig general. They both were galloping. When he saw them they were laughing. The lesser general was wounded in the groin. With every gallop the wound spurted blood. By the time Duncan had decided to shoot, they were out of range.

He saw Lord Cornwallis. Twice. Once was when the earl's horse screamed and pitched forward, a sudden monstrous cascade of hoofs and unnatural legs. Lord Cornwallis leaped and stumbled, and a redcoat steadied him, running at his side. And then brought him another horse.

The next time was when Duncan fell in with the Scottish Guards on a hillside before the artillery. The cannon were up the slope, the Guards being between them and the stubbornly fighting Whigs down the incline. It was the Guards' purpose to drive them back. They were threatening the cannon. Cornwallis galloped to the danger point and took charge. The great guns were slinging grapeshot over the heads of the Highlanders. Their thunder shook the ground, and their smoke was lifeless like ash and sharp like acid. But the Whigs did not fall back. The Guards, brilliant in battle as their history was, were falling. Duncan lay behind a stump and shot his lead and held his place. When the action began he was at the rear of the Scottish line. But now he was in front. The Whigs were creeping up. Already the grapeshot were falling behind them harmlessly. The Scots slowly were backing up the hill, leaving their dead and wounded along the slope. The cannon were in danger, and reinforcements had not come.

Duncan dashed from tree to tree, zigzagging back to the weakening line. Cornwallis was most imposing on his new horse. He was upright, gallant, unmoved by the thunder and the clash. He gave an order, and the officer who received it protested with upraised, shaking hands. Cornwallis shook his clenched fist down before the officer's face, and the officer turned away.

Duncan was in the line now. The Whigs, both Continentals and militia, bore on, firing, stepping up, falling and firing. The artillery spoke up with new shrill, desperate thunder. Grapeshot shrieked by him. He thought he could have touched them, no higher than his waist.

"In God's name!" he shouted, waving his arms toward the artillery. Then he grunted. The artillerymen had made a mistake. They wouldn't do it again.

But Duncan, in the trembling maelstrom of sound and smoke, suddenly had the sense that some ghastly error was in progress, the same feeling he had had when Lee had cut up Pyle's column.

To his left Scots suddenly were obliterated. Grapeshot struck them behind and splattered them down the hill toward the Whigs. Behind him, with Cornwallis unmoved on his horse, the cannon shook and thundered and poured salvos through the ranks of the guards in direct aim down among the Whigs.

"Stop it! I' the King's name, stop it!" Duncan shouted, waving his arms frantically, but he might as well have whispered. He turned to the Whigs. The cannon were cutting avenues through them, and they were in sudden disorder. Duncan felt something shocking and warming and sudden across the base of his neck, and he was lying at the head of a little gully. He stopped rolling when he reached this point. He was on his back, his head against the bank. It was as though he were in a shallow grave, looking out.

"I' the King's name!" He felt his mouth working at the words. He started to raise his hand and could not. He tried his other hand, and that was inert. So were his feet. He was paralyzed.

He breathed still. He tried that, fast and slow. Yes, he breathed. He twisted his mouth. Yes. He was not excited. Everything suddenly seemed hushed. Instantly he had been hurled into an abyss. He was through. This was the end. He could think. He could hear. He could speak. That was all. He was not a man any more. Merely a head, waiting to die. A word struggled on his tongue. Something inside him ardent and virile demanded to come out. It did.

"Mary!" he said imperatively. "Mary! Mary!"

His voice ceased. Duncan panted. The artillery was careening down yon hill, and redcoats were pursuing the grape-battered Whigs.

Companies of Loyal militia ran with the redcoats. They were near enough to recognize. Hector MacNeill led them. Archibald MacDougall was at his side.

"Hector!" Duncan screamed. Not loudly. His voice was muffled. But Hector had to hear. Hector would come, and he might live. He wished to live. "Hector!" he called.

As the companies went deeper into the woods, he called yet, but no one turned his way.

"Hector!" he whispered. His chin trembled, but he did not call again.

The afternoon was blowing cold and cloudy. The fickle March

day had promised the warriors warm sunshine merely to inveigle them into slaughter. And now that a thousand men lay dead and wounded on the ground, the clouds scudded in the whipping wind, rushing up their rain for the night, so that the water would freeze and stiffen the blood-soaked garments of the wounded men who retched and screamed.

Like that Irish redcoat not twenty paces from Duncan—screaming. He had a staff, a color staff with the flag gone. He attempted to pull himself upright upon it, but his legs were useless. He swore and screamed and called for water and attempted to stanch the flow of blood from his belly with his fingers.

But now there was no one to hear, except the wounded. And they wanted water. They would have snatched the Irishman's water from his hands if he had had any. He hadn't any nor did they have any. A Whig soldier came running across the field. Appeals for water followed him desperately, but he had no time to stop and quench the thirst of the King's wounded. But the wounded Irishman, nevertheless, cried: "Wather! Wather!"

The Whig stopped and sought the voice. "Where is the dommed sojer from auld Oireland?" he demanded.

"Here! Here! And God bless ye and keep ye, dommed Whig though ye be."

The Whig Irishman unbuckled his canteen and put it to the lips of the King's Irishman and held it gently while he drained it. Other wounded called. Duncan looked, but did not call.

"Ah," said the wounded man. "Thanks. Thanks, brither. I'm a sore hurt mon. The Whigs did it," he shouted. "God's damnation on the Whigs!"

"Don't forget, wid y'r curses," said his benefactor, throwing the empty canteen away, "I'm a Whig." He turned and walked off.

"Aye! And so ye be!" the wounded man shrilled in fury. He picked up his sharp-ended staff and hurled it with what strength he had. It struck the other on the shoulder, ripping his coat.

The Whig Irishman turned and looked and said nothing. He went back to the King's soldier, bayonet rising slowly, and plunged it through his chest. Then he walked on and did not look back.

Duncan did not know when it became dark. But it was dark. And raining. He could feel the ice-cold rivulet under his head as it ran down into the gully. His hair was matted with clay. He could feel it plastered against his face. The King's men had won the battle, for the King's soldiers had come marching back in the dark, not running. There were light spots, where the British had fire and attended to some of the wounded.

But nobody gathered up the wounded near Duncan. Some there were whose cries had ceased, but they had died. Some, doubtless, had drowned in the pools of icy water. The rain did not cease. Sleet mingled with rain and peppered the faces of those who constantly moaned. No longer were there Tories or Whigs in this sector, merely men screaming in a blizzardy night.

It was dark, so dark that except for the distant fire glows Duncan could have been blind. He had no pain, only a horrible sense of lack of pain. His face was cold. His ears stung, but that was the least of his cares.

"Mary!" he demanded of the blackness. "Mary!"

A woman's voice called. She was hunting someone. It was not Mary's voice. It was no voice that he knew. She called Archie. "Archie!" she called desperately. "Archie!" There was that desolation in her wail to make a man answer from the dead. "Archie!" And out across the sodden battlefield she went on and on in the darkness. "Archie!" Long after she had gone, the word echoed dismally in Duncan's ear: "Archie!"

He never knew when darkness came, and he never knew when the cold morning came. Men with stretchers stood beside him.

"What's the matter with this one?" one asked. "No blood."

They picked him up and cursed the mud that slumped from him to their boots.

They carried him through the trees and across a gap in the fence, their feet squashing in the wet earth.

"Wait!" said one of the stretcher-bearers. "Here's a man don't know the battle's over. Take his gun away from him. He is crazy."

Duncan could see the fellow, his arms braced in the fence, standing erect. One of the soldiers slapped him on the back. The man teetered over stiffly, cold dead.

It was hours yet before the doctors reached Duncan. Some of the wounded were in barns, some in churches, and some on the ground before campfires. Duncan was in a bed in a log cabin.

A young woman with a baby in her arms came and went, displaying horrified curiosity about him. She had the same look in her eyes as the Widow Jackson, down in the Waxhaws—blue and hard and clear and pitying. But she had black hair instead of red.

"Don't you feel nothin'?" she asked, bending over him, shaking her head for her own answer. "Nothin' at all?"

"Na." Duncan was weary of her searching.

"Looks like to me," she insisted, "there ought to be *some* way to fix you up."

"I'm done for," Duncan gasped. His head was sore, and his eyes hurt. "And I'll thank ye to let me die in peace."

"No!" she said, her eyes growing big over him.

The army doctor came in then, and two soldiers with him. They wasted no time asking questions. The soldiers stripped off the bedclothes and bared him to the waist. The doctor searched him for wounds.

"Neck," Duncan whispered. His throat hurt.

The soldiers turned him over. He felt the heat from the fireplace on his cheek.

"Only a bruise," the doctor said impatiently. "Get up and stop your soldiering."

The woman exclaimed: "Oh-h-h! You're brutish! The man's paralyzed. He can't move a finger!"

"Oh." The doctor pinched Duncan's arm and watched his eyes. Pinched his leg and watched his eyes. "That's right," he said. "Cover him up."

"But ain't you goin' to *do* something for the poor man?"

"Nothing *can* be done about that," the doctor said, and the soldiers followed him out the door. Duncan strained desperately to get up and follow them. He had that hopelessness of yesterday when he had called to Hector MacNeill marching away from him. He didn't want to die. He wanted to live.

The woman was pulling the pot crane from the fire, dipping chicken broth in a cup.

"Drink it," she said, as though he were a baby, putting a spoon to his lips. It was easier to let her than to resist.

"What is it? What is it?" she questioned him urgently.

"Hen broo," he grumbled.

"That's right! You *can* taste! Did it go down?"

He didn't answer. She put the spoon against his teeth and prized. He gave up and opened his mouth. The woman was unco worrisome. "It did!" she said triumphantly. She fed him the whole cup of broth before she would let him rest.

And then not for long, for the Scotch-Irish woman, as the Ulster Scots called themselves, had the urge to heal. She put pots on the fire, and she gathered cloths. She looked at him curiously, fearfully, and Duncan looked at her in fright, for he was helpless.

She took the quilts off of him, and Duncan gasped: "Stop! Stop, woman! I forbid ye!" But she pulled off her heavy shoes and mounted the bed. She lifted and tugged at his inert body until she panted and grew red-faced. She rolled him over on his belly, and his head hung down from the bed toward the fire. Duncan groaned and protested, but all his protests did not stop her. She was around him desperately, wrapping his feet in a quilt behind the bed, resting them in a chair. She was covering his body to his shoulders. She was placing a tub of hot water under his face. She bared his shoulders. She plastered a steaming hot wet sheet on his shoulders and neck. Then she washed the clay from his hair. He was not dead yet. That surprised Duncan. He groaned most mightily, but he had not determined in what way he was worse off than before.

Now the woman was frightened. She had done what she had set out to do, but whether for good or ill she did not know. His desperate groans sent her into mounting apprehension.

The heat around his head, somehow, felt comforting, and his fright became less. The bothersome woman, after all, was only trying to help him. He might even go to sleep. He might die while he was asleep. Perhaps this drowsiness was death coming on. The woman put another hot sheet on his neck.

Something clicked back of his shoulders, a soft, sliding click. Then, as though hot wires ran up and down his legs and through his arms and along his back, he had a most ungodly, excruciating pain. His shoulders felt as if someone had socked him with a splitting maul. His breath came and went in great puffs, and he screamed. He jumped out of the bed and staggered around the room. He fell and got up and dived back for the bed, his breath coming in shrill pants. The woman ran after him, screaming, too.

"See what ye hae done, woman!" he berated her in profound indignation, glaring at her from the bed. "Ye wouldna let well enough alone!"

Her eyes were frightened, and he, too, was frightened and panting, and they stared at each other in the excess of their fright. Then he was quiet. His arms moved, his toes wiggled; but they hurt in a most unholy piercing, tingling way.

"God's mercy be praised!" the woman murmured, scarcely yet believing. "God's mercy be *praised!*"

Duncan looked, and the woodswoman, whose eyes had been hard enough to take his life in her hands for pity's sake, now were angelic eyes of tenderness, misty at God's wonder.

"Amen," Duncan croaked, for his throat still was swollen. "And praise be to God f'r His makin' so wonderfu' a woman."

"Aw, that's all right," she said uncomfortably. It was the first time she had thought of herself as being at all responsible for the miracle. She wiped her anxious rough young hands on her apron and rushed for the broom and began to sweep the hearth.

Then she fed him cup after cup of hot chicken broth, and sleep came on him like a rising tide. It was as though the Cape Fear in its vast gentleness cradled him on its bosom and flowed with him away into a dismal place of peace.

He slept for a long while. He did not know how long. When he awoke he had the sense of having slept a long time. A great bulging pain centered in his shoulders. Before he had thought to do so, he had wiggled his toes. They worked.

It was dark, and the room was warm, and the fire was low, only a heap of glowing coals. The woman, her face drawn in lines, but red in the light, sat before the fire suckling her baby, looking at the door, startled.

A British soldier came in. Duncan frowned, trying to remember. He was one of those who had come with the doctor. The man's boots pounded as he crossed the floor, smirking. The woman shrank back, holding her baby tight, putting it in the crib, covering it, staring at the redcoat.

"What—what do you want?" she stammered.

"I came for that corpse." But his eyes lingered on her, he did not turn to the bed.

"He didn't die. He's getting well. He is almost well!" Her voice was rising. "He is strong. Strong!"

The man laughed shortly and glanced into the darkness where the bed stood. The baby in the crib began to cry.

"Think you that a King's soldier can be frightened from a kiss by such deceit?"

He bent swiftly and circled her waist with his arm. She fought back, straining, saying nothing, only a desperate: "Ugh! Ugh!"

"Come! Come!" the redcoat said. "Be kindly—be sweet—and save yourself distress!"

Duncan growled: "Stop it, soldier!"

The man was startled at the sudden voice. He whirled to the bed.

"Who—who are you?"

"I'm a courier f'r His Excellency, Governor Martin, and I wi' see to it that ye hang if ye harm the woman!"

"I thought you were dead."

"Begone!"

But the command was spoken to the soldier's red back. He was already through the door.

The woman was standing erect and stiff, her eyes hard and brittle. She hissed: "I could kill the bastard!"

"Where's y'r man?" Duncan asked.

"With Greene," she said, still looking at the door.

"Then I wi' stay till the armies pass."

Duncan stayed four days. For the first two he was so stiff and sore he could not rise from the bed. Cornwallis had moved south, a neighbor woman said, taking wagonload after wagonload of wounded. The near-dead Colonel Webster, the earl's most beloved officer, rode in a litter between two horses. The Whigs hovered near but they were too shattered to attack.

A Quaker let Duncan ride in his cart. The silent, wide-hatted man said he was following Cornwallis' army to sell tobacco. Quakers were triple-taxed by the Whigs because they were pacifists and would not bear arms. Therefore the Friends must work hard and trade closely for money to pay the taxes. It was a sore burden, he said, but they did not complain.

The tobacco maker said that Cornwallis had camped at a mill on Deep River. Duncan did not know until later that Martha McGee was hostess to the King's forces. They stopped there and ground corn meal night and day to build up their store of food. Foraging parties gutted the cribs for miles around, and the mill ran unceasingly. Duncan stood at her door. He asked admittance of the soldiers on guard. He had walked through an ocean of troops to get here, and now they stopped him. But Martha McGee heard, and she came to the door briskly.

"Duncan!" she gave him full-throated welcome. "You look like a camel, with that hump on your back."

"I come to ye again f'r y'r healing art, Martha McGee," Duncan said humbly.

"Huh!" she jibed him. "The last time you were here you offered me your proud protection. And now look! I've been captured by the whole damned British army, and you're as much help as a kitten. Come in and meet the general. He's not bad."

Martha was more proud than otherwise. If the British *had* to win, and they *had* to pass her mill, and Cornwallis *had* to have a headquarters house, then why not with her? It would be something for the grandchildren to talk about—long after the British had been driven from the country.

The general marched back and forth in front of the fire. His hands clasped over his coat tails, over his full rump, and his eyes swept out the open back door and across the rolling hills to the northwest. Every time he turned before the fire, his eyes jumped in that direction, and he seemed to hurry down and back so that he could look again.

"Now see!" Martha bustled by him to the door and closed it with a bang. "It is my door, and I want it closed! What if General Greene does charge in from those hills? If he takes you because of my closed door, so much the better. Besides, you'll take cold."

Cornwallis laughed, half troubled. "Have it your way while you are here, madam. When you leave, I'll have it mine. And—don't talk about General Greene's coming. I defeated *him*, not he *me*."

"Well, here's a man to congratulate you on your *great* victory."

Cornwallis turned and looked and remembered. "I know him," he said, extending his hand. "Duncan—Duncan——"

"Stuart."

"Of course. The Cape Fear Scot. Martin's man. Saw him aboard ship on the Cape Fear five years ago. Had more information and more sense about the country than all the King's staff. What's the matter with your shoulder, boy? Guilford?"

"Aye, sir," Duncan said grimly. "When ye shot the Scots in the back."

Cornwallis shook his head and twisted his lips and turned away.

Duncan was not bitter. It was all in the King's name. He said: "I would pass ye my compliments, sir, on y'r grand victory."

"I never saw such fighting since God made me," the general said.

Duncan said: "I hope y'r success means that the rebel cause is ended in all the South."

"Yes," Cornwallis said absently. "Yes. One more such victory would ruin me."

Martha laughed roundly. She laughed and swore like a man. And Duncan thought she would laugh and swear the same way in the presence of Auld Nick himself.

"Well," she said irrelevantly, "when you're gone, we Whigs have got a mighty sight of Scotch Tories to drum out of the land so we can start our country."

"Huh!" Cornwallis was abrupt. "What Tories? You could wrap up in the standard every one of them who came to it. They come, they shake hands, they wish me well, they go home. And"—he looked at Duncan—"I don't blame the Highlanders, after we failed to retaliate after Moore's Creek."

"I don' think you understand, General," Martha McGee said soberly. "You're just a damned interloper. So is the King. There's more nasty fighting left in this country than you ever dreamed of. When you're gone, the real fight will begin."

"I suspect you are right, madam, and God pity all of you."

Martha turned to go, but Cornwallis called her. "I take it," he said with studied casualness, "that you are passing no information to your friends on our disposition and plans."

Martha arched her black eyebrows and smiled saucily. "Don't you wish you knew?"

Cornwallis remained stolid, unresponsive to her levity. "The fate of spies," he told her, "isn't—shall we say?—pleasant. It would grieve me, madam——"

"Well, try to find out!" she snapped. Martha left them and slammed the door.

Cornwallis looked at Duncan speculatively, for a long moment, and then glanced at the door. "Your job," he said. "The woman has a distressing admiration for this Light-Horse Harry fellow. I suspect they are in communication, right under my nose."

It was too sudden and involved for Duncan to comprehend at once. He went out and sat at the roots of one of Martha's great trees and gave thought. Cornwallis was most moody for one who had gained such a great victory. It tended to blight Duncan's good spirits. True, Greene had fewer men killed than the British, but Greene was routed and disorganized, and his men were roaming the country, swapping their powder and balls for food. That army would never reassemble. Then surely the British had won a great victory. They were marching north triumphantly in the whole campaign—Savannah, Charleston, Camden, Guilford—laying waste the Whigs as they went. It was victory, of course. In a few days even Bladen would be under the King's rule again, and he could plow his land and serve the Crown and build his house. Aye—it was a fine, stout feeling. Cornwallis was but o'eranxious.

Duncan did not take the general's instructions to watch Martha too seriously. He had no aptness or training in espionage. But he did stay with Martha much of the time. Under her poultices and hot bathing his neck wound healed miraculously.

One jarringly suspicious circumstance bowled him over while he was there, and the outcome twisted his conscience for days to come. It was the night before the British were to march early next morning. No one knew their projected route, and the Whigs, certainly, were alert to discover it.

Duncan walked along the unfrequented path back of Martha's garden. He saw a man in the darkness hugging the fence, half hidden in its vines. His purpose was to pass on, for he had no will to interrupt any man's clandestine enterprises. But this man broke from hiding and ran swiftly without a word. Duncan stood there for a minute or more, looking, chuckling.

Then he heard a faint hiss inside the garden, and, in the same spirit of teasing, he answered. In the darkness he saw a hand thrust through the fence, under the vines. It held a letter, and Duncan, in a flash, grasped the wrist—for here was something to be seen to.

There was a gasp inside the garden. The wrist was soft and round, a woman's. Duncan gripped it until the woman moaned in pain, and all the while he was kicking out the wooden slats of the fence and made a most ungodly clatter.

He pulled the woman through. It was Martha.

"Duncan!" she whispered—and, by God, she was relieved.

He still held her wrist, pulled her close. "What does it mean?" he demanded.

She laughed lightly. "Read that letter and you'll know."

"'T' Light-Horse Harry Lee?"

"Yes."

Duncan's horror was tearing him inside. This was spy work. Spies were shot. He held her wrist and glared at her frantically.

"Well?" The woman was damnably calm, wi' his breast twistin' so. "What are you going to do with me?"

"Turn you o'er t' Cornwallis, o' course."

She drew a quick breath. "But, Duncan!" She leaned to him and smiled in his face—the same warm smile, the same helpless child plea she had made when she had leaned on his arm and pleaded when he had first seen her in Bladen. "He'll have me shot!"

Couldn't the woman know—couldn't she understand—it was a matter of honor? He couldn't help himself. She was a spy, caught red-handed. 'Twas not his decision. She must go to Cornwallis.

Soldiers stamped around the garden with torches to see about the noise. Duncan stuffed the letter into his sporran and waited, thinking violently.

"Ye did it y'rsel'!" he blamed her. "I winna shield y'r perfidy!"

The soldiers came running around the corner, and a torch made a long thin gleam along the barrel of a rifle—the same kind of rifle that shot bullets into spies.

Two soldiers took up short before them, with pointed bayonets. "Now what?" one demanded.

"Begone!" Duncan roared. "Canna a man hae a rendezvous wi' a woman wi'out the whole damn army spyin' on him?"

Martha tittered. The soldiers bowed back apologetically and left. Duncan, almost strangling, staggered away. He had to find a fire and burn the letter—he, wi' his face stingin' hot wi' the sweat poppin' out on it, feelin' like Judas Iscariot.

Governor Martin gave Duncan a horse, and the army moved by slow stages to Ramsey's Mill, to Cross Creek, to Elizabethtown and to Wilmington. At Barbecue Kirk Duncan wished that Flora MacDonald might look out its windows, as once she had done to see Caswell and his Whig troops, and observe the grand British Army move by in its power. In Cross Creek he wished that she might again sit on her white horse under the oak and review the mighty parade of the King's troops pushing down the Cape Fear in triumph. Flora was gone. But now, after this overpowering victory, with Whig domination on the Cape Fear broken, she would come back.

Colonel Webster got no better. When Cornwallis sent for him beyond Cross Creek, Duncan thought he might be seeking some local plantation where the desperately wounded man might be left in care of a physician. Gilbert Johnston's would be a good place. Governor Martin sat with Cornwallis when Duncan entered.

"I know of a Whig named Gilbert Johnston," Cornwallis said, "and I wish——"

"Gilbert is more the neutral than the active Whig," Duncan said. "He is nephew to our beloved Governor Gabriel Johnston."

"Yes? Well, anyway, you will accompany a troop of horse with wagons and point out this Johnston's plantation. The lieutenant has instructions to forage for supplies at this place—and it will be a part of your duty to see that he makes a thorough search. It is as essential that Johnston be stripped of all supplies. The King has need of them. That is all."

"But Gilbert is a good man," Duncan protested. "He has done no harm. He has abstained frae——"

"You have your orders, sir."

Duncan flushed. He looked furiously at Martin, but the governor did not face him.

Where Duncan would have preferred a controversy with Martin, he transferred his fury to Gilbert Johnston. Unreasoningly. For causing him to be in the despised position.

The troop turned up Gilbert Johnston's lane on the gallop, the same lane where on a moonlit night these years ago the High-landers had so proudly escorted Flora MacDonald. A soldier flung the gate open and, because the farm would have no need for gates when they left, he used it as a lever on its own hinges and wrecked it.

Gilbert Johnston came running up from the fields. He still wore his spurs. He did not dare ride his horse to the house.

Duncan alighted and strode angrily forward and met him.

"Gilbert," he said, not waiting for him to speak, "I do what I do because I hae orders. Now stand back and say nothing and it wi' be the better f'r *all*."

Gilbert stood straight and gripped his fingers, glaring into Duncan's eyes. And Duncan, because he was anguished, glared back ferociously.

The wagons backed up to the barns, and the soldiers began to gut them. Hay tumbled from the haylofts, and corn rumbled into the wagon beds. Grains scattered to the ground, and the chickens came squawking at such surprising good fortune. The soldiers caught the chickens as they came, wrung their necks and cast them into bags. Other soldiers came driving cows. Another soldier, expert in such matters, knocked them stiff with a maul and slit their throats.

Camp followers, the vultures of the army, streamed up the lane. They trooped into the house, women mostly, and a few civilian men. They filled the house. They shouted and yelled and laughed drunkenly.

Mrs Johnston ran out of the house, a buxom woman driving her, shouting stridently: " . . . and stay out, ye white ha'nt! If ye got silver, I'll find it. Talk or not, what do I care?"

Back in the house the ghouls were quarreling and fighting and tearing up chests and turning out clothes closets. Mrs Johnston crept up to Gilbert, and he put his arm around her and stood silently. Duncan walked away from them, more minded to shoot the camp followers than not. But Gilbert Johnston did not know that. Tom Hadley wouldn't know it. Nor Tom Brown. Nor could he tell them.

It was a desolate Brompton Hall that Duncan left that day when, staying purposely to see the last of the scullions away, he left the unhinged place with Gilbert standing with anger-dulled eyes, his arm about his wife. The house was open, the front door down, the inside stripped of everything worth having, and the outside dead, without a living thing left to crow or neigh or bark. What Gilbert Johnston might have hidden in the swamps against this day, Duncan wondered, and hoped it was enough. The British were triumphant in Bladen, finally, and Duncan had no pleasure in it now.

The army was marching by the highroad at the mouth of the lane, swinging on to Wilmington. Aye—it was the day he had prayed for. It was not as he had dreamed.

Cornwallis was riding beside the horse litter which bore Colonel Webster. Webster was dead. Cornwallis gave him such honor as was possible. They buried him miles down the road at Hugh Waddell's old place, Belfont, there to rest and sleep where the funereal gray moss swayed, and be forgotten.

Josiah Martin in Wilmington had the good grace not to go to the deathbed of that "foremost among the patrons of revolt and anarchy," Cornelius Harnett. Cornwallis had gone on to Virginia, and the Scottish Tories and other Loyalists were proclaiming vehemently the victories of the British and the subjugation of the state. Duncan Stuart, too, knew the mighty thrill of conquest.

Josiah Martin remained in Wilmington in the protection of Craig's garrison and awaited the unpleasant time when this wasted state would be his to govern again. His old enemies were gone. He had little desire to be governor now. The Highlanders were scattered and disorganized. The Moores were dead. Francis Nash was dead. Robert Howe no longer was a threat. John Ashe was hiding in the swamps, done for by illness. John Harvey was dead. James Hooper hadn't the old force. And now Cornelius Harnett, the greatest rebel of them all, lay dying. Josiah Martin had the chivalry not to go and gloat.

Duncan Stuart went to Hilton—humbly. Mary Harnett led him in quietly, in sad welcome. She was big enough to recognize a field of friendship which lay back of and beyond the harshness of the day. Tory though Duncan was, he was a friend of auld lang syne.

Cornelius Harnett was far gone when Duncan walked into the room. The paleness of death crept into the lines of his face, and the quiet hazel eyes which so well knew how to wait and listen now waited and listened for a faraway voice and were not afraid.

"Well, Duncan," Cornelius smiled. He lifted his hand weakly, and Duncan slipped his under it and let it rest in his palm. "I knew you'd come. I'm glad to see you. I wanted to—before I——"

"Na, Cornelius. Na. Ye but joke me. Ye'll be well soon."

"I feel craven, welcoming this chance to desert the cause of freedom, Duncan. Not that I matter now. No power on earth can stop it. Once I mattered, when the will to freedom was weak. I helped to nurture it. Maurice and James and John and Bob and Alexander —how we worked! But now it is done. All done! Done, except for the murder and arson and hate. I pity you, Duncan—all you who must live through it. But in the end you all will be free! Even you, Duncan."

Duncan sat stonily. One does not know how to converse with a man who is but half sane and, most certainly, no sane man could speak of a Whig victory now—after Cornwallis.

Cornelius continued weakly: "You are silent, Duncan. You don't believe me. Still, my friend, you shall know freedom."

"Aye," Duncan said hoarsely, meaning nothing.

"Freedom. Freedom in the minds of men. In the eyes of women. Planted in the thoughts of children. They will not know how to use it well, but it will be more precious to them than life, and they will learn to know. Freedom, Duncan—the most glorious thought that ever escaped your mind."

Cornelius stopped to breathe and rest, and then his thin voice continued:

"But I do not condemn. You, too, heed a high call. When the gush of change is spent, it is the bloody-headed Tory who must forget his fallen aims and his broken body and start building anew on the fresh location, lest the greatest enemy of all, chaos, overwhelm both him and his adversaries. The minions of change cannot. They haven't the knack. So you will build, my friend. As always. It is fate that you must build and rule and grow fat and make that clear, stable condition that we call the new civilization, and then you must be sacrificed again. For change will not be denied, my friend. Swamp water always reaches the sea, though it break your dam."

Duncan did not follow him, for he took the words to be the meaningless gabbling of a sick man, but then Duncan's ears were deadened with sorrow and his eyes with tears.

He pressed Cornelius' hand gently. He arose, for his old friend, in that lightness of sleep and awakening which belongs to the sick, closed his eyes and slept.

Hilton was the same glorious bank of trees and flow of water. But now it was bedraggled with grass and weeds. Duncan saw none of it as he blindly walked to his horse.

Flora MacDonald and, now, Cornelius Harnett—gone. Flora's desolation spawned victory. Or did it? And as Cornelius Harnett dies, so flickers the flame of revolution. Or does it? For the moment Duncan is not concerned. His heart is maist waefu'.

CHAPTER 8

IT CAME LIKE A PLAGUE. Like the smallpox that made a fevered, scabby path in Cornwallis' wake. Like the smallpox that struck Duncan Stuart and sent him to the Wilmington pest house to writhe and groan and burn and itch while frightened Negroes shoved food and water through the fence and pock-marked nursemen gave the patients attention wholesale. The smallpox was not such a plague as the other plague, but it was dismal and terrifying. Duncan watched them cart out the dead morning by morning. He counted them—one, two, three, four, five . . . nineteen, twenty, twenty-one—in the dead march that went by the door of his loose-boarded shack. It made no difference. Sometimes he would stop counting in the middle of the line from pure boredom. The fever had burned him, and weakness had made him pale, and the sight of the pock-marked nursemen retched him—so used to death and pain that they stood and chewed tobacco and talked about pay-day, while they waited for a man to die so they could move him out.

But smallpox was nothing compared to the other plague that swept the land. It began with Cornwallis' departure from Wilmington, where, away from the Loyal country, away from any hope of recruits, the camp followers—and soldiers, too—were permitted an orgy of rapine and pillage. That, finding ready soil in long-festered hatreds, spread and spread, crawling like a patch of smallpox sores.

From New Hanover it spread to Duplin, and from Duplin to Onslow, and up the Cape Fear to Bladen and Cumberland and into Chatham and Orange, to Anson and Montgomery. Hate, smoldering and growing deep, now blazed; but it was not honest hate, but slinking hate, that crawled by night hideously. It was the kind that made children cower in dark corners and wives hold the bloody heads of their husbands and scream at the shadows which faded into the night.

It was a sort which made a neighbor look upon the leaping glare in the sky as the lifetime home of his friend roared to ashes and plan vengeance; that which made men band together and hunt in packs, protecting their own only by exterminating their enemies. It kept them in the swamps and made them furtive, and he who dared stand up for the principles which men had grown to believe in was disbelieved and suffered from all. The time had come in the Cape Fear for the rule of fang and claw. It was a low point. A swing back. It was the breaking place between two ways of life. It was one road to freedom.

Duncan reached home from Wilmington just before daybreak. He did not go to his cabin, but like a homing otter dived into his secret cave and felt no safety until the deep darkness of the earth swallowed him. It was as he had left it. His rifle was there. His dirks. His canned cooked sausage. His buried store of powder and balls. He reached for them in the dark and felt them with his hands. Another night he would slip up the swampside and go home, to see if Gillie Black was still there, to see if the Whigs had stolen Donald Bane, to see if they had burned his cabin. This was July. He hadn't been home since February.

Much had happened since February. The Irish Catholic con-

gressman Thomas Burke, from Orange, John Pyle's territory, was
the new governor. His piercing eyes, his dark hair, his clear voice,
were rousing the Whigs to new efforts. But what could they do?
One paid $12,000 for a horse. The legislature paid $75,000 for a
month's rent for a house in which to meet. Government was a
mockery. Only men were significant, now that Cornwallis had
riddled the Whigs.

Colonel Colvill was in charge of the Bladen Loyalists. Duncan
knew him but slightly, but would report to him at once. Hector
MacNeill had a strong company, and it was getting stronger. Colvill's company was a part of it. And so were Archibald MacDougall's and Duncan Ray's. Up on Deep River, from where it flowed
into the Cape Fear on west nearly to the Yadkin, David Fanning
was performing atrocities so vile as to make the Highlanders
ashamed that he fought for the same cause. Yet, as occasion came,
they joined forces with him and the night resounded with their
mingled hoofbeats. It was the only way to make Cornwallis' victory
secure. The land had to be made so hideous for Whigs that they
would cease to trouble.

But Duncan never joined Colvill. That very night the colonel
was caught off guard by a squad of bushwhackers, and the morning found him quite cold and stiff. If it was revenge, it was for
raids and burnings and arrests which Colvill carried on with an
intemperate zeal. Everybody knew and nobody knew who had
slain him. Duncan himself had heard the shooting and the scream
in the darkness and wondered.

Softly he walked, late at night, but Gillie Black heard him nevertheless. Gillie walked out boldly.

"Are ye well, Gillie Black?" Duncan asked in low voice. He was
surprised at the catch which came in his throat.

"Yas'h, Mas' Dunk. I'm well an' doin' well."

"Ye hae na been stolen, I see."

"No, suh, nobody didn' want me."

"And Donald Bane?"

"He in de stable."

Gillie ran to the stable and led the horse out to Duncan and then
brought a pine torch. Donald Bane was sickly-looking. Duncan
had never seen him so distempered. His hair did not lie flat and

sleek, but straight out and dead. Duncan frowned and growled and looked at a great sore on his back and at a swollen foot swathed in a bluestone bandage.

"What hae ye done to Donald Bane?"

"Not much," Gillie Black grinned. "De Whigs, dey sarched and sarched when I kep' he in de swamp. I scared dey fin' him—an' me. So I fixed us bofe so dey wouldn' want us. I curry-cobbed de hoss wrong way, made he look sick, and I made a bluestone saddle sore on he back, and I tied a strip o' rag around he shank an' swell up he foot. Den I gied myse'f some bluestone sores—an' den dey let us alone. Dey come an' dey look an' dey say dey don' want no sick hoss an' no itchy nigger. So me'n Donal' Bane, we been doin' well. Wen one sore gits well, us make mo'."

Duncan chuckled. "God gied ye more wit than I kenned."

"You all can sleep home now," Gillie suggested. "Nobody don' come heah no mo'."

Duncan did sleep there. And the next day he took his rifle and walked boldly all over the fields and down by the tar kilns, pausing frequently and looking. The land, his redeemed land, was soft and restful under his feet. It pleased him to stop and look and plan in the shade of his own trees. He looked up at the weathered frame of his stout house, gaunt, hungry, begging for the life that he had once promised it. It was growing into twilight when he sat on a sill and gazed across the swamp that he planned to be his clear-water lake, to adorn the view from his house and to turn the wheels of his mill. Aye, 'twas worth fighting for. He had fought and he had won. Now he would have it. And Mary, too? Weel . . .

Someone was coming. He dropped back into the shadows of the trees. It was Sandy MacAlpin. Duncan could tell from the way he swung his shoulders. Sandy was a Loyalist. Had been. Duncan would wait and see. He followed quietly. Sandy met Gillie just this side of the creek.

"Did Duncan Stuart come back yet?" Sandy asked Gillie.

"No, suh. I ain' seed him since 'way las' winter."

"He is supposed to be back. We got information. We want him to help us tonight."

"What," Duncan asked at his back, "would ye hae me do to-night, Sandy?"

Sandy did not engage in the former cautious preliminaries to conversation known on the Cape Fear. He mentioned no weather, no crops, he made no talk of hunting.

"Colvill's dead. They bushwhacked him."

"Aye." The news was staggering, but those on the Cape Fear no longer were surprised at anything. "Perhaps I heard the shout."

"We're going after the Hadleys."

"Old Tom?"

"All of 'em. The whole rats' nest."

"Did they do it?"

"I don't know. We're goin' to clear out all the Toms—Hadley, Brown, Robeson, Owen. We can work on them while Craig is getting a new colonel up here. We've got to work fast, if we benefit from Cornwallis. How about you for colonel?"

"Na."

"Let's go. The Flea Hill men are waiting."

"I hae no horse."

"Nobody has. Come on."

Duncan had his rifle, his powder horn, his lead pouch, his dirk. He was ready.

It was as casual as that. It did not seem to him that he was on his way to raid the Hadleys on Carver's Creek. He hated Whigs, but not Hadleys. He liked old Tom. And Joshua. Joshua, they said, had done more than anybody else to keep down strife along the Cape Fear since Cornwallis had marched through. But Simon was the wild one, the cutthroat, the house burner. John, too, but not so bitter. Young Ben wasn't old enough. Old Tom was the master mind; he stirred up more Whig trouble than all the others.

The Flea Hill Scots were most bitter. Perhaps the Hadleys had killed Colvill. It didn't matter. Simon had driven every live thing from Peter MacLean's place, and Pete said he would get even if he had to burn the house. Avery MacNair said nothing but walked on in a queer silence. They weren't quite sure he was sane. Simon had called Avery's brother, Andrew, to the door at night and shot him dead. Since that time Avery had lived in the swamps and nursed his rifle.

Sandy MacAlpin was more talkative, more profane, more openly vindictive.

"Old Tom's my meat," he said. "Hadn't been for him, my dad would be alive. Ain't right, him alive and my dad dead. You boys leave him to me."

They filed through swamps, over sandhills, through Gray's Pocosin. The stagnant inch-deep water, still warm from the summer sun, splashed against their boots and soaked in to their feet. Mosquitoes rose in swarms and hummed about their heads poisonously.

"I allus said that the biggest 'skeeters in the world growed in Gray's Pocosin," one said. "Now I can prove it." This was one of the Witt boys. He suddenly had a bright idea and laughed about it in a falsetto snicker: "We ought to take old lady Hadley and tie her out here in her nightgown and let the 'skeeters eat her." Some of the men growled, and for a while he did not say more. Then he said: "Y'know, I'm gwine to jine up with this fellow Fanning. He fights war like a man to my notion."

Tom Hadley's high-roofed house was a tall black shadow in the night. The dogs barked, but having barked they ran under the house and hid. Then there was silence. Big trees stood in the yard, and each man found his own tree. The men were like shadows within shadows. No one made a noise in the house, but there was the vibrant feeling that the house was alive—but with what? If Daniel Beard and forty men slept there for the night, then the Flea Hill boys had a hopeless task. If only the Hadleys were at home, they'd stay.

They waited. They said nothing. The house remained still. The darkness creaked its ominous silence while men waited and wore on each other's nerves.

Duncan stood at the end of the house, where the steep roof peaked to a high gable. Others took the front. The house was surrounded. All stood silently behind trees, peering.

Out front someone called: "Hello, house!"

There was no answer. There was another hail. Still no answer.

"Come out, old Tom Hadley," Sandy called.

But all this was merely preliminary, a bait to arouse reaction, so the enemy could be gauged.

The Witt yelled, high and shrill: "Come out, ye old bastard, or we'll burn you down!"

The shuttered gable window high above Duncan's head creaked softly, but it was in the shadow. Duncan couldn't see it. He clung close to the tree. He heard old Tom Hadley's voice shrieking: "Dan Beard! Oh-h-h Dan Beard! Come a-runnin'—ride yo' hosses. The damn Tories have come!"

Intense silence followed. Everybody listened for the answering shout. There was none. It was a trick.

"Dan Bee-yerd!" old Tom yelled louder than before. There was a new note of anxiety in his voice. His women were in the house. His young son. His older sons were away, else from the vantage point of the inside they would have opened fire.

The situation was clear now. He was helpless. Old Tom yelled: "Dan Beard!" Duncan heard someone breathing near him. Panting. Sandy MacAlpin.

There was a single shot. Flame jutted from Sandy's rifle. Upstairs there was a clatter, like that of a gun falling down the stairs.

Around at the front was another crash. That was the door falling in. Duncan rushed in to see by the light of a torch. One of the Flea Hill men shoved aside an old woman and rushed up the stairs. Others did likewise. And Duncan.

Old Tom Hadley was half down the stairs, sitting crumpled, motionless, grinning at them, a trickle of blood down his cheek.

"Is he dead?" they asked.

Avery MacNair, his pale face now curiously alive and shining, shouted: "I'll make sure!" and sunk his sword deep into old Tom Hadley's body. That released air somewhere. The old body sighed and shriveled wearily against the steps. A bit of gray hair had been pinned against the window jamb by the bullet.

Downstairs a white-faced old woman stood, looking up. Her hands trembled. The sight made Duncan sick. He went outside.

It was not customary both to kill and to burn. The house was left as it was. The raiding party filed out into the yard, but two of them grabbed young Ben Hadley and took him along. They walked through the woods. No one spoke. No one questioned Ben Hadley's capture. A man might do very much as he pleased on one of these raids. If it was their purpose to hang him, very well. It was permissible.

But the warped mind of Witt, the swampman, clung to its mosquito idea.

"Strip 'im!" he cried, his voice leaping to high pitch in his relish. "Th'ow his damn clo'es away! Tie him out here in Gray's Pocosin and let him spend the night with the 'skeeters!"

They did that, young Ben cursing them with a steady, quiet bitterness that was his heritage from old Tom.

They left him there, standing barefoot in the warm, stagnant water, his wrists tied to a tree. The mosquitoes swarmed upon him. Someone the next day released him, swollen and sick.

MacAlpin's squad took to the swamps, but Duncan ran all the way home and hid in his cave. The Whigs were sure to ride before dawn, and their retribution would be grim. The repercussion would be like an explosion, from Tidewater to Cross Creek. Tories must die because Tom Hadley had died—and that meant only that other Whigs must die in retaliation. That was the way it had to be. That was the way old Tom Hadley had said it would be.

Duncan tramped the little circle of his cave again, but he was not alone now. Old Tom Hadley's blood-streaked, grinning gray face was before him. Always before him. A grisly, vivid, gray-bearded face in the dark, grinning. Above him, in the window, a lock of gray hair was pinned to the jamb with a bullet, and the gray hair waved in the wind. Duncan's shoulders hunched and his fist doubled and he strode faster, and he cursed the face with a vehemence that made him sweat and gasp, but the face never changed, but floated ahead of him, always grinning triumphantly.

He climbed out the tunnel to the top of the ground to escape it. It was not yet quite dawn. Up the river and down the river he could count the glares of five Loyal houses burning. Aye—Tom Brown was riding and howling like a maniac this night. Aye, weel, ride, Tom Brown.

The Whigs arose in such numbers that it was futile for small groups of Loyalists to confront them. Duncan dodged from swamp to swamp up the river. Duncan Ray had a company. He would join that. They would return and slay Tom Brown—and Tom Owen—and Tom Robeson.

He was far toward Cross Creek on an old road near Rockfish when he heard horses. Without more ado he dived into a gully and climbed under the vines. He had no more than settled himself when a man came running from the same direction he had come from, and the horses were nearer. Duncan recognized him. Allan MacSweene. He was a Loyalist.

MacSweene looked over his shoulder and left the road, diving for the gully.

"Come under the vines!" Duncan called. "I'm a friend!"

"Friend or foe, I'm comin' anyhow," MacSweene gasped. "It's death to stay out."

The horses galloped by, and just ahead of them a man staggered, exhausted. As one of the horsemen came by, he raised his sword and whacked into the skull of the running man. The horses kept galloping. The man dropped into the sand.

Duncan and MacSweene barely dared breathe. Then the horses were gone, and MacSweene laughed hysterically.

"It's the MacBride!" he shrilled. "The *MacBride!*"

"Aye? An' ye laugh?"

"Aye! Aye, I laugh! He's a Whig! They didn't know it. He's a *Whig!*"

They sat there, regarding the dead man, while MacSweene rested from his run. Between gasps he told what had happened.

Days before at Piney Bottom, not far away, Colonel Wade and some other Anson men returning from the Continental Army had been attacked by cunning John MacNeill. The Loyalists had killed a boy. Now Wade and a larger party had returned to retaliate. They spread terror from Drowning Creek to Rockfish. Their party had divided, and this part—the troop which Duncan had just seen ride by—had shot down John Clark and Duncan Currie and Daniel MacMillan and Peter Blue, and now, having twisted the thumb of an old man until he had told the hiding place, they were on the trail of Allan MacSweene.

"But they won't get me!" Allan said. "They will look, but I won't be there. I am going home, because they will think I wouldn't *dare.*"

Together they crossed the swamp—Allan to hide out near his home, Duncan to go to the house and notify his wife and get food.

The MacSweene house was quiet when Duncan approached. A boy was behind a stump, looking at him down a rifle barrel. Mrs MacSweene waited for him, her bitter blue eyes ready to welcome him, to order him away, to hear bad news.

"I'm from Allan," Duncan said.

She said nothing. Her hands went out awkwardly, impulsively, a gesture of sudden pleading.

"He is well."

She swallowed, still silent.

"He is in the swamp. He sent me for food."

She turned into the house, nodding for him to come. She hadn't spoken yet. Probably she couldn't.

There was precious little food to send. Some boiled field peas in a skillet. She raised this over a little bucket, to scrape out some with a spoon, to leave some for herself and the children. Then, with another of those queer, awkward gestures, she scraped out all the peas and left herself none.

Then she said: "Hurry! They are all around the place. They've been here twice already."

"Aye," reaching for the bucket. Duncan was hungry, but he wanted none of these peas. He wouldn't be able to swallow them for the haunted eyes of the woman.

She caught his hand before it touched the bucket. She listened, holding it. He heard the noise now. Horses.

She pushed him toward the ladder behind the door, and he scrambled into the dark space under the roof. He lay on his belly. He could look between the planks and see her standing there in front of the fireplace. She was a thin, pale woman, the thin corners of her mouth bent down in despair. The horses galloped close.

At that moment the back door crashed in, and Allan MacSweene fell through.

"A knife! A knife!" he cried to his mate. "I escaped, but they tied my hands. A knife—and my rifle!"

The poor woman had no time for either. The Whigs were pounding on the front door. It gave in, but she had dragged Allan MacSweene to the chimney corner and spread her wide skirt in front of his crouching form. She drew her children to her side. They made a screen.

The Whigs rode through the door. They filled the room with trampling horses. One nag nuzzled into the bucket and ate the peas. The riders had to bend their necks to save their heads from the ceiling. One's head was not six inches under Duncan. He could have jabbed his dirk point into the Whig's skull.

The horses lumbered on the floor. The men swore when they bumped their heads. They swore at the woman and demanded to know where Allan was. If she spoke, Duncan couldn't hear her. She looked at them and shook her head. One man threatened her with a sword, but she did not move. He could have struck her down and she wouldn't have moved. Duncan forgot his own danger, watching her unconquerable defiance.

Then one of the Whigs reached her shoulder and snatched her away between two of the horses. She shrieked—an unearthly, heart-rent, lonely shriek.

Allan MacSweene's terror-stricken face, with his wrists crossed, tied before him, remained in Duncan's sight a bare second.

Then Allan dashed through the horses, out the back door and toward the high stake-and-rider rail fence at the rear.

"Wait! Wait!" a Whig urged another. "Wait till he mounts the fence! Look! What a *jump!*"

A rifle fired. A body thudded to the ground. The Whigs laughed. They rode out the door, laughing still. The woman went to the back door in long, staggering steps, her arms reaching out.

Hector MacNeill descended on the section, riding hard. David Fanning came. Archibald MacDougall and Duncan Ray brought their squads. Together they made a large company. Few had horses. Duncan joined those on foot. They made for Raft Swamp to cut off the Anson men before they could leave the territory.

Fanning had just returned from taking prisoners to Wilmington. Craig had made him a colonel of militia, and he was arrayed in a vainglorious uniform of epaulets and streams of gold braid. In honor of his promotion, the Scots gave him the command.

They went into the swamp, and Duncan gave him reluctant admiration for the way in which he placed his men. Duncan and a large squad were placed in a bay thicket beside one of the causeways. It was their duty to fire on the enemy and drive them toward

Fanning or else draw their fire and divert them while Fanning drove into their flank.

The Whigs made a weaving column, coming down the long, straight water-flanked swamp road. Far ahead of them, not far from where Duncan was, a little Scot trudged along the road as though nothing impended. It was Angus MacCooish, the roaming piper, all unaware that he was surrounded by soldiers. Angus must have felt the oppression of the unseen Whigs, for he adjusted his bagpipes and blared forth in the wilderness: "The Campbells Are Coming, Oho, Oho!" Angus played that when he was displeased. Angus never knew how great and how interested an audience he had.

Back of Angus, where two roads came together, the banks-pony company of Scots came charging in ahead of the Whigs. Behind them, on the road from which they came, were other Whigs. It was a curious sight, the tiny ponies, with the long legs of men, charging madly up the road with the Whigs on bigger horses chasing them and laughing uproariously. Then the Whigs struck them, flaying with their swords and clubbing with their guns. The Scots leaped from the causeway onto the tussocks and ran into the swamp.

The little ponies, riderless, huddled there and blocked the road. The big horses charged into them and knocked them into the water. They were too short to reach bottom. On either side the lakes were dotted with the noses of little horses, reaching out for air.

Angus MacCooish looked back at the turmoil and began to run. He was little and short and old. A large man on a large horse galloped up behind him. The Whig laughed delightedly. Even when he reached Angus he did no more than trot beside him, teasing him, prodding him with his sword. Then, as though tiring of the sport, the Whig raised his heavy sword high, tipped in his stirrups, and split Angus down to the throat. The little fellow went down, a tiny, huddled heap in the mud. That was all of the roaming piper of Bladen. After the Whig horses went over him, he was never seen again.

Duncan's eyes never left the big Whig. With oaths that ground in his soul and never came to his grim lips, he swore to kill him.

The Whig checked his horse, wiped the blood from his blade on his palm, and sheathed it. Then he waited for the column to overtake him.

They came, laughing, never suspecting the other Scots in ambush. When the head of the column came opposite Duncan, he still had his eye on the big Whig who had killed Angus. He took the most careful aim he could. He waited for the order to fire. Six were to fire first, then, while they reloaded, six others, thus alternating in a steady fire until the Whigs reacted one way or the other.

"Fire!" the sergeant ordered, and six rifles barked. Only one man fell. The big Whig. He had six bullets in his head.

The next round emptied five saddles, and the Whigs broke madly, dashing across the more or less solid ground toward Fanning's concealed company. There they met the Scottish bullets with Fanning courageously exposed in his new uniform. The Whigs were in utter rout. The swamps suddenly were full of men, Whigs and Tories, and none could tell which was which. The battle ceased in confusion, but the Whigs were not to be found again.

Duncan found a horse and, joining a group going that way, rode over to visit the home of old Kenneth Black, not many miles away.

Maggie Black stood at the gate. Amiable and kind, now her eyes glittered blue, and she was silent—silent like the MacSweene woman—too bitter even for a smile of welcome.

"He's dead," she said.

Duncan said nothing, but sat with his hands crossed on his pommel, leaned forward, looking at her, waiting. He, suddenly, was empty—empty of thought, empty of words. Maggie's chill grief made him that way.

"He was riding a horse," Maggie said.

Duncan twisted his head. There was the coming of pain. Deep pain, the first bearable, ominous twinges of anguish. He loved old Kenneth Black.

"The horse was crippled," Maggie said. Her voice was dull. "They shot him. He tried to escape, but the horse was crippled.

He rode a little way, but he was wounded and fell off. One of the Deep River Whigs rode by and dropped a gun stock on his head and crushed it. We found him there."

Duncan rode swiftly to find Hector MacNeill. They must go into Deep River and find Phil Alston and hang him. Tom Brown and Tom Owen and Tom Robeson could wait. First they must take Alston. And hang him. Shooting would be too good. Duncan himself must be the man to put the rope about his neck. He was raging when he came to Hector MacNeill and the leaders.

"Come, Hector!" he demanded. "We wi' stop neither to eat nor sleep. I begrudge him every breath he takes till we kill him!"

Hector MacNeill was a man. A bold man and a sound man. Every Scot in his company leaped to Duncan's demand. Some ran for their saddles. They were about to stampede, for the killing of old Kenneth brought overflowing wrath.

"Na!" old Hector said. "Bide! Bide!"

Old Hector stamped among them, his robust body shouldering aside the sullen ones who would not move. His bold eye caught them and warned them. He turned to Duncan.

"Listen, lad! If ye loved auld Kenneth, then remember I hae loved him twice as long. But I canna act frae my heart—nor can ye. 'Twould gie me joy to grip the man wi' my bare hands and wring his neck. 'Twould be music to hear the bone snap. But I canna go rabbit-chasin' now, nor can ye. Colonel Fanning will attend to the man Alston and report to me at Cross Creek in two days. Duncan, ye will report to Colonel Slingsby in Elizabethtown and instruct him to harry Brown and Owen and Robeson wi' great diligence, till we come. When we hae taken Cross Creek, we wi' drive down both sides o' the river, sweepin' out the Whigs i' the valley. 'Tis the campaign, lad, not the incident, to remember. And God bless auld Kenneth and keep his soul. He was a good man. March!"

John Slingsby had been made commander of the Elizabethtown post, taking Colvill's place. Slingsby was a man of sense and of courage, and he hated no man.

Duncan reached Elizabethtown the next evening. Slingsby was

reading, and smiling at, a letter from Tom Brown to Governor
Burke, which had been intercepted and brought to him. Slingsby
read Tom's lament aloud:

*"'For six months we have been seeking to defend ourselves and
property, but the Tories . . . are daily plundering and destroying
. . . and we, being but few in number that stand in behalf of our
county, are not sufficient to stand in our own defense. Our number
is not a hundred and . . .'"*

"That shows!" Slingsby declared. "We will drive on. In a few
days no Whig will dare raise his head and we'll have peace, Duncan! Peace!"

The soldiers laughed.

Duncan shrugged. Bladen would not have peace as long as Tom
Brown was at large. "Send for my horse while I sleep, and gie me
ten rifles," he demanded, "and I'll bring Tom Brown to ye before
dark tomorrow."

John Slingsby considered that at length, dubiously. "Tom Brown
is fast and dangerous."

"All the more reason to catch him—or kill him."

Slingsby nodded slowly.

Duncan entered the fort and sought a cot. He did not want to
rest. He wanted to ride now, but he had not slept for two days,
and he was in no condition to meet the swift and resourceful
Brown. He would rest. It came on him that tomorrow was to be
the fateful day of the Whig revolt in Bladen. The day he would
take Tom Brown. That would end the revolution on the Cape
Fear. Perhaps it would be better to kill him. He thought of old
Tom Hadley's grinning, dead face. He hoped that Tom Brown's
face would not grin.

"'Tis needfu' f'r the King's cause!" shrieked in his mind. For
every pang he answered himself that. He felt like shouting it
aloud.

Tom Brown took flight just as they turned into the lane. The
long, double-decked, shady porch of Oakland was hauntingly
peaceful. There was no sign of soldier or slave or living thing. The
women must have gone to Duplin like so many others. Just then

Duncan saw Tom Brown's Jess leap over a back fence, stumble
and race on. Brown was low on his back, making for the woods,
alone.

The eleven men whirled on their horses and charged across the
field. Jess was like a brown arrow, and Donald Bane, now sleek
and well again, glided away from the other horses as though they
were pulling plows. Now! Now, Tom Brown!

Duncan bore to the left. To get between Tom Brown and the
swamps. To drive him toward the river so the other horsemen
could pen him in.

Now they were in the pinewoods. The other horses were far
behind. Duncan felt for his pistol in his saddle holster. It was
loaded, except for the powder in the pan. He could not use his
rifle, not yet.

Tom Brown, curiously, was not bearing to the swamp, but
straight for the river. Duncan was gaining. He had cut through a
thicket that Brown had skirted. Now they were within rifleshot
of each other, but neither had time to shoot.

Brown looked back and screamed. It was the wild scream of the
chase, and no wonder. He was a hunter, and here was the fox race
of his life—and he the fox. Behind him, curving across his wake,
riding like devils and yelling at every breath, was a line of horsemen
plunging through the pines, following their leader, penning him.
At their head Duncan Stuart, hair flying, shrieking like a savage,
sped surely between him and the swamp. Nobody could shoot at
that speed. It was a matter of horseflesh and God's blessing.

So, to the thunder of horse hoofs, went Tom Brown, six years
cock of the Bladen Whig walk, his followers scattered, his mansion
gutted, his plantation desolated, himself knowing hunger, rage-
maddened Tories bearing down on him with no more mercy in
their souls than hounds for foxes.

Duncan Stuart waved on his men and shouted: "I've got 'im!
I've got 'im! Close in!"

Tom Brown shrieked again and drew Jess to the right, for it was
true. A master in the swamps, he could not reach them. Duncan
Stuart had cut him off. Ten miles ahead was Elizabethtown and
hundreds of Tory soldiers to snare him. To the right was the river
—and far away, beyond Black River, was the doubtful haven of

Duplin. No wonder Tom Brown's defiant laugh also held a frantic note. The filth and disease of a British prison ship was the best he could hope for.

"A crazy fool!" Duncan stared dumfounded. Tom Brown had shot straight for the river, straight for a mass of bushes and briers that screened the bank. Duncan had a glimpse of him as he pulled Jess high and pitched far into the green and disappeared.

"Hy-yah! Hy-yah! Hy-yah!" Duncan forgot and called dogs to the lair. For Tom Brown was in hopeless position. Beyond him was a sand cliff, good for a broken neck if he attempted it.

"String out! String out!" Duncan shouted as the horsemen galloped in. "Make a line! Watch out for his rifle! He's in there and can't get out!"

Duncan raced up and down, around the little thicket, sizing up Tom's shape. "Fall on y'r bellies! He'll shoot!"

But Duncan did not protect himself. At this trembling moment he'd rather have Tom Brown's life than his own. He routed around the edge of the tangle, listening, peering, running, whining like a dog at a rabbit hole. He heard no sound. He could see no looming shape in the thick leaves.

"I got ye now, Tom Brown!" he howled. " 'Twas a long time comin', but y'r Whig jig is up! Come out, Tom Brown! Come out —else I ki' ye!"

He called to the men. "You, Blue!" he ordered. "Stand guard against the river at the ravine below there! Set fire t' the· thicket as ye go! Clark, take the upper end. If he jumps f'r the river, shoot t' kill! We'll burn him out!"

The dry leaves of a century rested on the ground. The trail of burning gunpowder led into them, and they began to crackle and roar and smoke, and the flame rose up to the top of the brush.

They waited. They hugged the ground. They cocked their guns, alert, ready, all set for Tom Brown, shooting or· not shooting, to stagger out and take his medicine.

But the fire swept from one end to the other of the thicket, and there was no sign of him.

"You reckon he took it—i' there?" Duncan asked solemnly.

"Mout of. Looks like it."

"Wi' his *horse?*"

The man in the ravine called him. Duncan ran, for if he had found Tom Brown, Tom was badly burned.

Duncan scrambled down the hill. The soldier pointed across the river—far up to the top of a long sand slope.

Tom Brown was there, in the saddle, looking back and laughing fit to kill.

Duncan set his foot on the solid wood block which was Mary MacLeod's doorstep and leaned on his knee. It had been a long time of disaster and grief since he had put that block there. They had trailed Tom Brown for miles, always toward Duplin, but they had not overtaken him. There were moments when he wanted to grasp him and throttle him and squeeze his breath out in pay for his outrages upon the Loyal, but—weel—he was gone. Broken. Pitifu'. Wi' no strength to make the hungry Whigs rouse again. Let him go.

"Mary!"

Mary opened the door and stood there. She was pale, and who wouldn't be—with the banks of the Cape Fear red with fire and blood? She ran her hand over her hair and looked at him hungrily. For him? For food? He couldn't tell.

"Howdy, Duncan!" Her voice tinkled, pleasant, as always.

"Hae ye eaten?" she asked. It was long past noon. Slingsby's men had gone on to the fort. They would now be eating heartily. Duncan was empty. "We hae some peas."

Peas! The same food that Allan MacSweene's woman had dished frae the skillet.

"Na. I'm na hungry," looking at her. Several things he wanted to say, chiefly to boast, wi'out venom, o' course, about Tom Brown.

"I hae run Tom Brown frae Bladen this morning," he said.

Behind Mary, Minnie Meacham hunkered in a chair and dipped snuff and gasped haggardly: "Lawd ha' massy!" Mary only stood a little straighter and said nothing. Peas! He wondered how long she had been living on peas. He said:

"A' the Whigs are flockin' out o' Bladen—like they made the Scots t' do four years ago."

"Aye?"

"Aye."

She looked down on the river, a little paler, but quiet. She was ungodly hard to talk to.

He said: "The Loyalists are comin' down the river, both sides, scatterin' Whigs as they march. Are ye na afeared o' their comin'?"

"Hector MacNeill is an honorable man. He wi' na stoop t' molest defenseless women."

"Aye—but on this side o' the river the man Fanning and his hoodlums hae charge. Ye wi' not content him wi' on'y a wee kiss —such as to the Gillespie boy."

Damn it, what was the matter wi' the woman? She wore a cold shell like an egg. Did she expect him, who had fought and conquered, to come to her, down to her last pea, crawlin' and beggin'?

For once her eyes flashed. "That," she said, "was nothing. Only a game. I wanted the letter to see what it might portend for——" She checked herself.

"F'r me?" he smiled.

"Aye!" She was angry for his forcing the word.

"Ay-y-ye?" and he put doubt in his tone, but he knew in his heart that she spoke truth.

"Aye!"

"Then," he said elaborately, "since ye were so good, I hae come to offer ye my protection when Fanning comes through. They are rough on Whig women."

She laughed scornfully. Duncan sighed. He had had no intention of engaging in this kind of conversation with Mary.

"A Tory protecting me from a Tory?" she asked and laughed again.

"Aye," he said woodenly. He had come wi' a glow in his heart, but the talk went wrong.

"Then," she said frigidly, "I thank ye most kindly f'r y'r magnanimous condescension f'r a puir lass, but I winna need y'r mercies!"

She closed the door, and he stood looking at it, worried. He had made no plan for such wrong talk. What was the matter wi' the lass? He wished now he hadna come.

CHAPTER 9

Duncan sang. It was monstrous music. Gillie Black gawked, big-eyed. Duncan's low notes blasted harsh and his high notes squealed. Sometimes he began to sing "Oh where, Oh where is ma little wee dog?" and ended singing "Oh, corn rigs and rye rigs . . ." But, despite the uncertainty of words and tune, he sang. Mostly he sang dolefully:

> *"If e'er I hae a house, my dear,*
> *That truly is ca'd mine,*
> *Though thou wert rebel to the King,*
> *And beat with wind and rain,*
> *Assure thysel' o' welcome love,*
> *Fo-o-r-r-r auld lang syne."*

Duncan was not exultantly happy. He sang, but he was not fully happy. Except in relief of worse plights than now. None could be happy completely with fresh memories dripping with blood and smudged with smoke and shrieking with the pains of the helpless. But there was a sense of betterment and promise. The plague of rebellion had ceased, but the wounds still bled.

It was later in August. He and Gillie, working in the hot sun, were cleaning up the place. They made piles of grass and weeds and dead limbs which had cluttered the lot these years of terror.

Duncan stopped and listened. "Thought I heard a baby crying." He laughed at the absurdity.

Gillie grabbed up a pile of weeds for the fire. "Wild cat, I reckon. Speck so."

Aye. No baby on the place—hadn't been even a woman since Martha McGee. He thought about her and her goodness to him. She had married a man named Bell, he had heard. One of Greene's soldiers. Weel—peace to her—and freedom from Steve Lewis' menace. Martha was a bonnie woman, but a Whig, and should hae been shot for a spy, by good rights. Ah—weel—he was na sorry.

He thought of Mary. He had not seen her since their bitter conversation the day Tom Brown had fled. He had seen to her welfare, nevertheless. No one had molested her, not even Fanning. He had come down the river and Whigs had flown before him like birds from a fire. When he had come to her, however, she would not leave nor would she tremble.

Fanning had not harmed her, though he had insulted many Whig women; had even given her admiring assurances of his protection. Later he had told one of the Cromartie boys that when he came back he expected to take the pretty filly to his cave on Deep River. Duncan had heard of it and had gone to him forthwith.

"I'll hae ye know," he had warned the renegade, "that the lass has my protection, and she's not to be touched."

Fanning's eyes had shifted, and that had been his answer. Then he had added:

"It's a lie! I *told* her she'd not be harmed," as though that ended it.

Duncan had kept a wary eye on him when he came up the valley, but Fanning had made no move to show that he even remembered her and had ridden on from Elizabethtown on the other side of the river. And so that threat had passed.

Duncan still had not seen her, but bided his time until passing days should show her that she was in the wrong and her common sense should return to make her amenable—which, God grant, should be soon, for he more and more yearned for her. When he thought of Fanning's threat he still took on madness.

Duncan heard no more of the new colonel's amours for several days, when Steve Lewis came through from up the country, taking some of Fanning's prisoners to Craig. Steve, as a huge joke, told of Fanning's great rage when he returned to his cave. Without ado David had dragged his kept woman out, and while she was on her knees pleading for her life, had shot her dead.

"But why?" Duncan and Slingsby asked together, shocked.

"Oh, jist tired of her," Lewis explained carelessly.

Quieter days permitted Duncan to spend much of his time at home. One more, final, trip up into Orange County, and Slingsby would give him full release.

The task at home made him both heart-heavy and joyful, and the mixed feeling found voice in melancholy song. The King still ruled, but Duncan was impoverished, the Cape Fear clan empire was shattered, Flora MacDonald had fled, hate and bitterness rode the river. Steadily, slowly, patiently, he would build back.

He was singing, thus, and planning, when Minnie Meacham, running and falling and gasping, staggered to him and told that Steve Lewis' gang, at Fanning's orders, had swept in from the woods, seized Mary and ridden away with her.

"Go, Duncan! Go!" Minnie wailed, pushing at him, but Duncan already was running for the stable.

Bay Doe was a beautiful mare. When she stretched her thin nostrils to the fore, and laid back her golden ears, and her small hoofs tinkled on the ground, the ardent David Fanning, even, asked for no more speed. She loved speed and she loved battle, and her soul was so akin to that of her master that to her, only, he·gave the small trickle of kindliness that flowed from his heart. Since he had scattered the Whigs he had lusted in his cave and Bay Doe had fretted in the stable. It was understandable then that Fanning, for once, had permitted another in Bay Doe's saddle. He had sent her down the valley as a relay horse to meet Steve Lewis and the Whig lass. That was why Duncan Stuart, approaching the Big Bend in Deep River, still forty miles from where Fanning might be expected, suddenly saw Bay Doe, her belly joyfully close to the ground and her heels flying, furiously in the chase. Steve Lewis was riding her.

It was near sunset, Thursday. Duncan for half an hour had been prospecting for the trail which led off to Sim Creece's cabin, where he might get news of Lewis. Suddenly, not a stone's throw ahead of him, a stalwart dark horse with powerful pumping legs thundered out of the green leaves which hid the trail, squatted and trembled in the sharp turn and dashed up the road ahead of him.

It was Martha's horse! Martha was riding him.

"Martha McGee!" he cried, and corrected himself: "Martha Bell."

He needed her. She knew the country. She could help find Mary. But something was wrong. Strangely wrong. The bold Martha was frightened, fleeing, and her face told it plainly.

He cried again: "Martha Bell!" but the noise was too great.

She had gone less than a hundred yards when Bay Doe, with the

litheness and lightness of a breeze, dashed out of the trail, and Steve
Lewis was in hot pursuit.

"Steve Lewis!" Duncan shouted, "I want ye!" but it was useless.
Duncan spurred Donald Bane, but that also was useless. The
nag, already overspent with the long journey, was in no condition
to race. Duncan could hope for no more than to follow slowly—
but it would not be long until Bay Doe came alongside. The chase
would end on that spot. Duncan leaned in the saddle and begged
and cursed and tried to pull the tired horse ahead by his own fury.

The two horses charged around a bend of the road, Bay Doe
gaining on Martha, and both were lost to Duncan's sight. When
he reached the turning point, they already were beyond the next
curve.

Now and then, between Donald Bane's slower hoofbeats, he
could hear the race and knew that Martha Bell was plunging on
through the woods, riding gallantly, employing every knowledge
of the good horsewoman she was.

It was a wilderness. There were no cabins. If there were, none
would have the men to stop Steve Lewis.

Duncan did not see them in the saddle again. He saw the horses
first. Bay Doe stood by a sapling, stamping, throwing her head, her
reins caught loosely in a fork. Martha's horse was in the road,
head up, ears pointed across a knoll.

Duncan crept up to and looked down the declivity. Steve, at
the foot of the hill, held Martha. They struggled. The grass was
stamped flat. Martha's right sleeve was torn at the shoulder and
hanging down. Her arm was bare. She twisted and plunged and
made him stagger with her strength, but he held her and laughed
and mocked her.

"You sweet hellcat! Stop fightin' and gimme a kiss!"

She was silent. And white. She was strong, but Steve Lewis was
stronger. For all her bending and bracing, he buckled her in to
him when he would. He played with her, wore her down, made
fun of her helplessness.

He opened his arms to let her run. She ran. He bounded after
her and caught her again. He snatched the back of her homespun
collar and tore it to the belt. He slapped her between the shoulders, and the smack came sharp in the brittle silence. She whirled

in his arms and dived for his eyes with her fingernails. He was too quick. He slapped her jaw. She fell to the ground.

He stood over her and watched her get up. She arose to one knee and paused. She was shaken, but her eyes still held courage.

"Damn hussy!" He was cool, deriding, holding his rage to enjoy his revenge. "Last time we locked horns, you captured me and made me the laughin'-stock o' Deep River, huh?" He put his hands on his knees, bent down, grinning. "I'll laugh now! You ain't nothin' but a woman! Big, fine woman. Hear me? Just a woman! Time you learned!"

Steve stood straight and thrust out his chest, lifted to his toes and sprang up, straddle-legged. He took his moment of male glorification and bent to her again. "Now you're goin' to learn what a *man* is. I'm goin' to learn ye!"

He cajoled and protested, pleading through his anger. "No sense, Marthy, in you gittin' banged up! I've wanted you the longest. Now I got you. I don't want to have to knock you around! Be willin'!" he begged, holding out his arms. "Come here!"

Martha Bell had a strange, expressionless look in her eyes. She stared beyond Steve Lewis, did not seem to see him, did not seem to see anything. She watched Duncan slip through the bushes, down the hill, back of Steve. She had the sense not to cry out, lest Steve have the chance to shoot before Duncan could reach him.

Steve gripped her hand and pulled her upright. She did not resist. He put his arms around her. "That a gal!" he approved her. She went limp and fell back, almost unbalancing him. "Hey, God damn it! Don't faint!"

Duncan could have shot him. He could have rushed on him with his knife. He did not. He had no thought of weapons. He wanted to feel the hard brawn of Steve Lewis go soft in his hands. It did not occur to him that Steve might be the better fighter.

Duncan clapped him on the right shoulder. Steve quivered stiff. He dropped Martha Bell, and she scuttled away. He did not turn to the right, but whirled to the left, and his fist hurtled in a curve. Duncan dodged, and it missed his jaw by an inch.

Duncan did not move from his tracks. Steve stamped around from his heave and faced him.

"I'll hae ye ken," Duncan said, scarcely more than whispering, "I

wi' beat ye till ye blubber like a bairn. Take heed. 'Twi' be a fair
fight. Ye're na t' gouge, na t' kick, na t' bite, na t' throw sand i' the
eyes. Ye ken?"

This always was said of the Lewises: one never shirked a fight,
one never broke his pledge.

Steve was surprised, suspicious. His face darkened. His eyes
roved and then held hard and sharp. He asked no questions,
bothered with no answers. He nodded, made his pledge. He
leaped at the same instant.

In that quivering flash in which Duncan felt Steve Lewis' fist
raking his neck, he felt his own fist slug, full and solid, against
Steve's ribs. Their first contact was thudding, jarring, loosening.
Duncan was lifted, intoxicated. He forgot the things which had
made him angry. He had but the one thought of battering and
crushing.

Both men fell back and became deliberate. Duncan crouched
over his left knee. His left elbow waggled, his right fist pumped,
his eyes fixed on Steve's.

The light still held. Half the sun blazed over the top of the hill,
but the shadows spread and night crept in. Steve Lewis stamped
his feet, winged his elbows.

Crows flew overhead for their night perches, cawing, disturbed.
Below them the two men threw off their shirts and dodged and
circled.

Martha Bell paced light-footed a little way off, back and forth,
leaning forward to watch.

Duncan spoke between his teeth: "I must know, too, where ye
put the Scottish lass ye stole frae Bladen."

Steve Lewis spat.

Duncan had but one idea, to get in and sink his fist against
Steve's left ribs. He had done that with the first blow, and he liked
the feel of it. He vaguely purposed to crash through the bony
structure, to hit him there until the spot became soft, until Steve
crumpled.

The agile Lewis was not easy to hit. His body was like a snake's.
It twisted. He took long steps. He danced around. He circled
Duncan. He rushed in and backed out. Duncan always was the
center of the fight, with Steve dashing in and out and around.

Duncan took many blows, more than he gave. He did not mind. Twice now he had taken terrific jars under his chin, and his head had snapped back, but he did not feel them. He felt Steve Lewis' fist sliding along his shoulder many times. Lewis did not seem to be able to land solidly there. All this was nothing. What Duncan treasured was that feel of his fist against Steve's ribs. Three times, now. He stood. He turned as Lewis turned. He waited, poised. As Lewis rushed in, Duncan's fist leaped out, aimed for that spot.

Lewis sought now to protect himself. He came in at different angles. Like Duncan's, his only strategy was to batter. He was beginning to feel hurt. His body writhed when Duncan's blows landed. Aye—Duncan had the right plan: to keep boring into the same hole. It gave him peace when his fist socked in with a rail-splitter's "ah-hunh!" Every cell in him now was concentrated on the one aim of throwing strength to his right arm, to wait, to maneuver, to hold steady and then shoot his fist like a piston.

The trees were not there any longer. Martha Bell was not there. Everything was vague except for the maddening thing that dangled just beyond arm's reach.

Duncan did not feel Steve's blow particularly. He merely felt light, but he knew that was disastrous. His head went back in a long, swinging arc, and his body followed it. He fell an interminable distance. He never seemed to stop falling, and then he hit the ground and struggled frenziedly against it.

He rolled over and bounced to his feet. His knees now were loose-hinged, protesting against the torture. Then his whole being centered again in his right arm, for through the dusk Steve Lewis followed him. Steve's body swung from side to side, staggering, still coming.

Suddenly Duncan was only an arm: an arm with bulging muscles and high-tension sinews. His fist was bone and power. That was all, for his body was weak and his legs trembled. His lungs shrilled for air. For one supreme moment he was an arm.

Steve did not stop—merely changed his course to the right when Duncan's fist landed. He stumbled to the ground, rolling, and lay on his back, quite still.

Duncan staggered and went to his knees beside his fallen adversary. Darkness whirled about him. Everything was vague. He had but the one desire to draw great clouds of air into his lungs. They ached. His body heaved and struggled at the task, and breath shrieked into him and out.

Slowly, very slowly, ideas became clearer, but things continued dark. His body did not pump so. Things were not so foggy, but they were dark. He looked up. It was night. That surprised him. Martha Bell was gone. That did not concern him. She was gone and, so, was safe.

He sighed, long and tremulously. The air was sweet again, not a harsh wind slitting his thrapple. He was tired. He sat on Steve Lewis' chest. Suddenly he was anxious again.

"Wake, man!"

He slapped Steve's face. Steve did not move. Duncan slapped him again, and Steve's eyes flickered and closed. Duncan slapped him a third time and bent down to watch. Steve's eyes opened. They were sullen and defiant.

"Speak, man! Where's Mary?"

Lewis said nothing.

"Where's the Hieland lass ye stole?"

Steve made no effort to speak, merely glared.

"I promise ye—ye can hae y'r one chance. Where's the lass? If harm comes to her, y'r death wi' be horrorfu'."

Steve's puffed lips opened. He strove to speak. He panted: "You'll never get her!"

Duncan nearly shrieked: "Where is she?" and grabbed Lewis' throat like a madman.

Steve made no further answer, and Duncan rose, dragging him half upright and dashing him back to the ground.

"Where is she?" he shouted.

Steve now was unconscious, and Duncan, crazed with his fear for Mary, worried over his body like a hound upon a dead fox at the kill.

"Duncan!" Martha Bell stood there, appalled at his murder lust. He looked around dazedly. He fell forward on his hands and knees and then slowly sat up and looked at them as though they were strangers.

"Doon-kan!" Mary breathed into his face.

"Mary," he said absently. "Mary."

He sat there a long time, looking at the ground. The women called to him, but he did not rouse. A great inertia held him.

Steve Lewis groaned, and Duncan jumped at him excitedly.

It took Martha's brain and brawn to clear the situation. She went to Duncan and slapped him smartly on the cheek.

He jumped back and shouted: "What ails ye, woman!"

She retorted: "Duncan, listen! You're crazy. Listen, now. You're crazy. Seize your mind and come out of your spell. You're crazy, understand? Everything's all right—a-a-a-ll right, you hear? Everything's all right!"

Duncan stood and squinted at her, uncomprehending. He looked at Steve Lewis and back at Martha. He shook his head.

"I must hae been crazy f'r the moment," he said.

"You've been crazy for seven years, if you only knew it," Martha chuckled, glancing at Mary.

He looked at Mary MacLeod and blinked, but said nothing. He stooped and took her in his arms, and his arms trembled.

"Duncan!" she screamed, frightened.

"Duncan!" she gasped, now no more than alarmed.

"Doon-kan!" she crooned, her arms creeping about his neck. "I knew ye'd come!"

She clung and clutched and wept and laughed hysterically.

Martha stood there and grinned.

"Maybe," she conceded, "you do have a glimmerin' o' sense."

But: "Here! Here!" she sprang to action. "The woods are full o' damn Tories! Let's scat!"

Martha Bell continued to have the practical sense of the three. It was she who had led Bay Doe into the bandit camp and convinced Steve's men that Fanning himself had sent her with his favorite horse for Mary. It was she who had made the plan of tying Steve Lewis to a tree so that he could not give the alarm before morning. And it was she who now planned for them to push forward all night toward Cross Creek and make for Farquard Campbell's house.

"Farquard Campbell," she said, "is the best Whig and the best Tory I know. Hell will be to pay in these parts tomorrow. Steve Lewis will be a wild man. David Fanning will foam at the mouth

when he finds his horse gone. Wouldn't surprise me if he kills Steve
Lewis." The prospect seemed quite agreeable. She chuckled. "Steve
never has no luck, nohow," she thought.

"Know what?" Martha Bell decided suddenly. "I'm headin' for
Duplin, where God made more Whigs."

They let the horses go. Their hoofs made music on the hard clay
roads. They threw dark miles behind them. Now and then they
stopped to listen, but the night told them nothing of pursuit. The
stars shone, a light mist rose to caress the low places, a breeze
played among the leaves. There was peace and quiet upon the
slumbering wilderness, and it seemed strange for the two women
and the man to stop and listen for the thundering hoofs of mur-
derers.

Dawn was graying when they rode down the steep west bank of
the Cape Fear. It was a narrow, nervous stream compared to its
lower, deeper, serenely powerful flow. But it was the Cape Fear,
and Duncan stopped in the middle of the ford and looked up the
long gray reach, with its lace of mist resting so still. This was something that belonged to him, something that through years of turmoil had remained the same. Everything else had changed. The
Cape Fear flowed on. Down below, the tides raced in and, faster
yet, raced out, but up here the water always ran downhill. Swamp
water always ran downhill. Cornelius Harnett had said that. Cornelius Harnett was dead, but the Cape Fear flowed on.

Farquard Campbell, his hair grayer and more stringy, the lines in
his face a bit deeper, the look in his eyes a bit more harried, still
was pink-faced, still was smiling; still saw the whole ghastly mess
as a macabre joke. He was agile. The sun was not quite above the
horizon when his tired guests straggled into his lane. By the time
it was fully up he had done several things.

The dangerous Bay Doe already was on her way back to Deep
River. His guests were sitting at breakfast, with Farquard Camp-
bell's daughters hurriedly coming downstairs to bid them welcome.
The Campbell women never were surprised, by day or by night.
Whigs or Tories, they bade all visitors welcome.

"Now you all go to sleep—go to sleep—rest," Farquard soothed
them when they had breakfasted. "Don't tell it now. Rest. We all

are dying to hear—but you must rest. Everything's all right now. But you must rest."

Farquard had a most wonderful way about him. It had been a dark and horrible night, but the shadows had flown. Everything was quite all right now. All they had to do was rest.

So, dazed and tired, and bruised and sore and torn and bewildered and upset, they were shown up the stairs to bed.

Duncan waked before Mary and Martha Bell. He wandered stiffly down the stairs that afternoon. He was sore all over. Farquard Campbell was waiting for him. The house doors were all open, but it was a cool day for summer. Enough to make welcome the stiff whisky which Farquard handed him.

"Aye," said Duncan with a satisfied "ah-m-m-m-m!" "One more, Farquard, and that will be enough. I'm doited sufficiently, as it is."

"Aye," said Farquard, pouring it. "Then we'll walk down the field road and talk."

Yellowing corn blades rustled. Pumpkins bulged out of the grass. The mellow sanded clay crumpled under their feet. Farquard's thin shoulders slumped more than formerly, and his coat tails stood out behind and crossed their flaps.

"Farquard," Duncan said desperately, "I have taken Mary."

"Ump?" the older man answered absently. "Yes. Of course."

"I dinna think ye comprehended," Duncan insisted. "I said I have taken Mary."

"But why not, lad? Ye've delayed too long, a'ready."

"But she is Whig and I am Loyal. Dinna ye ken?"

Farquard laughed. "Words! Just words! Ps-s-shaw! Is she na human? And are *ye* na human? And dinna ye love each the other? Then why should the words—sicklied o'er wi' nobility by the barons o' power but still empty when ye whack 'em wi' the rod o' intellect—come atween ye?"

" 'Tis a matter o' principle."

"What principle?"

"The same principle that made Flora MacDonald rally the Scots to the standard. The principle o' law and order and adherence to the Crown. The principle o' establishin' civilization and holdin' it strong."

"How can ye say that anither regime might na be as well? Ye dinna claim, I hope, that y'r woman-stealin' associates, Fanning and Lewis, are any argument f'r maintainin' the Crown?"

"They dinna truly represent——"

"Has y'r king a more admirable agent than the Whig, Thomas Jefferson?"

"Na, but he is misguided and——"

"Ps-s-shaw, lad, listen! Words! What does the King want o' ye? To wield power upon ye, 's what. And what does Thomas Jefferson want o' ye? First, to take ye frae the King, to gut the King's power and, second, to have ye subscribe to his leadership. A plague on both o' them, I say. I love people, and not the barons o' power— them nor their words. If them around about me, my neighbors, wish to serve the King, then I serve the King. If they wish tae be Whigs, then I am a Whig. But atween Whig leader and Loyal leader, I would na gie up one such bonnie lass as Mary for a legion o' 'em."

"Farquard," Duncan declared firmly, "a man who winna fight f'r his king——"

"Were ye fightin' f'r y'r king when ye fought yon Tory sojers f'r the virtue o' two Whig women? Na! Na, Duncan! Like many anither Scot, ye hae ruled y'r life by an oath long since empty. Ye redeem y'rsel' on'y by the exceptions to y'r rule. Y'r fight now is na whether ye wi' serve the King or the Whigs, but whether ye wi' put y'rsel' on the side o' liberty and law or on the side o' liberty and anarchy—f'r the King no longer rules America."

"What? Ye dinna speak sense, man. The King holds North Carolina from the Yadkin to the coast."

"Aye. The King claims he does. There is a great boast o' victory. The Loyalists delude themselves wi' their vauntie words. Cornwallis is doomed in Virginia. Any military man knows that. Greene is sweepin' South Carolina o' the redcoats. Whig leaders rouse the Ulster Scots in our own state, and they wi' hae Craig out o' Wilmington wi'in the month."

"Ah!" Duncan protested. "They canna e'en take Elizabethtown from Slingsby!"

"Huh!" Farquard Campbell dissented. "Tom Brown and Tom Owen and Tom Robeson wi' rush out o' Duplin one o' these fine nights and wi' a handfu' o' men knock the Elizabethtown post windin'!"

"Ah!"

"Duncan, ye canna kill the spirit o' men who hae the will to win. The King can pay and bestow titles, but he canna bestow the will to fight."

"I besought ye f'r wisdom, Farquard."

"Aye. And I hae gi'en ye wisdom beyond y'r capacity, Duncan. We go back tae the house now. The time wi' come when a' these things I said wi' come true."

"Na. Cornwallis wi' rout the Continentals in Virginia. South Carolina wi' hold Loyal. North Carolina a'ready is under subjection. I' the meantime, I wi' marry Mary—but on'y on condition she forbears to spread Whig doctrine."

Farquard shrugged and laughed. "She wi' do that. Mary has won her battle. She but waits f'r the result to be told."

Duncan did not tell Farquard, but, now that Mary was safe and arrangements had been made to send her and Martha into the comparative quiet of the Whig country in Duplin, he was anxious to ride again. Farquard did not know it, but Hector MacNeill secretly had gathered all the Loyal companies on the Cape Fear, save that of Elizabethtown, and even now marched up the river with the greatest Scottish force since Moore's Creek. They moved in the final, smashing drive which would utterly destroy all the North Carolina Whig strength and capture their government.

He told Mary good-by in the Campbell parlor. His black-and-blue arms no longer hurt, for they were around her and were eased with the healing of her love. The bruise on his cheek was not sore, for her cheek rested on his to make it well.

"It wi' na be long, now, Mary," he whispered, "till, as I told ye so long, long, long ago, at Gilbert Johnston's, we be wed."

She answered nothing, but clung the closer to him.

"Ye hae been misguided, Mary, but we winna remember that, but forget, and think o' what's to come."

Words . . . words. . . . They meant nothing. The eternal thrill of her, yielding to him, made his words discordant sounds in unheard music. His magnanimous forgiveness warmed him. She was disloyal, but she had lost, and it was not to be remembered.

"I go now," he said. Why must he make words? "We march to sweep the Whigs from the state. Then I wi' come for you."

She clutched him frantically. "Doon-kan! Don't——"

He laughed. "'Twill na be long! The Whigs weaken. We'll drive them out!"

"No, Duncan! No! No! You will not understand. You can't."

"Ye're doited wi' the crazy talk o' the Whigs, lass. They hae no ammunition, no food, no clothes. They're done for. They——"

Mary had his face in her hands, looking into his eyes. Her eyes were big and round and brown with the fear of her thoughts. But she said no more of that.

"Doon-kan," she whispered. "When ye need me, I'll come."

The night was cool, and the campfires blazed north of Cane Creek. Nearly a thousand Loyalists, most of them Highlanders, hugged the fires, for they all had been drunk that day in Hillsboro when they tore up the town and captured the Whig governor Burke and his counselors.

"I hae no love for Whigs," Duncan, beside a fire, said to young Dushee Shaw—the same who that long-ago night at Flora Mac-Donald's had voted with him for the Highland march out, "but I couldna see the point today when Fanning turned the Loyal prisoners out of jail to bayonet their Whig guards. The cruelty was unnecessary."

"Well"—Shaw grimaced at the memory—"as long as we must fight wi' men like Fanning, we must endure the consequences."

Duncan had not seen Fanning in the line of march, had heard nothing from him on the score of Mary's release. Duncan did not wish to see him, for fear that his wrath would go beyond control.

They met, soon enough. Even as Duncan and Dushee were talking, old Hector MacNeill and Archibald MacDougall, Duncan Ray and David Fanning came to their fire. Archibald and Ray and Fanning were in high spirits over the dramatic success, but old Hector was silent and preoccupied. The camp was shipshape for the night. The Loyalists were in a circle around their distinguished prisoners. "Sober John" MacLean, who would have no part in breaking in the Hillsboro grog shops, was in charge of the captured men. The officers in command were strolling from group to group, inspecting.

The first Duncan knew of Fanning's presence was when the Deep River man slapped him on the back jovially.

"You sure God gave Steve Lewis a grand larrupin'," Fanning said. His eyes were hard, but he smiled broadly. "He's on crutches yet."

Duncan shrugged the hand off his shoulder and said nothing.

Fanning continued: "No hard feelings about the Whig woman, I hope. I didn't know she was *your* strumpet."

He struck before he knew it, and then wished he had hit harder. Fanning staggered back and would have fallen had he not caught a sapling. Archibald and Duncan Ray leaped in angrily to make peace. Despite Scottish contempt for Fanning, no disruption in the command could be tolerated now. Archibald swung to Duncan's collar, shouting in his face. Duncan held him to one side with his left arm, poising his right, waiting for Fanning to return.

But Fanning was too wise, too proud of the prestige which the Highland relationship gave him to endanger it with a personal brawl. He held to the little tree a moment, rubbing his jaw, steadying himself, and came out.

Duncan Ray pleaded with him: "Think nothing of it! Think nothing of it! Let's not fight among oursel's!"

Fanning was not even apparently ruffled. He waved Duncan Ray aside, smiling. "Stuart's been beating me up ever since he first saw me," he complained humorously. "He kicked me through the crowd at Cross Creek. He kicked me off his boat below Elizabethtown. Now he clouts me again. It is getting to be a habit."

The Scots laughed loud in relief. Except Duncan, who turned and walked away. Old Hector followed him.

"I'll na be y'r commandin' officer for long, lad," old Hector rumbled from his big chest, "but it is a sweet thought to carry wi' me, the knock ye gie the Deep River carrion. Aye! I hae often wished to do the same."

"Why na f'r long, Hector?" Duncan still was white and angry, but his senses were returning. He wanted no conversation about Mary and Fanning. Every time he thought about Mary in Fanning's

Deep River cave he went crazy. He would talk of something else.

Old Hector did not answer directly. Or quickly. The old man's melancholy air weighted him to silence. "Wi' victory in sight, I go," he said, as if to himself. His voice had a frantic note in it. "Not the victory Flora MacDonald dreamed—one o' peace and plenty, wi' the clans dominatin' the Cape Fear and buildin' a new Caledonia. Na. Not that."

Duncan frowned on him fiercely. "Hector, what the Auld Nick are ye saying?"

They went to one of the cannon they had captured in Hillsboro and sat on the carriage, looking down on the campfires which dotted the slope.

"Na," Hector continued, still as if talking to himself. "We fought to hae our kilts and our bagpipes and our clans. We fought for plantations and strong houses and slaves and fine horses and the glory o' tradition. We hae victory, but we hae for our prize a land o' poverty and hate and hunger and broken clans and burned houses and desolation. 'Tis an empty victory. 'Tis na worth my blood, and I make the trade in protest."

Duncan shook Hector's shoulder. The old fellow had lost his spirit. Duncan had the same feeling of dismay as when Flora MacDonald gave up to go.

"F'r God's sake, Hector! Ye're doited! We march to the coast, deliver our prisoners and, save for cleanin' out a snakes' nest o' Whigs out back, the land is ours! Come out o' it! Where's y'r good sense?"

But old Hector did not respond. He said: "We wi' march into battle. None knows it, but it has come to me to know it—by what caprice of the fates I dinna ken. I see it, as plain as it were there before us now. There's a creek, wi' a bank beside it, and a tree in the bank—a bonnie, green tree, leanin' o'er the trail, peaceful, like something to adorn a grave. I wi' know it when I see it. I die there."

Duncan was troubled. He had respect for premonitions. Yet he dared not agree with Hector. He led him back to the camp for the counsel of better wisdom.

Old Hector related his upsetting prescience to the officers, but they scoffed. They grouped around him in the tent, angered and contemptuous.

"When I see the tree and the bank and the creek," Hector said fearfully, "I'll know my time has come."

Archibald MacDougall led the attack on him. Dushee Shaw was quiet and sympathetic, but Duncan Ray and David Fanning sneered. Archibald's voice rasped with his condemnation.

"F'r a' your record o' courage in battle, f'r a' y'r unflinchin' charges into the ranks o' enemy after enemy, here ye are, wi' y'r battles all won, wi' peace comin' like the sunrise, shakin' an' quaverin' an' droolin' like an auld carlin! Shame on ye, Hector MacNeill!"

"I dinna wish t' dee! I dinna wish t' dee!" Hector's old head was low, and he looked at the ground in anguish.

"Come out o' it, Hector!" Duncan Ray snapped. "Where's a battle? Ye'll hae no fight. Who's to fight? Would ye blot y'r fine record at the last minute among y'r men? Shame f'r y'r strange cowardice!"

But old Hector would not take umbrage at charges of cravenness or rouse from his fears. He sat sleepless through the night. When he marched with the column the next morning, he had shed his uniform and marched in plain garb, hidden among the private soldiers. He looked fearfully ahead, and Archibald MacDougall marched near him and watched him.

The Highlanders were at the front. The prisoners were in the middle, and Fanning brought up the rear. They marched upon Cane Creek, to cross it, and press on that day far into the Highland country. No trouble was expected, for the Whigs were disorganized and hadn't yet time to reassemble even though they foolishly might try it.

It still was morning when the Highlanders turned down the hill to the peaceful Cane Creek ford. The trail went down the bank and turned upon a level space beside the creek. A tree on the bank leaned over to shade the trail.

Old Hector looked up and gasped and went white. Duncan was only a few feet from him. Hector's prayer almost was a shriek.

"God hae mercy on my soul!"

Not many heard it, for at the instant Butler's Whigs, hidden in the trees across the creek, opened fire and riddled the head of the column.

Highlanders pitched headlong into the creek, and their wounds made wavering red streamers in the clear water.

Old Hector's great cry rang out: "Fall back! Fall back!"

Archibald MacDougall rushed up, shouting at the top of his voice: "Forward! Charge!"

Old Hector's retreat order was his death signal, for five bullets spun him around and dropped him. Dushee Shaw ran to him, but Dushee jerked and stumbled and fell to the ground beside Hector, quite as dead as he.

A soldier shrieked: "Old Hector's dead! Old Hector's dead!" and a surge of confusion swept through the line, until Archibald cried out: "It's a lie! It's a lie! Old Hector leads us on!"

The Whigs, fighting to recover their governor, fought bitterly. The Highlanders wavered, fell back, charged again, and battled stubbornly at the ford. But the Whigs were in better position, and they were desperate. Though with smaller forces they might yet have routed the Scots, but Fanning crossed the creek higher up and smashed into their flank and won the day—and a broken arm. The governor still was captive, but old Hector's corpse held the minds of the Scots as the column mournfully moved into the sandhills.

CHAPTER 10

DUNCAN, STARTING HOME from Elizabethtown, turned back to Colonel John Slingsby to speak again of those things of which they had spoken before. Duncan, unaccountably, was uncertain. So often thwarted, he viewed with misgivings the green and mellow prospect of peace.

Though his horse was saddled and he was ready to go home, he mounted the steps to the platform on the outside of the prisoners' stockade and joined Slingsby there. The Whig prisoners, nearly a hundred of them, lay on the ground, snoozing, enjoying the midday sun. More than three hundred Highlanders and other Loyal soldiers lazed about the fort, many of them sitting on the sunny side of the ammunition house. The early-fall chill made the sun a luxury.

"Have no fear, Duncan," Slingsby said to him kindly. "Go on home—and make ready for Mary. I release you, except to keep alert and notify me of suspicious circumstances. The war is over. Peace has come, except for the armistice."

"Aye, John," Duncan said doubtfully. "So it seems. But I couldna stand it, I tell ye, should this fair promise turn into another delusion. I hae been buffeted and disappointed and unhinged and battered so long that now, should this pure ray o' hope turn dark, I fear I should collapse. I hae ne'er yet been so torn between hope and dread—and I do not see the sense o' having dread, do ye, John?"

Slingsby laughed and slapped his shoulder. "Go home, Duncan, and forget your fears. You're tired and nervous, and you have so much to hope for. I understand, but now listen." Slingsby checked the items on his fingers, recounting his reassurances. "Cornwallis soon will close in on the young LaFayette in Virginia, and then crush General Washington between the Northern and the Southern armies. In South Carolina the Whig general Greene meets defeat after defeat. In our western counties the Whigs struggle to rally around the man Rutherford, but Archibald MacDougall only waits until their number is great enough to scatter. On the Cape Fear not a Whig dares raise his head. This garrison is three times as strong as their utmost number. Around Wilmington their only semblance of arms is Alexander Lillington's hungry band, so short of ammunition that they can't shoot wild game for food. It is just a matter of time, a little while. So you go freely. You've won your fight—and I would to God I had your record."

Duncan smiled. He dared hope—a little. He dared not scream aloud with joy, as he had the impulse to do. He had been so often balked.

"These prisoners . . . " He nodded into the pen, finding doubt anew. Slingsby laughed. "There's ammunition there," said Duncan, pointing to the storehouse, "f'r a thousand Whigs if they could get it."

"They are not fools. I could open the gate, and they would not leave. They eat, three times a day. Outside, they would nearly starve. They know that."

"John"—Duncan chuckled; the sound rippled and flowed, and

he could barely stop it; he felt like a fool—"I swear to God I'm about to get so happy I could shout. But I won't! I daren't! If something should happen——"

"Go on, Duncan!" Slingsby pushed him down the steps and laughed at him as he rode away.

Gillie Black had a surprise, a fearfully and proudly displayed gift. She was a squatty little brown girl, placid-faced, somehow both shrinking and unafraid, holding a baby no bigger than a rabbit.

"Mine!" Gillie boasted, stamping his feet.

"Like hell," Duncan was dubious. "How come she's yours?"

"I stole 'er!"

Duncan looked her over—good arms, good shoulders, small but strong. He frowned at her quizzically. "Who do you belong to, girl?"

"She don' know who she belongs to, does you, Millie?"

"Shut up. Who do you belong to, girl?"

"I don' know, suh. I come fum way down yanduh in South Ca'lina. Wen de soldiers kill ole mas' and took all us nigguhs, I don' know who I belongs to."

"Whose baby?"

"My baby!" Gillie asserted. "I got it."

"Good Lord! How long have you been keepin' this girl?"

"Since las' winter. Some king's soldiers camped on de river wid a whole passel o' nigguhs. I got me one."

Duncan chuckled. Gillie chuckled. The girl smiled.

Duncan looked at the baby and tickled its chest with his finger. "Kitchy-kitchy-kitchy!" he said, and Gillie and Millie wailed in laughter.

"Das it! Das it!" Gillie shouted.

"That's what?"

"Dat's she name! Kitchie! Fust word you said to huh—Kitchie! We'll call huh dat! Kitchie! Good name! Mas' Dunk," Gillie now pleaded, "kin I keep huh? Please, Mas' Dunk!"

Duncan shook his head doubtfully. "We'll see."

He walked off. He felt like an unchained prisoner. A thousand things to do, and nothing to do them with. He was most pleased about the little black baby. It was a good omen. On the first day of his freedom from war, the place began to bear fruit. It portended increase and prosperity.

"Gillie!" He turned in gruff good humor. "That *was* a baby I heard last week."

Gillie and Millie broke down in new laughter. "Yas, Mas' Dunk, sho was!"

Duncan leaned on a rail at the stable and laughed long. Gillie had beaten him to it. Gillie had a family.

Weel—soon, now . . . Still, there was common sense in delaying his trip for Mary a little while. A very little while. Not near so long as a fortnight. Perhaps not as long as a week. Two days might be long enough. If he could wait that long. The longer she stayed in the misery of the ragged and hungry Whigs in Duplin, the more it would come on her how miserable a cause she had joined and how wretched its end. Perhaps tomorrow would be long enough.

"But the place should be fairly decent before it's fit for her to come to," he protested to himself. "God!" he groaned. " 'Twas my plan to fetch her to ma stout house!"

He started up, looking wildly over the lot. A thousand things had to be done, and every one of them impossible. Tar kilns to clean and fill and burn. Trade would soon open. But he had no oxen. The Whigs had taken them. Even if he had oxen, he had no cart. It was falling to pieces. He could repair that, but he had no tools. He could make shafts for Donald Bane with an axe, but he had no auger to bore the holes.

Duncan frowned and shook his head and turned away. Everything he thought of to be done turned to the same deadening channel.

He began to walk the place. They were not the discouragingly impossible things which he had encountered almost through the whole war. These were things which he would do. In his breast was the determination to do them, so they would be done.

The more he gave his mind to them, the more he forgot the war, the more he thought of the future, here, with Mary, and the more the future glowed. John Slingsby, the King's colonel, was right. The war was over. Let the soldiers bother with the armistices. That was their business. All he wanted now was to be let alone.

He was in his stout house again, walking from sill to sill. It would be many a day before he could build again, but here it was, waiting. Hope and faith and confidence swelled his chest, and he looked over the swamp—and the whole radiant dream flamed anew.

The King was on his throne. The Whigs were subdued. The Highlanders would come back. Flora MacDonald would return to Killiegrey. Aye—she must! The Cape Fear would make up again as a Little Caledonia—and his stout house waited to be built—and his mill waited to be built—and his lake waited to be built.

Duncan hurried back across the footlog, shouting—senselessly, he knew—to Gillie to sharpen the axe and get ready to split kiln wood. Time would come for that. But he loved to hear the sound of his own voice giving orders.

His mind was a riot of plans, and sleep wouldn't come that night. The plowing. Pigs to be hunted from the swamp. Oxen to be bought. Turpentine trees to be chipped. Logs to be cut and rafted. Cart wheels to be repaired.

He got up from bed and walked in the fields. It was good soil, freed from the scourge of the Whigs. What would happen to Tom Brown? And Tom Robeson? How would he deal with them when he saw them, conquered and contrite? Or would they be sent to prison in London? Or shot?

How about the Whig families? How long would the King be content to maintain the garrison at Elizabethtown? Aye—well—these things would work out. Still, it would be better to hold to the fort for some months.

He was worrying again. There were thousands of Whigs in North Carolina yet. Farquard Campbell had said that Tom Brown would capture Elizabethtown. If he did, that would be serious, for he could rearm a thousand Whigs from the Elizabethtown ammunition house. But it was a silly thought.

He considered these things as he walked silently in the pines and oaks back of his field and looked at the clear crescent of the quarter-moon going down.

Then, suddenly, he drew into the shelter of bushes and held his breath and listened, prickly. Ahead of him, silent except for the soft shuffle of their feet in the sand, a column of men moved.

He could see them now. They were like ghosts in the faint light.

They were not hunters: they were soldiers on the march. They were ragged, and half of them limped. They were like starving men moving on food. At their head was their captain. His shoulders were stooped and his feet weary, but he drove ahead as though nothing could stop him. Was it Tom Brown?

Duncan looked after them with his mouth open and a great empty feeling in his belly. It was not over. The war was *not* over. The damned Whigs had come to Bladen again.

He waited until he could run without being heard and saddled Donald Bane, cursing every foot of the way which delayed his ride to John Slingsby. He rode circuitously, so as not to encounter the little column. He reached the river above the ferry and found a boat and left the horse on the home side. It took time, but he had to ride safely.

He ran down the river with what speed he could. A sentry let him by. He was winded when he reached the post and found Colonel Slingsby's quarters. The orderly would not immediately let him in. Then he was admitted to the colonel's bedroom, with Slingsby sitting on the side of the bed yawning, lighting a candle.

Slingsby frowned and shook his head. "It couldn't be, Duncan. Those fellows couldn't muster a handful of men. It must have been some hunters."

"But, I tell ye, I counted at least fifty men, and I don't know how many ithers I missed. Maybe Lillington's whole army."

"Well"—Slingsby yawned again and spoke doubtfully—"we shouldn't take chances, I suppose. Let me put on my clothes and we'll go out and toot a bugle."

While he dressed he continued to insist that Tom Brown and the other Toms wouldn't be up to such madness. "Why, we'd surround them and drive them into the ravine!" John Slingsby said.

In less than five minutes after Duncan had entered the room, they stepped out the door together. The orderly raised the bugle to his lips, but just then a sentry came running across the yard.

"The enemy!" he yelled. "The enemy! We are surrounded!"

The bugle's blast was lost in the turmoil of three hundred soldiers shouting and rushing to their posts. The whole dark area was filled with their confusion.

The high, ringing voice of Colonel Slingsby rose above the rest as he tried to bring them to order: "Steady! Steady, men! First company to the right, second company to the left—third company . . ."

Colonel Slingsby was running across the hard-packed sand of the area, shouting as he went. Colonel Godden, his second-in-command, was marshaling the third company. There was the clatter of weapons as men buckled on their swords and tested their rifles in the darkness and looked uneasily about for the incredible enemy of which the sentry had shouted.

Duncan raced with Colonel Slingsby, their feet pounding in unison. He had a rifle. He didn't know where it came from. He felt his shot pouch and shook his powder horn at his ear. Slingsby would take the front line. Duncan would be in there with him.

He was looking straight ahead at the dark blotch of trees which were blacker than the night. He saw the trickling spurt of flame—like the little points of light like fireflies which had played such havoc before dawn at Moore's Creek. Here they were again, before dawn at Elizabethtown. A big Scot from up the river screamed and ran and fell. The tumult in the Scot ranks suddenly thinned, and a thrusting, fighting voice sang out from in the trees:

"Colonel—Robeson—advance—and—fiah!"

It was Tom Brown. Tom Brown! It *was* Tom Brown. They said it couldn't be, but it was *Tom Brown!* Duncan listened and disbelieved, and as he listened, the spurting "fireflies" blazed from the trees at the left. There were thudding noises among the men near him. One coughed and staggered and fell. Another emitted a shriek of pain.

"Colonel—Morehead—advance—and—fiah!"

It *was* Tom Brown. He must have a regiment. Duncan's brain reeled. The post soldiers were going panicky. This time the volley came from the right.

"They've got us surrounded!" a soldier cried. The Tories were ready to shoot, were awaiting the word to shoot. They would fire, anyway, but there was no target. All they had was a charging voice in the darkness and twinkling beads of light. As fast as one Whig company fired and fell back, another company advanced under the battling voice of the commander and performed its destruction. The Whigs operated with the precision of perfect training and of large numbers.

"Colonel Godden has been killed," someone shouted in Duncan's ear. "You will take the company."

Duncan turned to go, and Colonel Slingsby made a whistling, gurgling noise and fell over, clutching his throat. Duncan caught him and laid him on the ground.

Duncan rose up and shouted, a sudden idea blazing: "It's a trick! It's a Tom Brown trick! Steady! We'll get him yet. He's not got but one little handfu' o' men that runs around and shoots frae every direction!"

The rattle of rifles kept up. Their flame spat closer. The men could not hear him, could not see him. It was dark. . . . Something thumped and burned. Running feet pounded by like horses. Dark figures thumped by toward the river. Over his shoulder he could see them running to the lip of the ravine and leaping. Some of them screamed as they leaped. But mostly they ran by him, dark, shadowy figures, thumping the ground, running and leaping into the ravine. A great horde of them. Running by him and by John Slingsby's gurgling throat. They ran by him and then disappeared over the lip of the ravine. Some of them screamed as they leaped. They set up a rhythm, shadowy, dark figures in the dawn . . . thump . . . th-h-h-ump . . . th-h-h-ump . . . th-h-h-ump . . . th-h-h-ump . . . th-h-h-ump . . . th-h-h-ump. . . . Some of them screamed . . . and leaped . . . th-h-h-ump. . . . There were thousands of them. . . . Their number never ceased. . . . They ran and leaped and screamed for hours—days—eternally —th-h-h-ump . . . th-h-h-ump . . . th-h-h-ump. . . .

And gurgled . . .

Th-h-h-ump . . . th-h-h-ump . . . th-h-h-ump. . . .

Tom Brown, faintly, was saying: *"That's* right! Keep a stiff upper lip, lassie. But no use tellin' you that. You're just a natural-born gallant little Whig."

Tom Owen said: "But you *must*—positively *must*—let us help. You can't sit up with him every night, night in and night out."

Mary said: "But Dr Cobham said it was—— He said it was——"

"Yeah, I know," Tom Brown said bluffly. "He said it was hopeless, but doctors ain't wuth *that*"—he snapped his fingers. "Dunk's too good a man—he's too stout—and you love him too much—and we all love him too much—for one little bullet to take him off. He'll be all right."

"Well, I feel"—Mary said and hesitated, "that maybe, because I do love him so, if I stay with him every minute—perhaps the good God wi' gie him some o' my strength f'r his own use and——"

"Yeah! Yeah!" Tom Brown comforted her. "Well, he's wuth workin' for, and if anybody kin pull him through, you kin."

Tom Owen said: "My wife will bring that sheet—— By the way, nobody's mentioned it. You'd heard that Cornwallis surrendered?"

Mary said: "Cornwallis? Oh—Cornwallis. No. I hadn't heard." She didn't seem to care one way or the other.

The voices were vague. They were growing clearer. The thumping was growing dim. The men weren't leaping over the lip of the Elizabethtown hole any more.

CHAPTER 11

It was a dark winter. A gray winter. There was no light. His food tasted like ashes, and he breathed the dead, lingering smoke from the swamp. His eyes beheld shadows, and his ears drummed against the echoing yammer of the Whigs. Whigs! The land was filled with Whigs—snarling—gnawing—like rats crawling on the ash heap of all that mattered. The wound in his side had healed. He gave it no thought. It never was important, for when he awoke from unconsciousness he was not concerned with a mere wounded body but with the specter of defeat which dangled before him by night and day to stab his soul.

As November went into December and December into January he, sometime in that period, regained his strength. He walked about the place. He never spoke. When someone spoke to him his tortured eyes glared back, but he said nothing. Sometimes he mumbled to himself, crying out against this incredible thing that, in one swift stroke, had swept his life bare.

Mostly he sat before the fire and glowered into the coals. Mary made him eat, and that angered him. 'Twas another Whig trick to force him against his will. As when Tom Brown with a wee handfu' o' men, by artifice and subterfuge, when he was beat and had no right, fell upon Elizabethtown and slaughtered good Loyalists and turned the Whigs back into Bladen.

"But ye must eat, Doon-kan!" Bah! Mary's clear, insistent little voice dinned on his consciousness day and night. "But ye must eat!" He didn't want to eat. He wasn't hungry. But he ate. The Whigs made him eat—the same way they had banished Flora Mac-Donald and the Highlanders, and murdered old Kenneth Black and old Hector MacNeill and split little Angus MacCooish's skull. Damn them! They were a plague on the earth, tearing up and routing out and trampling down. He had no strength to balk them, either in his will or in his arm. They made e'en the King's power impotent.

They came to the cabin. His cabin. Incessantly. There was no clear relation between those who came now and those who wrecked the stout civilization of King George. The Tom Brown who came now, bluff, hearty, generous, bringing food to Mary, somehow was not the Tom Brown who had galloped roaring through blood. Or the Tom Robeson. Or the MacKeithans and the MacMillans and the MacCollohs. They were not harsh. There was a difference. It was confusing but not a thing of moment. He did not trouble to think of it. They were Whigs and had desolated all that he had dreamed of and left nothing stable.

Duncan spoke no word until January. The Whigs came in and sat at his fire and jangled. They had great enterprises. Duncan shut his ears, but what they said seeped in, unwelcome. "Thomas Jefferson says . . ." they cried. "But Alexander Hamilton refutes . . ." They yelled of Locke and of Hobbes and of strong governments and weak governments and of the glories of popular rule. They quarreled among themselves, put their wormy little brains to the high tasks of statecraft. Bah! Every nobody his own king!

One day in January Mary's voice tinkled into his mind. The preacher was there, and others.

"Ye're well, now, Doon-kan—but again ye're na well. I must be wi' ye. But people wi' talk. The minister wi' make it right. Stand up, Doon-kan."

When the preacher asked him: "Do you take this woman . . ."

he answered "Aye!" and walked out of the cabin. Mary did not
follow him. It made no difference. It was another Whig trick. At
the threshold he turned back to frown. Mary stood before the
preacher alone. She was pale. Her chin was up, and her brown eyes
held on the preacher's lips desperately, as if clinging there for
strength.

"I do," she said.

"Romance!" Duncan went down the step. A great harsh laugh
made up in him, but his taut lips did not quiver. Words rose in his
mind like cold, hard tombstones. "Romance!" was one. "Property!"
. . . "Big house!" . . . "Plantation!" . . . "Slaves!" . . . Each rose
like something in the dark to haunt him, and then faded, and
another took its place. . . . "Flora MacDonald!"

The laugh was sardonic, hard, brittle, wholly in his soul. His
belly muscles never rippled. "Romance!"

Duncan rarely went off the place. When he did, he spoke neither
to friend nor foe. Attainted friends were too much in gloom to
give him cheer. Or did he want cheer? Foes of the cheaper sort
jeered at him. They were like cur dogs showing their teeth, without the courage to bristle. He walked through them silently, with
his ears deadened. The better ones had the good grace to avoid
him, but their chill evasions did more than the snarls of the riffraff
to build the frozen wall which imprisoned him from human
warmth. They were the leaders, but they could not lead. They
only spoke the voice of the mob.

Sometimes, even on his own land—which the Whigs left un-
seized because of Mary—the prison became smaller. As today,
when they made him marry. When it cramped him anew, he
glowered in silence until resignation came again. In the more
peaceful moments of his tribulation he pottered about the farm.
He liked to handle his drawing knife. Its blade was dull and
rusty, but he could look on it and feel the vibration in his arms
and hear the buckling and purling music, and see the creamy
white shavings circling over and falling to the ground. That had
meant something once, something real, the flow of his own heart's
blood into the processes of achievement. Barrel staves, and barrels,
and tar, and wealth, and slaves, and position. He liked to look at
his broken plow and the rust-eaten tires of his collapsing ox cart.

It gave him morose pleasure to look at the rotting roof of his
barn and think when, by his own hands, it was new and stout and
sound. Many times he thought of his corroding broadsword at
the bottom of Moore's Creek. Come a day, he would go and fish it
out. These things were like the funereal gloom which made the
peace of a graveyard.

Sometimes he rebelled. Sometimes, still silent, he defied the moil-
ing Whigs and walked among them in Elizabethtown. He did so
this day. He tied Donald Bane on the swampy side of the Elizabethtown ferry. A Whig ran the flatboat and Duncan would not pay
the fee. He found a bateau and paddled across. He looked grimly
to the right. Not to the left. To the left was the ravine into
which Tom Brown had routed the Loyalists and slaughtered them.
They called it the "Tory Hole." He would not look. He could
stand among the other wreckage of his civilization and survey it
and not shrink, but when he saw the Tory Hole he trembled in
his stomach. So he would not look.

This was court week. Had he known that, he wouldn't have
come. The Whig soldiers filled the commons, back home from the
battlefields. Many of them were drunk. They returned to find
burned houses and murdered fathers and desolated sisters. Many
of them were vindictive. Most of them drank and forgot. They
fought cocks. Traded horses. Some accosted Duncan, as when
Simon Hadley, son of old Tom, faced him in front of the courthouse and swore bold oaths and dared him to resent the insult.
Duncan only turned aside and walked on. He was not hurt. He
was numbed by greater things than the hate of the Hadleys. If
by responding he could have given Simon the power to take away
the memory of old Tom's grinning dead face, he might have.

Lawyers, posing, talking loud, making gestures, always alert
for popular acclaim, went and came through the door of the
courthouse. Some were from Wilmington. Some from Hillsboro.
Some from Halifax. They were not finely dressed. No one was
finely dressed, but they took on vain airs of distinction as one of
their stocks in trade.

Everyone, including the hangers-on, mouthed the words of the
day. "Free and equal . . ." "Human rights . . ." "Vested interests
. . ." Even that early they had ceased to inveigh against the

Crown and were berating the "interests" and the usurpers. One of these mouthing crowds swirled around Duncan now. Tom Brown was among them, and the rabble was buffeting him with questions. Some of them were drunk, celebrating what they considered liberation, and were in boisterous humor.

"No damn kings and weaslin' princes in *our* country, eh, Tom Brown?"

"No, *suh!*"

"Damn right! And there ain't gonna be none."

"Ev'y man free and equal!"

"Free! E-e-e-e-e-yay!" shrilled a drunken, unwashed swampman, his tall, gangling body staggering loosely as far as more stalwart shoulders would permit. "AND," bending far down to look up with gleaming eyes and point a finger suspiciously into Tom Brown's face, "EQUAL!"

"Free and equal!" Tom Brown said stoutly.

"That means," said the swampman, "that I'm as good as you is —free and equal?"

"*Born* equal!" Tom Brown said, as though that made it stronger.

"Then I'm as good as any goddam stuck-up Highlander, eh?" The swampman turned to Duncan, grinning yellow-toothed hate.

"All men!" another demanded of Tom Brown. "Don't that mean nigger slaves, too? Don't that mean that all the slaves will be free, and the slave*owners* will have to work like us po' folks? Huh?"

But Tom Brown was looking away, as though he had not heard.

"Na!" Duncan spoke, in protest. It slipped out. He had not intended to speak.

"Shet up, damn Tory!" someone snarled. "Who axed you to dip in? Hey, Tom, how about the niggers? Free?"

Tom Brown jerked at his belt and stamped about, still not hearing. A new man, one of the lawyers from the courthouse, stood beside Duncan and looked on, smiling amusedly.

"Tom!" impatiently. "We want to know! What about the niggers? They free?"

The time had come for Tom Brown to answer. A leader had to have the answers. "Certainly!" he said impatiently. "That's what Thomas Jefferson said—free 'em soon as *possible*."

"Niggers free! E-e-e-e-yay!" yelled the drunken one. "Free and equal! Ev'ybody free! How ya gonna make 'em white, Tom?"

"Damn if I believe it!" one in the crowd snorted.

"Sho-o-o not!" the cringing, drunken swampman smiled, poking him in the ribs, as though exposing the trick. "But you wait until I git that uppity black son of a skonk that drives the carriage over to the Waddell place free and equal. *I'll* equal 'im—with a six-inch blade right bechune his ribs—see if I don't!"

"Hurray for Tom Jefferson!" another cried.

Everyone was talking at once, and Duncan became conscious of a low, hate-filled undertone of billingsgate at his side. A half-crazed Whig soldier, back home to find it desolate, cursed him for a Tory Highlander. These Whig soldiers back from the war couldn't see Loyal ashes—only Whig ashes.

The tall lawyer who had come up and stood beside Duncan took him by the arm and led him away. Duncan sensed it as an act of friendship and made no objection. The Whig looked after the lawyer and spat: "Monocrat!"

The tall one's clothes were of fine quality, but they were old. His black broadcloth coat had a greenish cast. He wore his clothes well. He had the air of distinction. He reminded Duncan of Cornelius Harnett, except that Cornelius was more rugged. This man was finer-grained and younger, but he had the same benign expression in his eyes, the same listening attitude, the same far-seeing manner.

"I thought," he said, and his voice was musical and strong, "it might be pleasanter away from the—mob." He hesitated in saying the word, and his sensitive lips curled as though its sound was as distasteful to him as the rabble itself. "Mobocrats!"

Duncan said nothing. After his long silence he had found silence not bad, although the courtly grace of the man walking beside him was not unpleasant.

"My name is Davie. Perhaps you may have heard of me. William R. Davie."

Duncan had, and felt his rancor heave. Davie was a Whig colonel. He had been the scourge of Cornwallis entering Charlotte-town. Davie had been General Greene's supply officer and ably kept him rationed when Cornwallis' men went hungry. Davie was an aristocrat and a man of courage and culture. He was the man who had said and insisted and repeated over and over again that the state must create a University of North Carolina, for freedom would consume itself without education. He spoke with uncommon good sense for a Whig, *but* he was a Whig.

"I have taken you aside, my friend"—Davie now spoke more freely; they were picking seats on the coupling pole of a settler's wagon—"because of one word you said. Perhaps I am presuming too much. You said 'no' when the rabble proposed freeing the slaves, and I take it that you are the kind of man I seek."

Duncan glared at him, still silent. He wanted to be sought by no Whig. Whigs flattered you and stabbed you in the back.

"Now I am not particularly concerned on which side you fought in the war," Davie's voice flowed on. "All that is in the past. I happened to be a Patriot. I think you will understand when I say that there were times when it was distasteful. With my own hands I helped to throttle associations and institutions which I held most dear. But war is ruthless and does not make fine distinctions. With every gain there also is a loss. I accept them.

"But now comes a time, whether you welcome it or not, when you must realign your loyalties—I, mine. One conflict is over. Another begins. This time, God grant, you and I will fight on the same side."

The man had the power to bring up old things and make them live again. The numb anguish in Duncan's soul came quick, with an ache. The awful perfection of the disaster blazed anew, for it was as if he hugged a grave and the man dragged him away.

"I wi' na fight! I wi' espouse no cause!" Duncan's voice was a croak, and he did not care.

"See, my friend," Davie's words flowed on yet, and fired, yet, the feelings of other days. "It is a duty. Are you content to let mob rule be your master? Chaos? We know, you and I, that the ragtag-and-bobtail has no ability to build an empire! It would be anarchy. Do you consider the scarecrow from the swamps back yonder your equal or mine? Tom Brown admits to it, with tongue in cheek, because he blindly follows the most dangerous mobocrat of them all, the man Jefferson—who sees the mass of the people as a spawning ground of wisdom. But I deny it! Every cell in me cries out against the subjection of the well-born, the rich and the able to the will of the rabble.

"And I call to you, my friend, by a call stronger than that of monarch or tradition, to assume your responsibility—for the fraternity of those who are born to have and to rule demands it of you. Join me, and Alexander Hamilton, and our own Samuel Johnston and William Hooper. The battle faces us, and we are outnumbered."

William R. Davie's plea swept on, and it was like distant music. Every note struck response in Duncan—dull and faint at first, then clear and thrilling, like a battle march of the Highland clans of old. But this was secret to him, and he gave the Whig no satisfaction.

"I do not deny any man equality," Davie said. "But I tell him to achieve it rather than boast it. When he fits himself for the higher order, none will welcome him more warmly than I. I offer him, not equality, for I cannot, but equal opportunity."

"Aye!"

"I see, gratefully, that you consider what I have said as honestly spoken, and not mere snobbery, sir."

"Aye." The man was unco persuadin'.

"Remember, then, that the rabble now in power sees more virtue in lawless license than in self-restrained liberty. Their government inevitably must be unstable, irresponsible and disintegrating. For our own purposes, and for their good, we do insist, we must bend them to law, to an orderly society, to respect for private property. We, sir, must federalize the states and establish strong central power, that the decisions of the best people may be imposed upon all."

"Aye!" Duncan jumped with his vehemence. The man Davie's words were different words for what he had said all the while. Davie smiled.

"What the North can do, I know not," Davie continued, "but I envision a South country of great plantations, each manor house a citadel of its own, each swaying the common people of its shire by prestige and patronage, holding them to lines of right thinking. I see strong families, supported by masses of slaves, controlling the government, living in luxury and achieving culture and wealth, to be the envy of all the world. Its gentlemen shall know chivalry and its ladies all the graces. And, my friend, it shall flourish while the rabble still shouts its catchwords and mouths its prejudices. Are you with me?"

Duncan frowned heavily. He blinked, for tears threatened to stand in his eyes. It was on his tongue to blurt: "Aye! I hae been wi' ye a' the time. *I* and *mine* hae been wi' ye a thousand years!" But na. It was na well t' decide wi'out pondering.

So he frowned silently and twisted his mouth. He flicked a straw from his kilt. He rubbed a brier scratch on his leg and peered at it a long time, as if it were most important. He stood out from between the wagon wheels and stamped his heel and flung his hair. He needed room.

"The well-born . . ." he repeated profoundly. "And the rich . . . and the able."

"First," Davie continued, persuasively, "we must begin to organize our group. We are not alone. It will be a new party. Doubtless we shall be known as the Federalists."

"Aye . . ." Duncan thought on. "The well-born. They, by good rights, should be the rich—and it wouldna harm them to hae the aid o' such accidental able as may come frae the masses. So it boils down to rule by the well-born."

Duncan gripped his lips and nodded. "Aye," he accepted that thought.

"Well, to a large extent, at least—naturally," Davie temporized, raising no issue. "But don't discount the able, with equal opportunity. That should be emphasized."

"Rule by the well-born," Duncan insisted stubbornly.

"Well," Davie chuckled his assent, "if they are able enough to take it."

"But i' *this* country," Duncan went on dubiously, and scratched his ear, upbraiding himself—for he was talking government like a daft Whig, "that means takin' in the well-born o' the French—and the Dutch—and the Irish—and"—looking at Davie accusingly—"the English—when everybody knows the Hielanders are the highest-born o' a'."

Davie laughed gleefully, and Duncan joined him with a perplexed smile.

"I wi' think on it," Duncan agreed, shaking his head uncertainly, turning to go, now suddenly eager to be on his way. "I mistrust that Flora MacDonald would come back to such a rabblish government as ye speak of, but, e'en so, a man could concede a wee bit now and then, I ween, if a thing promise stability."

Duncan walked slowly away, then turned back with a new doubt. "But what of the North—wi' they acquiesce in the South's way o' life?"

Davie shook his head. "Possibly not for long, but that issue can be delayed for many years."

"Aye. By then we wi' hae our dam built—strong enough t' hold against 'em."

Duncan rushed home from Elizabethtown. He rode Donald Bane as fast as ever he had chased Tom Brown. Something new had burst alive in him, something light and blazing and compelling. He was as bound to it as he was to the old oath. It *was* the old oath in a new day. The stalwarts of the fiery cross even now moved to battle. He belonged. He urgently had to have Mary, to hold her, to tell her, to share with her the joy of the noble new dream. He must plan with her and start building Stuart's Hall, and the plantation, and the mill, and buy slaves, and a fine carriage —all impossible, he wi' barely a good grubbin' hoe. But it would be done. He would do it.

He dashed under the trees by the square solid sills and yawning frame of his stout house, and Donald Bane crossed the creek in one bound. Duncan leaped off near the cabin and sent him, with a jovial slap on the rump, galloping to Gillie Black to unsaddle and stable. Duncan ran eagerly through the sand to the cabin. He had left there sore and distrait, mourning the loss of all good things. He came back urgently, with zeal and hope and vision. He had found his cud again. Stability.

He opened the door. Mary sat unmoving before the fire. She did not look up. She had learned to avoid his frowns. The fire shone into her hair and made a halo of brownish gold. Her cheek was pink, like a rose, but Duncan knew the fire made it so, for she was pale from long distress. Her eyes were brown and disappointed and wistful. And she was so little—and so lonely.

Duncan forgot his glowing message. His heart turned over. He stared in sudden, consuming hunger for her, and in self-abasement. Old Gilbert was right—she had so much to give it made a man ashamed that he had so little to give in return.

"Mary," he whispered, humbly. "Mary!"

She stood and looked at him. And was startled. And fearful. Her eyes held on his searchingly. Her hands crept out, timid—hesitating—her face lighted. She came.

THE END